Praise for the novels o

"*Poison Study* is a wonderful and lively
—World Fant... ...ard finalist Kate Elliott

"Snyder's clear, straightforward, yet beautifully descriptive style is refreshing, while the story itself is completely engrossing."
—*RT Book Reviews* on *Magic Study*

"Snyder delivers another excellent adventure."
—*Publishers Weekly* on *Fire Study*

"Snyder deftly weaves information about glassblowing into her tale of magic and murder."
—*Library Journal* on *Storm Glass*

"A compelling new fantasy series."
—*SFX* magazine on *Sea Glass*

"Snyder's storytelling skills continue to build an involving story line."
—*Library Journal* on *Spy Glass*

"Filled with Snyder's trademark sarcastic humor, fast-paced action and creepy villainy, *Touch of Power* is a spellbinding romantic adventure."
—*USA TODAY*

"The action in this book is nonstop, with many twists and turns to keep the reader guessing about what's in store on the next page."
—*Examiner.com* on *Scent of Magic*

"Snyder draws us in with her excellent, efficient storytelling, amusing dialogue and distinctive characters, all set within a well-crafted plot. A delight of a read!"
—*RT Book Reviews* on *Taste of Darkness*

dawn study

NEW YORK TIMES BESTSELLING AUTHOR

MARIA V. SNYDER

Recycling programs
for this product may
not exist in your area.

ISBN-13: 978-0-7783-1985-6

Dawn Study

Printed in U.S.A.

First printing: February 2017
10 9 8 7 6 5 4 3 2 1

To my husband, Rodney. You were there in the beginning when Yelena's story was just an idea. Thank you for enduring the countless revisions, writing retreats, conferences, extended travel, bad reviews, strange visitors and the million other things that come with living with an author!

dawn
study

1

YELENA

I ghosted through the quiet Citadel streets well after curfew.
Dressed in black from head to toe, I stayed in the shadows
to avoid detection and lamented the necessity of having to
skulk about like a criminal. The row of Councilors' houses
appeared to be deserted—we'd received intel that the Cartel
had "relocated" the Sitian Council for their safety. Not trusting the darkened windows or the info that the houses were
empty, I looped around to the back alley and waited. No signs
of movement. Were the houses vacant, or did a professional
ambush wait inside?

If I still had my magic, there would be no need to guess.
But the baby in my belly was blocking my powers—or, at
least, that was the current theory. My pulse skittered with
the thought of the baby. Valek's request that I be very careful
echoed in my mind. I drew in a breath to steady my heart as
I approached Councilor Bavol Zaltana's home, located in the
middle of the row.

Without the light from the street lanterns, the darkness
pressed around me. A cool night breeze diluted the stink of
garbage left too long in the sun. I knelt by the back door and
felt for the keyhole, then inserted my tension wrench and dia-

mond pick. Lifting the pins into alignment, I twisted the tumbler and the door swung open into the kitchen that during my previous visits had been filled with heat and light and the scent of jungle spices. Instead, a cold, quiet mustiness greeted me.

I tucked my tools away and stepped inside and to the right. Standing in the threshold, I would have been an easy target. I sniffed the air for any hint of perfume, cologne or shaving cream, or anything that would indicate another person or persons crouched in the shadows.

Only the dry scent of dust filled my nose.

That ruled out the amateurs, but I knew The Mosquito remained a threat and wouldn't make such a rookie mistake. He'd been paid to assassinate me, and he would hunt me until he finished the job. No surprise that Valek wasn't happy about this mission, but due to our limited resources, personnel and time, he'd conceded the need to send me here while he searched Bavol's office in the Council Hall. Since Bruns Jewelrose and his Cartel had moved into the hall, Valek had the far more dangerous task.

We both sought any information on how Bruns's Cartel had been able to procure enough Theobroma to lace the food at the Council Hall, the Magician's Keep and four military garrisons. Their magicians then used magic to turn all those who consumed the sweet treat into compliant and obedient members of the Cartel.

When no obvious dangers materialized, I walked through the house, checking every corner for intruders, including the ceiling. All clear. Breathing became easier as I drew the curtains tight before concentrating on my task. Lighting a small lantern, I started in Bavol's home office, looking in his desk drawers.

Bavol had been given the assignment of determining a way to mass-produce Theobroma for the Sitian military. Once the

MARIA V. SNYDER

Council learned that the Commander had barrels of Curare, they'd panicked. Curare was an effective nonlethal weapon, causing full-body paralysis. The substance that counteracted Curare was Theobroma, which wasn't ideal due to it rendering a person vulnerable to magic, but it was better than being paralyzed. The other problem, however, was that it only grew in the Illiais Jungle, and at a very slow rate.

Or so everyone thought.

Bruns and Owen Moon had managed to increase not only the quantity but also the growth rate, using glass hothouses and grafting techniques. But just how had they learned this technique remained a mystery.

Finished with the drawers, I moved on to Bavol's cabinet. A couple of the files included diagrams of plants, and I stacked them next to me. The last time we visited Bavol, he'd acted... odd. Leif's magic picked up a strange vibe from him, but we hadn't pressed the issue. Now, with Bavol "housed" at the Greenblade garrison and unreachable, I hoped any information we found would help us determine not only where Bruns had procured the Theobroma but also how.

I collected a nice-size pile, but spent a few minutes checking the living area and his bedroom, too, just in case he had hidden files elsewhere.

Satisfied that I'd covered all possible locations, I grabbed the stack and slipped out the back door, relocking it behind me. I waited for my eyes to adjust to the darkness as the air cooled my sweaty skin. I'd left my cloak back at HQ. It was the middle of the warm season. The night air remained a reasonable temperature a little longer each evening. And since I was three and a half months pregnant, I stayed warmer as well.

An extra-deep pool of black appeared next to me. Instinctively I dodged to the side as metal flashed, and a sharp coldness nicked the left side of my neck before striking the door behind me. I dove to the right and hit the ground with a thud. The blackness cursed and followed me. I hissed as a blade seared a path along my left bicep. I kept rolling deeper into the darkness—my only defensive play at this point. Fear pulsed, urging me to hurry.

A narrow beam of yellow light sliced through the darkness. My attacker had come prepared. Lovely. The light swept the ground, searching and then finding me. Caught in the beam long enough to be a target, I somersaulted to my feet as the *thwack* of a crossbow sounded. Debris pelted me when the bolt ricocheted off the ground nearby. Too close. My heart jumped in my chest. Another bolt clipped my right side, the pain a mere nuisance in the grander scheme of things.

I raced for the end of the alley, zigzagging as much as possible and hoping with all my soul that a second ambusher didn't wait for me at the end. A third bolt sailed past. I shot from the alley and increased my pace, no longer caring about staying in the shadows. Glancing behind, I spotted a black-clad figure aiming a crossbow in my direction. Ice skittered down my sweat-soaked back. I changed course, spinning to the left just as the bolt whizzed by my ear. The air from its passage fanned my face. Not stopping to marvel at either my good luck or his lousy aim, I dove for the shadows and ran.

Hours later—or so it seemed to my starved lungs—I slowed and ducked into a dark shadow. Bending over, I gasped for breath. So much for staying in shape. Although running for your life wasn't exactly something you could train for. Plus I'd gained a few baby pounds. The thought sent a new spike of fear right through me. I ran my fingers along the gash on my side, seeking its depth. I sighed with relief—only a flesh wound. Then I remembered my other injuries, and they flared to painful life. The one on my neck was also shallow, but the cut on my arm would need to be sealed. I sagged against the

MARIA V. SNYDER

building for a moment. Not only my life but also the baby's had been in danger.

Once I recovered, I realized I still clutched the files from Bavol's office. I would have laughed, but the sound might have attracted the wrong attention. Dozens more soldiers had been patrolling the streets since the Cartel declared martial law and set a curfew. To avoid them, I took the most round-about path back to HQ, ensuring no one followed me. By the time I tapped on the hidden door, the first rays of dawn lit the white marble of the Citadel.

Hilly, one of the Helper's Guild members, let me in. She raised an eyebrow at my disheveled and bloody appearance.

"I ran into a bit of trouble," I said.

She quirked a smile. "Not as much as when Valek returns."

Oh no. "Did he…"

"Yep. He stopped in about an hour ago, but when he heard you hadn't returned, he took off to look for you."

I wilted.

Hilly took pity on me. "Come on. We'll wake the healer and get you cleaned up before he comes back."

I followed her through HQ. Since the building Fisk had once used to house his Helper's Guild had been seized by the Cartel, he'd found another empty structure tucked almost out of sight in the northwest quadrant of the Citadel to use as a temporary base of operations. Now his people helped us in our efforts to stop the Cartel from taking complete control of Sitia. The so-called resistance.

Sleeping barracks occupied most of the lower level. The members of the guild spanned in age from six years old to eighteen. The kids didn't mind the close quarters, and some happily shared a bed. The extra-large kitchen took up the rest of the level. The two upper floors contained Fisk's room and office, a small suite for Valek and me, and a number of guest rooms for our growing army. Our farmhouse in the Storm-dance lands had been a useful place to plan and recuperate during the last month, but we'd quickly learned that we needed to be closer to Bruns.

The healer was a sixteen-year-old boy named Chale who'd recently developed magical powers. Since all the magicians at the Magician's Keep had been conscripted and sent to the Cartel's garrisons, there had been no one to teach him how to use his power—except me and Valek. Even though I lost my powers over three months ago, I hadn't forgotten my lessons from the Keep. Valek, on the other hand, had freed his power only recently and almost flamed out, killing us all. Now he was reluctant to use it until he learned how to fully control his powers. Not an ideal situation, but we tried.

I sat at the kitchen table in my undershirt as Chale cleaned my wounds. The gawky teen was all thumbs. He peered through a riot of black hair that my fingers itched to trim. As I suspected, the cut on my biceps needed more than just a bandage. At least talking Chale through the steps needed to heal it with his magic distracted me from the pain. As long as he didn't touch me skin to skin, he could use threads from the power blanket to stitch the cut closed.

"I have to keep pulling power to knit the skin together," Chale said with concern. "Something is tugging it away. Is that normal?"

"No. I think what is draining your power is what is blocking mine. At least, I hope that's the case."

"Is it the baby?"

I stared at him. Not many people knew.

He blushed. "Sorry, I just—"

"No, don't apologize. You're a healer. Sensing the baby is a part of your powers."

"It's healthy, if that helps?"

MARIA V. SNYDER

"It does," Valek said from the doorway. He still wore his black skintight sneak suit, which highlighted his long, lean and powerful muscles. "Can you say the same about my wife?"

A dangerous glint lit his sapphire-blue eyes, but Chale failed to notice.

"Of course. It's just a couple scrapes." Chale's light tone downplayed my injuries nicely—perhaps he'd noticed more than he let on. "We're almost finished."

"Good," Valek said, but his gaze seared into mine.

And though his angular face revealed none of his thoughts, I knew he suppressed a whole gamut of emotions. In a few graceful, almost predatory strides, he was by my side. He laced his fingers in mine as Chale completed his work. Bandages were fine for the shallow cuts. I didn't want Chale to exhaust his power on the minor abrasions—one of the guild members might need him tonight.

Valek let go of my hand as I shrugged on my torn and bloody tunic. He studied the garment without comment—another dangerous sign. But by this time, the kitchen bustled with the morning crew, and soon piping-hot sweet cakes were set in front of us. My stomach roared with sudden hunger, and even Valek wasn't brave enough to get between a pregnant woman and food.

Only after I stuffed myself did he reclaim my hand and tug me to my feet.

"Upstairs," he said.

Feeling much better with a full stomach, I trailed after him as we ascended the stairs to the third level and into our rooms. Valek closed the door and I braced for his lecture. Instead, he wrapped his arms around me and pulled me close. I rested my head on his chest and listened to his heart beating, soaking in his warmth, breathing in his musky scent, feeling safe. At six feet tall, he was eight inches taller than me.

I'd known Valek for almost nine years, and the only thing that scared him was the threat of losing me. "What happened?" I asked.

He leaned back and lightly brushed the bandage on my neck with his thumb. "I found out The Mosquito is in town."

Ah.

"Did he attack you?" he asked.

"It was too dark to see, but the first strike was aimed at my throat." The Mosquito's signature way to kill was to stab an ice pick into his victims' jugulars and let them bleed to death. Nice guy.

"Tell me what happened."

I detailed the attack and the reason it took me so long to return. "But I managed to hold on to the files. Did you learn anything else while you were in the Council Hall?"

"I grabbed a few promising files from Bavol's office, but I'm more concerned about what I overheard Bruns and his sycophants discussing in the hallway."

I stepped back in alarm. "You weren't supposed—"

"They didn't know I was there. Besides, the information was worth the danger."

"About The Mosquito?"

"Yes. That, and Bruns knows you're in the Citadel. He's offered a large bounty to the person who kills you."

No surprise. "How much?"

"Yelena, that's not the point."

"It's not the first time someone's put a price on my head." Master Magician Roze Featherstone had offered five golds as a reward for my capture when she tried to take over the Sitian Council seven years ago.

"This time is different. You're..."

I waited.

"Vulnerable without your magic. And it's no longer all

MARIA V. SNYDER

business with Bruns. He took Ben's and Loris's deaths and our escape from the Krystal garrison personally. You need to go back to the farmhouse in the Stormdance lands. You'll be safer there."

"And what about you?" I asked. "As you said, *our* escape. Did he set a bounty for you, as well?"

"No."

"How do you know?"

Valek paced the room. I crossed my arms to keep his lingering warmth close. Plus, judging by the agitation in his steps, I sensed he was working up the nerve to deliver more bad news.

He stopped. "Bruns has offered fifty golds to the person who kills you."

That was a fortune. I whistled, and he shot me a glare. "You didn't answer my question," I said.

Another scowl, and then his shoulders drooped as if in defeat. "Bruns has been in contact with Commander Ambrose, and…" Valek paused. "The Commander has agreed to send Onora to assassinate me."

2

VALEK

Yelena's mouth opened slightly in surprise, and concern flashed in her green eyes over the news. But Valek had expected something like this. If he focused on the logic, the move made perfect tactical sense. The Commander had warned Valek that leaving Ixia would be an act of treason. And acts of treason, no matter what the reason, were punishable by death. Plus, he now had magic, of all things. He'd inadvertently traded his immunity to magic for the power to wield it. And the Commander had a standing execution order on all magicians found in Ixia.

Except he and the Commander had been close friends, and he was unaware of Valek's magic—only a handful of people knew. He'd hoped the Commander would give him the benefit of doubt and not send an assassin after him.

Yelena put her hand on his arm. "He's being influenced by Owen's magic."

"We don't know that for sure." There had been a few inconsistencies, like when the Commander had tried to protect Valek from Owen by sending him to the coast to deal with the Storm Thieves. He was also supposed to be protected from Owen's subversion by the null shields that Leif had woven into his uniforms, but the Commander could have lied to Valek about wearing them.

"He has to be," she said.

He pressed his hand over hers and enjoyed not only her touch but the respite from the constant presence of his magic. With his mental shield in place, it wasn't as bad, but contact with her turned it all off, and he returned to the man he'd been for the last forty-one years of his life.

"Are you worried about Onora?" she asked.

Was he? They had sparred a number of times, and each time he had defeated her. But perhaps she planned to ambush him. "No. She's the best to come along in the last twenty-four years, but unless she catches me off guard, I don't expect her to cause me any trouble."

"And you're never relaxed," she teased.

"I am when I'm with you, love." He picked up her hand and kissed her palm.

"Really? And those knives under our pillows, the swords on the floor, the darts in the headboard?"

"I said relaxed, not stupid. Being prepared is never a bad idea."

"No." Her gaze grew distant as she rubbed her side.

Probably remembering The Mosquito's attack. While Valek was proud she was able to get away, he planned to ensure that would be the assassin's last attempt on her life.

"Speaking of being prepared," he said, "you need to leave the Citadel until I've taken care of any bounty hunters coming after you. Either go to the Stormdance farmhouse, or travel to the Illiais Jungle to visit your mother. Both are safer than here."

She gave him a tight smile. "Nice try, handsome, but I'm not going anywhere. At least not until Leif and Mara return from Broken Bridge with my father, and we've looked over the information from Bavol's."

"At least promise me you'll stay in HQ until they arrive." He leaned close and kissed her neck, then whispered, "Do it for your handsome husband."

Laughing, she said, "I promise to stay in bed for the rest of the morning as long as you stay with me. After that...no promises."

"What if I give you a *very good* reason to stay in bed until I squash The Mosquito?"

She drew back, and desire burned in her gaze. "What's the reason?"

"Me taking care of you until you're out of breath and a puddle in my hands. A service I'll be happy to perform anytime during your...bed rest." He nibbled on her earlobe.

"Oh, my. Someone certainly has a high opinion of himself," she teased.

"Is that a challenge?"

"Oh, yes! Show me what you can do, and I'll consider your request."

He grinned. "Accepted."

Not giving her time to reply, Valek pulled her to their bedroom and made short work of her clothing. A few bloody scrapes marked her back and a number of bruises peppered her arms. Valek suppressed his fury with the knowledge that The Mosquito would soon be crushed.

Valek scooped her up and laid her on the bed, then kissed her for a long moment. She plucked at his clothing, and he grabbed her hands. "This is for you, love."

"Exactly. Now strip."

He peeled off the tight garment, but his gaze never left her. Once divested of his clothing, he joined her on the bed. He trailed kisses down her neck. Valek had been convinced he'd

MARIA V. SNYDER

lost her when she hadn't returned from her mission, and he planned to savor this time with her as if it were the last. His efforts left her gasping, and he gave her three very good reasons to stay in bed.

She stretched like a cat and curled up next to him. Yelena met his gaze. "You're really worried about the bounty on me?"

Valek traced the recently healed cut along her side with a finger. Purple bruises ringed the bright red line. "I know you can handle an assassin." He quirked a smile. "Or two, but with fifty golds at stake...a gang of wannabe bounty hunters could come after you together and split the money."

"All right, I'll stay in HQ until you've dealt with The Mosquito," she promised.

A weight lifted from his shoulders. He pulled her close. She snuggled against him and fell asleep almost immediately. He smoothed her long black hair back from her beautiful oval face. The knowledge that he'd do anything to keep her and the baby safe comforted him, since it required no thinking, no weighing the consequences of his actions and no hesitation.

Valek had once felt the same uncomplicated feelings for the Commander, but not anymore. Even if the Commander's behavior had been caused by Owen's magical hold on him, Valek could no longer return to that place of blind loyalty. His new magic complicated everything, of course. However, that would just be an excuse. No. Yelena meant more to him than his own life and happiness, and much more than the Commander's.

Valek woke a few hours later and slid from the bed without waking his wife. An automatic smile still spread over his lips every time he thought of Yelena as his wife. Not many people knew of their marriage, and even fewer were aware of the baby, but the fact that they had exchanged vows continued to thrill him, as if he'd won the biggest tournament in the entire world.

Going down one level, Valek stopped in Fisk's office. The stark room contained a desk, a couple chairs and a table. The young leader of the Helper's Guild bent over his desk. The fingers of his right hand ran through his light brown hair, leaving behind rows of spikes, while his left clutched a stylus. He frowned at a sheet of parchment spread over the desk.

Valek tapped on the open door, and Fisk glanced up. Dark smudges marked his light brown eyes. The poor boy appeared years older than seventeen.

"When's the last time you slept?" Valek asked.

Fisk blinked at him. "Sleep? What's that?"

"Not funny."

Fisk dropped the stylus and rubbed his face. "Wish I was joking."

"Bring me up to date, and then take a break."

"But—"

"It's not a request. Exhaustion will only lead to fatal mistakes. I'll collect the information from your guild while you rest."

He grinned. "Half of them are terrified of you and won't report."

"Then they can wait until you're awake. What's the latest intel?"

Fisk filled him in. "We think Hans Cloud Mist is a member of the Cartel. He's been spotted at the Moon garrison twice, and we've confirmed Danae Bloodgood and Toki Krystal as members."

Valek considered this for a moment. They were all influential businesspeople who thought their accumulated wealth and business acumen meant they could do a better job of running Sitia than the appointed Councilors. "I'm beginning to sus-

MARIA V. SNYDER

pect there are eleven members, one for each clan, with Bruns designated as their leader," he mused.

"Sounds like something they'd do to justify their actions."

Interesting comment. "What do you mean?"

Fisk leaned back and spread his arms. "They decided that the Sitian Council was not doing a proper job of keeping Sitia safe from the Commander. Plus the Council also failed to rein in the Sitian magicians, letting them go about their business willy-nilly."

"Willy-nilly?"

"Yeah, you know." Waving his hands, Fisk elaborated, "Selling null shields to anyone, using their magic for selfish reasons. I think the Cartel feels they can do better than the Councilors, but they still honor the structure the clans have established long ago. So they're not really usurping the Council—just replacing them."

"And that helps them sleep better at night?"

"Exactly." Fisk rubbed the stubble on his chin. "Why is identifying the other members of the Cartel so important when Bruns has brainwashed them along with everyone else? They've no clue that Bruns is collaborating with Owen and the Commander."

"You tell me."

He huffed. "I don't know, because in order to stop the Sitian takeover, all we have to do is stop Bruns, Owen Moon and the Commander."

Valek suppressed a smile at the "all we have to do" comment. If only it were that easy. "Why are these people members of the Cartel?"

Fisk shot him a sour expression. "Okay, I'll play. They're rich and powerful. Which is why the Cartel has been so successful in getting resources and converting the garrisons—Oh!"

Valek waited as Fisk followed the logic.

"So we identify them all and wake them up to what's really going on, so they can use that influence and power to help us instead of Bruns."

Smart boy. "Or we assassinate them all and take them out of the equation. The added benefit is that we scare their support staff."

Instead of a knee-jerk reaction to the thought of killing ten people, Fisk paused to consider it. "Yelena would never allow that. She doesn't want any of the brainwashed to be killed. Besides, I think they'd be more useful alive than dead."

"And that is why we need to know their identities."

Fisk yawned. "We're getting reports back from the garrisons and will soon have a complete list of personnel at each one."

"Good. I need your people to locate a bug for me."

"The Mosquito?" He straightened in his chair, looking more awake.

"Yes."

"Where?"

"Here in the Citadel."

"Ah, hell. Is that why Yelena needed…" He stopped. "Won't he be with Bruns?"

"From what I heard last night, either he's been fired, or Bruns thinks the competition will compel him to finish the job." Valek told Fisk about the bounty.

"She has to leave now and go some—"

"I already tried that. Best I could do was get her to promise to stay at HQ until I've dealt with The Mosquito." In other words, once Valek plunged his knife in The Mosquito's heart and scared all the others away.

"That's some relief." Fisk ran both his hands through his hair. "But the Citadel will be overrun with assassins, and it's gonna be hard to find the bug. He's smart, and my people aren't as effective in the Citadel. Rumors that they're doing

MARIA V. SNYDER

more than helping carry packages for shoppers are spreading. Before, everyone ignored my kids, thinking them harmless and stupid. Now..."

"Just tell them to keep an eye out for him. I only need a general vicinity."

"All right. And now that Yelena is under house arrest, so to speak, she can take over collecting the information from my people, since they trust her, and I can do a bit of reconnaissance on my own." Fisk paused. "Are you sure she's going to be happy hanging around here all day?"

"Don't worry. *I'll* keep her happy."

Fisk shot him a dubious look before heading to bed. Valek settled behind the desk and studied the map Fisk had been marking. The other Sitian garrisons were highlighted. Members of the Helper's Guild had infiltrated them all. Since the Cartel controlled the Citadel and the Moon, Krystal, Featherstone and Greenblade garrisons, they'd put the military soldiers in charge of all the civilian security forces in those lands. Rumors that the Cloud Mist base was also compromised hadn't been substantiated yet.

The garrisons farther south still hadn't been indoctrinated, and Valek had agents working in the kitchens to ensure they remained uninvolved long enough for Valek to recruit them to their side. The agent in the Jewelrose garrison hadn't reported in weeks, and Valek suspected the man had been captured or converted. Heli the Stormdancer was keeping an eye on the base in the Stormdance lands, but the storm season would start at the beginning of the heating season, and he'd need to find another agent then.

Ari and Janco had been assigned to the Greenblade base to keep an eye on the Sitian Councilors and First Magician Bain Bloodgood. Eventually, they would need to be rescued. Meanwhile, his sister Zohav and his brother Zethan—a concept that still amazed him—worked on exploring the extent of their powers with Teegan and Kade on the Stormdance coast. They were safe for now.

Valek reviewed his to-do list—identify the Cartel members, find and cut off the source of the Theobroma, rescue the Councilors, recruit the southern garrisons and free the magicians in the other garrisons. Oh, and find some time to rescue the Commander. Knowing *what* he needed to do was the easy part. Too bad he didn't quite know *how* these tasks would be accomplished, with only Fisk's Helper's Guild and ten others to help. They needed more bodies. More allies. Yelena wished to recruit Cahil, believing the man might be smart enough to see the truth. Valek hoped she was right. Then there were Devlen, Opal and her soldier friends, Nic and Eve. As long as Reema was safe, they might be willing to help. Perhaps when Leif, Mara and Esau returned, he'd send another messenger to Fulgor, the capital of the Moon Clan's lands and ask.

Leif and Mara had left ten days ago to collect Esau and the plants in the glass hothouse near Broken Bridge. They should be at the farmstead where Leif had left his father by now. However, the return trip to the Citadel would take them twice as long since they'd be pulling a wagon.

Fisk's people honed in on a potential location for The Mosquito three days later and provided him with a current description. Valek had been collecting information in the Council Hall in the evenings, much to Yelena's annoyance at the risk he took while she was stuck at HQ. He refused to feel bad. In fact, knowing she was safe after learning Bruns's plans kept him from being overwhelmed with all that had to be done. Plus, when he returned each morning, he woke her with more reasons to stay safe.

"You're going after him," Yelena said. It wasn't a question.

MARIA V. SNYDER

She watched him as he dressed in nondescript Sitian clothing—a gray tunic and charcoal-colored pants—and tucked a number of weapons into the various pockets and hidden holders.

"If you kill him, does that mean I'm no longer under house arrest?"

"Technically, yes. But there's still the bounty," he said.

"What if he kills you?"

"He won't."

"Cocky bastard."

Valek pulled her close and kissed her. "He won't, love."

She melted against him. "I feel so useless."

"Don't. The kids love you, and Fisk is getting better intel by being out in the Citadel."

She managed a half smile. "You're right."

"I'm going to put on quite the show today and attract lots of attention and scare the other bounty hunters off for a while, so if you really can't stand being inside and want to get some fresh air this afternoon, it should be a little safer."

Yelena's face lit up.

"I'd rather you didn't, but if you do, please don't go far or alone. All right?"

"Yes." She hugged him tight.

He nuzzled her neck.

"Tell The Mosquito to enjoy the fire world for me," she said.

"It will be my pleasure."

Once outside, Valek moved through the busy market with ease. He spotted a number of Fisk's guild members working the crowd and darting between shoppers. The market was located at the very center of the Citadel. Factories and businesses ringed it in ever-widening circles and occupied the two center sections of the Citadel. The Magician's Keep encompassed the northeast quadrant, and the Sitian Council Hall and other government buildings were located in the southeast corner. The Citadel's citizens lived in the labyrinth of homes in the northwest and southwest quadrants.

A few of the abandoned warehouses and factories had been converted into apartments, and according to Fisk, The Mosquito lived on the top floor of one of them. Normally Valek would attack at night, but The Mosquito knew that trick and would be ready.

As he crossed the market, Valek noted three people taking an unhealthy interest in him and sensed another, but was unable to locate the fourth—a professional. He considered his options. Lead the three on a merry chase to an unfortunate dead end, or lose them?

When he spotted The Mosquito standing near the entrance to an alley, Valek recognized the setup. Those three worked for the bug. Like a pack of sheep dogs, their job was to herd him toward that alley, where Valek's prey would conveniently dangle like bait on a hook. Then the bait would slip down the alley and draw Valek right into an ambush. Classic.

He judged his odds. The Mosquito plus three—doable with darts, but just how many waited? A brief thought of using his magic to sense the others flashed before he dismissed it. Too many people around. Even though Teegan had taught him to control his magic in order to prevent a flameout back at the Stormdancers' safe house, he was reluctant to use it. According to Teegan, his mental barrier was strong enough that he didn't need to wear a null shield. Besides, he liked being able to detect when magic was in use around him.

Instead of using magic, he decided to take the high ground. Valek returned to the heart of the market and lost his sheepdogs, then cut down the street next to The Mosquito's chosen alley. When no one appeared to take an interest in him, he climbed the nearest building and reached the top.

MARIA V. SNYDER

When he straightened, he spotted The Mosquito waiting on the roof two buildings down on his left. Fisk did say the man was smart. So how did Yelena get away from him with only a few cuts?

It occurred to Valek that perhaps Yelena wasn't his target.

Valek drew both his daggers and faced The Mosquito as he lightly hopped buildings.

The Mosquito halted six feet in front of Valek. "Please tell me you really didn't think I'd set up such an obvious trap for you."

"You took a contract to kill Yelena. That makes me question the level of your intelligence."

"Fair enough." He swept a hand out.

Sensing movement behind him, Valek angled his body to keep the bug in sight while he glanced back. Four black-clad figures stood up from where they'd been lying on the right side of the rooftop. Nice.

"What about now?" The Mosquito asked.

"It depends on who you brought for backup."

"Well, this is Sitia. Not a ton of trained killers here. But there are plenty of magicians. Four might be excessive, but…" He shrugged. "I'd rather too many than not enough."

Ah. Smart move. Around Valek, the presence of magic disappeared suddenly. The magicians must have surrounded him with a null shield. Valek dropped his arms to his sides, as if an invisible hand had wrapped around his torso. When he'd been immune to magic, a null shield could immobilize him like a rat stuck between the jaws of a trap. Now…not at all. However, he didn't want the bug to learn this fact until the perfect moment.

"Now I'm questioning your intelligence, Valek. Why would you come after me alone when everyone knows how easy it is to trap the infamous assassin?"

"Who says I'm alone?"

The Mosquito opened his mouth, but snapped it closed as his gaze slid past Valek's shoulders. Four thuds sounded behind him. The presence Valek had sensed in the market stood among the prone forms. As usual, Onora was barefoot.

"You do realize she wants the same thing I do," The Mosquito said.

Valek rolled his shoulders as if he'd been released from the pressure of a null shield. "I do," he said. "But she'll wait her turn. Right, Onora?"

"You can play with your bug first," she said.

Valek didn't hesitate. He flipped his dagger and flung it at The Mosquito's chest with all his strength. Shock whitened the man's face as the blade pierced bone and buried deep into his heart. The force slammed The Mosquito to the ground.

Shuffling close, Valek crouched beside the assassin. Valek met the bug's horrified gaze. "I'm sorry we didn't have a proper match, but I need to save my energy for the next fight."

For Onora to show up in broad daylight meant it was going to take all his skills to defeat her. If he even could. She must have downplayed her abilities when sparring with him before. "Oh, and Yelena says enjoy the fire world."

Valek yanked his knife from The Mosquito's chest and stood to face Onora.

MARIA V. SNYDER

3

LEIF

"You can't pack an entire hothouse's worth of plants onto one wagon, Father," Leif said for the billionth time. Sweat rolled down his face as he helped Esau pack the plants' roots into large terra-cotta pots filled with soil. They'd been at it for two days now. "Just collect the important ones and those that you think can survive the trip."

Esau knelt among the greenery. Dirt streaked his face and smeared his coveralls. His tragic expression over leaving any of the shrubbery behind was almost comical. "If Mara makes me glass panels for the wagon, we could construct a hothouse on wheels and—"

"It would weigh a ton and take a team of oxen to drag it to the Citadel. Not to mention draw attention to us, and right now, we can't afford to be noticed." Leif and Mara had to dodge a number of military patrols on the eight-day trip here. Traveling with a full wagon was going to be a nightmare. "We'll probably have to put a tarp over the plants we do take in order to blend in."

Esau gasped in dismay, and Leif suppressed a sigh. His father was the best at identifying and working with plants, but sometimes the man's devotion bordered on obsession.

"We're leaving in the morning, Father. So tell me which ones to pot, or I'm going into the farmhouse and—"

"Take the crossbreeds and the grafted Theobroma trees." Esau stabbed his finger at the plants. Soil filled his nails, which had grown long, along with Esau's wild gray hair.

Leif hadn't wanted to leave his father behind in Broken Bridge when he'd returned to the Citadel two months ago, but that Zaltana stubbornness won out, and Esau had remained at the farmstead. And it appeared that he had practically lived in the glass hothouse and only spent the minimum amount of time on things like basic hygiene, sleeping and eating.

Then again, it was probably a good thing Esau hadn't accompanied Leif. Considering he'd been ambushed, kidnapped, brainwashed and shot in the chest with a crossbow bolt, Leif thought his father had fared better, even with the malnutrition. Leif rubbed the scar on his chest, remembering the pain and the knowledge that he was dying. That he'd never hold his beautiful wife in his arms again. Then, from nowhere, Valek had appeared and saved his life. With magic! A month later, Leif still couldn't get his mind to accept it. Valek, who'd been immune forever, and now...a magician of considerable strength. Weird.

Leif finished potting the plant and several more that Esau gave him, then stood. Stretching his back, he wiped the sweat from his face and headed toward the house to check on Mara. Ever since his near-death experience and seeing her a prisoner of Bruns, he grew nervous when he'd been separated from her for more than a few hours.

The trip to the Citadel was going to be tricky. He planned to let her ride his horse, Rusalka, with instructions to head back without waiting for them. It was safer for her, and she'd have a better chance of avoiding the patrols by traveling alone.

MARIA V. SNYDER

The time apart would be torture for him, but it was much better than letting Bruns capture her again.

Mara was in the farmhouse's large kitchen, cooking supper. He paused in the threshold and watched his wife. Honey-colored curls framed her heart-shaped face. She was gorgeous on the outside and equally as beautiful on the inside. He'd never met a sweeter soul. But he'd learned she wasn't as soft as she appeared. Her run-in with Bruns had brought out her inner strength.

She spotted him hovering and flashed him a huge grin, her tawny-colored eyes shining with love. His heart melted at the sight, and he rushed to gather her close.

Mara nuzzled his neck. "You smell of earth and sweat."

"Does my man-odor turn you on?"

She leaned back to meet his gaze. "You've been spending too much time with Janco."

"I haven't seen Janco in weeks," he protested.

"Doesn't matter. The damage is done," she teased. "Go get cleaned up. Supper is almost ready, Man-Odor."

"Come with me? Father is busy."

"And let the roast dry out?"

"Yes." Food had lost its appeal. Almost dying had a way of rearranging a person's priorities.

"I won't serve a meal that tastes like shoe leather." She squeezed him. "We'll have time later. This house has lots of bedrooms, and we'll probably need to check on the horses sometime this evening."

He laughed. "Is 'check on the horses' going to be our code?" Leif imagined a house full of kids and a future Leif announcing that Mommy and Daddy needed to "check on the horses" and would be back.

"You've no sense of romance."

"That shouldn't be a surprise."

She shooed him away in mock disgust. Smiling, Leif cleaned up and helped her finish cooking dinner. He brought a tray of food outside for his father. After Esau ate, they loaded the wagon and watered the plants.

"Poor things." Esau tsked. "Out in the cold. Maybe I should—"

"No. You're not sleeping here with them. We'll be on the road for—" he calculated "—sixteen days, if the weather cooperates. You'll have plenty of time to coddle the plants. Tonight, you should get cleaned up and have a proper night's sleep in a bed."

But Esau fretted anyway, and Leif offered to put the tarp on that night instead of waiting until the morning. By the time he finished securing the fabric to Esau's satisfaction, Leif really did have to check on the horses. He sent his father into the house with strict orders to wash up and go to bed, then headed to the barn.

He breathed in the comforting scent of hay, horses and manure. Rusalka greeted him with a soft nicker. He topped off her water bucket and added grain to her feed. Then he tended to the other two. Fisk had lent them a hardy sorrel quarter horse named Cider for Mara to ride, and who had also been trained to pull a wagon. Leif had traded in his father's horse for a barrel-chested black draft horse named Kohl. The brute could probably handle the wagon on his own, but, due to the distance, Leif felt better with two.

Mara arrived just as he finished cleaning Kohl's hooves.

"Come to *check on the horses*?" He leered.

She ignored him. "I tucked your father into bed, but I had to promise to tug on the fabric over the wagon to ensure it doesn't come loose."

"Sorry."

"Why are you apologizing?"

MARIA V. SNYDER

"'Cause you're looking at your future. I'm going to turn into an obsessed old man who will demand that each bag of tea I make will have the exact same number of leaves while hair sprouts from my ears seemingly overnight."

She cocked her head to the side and stared at his right ear. "And how's that different than now?"

He growled. Mara squealed and ran for it. He caught her easily and carried her to the piles of hay. "Time to check on the horses," he whispered in her ear.

The next morning didn't go as smoothly as Leif had imagined.

"No." Mara crossed her arms, emphasizing her point.

Leif tried again. "But it'll be dangerous."

"No. Where you go, I go." She climbed into the wagon and sat next to Esau, picking up the reins. "We'll avoid populated areas and keep to the back roads. We'll be fine."

"Do you even know—"

"Leif Liana Zaltana, if you don't mount Rusalka, I'm going to run you over."

Esau covered his mouth but couldn't quite stop a chuckle. Great. This was just great. Didn't she know Leif wouldn't survive if something terrible happened to her? However, her stern expression meant he'd have more luck convincing the Commander to welcome magicians into Ixia.

Leif bit back a childish retort. Instead, he said "Fine" in a peevish tone, then mounted Rusalka and took point. The wagon team followed him from the farmstead.

They stayed close to the Sunworth River and kept to the back roads. Making steady progress to the southwest, Leif decided to remain well north of Fulgor and skirt the edge of the Snake Forest until they crossed into Featherstone lands. A solid plan, until it started to rain.

They'd been traveling about eight days when the skies opened and sheets of rain turned the road into a quagmire, forcing them to go south to access the stone-covered ground of the well-traveled east-to-west route.

Blending in with the other miserable travelers was the one benefit of being on a popular route. However, the presence of more patrols was the downside. But with the three of them huddled under cloaks and the plants hidden by the tarp, no one paid them much attention.

Two rainy days later, they were just about past the outer limits of Fulgor when the scent of burnt sugar stung Leif's nose. Magic. He tightened his grip on the reins but stayed still as the strong aroma swept over him. Rusalka jigged to the side, agitated by the sudden wave of magic. Leif kept his mental barrier firmly in place but was ready to build a null shield if they were attacked by a magician.

Nothing happened, and the scent disappeared. But just in case, Leif pressed on longer than normal, trying to get as far away from Fulgor as possible before they stopped for the night.

The next day dawned bright and beautiful. Too bad it didn't last. Two hours after they set off, Leif spotted a patrol of ten soldiers blocking the road, as if they'd been waiting for them.

Leif slowed Rusalka and opened his magical senses. When Mara caught up to him, he told her to stop the wagon.

"I'll go talk to them. Stay here, but be prepared to jump off the wagon and run into the woods if I give you the signal," he said.

"What's the signal?" she whispered.

His magic detected the sweet scent of her anxiety. It smelled like molasses. "I scream, 'Run.'"

"Clever."

"That's why I'm one of Valek's go-to guys for spy stuff."

She managed a smile. "Just be careful."

Leif nodded and spurred Rusalka into a gallop. Ideally this was just a routine road check and he could talk his way past them. When he rode into a fog of black licorice, his magic detecting deceit, he knew they were in trouble.

Big trouble.

He spun Rusalka around and drew breath to warn Mara, but the words died in his throat. Another patrol stood behind the wagon. Mara spotted them as well, and the bitter tang of her fear stabbed right through him.

Ah, hell. He grabbed the hilt of his machete.

Mara stood up and yelled, "Rusalka, go home."

"No!" But the well-trained horse grabbed the bit in her teeth, cut to the right and plunged into the woods at top speed, leaving Mara and his father far behind.

4

YELENA

After Valek left, I paced from the door to the kitchen and back again. The Mosquito was smart and well aware of Fisk's network. There was no way he'd let them find him unless he wanted them to. He probably had an ambush set up for Valek. At least a null shield no longer trapped him, but he was vulnerable to other magic. An intelligent magician would be able to adapt once he or she realized the shield didn't work.

I really wanted to get some fresh air, but I was trying to be sensible. There was no reason for me to go out. Turning around, I almost walked into Hilly. She blocked my path to the kitchen.

"Lovely Yelena, there are two runners upstairs waiting to report in."

I glanced at the door.

She inclined her head. "Do you think staring at the door will make him return faster?"

"No." In fact, he'd warned me he might not be back until the morning.

"Then why do it?"

"Because emotions don't always follow logic."

"Ah."

"And I'm going crazy."

"That I understand. Perhaps you need something to keep your mind occupied."

"The reports—"

"Not enough. What about all that plant information you and Mr. Valek collected?"

"I'm waiting for my father and brother."

She remained quiet.

I sighed in defeat. "But that doesn't mean I can't take a look at it now. Thanks, Hilly."

Flashing me a smile, she returned to the kitchen as I headed to Fisk's office. The two young boys sprang to their feet when they spotted me. Words tumbled from their mouths before I'd even settled behind the desk. I raised a hand, and they stopped.

Once I was ready, I asked them to repeat the information. Noting it down in Fisk's log book, I thanked them for the good work. I assumed it was vital. Fisk had his members gather an eclectic range of data. And from this variety, he was able to make connections and discover golden nuggets of intel.

I collected the files Valek and I had taken from Bavol's residence. Ignoring the dark brown stains of my own dried blood, I returned to the office. During my initial pass through, I organized them into three categories—useful, useless and beyond my expertise. I marked the third pile for my father.

Getting comfortable, I read through the notes in the useful stack. Bavol had considered the grafting techniques that Leif said Owen's unknown Master Gardener used to increase the production of Theobroma. He had sketches of how to cut into the tree's bark and insert a limb from an older tree and then bind them together. The older limb would produce pods quicker than the new host tree, cutting down on the two-year wait for the tree to mature.

I wondered if Bavol had tried it. There hadn't been any

plants in his home or office. Would he have used another location? Maybe in the Council Hall? No. Not enough light. Perhaps the Magician's Keep? The gardeners who worked for the Keep had an impressive amount of knowledge.

Another hour passed as I continued reading, marking some pages for my father to explain. But one sketch drove me to my feet. I ran to our rooms and hunted through my travel pack, hoping that it was still there after all the insanity of being captured by Bruns.

It was. Thank fate!

Dashing back to Fisk's office, I compared Onora's drawing from the Commander's castle to the sketch in Bavol's file. They matched. I sank into the chair, mulling over the significance. Onora had drawn the saplings that Owen had carried all the way from Sitia. He called them Harman trees, and they had to be important with a capital *I*. Now Bavol also had a picture of them, but there wasn't an explanation to go with it.

I growled in frustration. So close! However, this could be a clue that Owen's Master Gardener might have worked with Bavol at one point. And they needed a place to work close by. Maybe even one of those glass hothouses. I returned to my reading, hoping for another clue.

"What are you scowling at?" I jumped at the sound of Fisk's voice. He stood in the doorway.

"Bavol's notes. Did you have a productive afternoon?"

His light brown eyes shone. "I finally found Lovely Adara the perfect dress for her wedding."

"You're seriously excited about that? At a time like this?"

"Yes. She is extremely picky, and her father promised me double payment if I found her one within the week." He tapped his bulging pocket and coins rattled. "He hated to pay, but once again I proved I can find *anything* in the Citadel."

I grinned at him.

Fisk held his hands up. "Oh, no, what did I say?"

"Have you found a structure made of glass in the Citadel? Or maybe a building with lots of windows? Perhaps with greenery growing inside it?"

"No, but..." Fisk moved to his desk and dug through the drawers. "Tweet mentioned a green glass roof, but I thought I'd translated his report wrong."

"I'm amazed you understand him at all." Tweet's tongue had been cut out at a very young age, so he communicated with a variety of hoots and whistles. Hence the nickname.

"We both grew up on the streets," Fisk said, as if that explained everything. He withdrew a notebook and flipped through the pages. "Ah, here it is. Tweet tried to look inside, but a man spotted him and chased him off with threats of harm if he returned. I figured he'd found a skylight and was peering down into someone's bedroom. People don't like it when you spy into their private rooms." His tone made it clear that the very concept amazed him.

I suppressed a smile. "Where was this glass roof?"

"Not far from here. I can have someone take another look."

"I need to go and see it for myself," I said.

"But Valek—"

"—said I can get some fresh air. Besides, once he kills The Mosquito, the others will be too frightened to come after me. Plus it's close, and you'll be with me. Right?"

"I don't know."

I tried another tactic. "We can bring along a couple bodyguards, if that makes you feel better."

"Bodyguards? You do realize most of my people are underage."

I stared at him.

He fidgeted under my scrutiny. "Well, I do have a few members who are skilled fighters."

"Please, Fisk. I'm going crazy in here. Valek was okay with me leaving as long as we stay nearby."

"If anything happens—"

"It won't."

"—Valek's going to kill me."

"I'll kill you if I have to stay inside one more moment."

"Sorry, but Valek scares me more."

"That's 'cause you've never seen me cranky." I stood.

"All right, but we'll need disguises. And if Valek asks, you forced me at knife point."

"Chicken."

"Damn right."

Our disguises turned out to be a family. Fisk played the father, I took the role of mother and the bodyguards, Lyle and Natalie, were dressed as our children. The irony was not lost on me. With blond curls and chubby cheeks, Lyle was so adorable, I had to resist picking him up and hugging him.

As Fisk and I strolled hand in hand, I asked, "Are they even armed?"

"To the teeth."

"Must take after my side of the family."

Fisk chuckled. "They've been bugging Valek for lessons, and he's been kind enough to work with them when he has time." He squeezed my hand. "He's going to make a wonderful father."

I squeezed back in agreement. We walked for a while in silence. I enjoyed the fresh air and the afternoon sunshine warming my black hair. One of the guild members had pinned it into a sedate bun and used makeup to age my face. My future had stared back at me in the mirror.

Fisk navigated the maze of streets and buildings that comprised the northwest quadrant of the Citadel. Constructed

MARIA V. SNYDER

from a variety of building materials, the once-organized grid of residences was now a labyrinth of homes, apartments and shacks.

"Tweet said he'd meet us near there," Fisk said. "It's a bit tricky to find."

"Good. Is anyone following us?"

"No one has taken the least bit of interest in us."

I considered the speed of his reply. "You have more people shadowing us, don't you?"

"Of course."

"How many?" Or rather, just how scared of Valek was he?

"Two scouts and two sweepers."

"Sweepers?"

"They follow behind and ensure no one is trailing after us."

"Ah."

When we drew closer to our destination, Tweet appeared as if from nowhere. He took my other hand and smiled shyly. We strolled another couple blocks in silence.

"Go with Tweet," Fisk said. "He'll show you and Lyle where the glass roof is, and the rest of us will meet you on the flip side."

"All right."

Fisk released my hand, and I allowed Tweet to lead me. Lyle, the chubby-cheeked blond, trotted at my heels like a lost puppy. We cut through a narrow alley, climbed a rickety series of steps and cat-walked between buildings until we reached a roof. Tweet stopped and pointed to an adjoining roof that was made of glass. Sunlight reflected off the surface, so I was unable to see inside.

Tweet put a finger to his lips and mimed tiptoeing. Understanding the need to be quiet, I crept toward the glass roof. My pulse raced as I drew closer and spotted green shapes. But when I reached the edge, disappointment deflated my excitement.

Algae coated the inside of the glass. All the plants Bavol had been interested in would need sunlight to grow. I peered through a couple clear spots, but dead plants and shriveled leaves occupied most of the room. It appeared nothing but mold and fungus grew inside.

I returned to Tweet, who shrugged as if to say it was worth a shot.

Not about to give up, I crouched down and described the glass hothouse to Tweet. "In order to build it, they would have needed large sheets of glass. Maybe you or one of your friends saw a glassmaker delivering them?"

He met my gaze and nodded. Lyle and I followed him off the roof and joined Fisk. I shook my head at his questioning expression.

"Back to HQ?" he asked.

Tweet piped up with a series of hoots.

Fisk groaned. "Why didn't I think of that?"

"What did he say?" I asked.

"There's a glassmaker with a factory in the fourth ring of the Citadel who has been specializing in sheet glass for windows."

"Great. Let's go talk to him," I said.

"I don't know," Fisk hedged. "The bounty hunters have been watching the market. And you said Valek only approved a short trip."

"We'll avoid the market. Besides, with these snazzy disguises, no one will suspect a thing."

"You're killing me, and not with your humor," Fisk muttered. But he led the way, once again taking up his fatherly role.

We stayed away from the popular routes and avoided the deserted streets. Half the time I didn't know where we were, but I trusted my guides. I smelled the sweet odor of burning

MARIA V. SNYDER

white coal before I spotted the small factory tucked between two warehouses. The sign above the door read Keegan Glass.

A chime announced our arrival. Glass wine goblets, vases and pitchers decorated the display shelves. I gathered the "kids" close and told them not to touch anything.

A middle-aged man glided from a back room. He gave the kids a stern glare, as if daring them to misbehave, before asking if he could help us.

"I hope so," Fisk said. "We are building onto our house, and my wife wanted to put in big windows in the new kitchen. She loves her plants and would really love just a wall of glass, but that's impossible. What's the biggest size you can make?"

Well done. Fisk was flawless.

"Actually, sir, I can make you a wall of glass, if you'd like."

Fisk and I acted shocked. "But Crystal Glass said—"

"It's impossible?"

Fisk nodded.

"It is. For *them*. Not for Keegan Glass. *I've* made an entire *house* out of glass."

Yes! Keeping up the act, I furrowed my brow in suspicion. "Surely you jest."

"It's quite simple, actually." Keegan then proceeded to explain how he made sheets of special glass that were used to build a structure. "Mind you, it wasn't very big, but with enough support, it could have been bigger."

"Was it part of a house?" I asked.

"No. It was the size of a large shed, but I can make yours to attach to an existing structure."

Excited, I turned to Fisk. "With all that sunlight, I could grow all my own herbs!"

"You could," the glassmaker assured me. "In fact, the guy who ordered it mentioned something about vines."

Fisk pressed his lips together. "I'd like to see it first. Is it in the Citadel?"

"No. We delivered it to a farm south of the Citadel."

Fisk glanced at me. "Doesn't your cousin own a farm? She's also a plant nut. Maybe..."

But Keegan didn't fall for it. "Not likely. My client prefers that I don't discuss the specifics of his order."

Backing off, Fisk inquired about prices. Keegan wrote down the estimated measurements of the wall and returned to his back room. Fisk waited a few minutes before signaling the kids, who immediately started to bicker and then mock-fight. He gestured for me to intervene. I played the aggrieved mother trying to get her kids to stop. When they knocked over a couple vases, Keegan flew from the back room to admonish us.

I apologized and tried to clean up the mess while the kids continued their argument. As if on cue, the kids settled down, and we paid Keegan for the broken pieces. He was probably so glad to see us go that it would take him a while to realize that in addition to losing a sale, he'd lost an invoice as well. During the chaos, Fisk had slipped into Keegan's back room. Keegan would have used the invoice for the other job to estimate the price of our project. At least, that was the hope.

"Did you get it?" I asked Fisk when we turned the corner.

"Yep."

"And?"

He pulled a folded piece of parchment from his pocket and studied it. "No client name."

I cursed.

"Language, Mother," Lyle scolded.

"Be quiet, or I'll pinch those adorable cheeks of yours."

"Wouldn't be the first time," he muttered sourly.

"There is an address for delivery and a date," Fisk said.

Better. "Where was it sent?"

"A farm right along the border of the Avibian Plains."

Of course. The plains would be the perfect place to hide a glass hothouse. Only the Sandseed Clan and Zaltana Clan could travel across the plains without getting lost, and there were only a couple dozen Sandseeds left. But that meant if Bavol had been working with Owen's Master Gardener, then the mystery person had to be a member of the Zaltana Clan. My clan. My elation died.

"When was it delivered?" I asked Fisk.

"A little over three years ago. Do you think it's still there?"

I told him about my theory.

"Makes sense. No one would accidently discover it in the plains," Fisk said. "Too bad the plains are so huge. It'd be impossible to find."

"No, it wouldn't. Bavol would build it only far enough in to hide it from the roads. No reason to go any deeper."

"There's still a lot of ground to cover."

"Shouldn't be a problem for a Sandseed horse like Kiki."

"You can't go unless you have permission from Valek."

I laughed. "I'd like to see you stop me."

His face creased as if he was about to get sick to his stomach. "Yelena—"

"Relax, Fisk. I'm kidding, and I'm sure Valek will approve of the trip, since I'd be leaving the Citadel and going where only a few can follow."

"You're going to give me a heart attack one of these days. Do you know that?"

"You love all this intrigue and drama. You're the Sitian Valek."

Fisk laughed and started to shake his head, but his expression sobered. He glanced at me. "Do you think if we manage to save Sitia from the Commander, the Sitian Council would hire me as their Chief of Security?"

"They'd be idiots not to. But would you really want the job? You'd have bosses."

"Ugh. I didn't think of that. Hmm... I guess it would depend on the salary."

We walked toward HQ in companionable silence. The lamplighters began their nightly routine, moving from one lamppost to the next like synchronized fireflies. The sun had disappeared behind the Citadel's walls, which meant we'd been gone a few hours. Ideally we would return a few minutes before Valek, so I wouldn't have to worry about him. However, I'd be thrilled if he was already there, waiting for us, even if it meant I'd be in trouble for this extended trip. Although promising to remain in HQ had its...perks.

When we entered the northwest quarter, we caught up to the lamplighters. Amazed by their dexterity, I watched as one woman climbed the post one-handed, holding a lit torch in the other.

Fisk grabbed my elbow and pulled me along at a quicker pace. Concerned, I hurried to keep up and noticed that there were far more lamplighters than this street required, and yet half the lanterns remained dark. I glanced around. We were surrounded by a ring of figures holding blazing torches, and I was unarmed. I'd left my bo staff back at HQ because it didn't fit in with my disguise.

We stopped. I reached for my switchblade as nasty-looking curved daggers appeared in Lyle's and Natalie's hands. Even Fisk pulled a short sword from his tunic. My thoughts flashed to Valek as I slid my feet into a fighting stance. If I escaped, I'd never dismiss his concern for my safety as being overprotective again.

Undaunted by the display of weapons, the ring of fire tightened. My blood sizzled with fear. I shrank back as the lamplighters closed in on us. Even when I had magic, I had no control over fire. And, although I knew that the Fire Warper had been captured and imprisoned in a glass prison years ago, an irrational part of me expected to see him smirking at me through the flames.

Lyle, Natalie and Fisk formed a protective circle around me. They brandished weapons, but I'd bet all the coins in my pocket that they didn't have any experience fighting against a flaming torch. Neither did I. I held my switchblade, even though its nine-inch blade was inadequate. Fisk had the best shot with his short sword.

One of the lamplighters gestured to a small gap opening in the circle. "Fisk and the kids can go. We don't wish to harm them."

"No," Fisk said.

"Yes, go," I said at the same time.

"No."

I put my hand on his shoulder. "Go and bring back help."

"The sweepers should already be on the way for help." He glanced at me with a grim expression and whispered, "We need to delay as long as possible."

"I'm not worth your life."

Surprised, he said, "Sure you are. Without you, I wouldn't *have* this life."

"Fisk—"

"Time's up," the lamplighter said.

The gap closed, and the lamplighters rushed us. Although the kids showed an impressive amount of skill, the math just wasn't in our favor. Shorter weapons and a dozen against four. My switchblade was knocked from my hand, and it didn't take long for the four of us to be backed against the building.

A torch was thrust at my chest. "Hands up, or we'll set your clothes on fire."

I didn't need any more incentive. I held my arms up as heat

brushed my face. The bright light seared my vision, turning everything behind the fire black. Next to me, Fisk punched one of the lamplighters, but another ambusher swung his torch at Fisk's temple. Knocked unconscious, Fisk collapsed to the ground with a heart-stopping thud. Lyle and Natalie dove through the lamplighters' legs, and four of the attackers chased them. I hoped they escaped.

"Lace your hands behind your head," a voice ordered me.

I did as instructed, not only hooking my fingers together, but through my bun as well.

"Turn around."

I faced the wall. Someone grabbed my wrists. Then each one was pulled down behind my back and snapped into a cuff. These guys weren't taking any chances. But they failed to check my hands. I held two fistfuls of bobby pins.

Dousing their torches, they ignored my questions as they led me through the Citadel without saying a word. I hated to admit it, but posing as lamplighters had been a smart move. No one so much as glanced at us. Six of them kept me boxed in the middle, hidden from casual view. I dropped one bobby pin after each turn, hoping that Valek could follow my trail and I didn't run out before we reached our destination.

I wondered just how long they'd been waiting for me to leave the security of HQ. The ambush must have taken some planning. Did they set it in motion as soon as I was spotted this afternoon? How did they know I'd still be out at twilight?

Did it really matter at this point? No. All that mattered was that it had worked, and I was caught.

We entered the rings of warehouses, factories and businesses in the central area of the Citadel. Looping around to the alley behind a sprawling structure, the lamplighters led me inside. Before I stepped over the threshold, I dropped my last two bobby pins. Piles of crates littered the floor, and we

MARIA V. SNYDER

wove around them before stopping at a set of stairs that disappeared down to the dark basement.

One of the group found a lantern and lit it. A skittery prickle coated my skin as we descended. My imagination conjured up visions of a dank cell and being tortured. I slowed. Hands grabbed my arms and pulled me along. At the bottom of the steps was a narrow hallway, and at the end was another door. My insides turned to goo and I braced for the horrors that waited for me within.

5

VALEK

"That's it?" Onora asked, sounding disappointed. "Thought I'd get to see a show. You versus The Mosquito on a rooftop venue."

Valek gestured with his bloody dagger to the four prone forms around her bare feet. "Thanks for the help."

She shrugged. "Trapping you in a null shield wasn't fair."

"Are they dead?"

"No."

"The Commander send you?"

"Yup." Onora studied Valek without emotion. She had pulled her long brown hair into a bun on top of her head. "But you knew that already."

"It never hurts to pretend ignorance."

"Or to have people underestimate you."

"Yup." Valek wondered if that was a hint about her true abilities. He'd expected her to ambush him, not square off against him in a fair fight. That meant she was either crazy, brave or very confident. He'd put his money on confidence.

Onora stepped over The Mosquito's sleeping goons. When she was within six feet, she pulled her daggers. Valek excelled at knife fighting, but Onora had been trained by the same teacher—and she was about twenty years younger than him.

He met her gaze. "Stay in Sitia with us. We need you."

There was a split-second flash of hesitation in her gray eyes, and then it was gone. "I gave my loyalty to the Commander. *I* don't go back on my word."

"The Commander is not the same man I pledged my loyalty to. Even you have to admit he's changed." When she didn't respond, he added, "You're taking orders from Owen Moon now."

"I thought only Janco talked this much before a fight."

Valek shrugged. "Just trying to prevent an unnecessary death."

"Keep it up, and I'm gonna *die* of boredom."

Valek laughed. "Now who's picking up habits from Janco?"

She pressed her lips together and slid into a fighting stance. He waited for her to make the first move. Good thing he didn't blink, because when she came at him, he barely blocked her knives in time. His suspicions were correct—Onora *had* been hiding her skills.

This was going to be...interesting.

At five feet eight inches, Onora was four inches shorter than Valek, but she made up for her height disadvantage with speed and agility. Valek remained on the defensive as she shuffled in close, executed a flurry of strikes and danced back before he could counter. Then she switched tactics, circling him and coming in at an angle. Worry flickered in his chest.

"The Commander's been training you," he said.

"Yup."

A brief stab of hurt and jealousy almost broke his concentration. While the Commander had always been willing to spar, he'd never offered to teach his fighting techniques to Valek.

Fire raced across his neck as her blade skimmed over the

skin, snapping Valek back to the fight. He returned his full attention to Onora. But an impressive number of cuts peppered his arms and ribs by the time Valek had seen enough of her tactics to plan a counterattack. The next time she stepped forward, he also shuffled in close.

Valek launched an aggressive offensive of strikes with not only his blades but also his feet. His longer legs kept Onora at a distance.

She grinned at the new challenge. *Grinned.* Ah, hell.

He kept the pressure on her but knew he wouldn't be able to maintain the pace for long. Already he sucked in breaths, while she appeared unfazed by the exertion. Real fear pumped through his heart.

He changed tactics again, this time trying all his tricks. He hooked her ankle and sent her to the ground. She rolled and regained her feet with ease. Valek poured on the speed and backed her toward the edge of the roof. She dodged and sidestepped.

Then he started fighting dirty. She growled, but countered. In a flash of understanding, Valek knew he wouldn't win unless he used magic.

No.

With the last of his strength, he knocked the blades that had been aimed at the center of his chest, just wide enough to miss his vital organs—he hoped. Valek dropped his own weapons, shuffled in close and grabbed her wrists as she stabbed one blade into his shoulder and the other into his left hip.

Ignoring the explosion of pain, Valek fell back onto the roof, pulling her with him. He wrapped his legs around her torso and squeezed her to his chest. Onora struggled to free herself. He tightened his grip, making it difficult for her to breathe and proving that he'd won the bout. He didn't want to squeeze the life out of her, but he'd do it to save his own life. Yelena and the baby needed him.

She stopped resisting. "I…wasn't going…to…kill…you," Onora gasped.

"Oh? You sure…looked like you…wanted to kill me," he puffed. The pain and effort of the fight had caught up to him.

"I wanted…to…see if I…*could* beat…you." She relaxed. "I can't."

Valek eased up on the pressure but didn't let her go. "You came closer…than anyone. Only the Commander…has beaten me one-on-one." He considered her earlier comment. "If you weren't going to kill me…then what did you plan to do… when you had your knife at my throat?"

"Make you promise to come back to Ixia with me."

Not what he was expecting. At all. He thought about it as his breath steadied. "The Commander is getting worse."

"Yes. Obviously it's due to Owen Moon, but I can't *do* anything. Your corps won't acknowledge me as their boss, so I've no help except Gerik. I swore to protect the Commander, so I thought if I let you live, you'd return with Ari and Janco and help me free the Commander."

"You'd have to tell him you assassinated me." He wondered if the Commander would be upset by the news. Probably not while under Owen's influence.

"Yeah. Otherwise all Owen would have to do is use one of those shields, and you'd be skewered."

He huffed in amusement at her use of another Janco term. The motion hurt like hell. "Like I am now." Valek released his hold on her.

She extricated herself and sat up. "Sorry. I really didn't expect that last move."

He waved away her apology. "Desperate times…"

"Do you want me to…" She made a yanking motion.

"No." Valek tried to sit up. Pain forced him back down. "Yes. I'll need some bandages." He could heal his wounds with magic, but not on top of a roof without Yelena nearby to give him instructions.

Onora picked up one of Valek's knives. He tensed, but she crossed to The Mosquito's goons and cut strips of cloth off their tunics. It would take a while for Valek to trust her. He'd won, but it had cost him. If they'd fought again, she'd win. Of that he had no doubt.

Returning with the bandages, Onora set the knife aside. "Which one first?"

"Hip." He braced for the pain as she wrapped a hand around the hilt. Even so, a gasp hissed between his clenched teeth as she yanked it free. Blood poured out.

She helped him staunch and bandage the wound. Then she moved to his shoulder, and he experienced a whole new kind of agony. He was too old for this shit. When she finished securing the bandage, Onora let him lean on her as he stood. A moment of dizziness spun the Citadel around him. When the world steadied, he realized the sun balanced on the edge of oblivion. They must have fought for half an hour, at least. No wonder he felt as if he'd been run over by a herd of horses.

Onora picked up his daggers with exaggerated slowness and handed them to him hilt first. Smart. He met her gaze as he tucked them away. Then she cleaned hers and slid them back into their hidden sheaths.

"Can you climb down?" she asked.

He walked to the edge and peered into the dark alley below. The descent was doable, but it was going to be torture. "Yes."

"What about the bug and his people?"

"Leave them. His people will eventually wake and need to decide what to do with his body." Speaking of deciding, Valek glanced at Onora. "What are you going to do now?"

"Go with you, if your offer is still good."

"And if it isn't?"

She didn't blink. "I don't know. I can't go back to Ixia. Guess I'd have to find a job here."

And he was sure Bruns would be happy to employ her. "My offer stands, but it's going to take me a while to trust you again."

Onora looked up in surprise. "Again? I thought you *never* trusted me."

"That's what you were supposed to think."

Crossing her arms, she studied him. "So, to me, nothing's changed."

"Yup. Except when I do trust you, we'll go rescue the Commander."

She smiled, and it reached her eyes. It was that smile that convinced him she'd been telling the truth. However, he wasn't going to let her know. No. He'd let her sweat it out for a while.

As expected, the climb to the alley was a test of his pain tolerance. Twice he clung to the wall and fought off unconsciousness as fire burned along his shoulders and ringed his waist. Thank fate the trip down didn't take long. Onora waited for him below.

Once he recovered, he asked, "Do you know where we've been staying?"

"Yes."

"How long have you been in town?"

"A couple days."

He cursed. "Fisk will need to relocate his headquarters."

She agreed. "There are a number of assassins in town. I don't know if that's normal, but it's a good thing they're not the brightest."

Small comfort. Valek told her about the bounty.

"Yelena needs to leave the Citadel," Onora said, alarmed. "The city is contained by an unclimbable wall and has only so many hiding places. Even those idiots will find her eventually."

He barked a laugh that turned into a hiss. "I tried logic."

"Try again."

He admired her optimism. She followed him as he crossed the Citadel, staying in the shadows. Her passage was soundless, and when he glanced back at her, her skin and clothing appeared darker, as if she was turning into a shadow. Valek remembered Janco commenting on how well Little Miss Assassin blended in with her surroundings. Janco hadn't detected magic, but he didn't always pick up on the more subtle users, like Reema. It was a bad time to open his magical senses so Valek added it to the list of things he still needed to discover about Onora.

When they reached the secret entrance to Fisk's HQ, Valek said, "Here's the story. My injuries are due to a fight with The Mosquito. He used magic and, if you hadn't come along to help, I'd be dead. Oh, and you had no intention of carrying out the Commander's order to assassinate me."

"Except for the fight with the bug, it's true. Why the change?"

"You tell me."

It didn't take her long. "You don't want Yelena to be mad at me." Her brow crinkled. "Why?"

He waited.

Onora shook her head, truly puzzled.

"Because she considers you a friend. Yelena doesn't have many friends. And none who have also been—" there really was no way to say this gently "—raped. You share that in common, and it forges a bond. I don't want to ruin that for her... or you." He sensed she needed it more than his wife.

"Thanks."

He nodded and tapped the code on the door. Hilly opened it. Her gaze slid to Onora.

"This is Onora. She's going to be staying with us."

She stepped aside, letting them in. Hilly took one look at his bloody tunic and said, "I'll fetch Chale."

"Thanks. Can you tell Yelena I'm back?"

Hilly paused and turned around. Her tight expression warned him before the words left her mouth. "She's not here."

He stilled as a number of emotions fought for dominance. Fury rose to the surface, but his battered body couldn't produce the energy to sustain it. Instead, a tired anger laced his voice. "Where is she?"

"She's with Fisk, two bodyguards, Tweet and a four-person surveillance team. They're wearing disguises. She's fine."

"That's not what I asked."

"They went to check a glass roof in this quadrant. They should be back any minute—"

"Not helping."

"I don't know."

Valek tightened his grip on his knives. He hadn't realized he'd drawn them.

"I'll go," Onora said.

"No. She knows the Commander sent you. We'll go together."

"Renée! Innis!" Hilly called into the kitchen behind her. "Report for backup."

"We don't—" Valek tried.

"They know all the problem spots. And they can fight."

Two teens raced into the room. Both were about sixteen years old. Renée was a sturdy-looking girl with pale skin and red hair, but Innis looked like a stiff wind could blow him over. Nonetheless, their determined expressions warned him that arguing would involve too much energy. And he needed every ounce to find Yelena. They tucked daggers into hidden sheaths. Valek figured he'd ditch them if they couldn't keep up.

Without a word, he strode to the door and headed out. It took another minute for his brain to catch up with his body. He had no plan, and therefore no direction and no way of finding Yelena. Valek stopped and sorted through the limited information. Hilly mentioned a roof. A rudimentary plan formed.

"I need to get onto a roof, or the highest point in this quadrant, without scaling a wall. Can you get me there?"

Renée and Innis exchanged a glance.

"Penny's Arch?" Renée asked.

Innis nodded. "Safest bet."

"This way," Renée said before taking off with a ground-eating stride.

Valek, Onora and Innis followed. After ten minutes, he hoped the teens wouldn't ditch *him*. At least the effort to maintain the pace kept his mind occupied. His injuries throbbed with pain, and he didn't have any spare energy to conjure up various dire scenarios for his missing wife.

The street lamps emitted enough light for them to skirt security patrols, avoid busy intersections and cut through an impressive number of alleys. Then it turned tricky.

Renée scrambled up a dilapidated shed and crossed a high fence to get onto the roof that was connected to a row of houses. Innis accomplished it with equal ease. Valek sweated as he climbed and almost lost his balance on the fence. Onora touched his elbow to steady him.

Once on the roof, they stayed on the top of the buildings, winding through the quadrant. The place resembled a maze, and Valek didn't have the strength to track their location.

Penny's Arch turned out to be a thick walkway between

MARIA V. SNYDER

two buildings. It arched high up in the middle, as if the structures had shuffled closer together and bowed it.

Valek scanned the area, noting the brief patterns of the original structures that emerged from the unorganized mess. He didn't know what he'd expected—a giant hand pointing to a specific section? Maybe if he used magic...

Valek lowered his mental barrier and was immediately assaulted with the thoughts of the thousands of people all around him. He raised his shield again, cursing. The entire endeavor had been a waste of precious time.

About to ask Renée to lead them back to HQ, Valek noticed that one area was darker than the others, but there was a bright glow right next to it. As if all the lanterns had decided to huddle together instead of spreading out.

Assassins were creatures of night and shadows, and if they'd set up an ambush, it would be in the darkest part of the city. And if there wasn't a naturally dark spot, then they wouldn't hesitate to create one.

"Renée, can you get us where it's dark?" Valek asked, pointing to the spot.

"Yes. It's near the entrance. There are two routes. Which one?"

"The fastest one."

"There's a wall."

"Up or down?"

"Down."

"I can handle it. Let's go."

Another race through the city. More pain and the conviction that his arm was about to rip from his shoulder. The trip blurred into one test of endurance. He kept his gaze trained on Renée's back, concentrating on the next step.

Shouts pierced his fog. Two more of Fisk's guild members

joined them. Their mouths moved, but it took him a moment to decipher their words. And when he did, they made no sense.

"Slow down. What's this about sweepers and lamplighters attacking?" he asked.

"They're the sweepers for Fisk and Yelena's surveillance team," Innis explained. "They were running for help. Guess the scouts missed the ambush."

The word zipped through him. "What ambush?"

"The lamplighters. Or people dressed like the lamplighters. They attacked with…" He swallowed, afraid to continue.

"With what?" Valek kept his fists pressed to his side to keep his hands from grabbing the boy's shoulder and shaking him.

"Torches."

Cold dread numbed Valek's pain. "Where?"

"This way."

He pulled his daggers and noticed Onora and the others doing the same. They raced after the two sweepers, heading toward the bright spot he'd seen from Penny's Arch.

Except when they arrived, it was no longer ablaze with light. Instead, the dark area had spread, encompassing the entire street. Valek signaled for everyone to slow down. No sense rushing into another ambush.

They found the scouts first. The two young men had been knocked out, but their pulses were strong. Fisk lay crumpled on his side next to one of the buildings. He was unconscious as well, and had a large, fist-sized burn on his left temple. Blood dripped from a cut on his cheek. Valek suppressed his fury, keeping a firm grip on his magic.

"The lamplighters formed a circle around them and forced them up against the building," one of the sweepers explained.

"How many of them?" Valek asked.

"At least a dozen."

Lovely.

MARIA V. SNYDER

"Over here," Renée called. "I found Lyle and Berk."

Valek crouched beside them. Peppered with cuts, bruises and burns, the two...boys looked in worse shape than Fisk. But their chests rose and fell with even breaths. "Are they the bodyguards?"

"Yes."

Incredible.

"They're good," Renée said in their defense. "They were just outnumbered."

"Any sign of Yelena?" he asked the group.

No response.

Onora appeared next to Valek. "A word?"

They moved away from the others. "Did you find something?"

"I've an idea of which direction they're headed."

"Let's go." He stepped past her, but she touched his shoulder and he bit back a scream of pain.

Onora showed him her bloody fingers. "You're in no condition to go anywhere. I'm surprised you made it this long with the amount of blood you've lost."

Valek growled at her, "I'm fine."

She stared at him. "Twelve of them. Two of us. Think you can handle six with that shoulder?"

He sighed. "I'm listening."

"Go back to HQ and take care of your injuries. I'll discover where they've taken Yelena. Then I'll return, and we can plan a way to get her back. Together."

She was right. Yet his heart didn't agree. It slammed against his chest, trying to rally the troops, get the body moving, or else it threatened to break out and go on without him. "What if she doesn't have the time to wait for us to plan?"

"If they wanted her dead, we would have found her body."

She was right. But could Valek trust her?

Onora met his gaze, sensing his hesitation. "She's my friend. My only friend. Ever. I'm not going to let *anything* happen to her."

"What about Sergeant Gerik?"

"He's not my friend. He's my brother."

MARIA V. SNYDER

6

LEIF

By the time Leif wrestled control back, Rusalka had taken them far away from the wagon and its precious cargo—Mara and his father. None of the patrol members had chased after him. Leif dismounted and walked Rusalka, letting the horse cool down. He needed to cool his raging thoughts, as well.

Impotent fury burned in his chest over what Mara had done. She'd commanded Rusalka to go home, and the horse hadn't hesitated. Damn. This was the exact reason why he'd wanted Mara to ride Rusalka. So she'd be safe. But she'd refused, and now she was caught, along with his father. Double damn.

Trying to suppress his fear and anger, Leif considered his next move. The patrol would most likely take them to Fulgor, to either the security headquarters or the garrison. If he could intercept them before they arrived…

No. Too many of them. Plus the soldiers were on horseback, and Leif would need to bring along a couple mounts for Mara and Esau. Doubtful he'd find any extra horses in the middle of nowhere. Leif glanced around at the forest and realized he had no sense of his location. As much as he hated—no, despised—the idea, he'd have to wait until they were taken to a specific place before he could rescue them.

At least he had friends and family in Fulgor. Opal, Mara's younger sister, wouldn't hesitate to help him, and neither would her husband, Devlen. Leif checked Rusalka's legs and gave her water, but his mind was already planning his next move.

Only later, with Rusalka headed toward Fulgor, did Leif grudgingly acknowledge Mara's quick thinking and intelligence. Of the three of them, he had the best chance of coordinating a successful rescue. He had magic, connections and the most experience. It made sense that he'd be the one to escape.

But that didn't mean he had to like it.

Opal's glass factory appeared to be abandoned. No light shone from any of the windows. The sweet smell of burning white coal didn't float downwind. No one had entered or left since he'd started surveilling the place around midafternoon. Leif looped around the building one more time, checking for other watchers, and spotted a couple with a view of the front doors. Interesting.

He ducked down the alley and picked the side door's lock. Inside, he confirmed his suspicions. Dark, quiet and cold—three things he'd never experienced when visiting Opal's factory previously. The four kilns had always remained blazingly hot, day and night. Heating glass to its melting point took too much time and effort to let the cauldrons cool.

Leif lit a lantern and checked the apartment on the second story. Opal, Devlen and their two adopted children, Reema and Teegan, lived above the factory. A sick feeling swirled in his stomach when he spotted the overturned chairs and broken table in the kitchen. The military must have taken them. With Devlen's superior fighting skills and Opal's ability to

MARIA V. SNYDER

make magic detectors, they would be an asset to the Cartel. Once they were brainwashed, of course. And even though Opal was immune to magical subversion, she would do anything to keep Reema safe.

Yelena had sent a messenger to Opal weeks ago, warning them of the Sitian takeover, but Leif guessed they didn't get it in time. Good thing Teegan was currently safe on the coast.

Leaving by the same door he'd entered, Leif headed toward the headquarters for Fulgor's security. Nic and Eve, two officers and friends of Opal, might be able to help him. But once he arrived, the number of uniformed soldiers coming and going at HQ meant the military had taken control of the local security and would likely arrest Leif on sight. No surprise, as martial law had been declared, but it had still been worth checking. Leif watched the flow in and out for a couple hours, just in case he spotted Nic's broad shoulders or Eve's short hair. No luck.

Leif had one last place to go before he ran out of options. Then what?

He pushed down the panic. He'd worry about that later.

The Pig Pen bustled with customers despite the late hour. Leif noted four Sitian soldiers, but he'd altered his appearance as much as he could under the circumstances. It was hard to disguise his square face or his stocky build. No sign of Nic or Eve, and their two stools remained empty. Nic's twin brother Ian owned the Pen and nobody would dare to sit in Nic's or his partner's space. Leif settled on one of the empty stools and waited.

"Those stools are not for you," the man next to him said. "You better find another place to sit."

"I like this stool," Leif said.

"You're either brave or stupid."

"I like to think I'm a little of both. It keeps people guessing," Leif replied. Then he waved at Ian, who was tending the bar. "An order of beef stew and an ale."

His neighbor laughed and muttered, "This ought to be good."

Ian didn't acknowledge Leif's existence. Didn't make a move, as far as Leif could tell, but within a minute, four thugs surrounded Leif.

"You're leaving," Thug One said.

They grabbed Leif under the arms and carried him to the door. Then they tossed him to the sidewalk. Leif rolled on impact and regained his feet.

"Tell the proprietor that I will no longer frequent his business. He doesn't get a second chance."

"Don't come back, Meat," Thug Two said.

They remained in front of the entrance. Leif brushed his pants off, glared at the impenetrable wall of muscle, and walked off in a huff. He took a circuitous route to the Second Chance Inn and found a hidden place to keep an eye on the inn's entrance. He settled in for a long wait.

If Ian hadn't been influenced by the Cartel, he would relay the message to Nic and Eve that Leif was at the inn. Provided Nic and Eve were also free. If Ian had been converted by the Cartel's special indoctrination methods, then Leif expected a number of soldiers to storm the inn, looking for him.

When the sun rose in the morning without either scenario developing, Leif realized he'd have to rescue Mara and his father on his own. An almost impossible task.

Leif wandered the city, reviewing his options. He could return to the Citadel and recruit helpers. Or he could turn himself in and offer his cooperation and loyalty in exchange for Mara and Esau's freedom. The Cartel was run by business people who honored written contracts.

Or he could go in undercover as one of the soldiers. With

MARIA V. SNYDER

a null shield around him, he'd be able to avoid detection for a while. Then Leif remembered Fisk already had people undercover in the garrison. If he could just contact one of them—

"Spare a copper, sir?" a street rat asked him, holding out a grubby hand.

"Uh…sure…" Leif fished a silver coin from his pocket and gave it to…her? It was hard to tell under the grime.

"Thank you, sir. I have something for you in return," she said.

"Oh?" He opened his magical senses, but only the clean scent of honesty reached him.

"A bit of advice. You need to leave Fulgor. Right away."

"I'm not going anywhere."

"You can't stay here. You've been spotted all over town. It's amazing you haven't been arrested already." Her tone was a combination only a young teen girl could pull off—equal parts annoyed, dismissive and incredulous.

In any other circumstance, Leif would have been amused. "Maybe you can help me? I'm—"

"You're too hot, Mr. Leif. You really need to leave."

Ah. She was a member of Fisk's guild. "Not without my wife and father. They were captured and brought to the garrison."

Understanding smoothed her dirty face. "Oh, so you're *trying* to be arrested. No need. They're not here."

7

YELENA

My captors opened the door into the basement of the warehouse. The bright warmth spilling from the entrance threw me off balance. I blinked and, for a moment, thought I'd been transported to the Commander's throne room or a security office. Lanterns blazed from desks. Men and women bustled about or grouped together, discussing what must be important things, if I read their expressions correctly. A few glanced at us but didn't think my arrival all that noteworthy.

Weaving through the people and furniture, our group—now down to four, plus me—headed toward an open doorway, where more light and voices poured out.

Entering the room, my captors stopped. Three men hunched over a blueprint on a table, arguing over the best way to bypass the building's security.

The guy holding my right elbow cleared his throat to catch their attention. "You were right, General, she's terrified of fire."

The man with his back to us turned around, and my emotions seesawed between terror and relief. Cahil. My survival would depend largely on his state of mind, but at least there was some hope when dealing with him.

"Good. Any trouble?" General Cahil asked.

"Nothing we couldn't handle."

"Valek?" He spat the name.

"Occupied with his own ambush."

Worry for him eclipsed my own fears. Did Cahil set up an ambush for him, as well, or had someone else? Was it Onora?

I kept the questions—and my rising concern—to myself. I wouldn't give Cahil the satisfaction.

"Weapons?" Cahil held out his hand, and the lamplighter gave him my switchblade. He shook his head. "Hanni, search her. Be careful. She'll have a number of darts—some filled with Curare—a blowpipe and a couple sets of lock picks. Check her hair, too."

Damn. Cahil knew me too well. Hanni, who had been standing behind me, did a thorough search and found almost all my hidden surprises. She laid them on the table, and the other men stared at the amount in amazement. As Valek said, it never hurt to be prepared. Too bad I hadn't listened to all his advice.

Cahil's gaze, though, never left mine. His blond hair was military short and he'd shaved off his beard, but not his mustache. Amusement lit his washed-out blue eyes. "This reminds me of the first time we met."

That time I'd been ambushed in the woods. Cahil had believed I was an Ixian traitor and planned to deliver me to the Sitian Council in chains. We'd gone on to become friends, then enemies, and finally called a cease-fire when he was promoted to be a general in the Sitian army and I was named Liaison. However, the last time I saw Cahil, he was taking orders from the Cartel. Was he still under Bruns's influence?

"And I escaped."

"True. But you had your magic then."

He had a point. I studied him. Was Cahil aware that the Commander's invasion was just a ruse to give control of the garrisons to the Cartel? That Bruns planned to use the Sitian military to take over Sitia without ever going to war? That Owen Moon practically ruled Ixia?

Now might not be the best time to broach the subject.

"What? No smart comment?"

I shrugged. "Too easy."

He laughed. "Some things never change."

Tired of the game, I asked, "Can we skip all this? What do you want, Cahil?"

Cahil gestured to the wall. "Secure her," he ordered his people.

Resisting netted me a number of bruises, but I managed to knee one of the guys in the groin and kick another in the shin—a small victory, considering they chained my wrists to the rough stones with my arms spread wide. My ankles were manacled together and secured to the wall, as well.

While my situation had gone from bad to worse, I just couldn't contain my amusement. "Are you *that* scared of me, Cahil?"

His cheeks turned red, and he ordered the others out of his office. Closing the door, he turned to me with a dangerous expression. "I know you, Yelena. I know what you're capable of. What situations you've escaped from. This—" he swept his hand at me "—is excessive for a normal person, but you're far from normal."

"Is that a compliment, Cahil?"

"If it makes you feel better, then yes. It is."

"Good to know you wish me to feel better. I was beginning to worry that you meant me harm, Cahil." I kept using his

MARIA V. SNYDER

name to remind him of the time when we were once friends. A trick Valek had taught me.

He rubbed his hand over his jaw and leaned on the desk, as if suddenly tired. A haunted emptiness clouded his expression, and for the first time since seeing Cahil, I feared for my life.

"What do you want, Cahil?"

"To talk with you."

I bit back a sarcastic comment about having to work on his invitation skills. "I'm willing to talk to you, Cahil, but am I talking to *you* or to *Bruns*?"

"That doesn't make any sense. I report to Bruns."

"Does Bruns know you're here?"

"Of course."

Not good. "What is this place?"

"My base of operations." He quirked a smile. "I never felt secure in the one they assigned me in the Council Hall, so I constructed my own. And I took a page from Valek's spy book and recruited a group of loyal people."

"And you used this network to help Bruns and the rest of the Cartel."

"Yes. They wanted to protect Sitia, and the Council refused to see the need."

Old news. "And now?"

"Why are you fighting the Cartel? Don't you want to see Sitia safe for your child?"

A loaded question. "I'm fighting Bruns to keep Sitia safe."

"Yet another statement that doesn't make sense."

"And I won't be able to explain it to you, Cahil."

"Why not?"

"You won't believe me. You've been indoctrinated."

He paced in agitation. "What the hell does that mean?"

"It means that since you've been ingesting Theobroma for

seasons, you're *all* under his control. None of you can think for yourselves any longer."

Cahil shook his head, stopping in front of me. "No. The Commander is a threat to Sitia. And Bruns is a genius. He's combined our resources, and we finally have an advantage over the Commander's army. We don't have to be afraid anymore."

"I agree, he's innovative. But what happens if the Commander doesn't invade Sitia?"

"Our intel says he's planning to attack soon after the fire festival."

"Which Bruns learned from Valek."

Cahil frowned.

"And why did he order you to the Citadel to find me? Aren't you supposed to be leading the Sitian army against a major attack in four months?"

"Because he knew I'd get the job done. You can't argue about that." He gestured to my chains.

"Fair point. But couldn't you have told someone else how to trap me? I'm sure you have more important things to do."

"It doesn't work that way. Can you just tell someone how to find souls?"

Score another for Cahil. I changed tactics. "What happens if the Commander doesn't wage war?" I asked again.

A mulish look settled on his face.

"Nothing happens, right? If the Commander is such a threat to Sitia's safety, then why doesn't Bruns plan to invade Ixia and take care of that threat once and for all?"

"We're not like the Ixians. We value life. As long as we're ready, the Commander won't invade."

I sagged against the wall. He'd been fully brainwashed. Nothing I could say would change his mind. "When is Bruns coming to kill me and the baby?"

Cahil stilled. "I haven't told him you're here."

MARIA V. SNYDER

Oh? I waited.

"The Commander's new assassin is in town. She and Valek were spotted having quite the battle on the rooftops and, I'm not sorry to say, your husband wasn't doing very well."

I kept my expression neutral despite the pain squeezing my heart into pulp.

"Our intel says that after she kills Valek, she'll be coming after you next."

Not a surprise, but still it felt like a kick to my stomach. "You're going to let an Ixian do your dirty work?"

"Yes. You see, despite your current efforts to undermine Bruns, Sitians like you. If Bruns or I were to execute you, it wouldn't be well received. But if the Commander is responsible for your death, the people will be upset and continue to support our efforts."

Ah, hell. A smart move, although I was surprised Bruns agreed. Or had he? "Bruns doesn't know what you plan to do."

"Bruns had his chance to kill you, and he screwed it up because he wanted you as a showpiece."

"What if Valek kills Onora?"

"Then I let one of the assassins in town score fifty golds. Now, if you'll excuse me, I've work to do." He headed for the door.

"Cahil."

He paused without looking at me.

"If Onora comes for me, can you free me from these chains and return my switchblade?"

"You won't beat her."

"I'd rather die fighting than chained to this wall."

He met my gaze. "All right."

Waiting was never fun. However, when I considered what I was waiting for... I forced my thoughts away, but of course they just circled right back around. If Valek won the fight with Onora, I might emerge from this situation alive. If he didn't, I wouldn't. Unless Fisk's people moved in before Onora could. My emotions flipped from optimistic hope to fatalistic numbness and back again.

In order to remain sane, I focused on how I could protect the baby. I concentrated on what I could do. Me, and not any what-if scenarios about being rescued. But after looking at every possibility, I conceded that my chance of survival was close to zero.

Time limped along, and one of Cahil's agents came by to feed me a handful of grapes. The voices in the other room eventually died, and the lanterns were turned down. They must be stopping for the night.

The thought of a night spent chained to the wall produced mixed feelings. The longer I remained alive, the greater the hope of rescue. Besides, stiff muscles and discomfort were a mere inconvenience if it meant Valek lived.

Another agent strode into the office. He extinguished the lanterns and muttered a hasty good-night before bolting. There were a number of words to describe this night, and *good* wasn't one of them. Nope, not even close. I managed to doze briefly, at least until a burning pain in my shoulders woke me.

Cahil returned in the morning, or what I assumed was the morning, as he appeared awake and clean-shaven. He stood staring at me while one of his men lit the lanterns.

Unable to endure the silence any longer, I asked, "What's the verdict?"

"The Mosquito is dead."

"That's good news."

"I'd thought you'd like that."

"What's the bad news?" I braced for his answer.

"Onora was spotted in the Citadel late last night."

MARIA V. SNYDER

My legs trembled with the effort to hold my weight. The chains prevented me from sinking to the floor. Valek would never have allowed her to walk away from a fight. The fact that she lived meant…

"We were unable to locate Valek's body."

"Why would you care about that?" I asked, leaning back on the wall as the rest of my world melted.

"Confirmation. We think she's hidden the body to keep everyone guessing long enough to avoid any retaliation from Fisk and his people."

The body. No longer being referred to by name. I concentrated on Cahil's comment to keep from screaming. My focus narrowed to one thing—keeping the baby safe. "Why would she worry about Fisk's guild? If she can…beat Valek, no one else can touch her."

"Fisk has the numbers, plus Stormdancers."

"Stormdancers?" This kept getting worse. If Bruns suspected the Stormdancers, then they needed to disappear. Fast.

"Don't act stupid, Yelena. A huge thunderstorm roared over the Krystal garrison at the precise moment you needed a distraction to escape. You couldn't have done it without their help."

"We would have figured something out." Eventually. Maybe. Probably not. Bruns had us pinned.

"You know, I was about to disagree, but I'm sure you would have, which is exactly why keeping you alive is a bad strategy."

"Trying to rationalize your decision so you don't feel guilty, Cahil?"

"I won't feel guilty. I'm protecting over a million people. If only you understood that we're doing the right thing—" he gestured vaguely "—none of this has to happen."

"I understand that's what you believe." I straightened as a

sudden notion popped into my head. Perhaps a way to save the baby. "How about a deal?"

"No deals."

"Okay. How about you prove me wrong?"

Cahil gave me a just-how-dumb-do-you-think-I-am look. "Okay, I'll bite. How would I do that?"

"You stop eating the food Bruns's people cook and wear a null shield for ten days. After that, if you still think Bruns's strategy is beneficial for Sitia, then I'll sign up and help you convince Fisk and all his people to join up, as well."

"And why would I trust you?"

"Because I'd give you my word, Cahil. And you know me. I've never broken a promise. Not even to the Fire Warper."

A contemplative purse rested on Cahil's lips. Then he chuckled. "You almost had me, Yelena. But I'm not falling for any of your tricks."

"It's not a trick. I'm serious. Think about it. There's no downside for you."

"Yes, there is. I'd have to let you live for ten days. Plenty of time for Fisk to send in his troops and rescue you."

Good point. "I'll send them home. I'll stay with you."

"Why would they listen to you? You could have been… what's the word you used?…*indoctrinated* to the cause."

I balled my hands into fists. Another valid concern. "It takes more than a few days to be brainwashed. How about if I sign an agreement, so you have written proof that I've given you my word? And we can also leave the Citadel before they try to rescue me. We can go to the Featherstone garrison. Isn't that where you need to be to prepare for war?"

"So you can steal all our secrets."

"Lock me in a cell. I've been in so many, it'll almost feel like home."

MARIA V. SNYDER

He studied my face for a dozen heartbeats. "You are serious."

"Yes."

"And if I write up an accord right now?"

"I'll sign it."

"What if I'm cured, but I still believe Bruns is the best for Sitia?"

"Then I lose. I'll help you and Bruns, like I promised."

"You're that confident of my response once free of the Theobroma?"

"I know you, Cahil. I know that you would be upset by Bruns's methods of robbing people of their free will and ability to make their own decisions."

He strode to his desk, found a clean piece of parchment and wrote up our deal. It was simply worded. I would agree to go with him, without trying to escape or interfere with any of his plans, and to cooperate for ten days. No one but his loyal people would know who I was. In exchange, he would wear a null shield pendant at all times and no longer consume food cooked with Theobroma for ten days.

"How do I know if the food has Theobroma or not?" he asked.

I gave him a wry smile. "I can taste your food like I used to do for the Commander."

He snorted in amusement and continued writing. At the end of the ten days, if Cahil remained loyal to Bruns, I would agree to join their cause, do nothing to sabotage their efforts and be an active participant.

"Like a cheerleader?" I asked.

He was not amused. "More like a spokesperson. And help us with strategy and planning."

If he was no longer loyal to Bruns, then Cahil would join

our side and be as engaged in our efforts. Cahil held up the finished treaty for me to read.

"We'll need witnesses, and you need to release me." Seeing his dubious expression, I added, "If I'm chained to the wall when I sign, then even a bad solicitor can argue that I signed it under extreme duress and that I don't have to comply." Not like I'd ever break my word; signing the parchment was a mere formality and for Cahil's peace of mind. But I really wanted to be free of these chains.

Cahil disappeared and returned with two of his people. He introduced Faxon, and I already knew Hanni. Faxon unlocked the cuffs, and everyone stepped back a few feet with their hands on the hilts of their weapons. Amused by their skittishness, I rubbed my wrists, working feeling back into my fingers.

When the pins and needles ceased, I signed the agreement, then handed the stylus to Cahil. He paused for a moment—probably trying to uncover any loopholes—and added his signature to the document. Hanni and Faxon affixed their names, and it was official. I focused on the fact that the baby would remain alive. At least for the next ten days. If this ended well, we'd have a powerful ally. If not...

Best to focus on one thing at a time.

I drew in a breath. "We need to leave," I said. "Right away."

"Why?"

I told him about the trail of bobby pins.

"Shit." Cahil barked orders to his people, harassing them to hurry and grab their things. We were leaving. Now.

Keeping out of the way, I hoped I'd have a chance to send Fisk a note. One of the agents handed me a cloak to wear, and while everyone was occupied, I reclaimed my weapons and lock picks. Grief threatened to drown me, but I chanted *keep the baby safe* over and over in my mind to block the emo-

MARIA V. SNYDER

tion. Also there was the possibility that Cahil lied about seeing Onora in the Citadel.

Cahil returned. "Time to go." He grabbed my elbow as we headed to the stairs. A number of his people preceded us, and the rest followed. Twelve total.

"Can one of your crew deliver a message to Fisk?"

He slowed. "Why?"

"So when I'm spotted at the Featherstone garrison, he doesn't risk his people trying to rescue me."

"Why would you be…" Cahil's grip tightened, and he muttered a curse. "He has people in the garrisons, doesn't he?"

"There are many public roads to the garrison. We could be spotted at any place en route."

"Nice try, but you're a lousy liar. Do you know who they are?"

Now it was my turn to curse. "No."

"And you won't tell me until the ten days are over."

"No, I really don't know."

I wasn't sure if he believed me, but he remained silent as we climbed the stairs and exited onto the warehouse's ground floor. A few beams of sunlight pierced the blackened windows, providing just enough light to see the words written on the crates. Our group wove through them as if navigating a maze they'd been through a thousand times. I glanced at the floor. The dust was thick between the piles, but underneath our feet, the path was clean. Even I could follow this trail.

"Head to the Council's stables," Cahil ordered when he spotted the entrance. "Yelena will ride with me on Topaz."

The door opened, almost as if on cue. Everyone grabbed their weapons as Onora strode into the building like she owned the place. I stumbled. The dam inside me broke, and grief ripped right through my body. The tiny spark of hope that Valek still lived died.

Cahil's hand steadied me. "Don't worry. I won't let her kill you."

I didn't have the strength or the ability to correct him. Emotions lodged in my throat, cutting off my air.

He faced me. "Breathe, Yelena. We might need you if this gets...ugly."

Right. I focused on Valek's killer. Barefoot, and with her hair tied back, she looked years younger than twenty. Cahil's agents spread out as much as they could among the piles of crates. Two of them held crossbows and they pointed their weapons at her, even though her hands were empty.

No, that wasn't correct. She played with two bobby pins, spinning them through her fingers. Ah, hell.

Cahil strode forward. "You're too late. Yelena's in our protective custody. Go back to Ixia."

Onora cocked her head to the side. "Why isn't she dead?"

"None of your business."

"But Bruns wants her eliminated."

"Bruns? Are you working for him now?" Cahil asked in surprise.

"No. Bruns asked the Commander to send me to take care of Valek and Yelena." She met my gaze. "One down. One to go."

I drew my switchblade and advanced. The desire to plunge it into her heart pulsed through me. Cahil put a hand on my shoulder, stopping me.

"Bruns would never turn to the Commander for help," Cahil said.

"Then maybe you need to have a chat with your boss."

Frowning, Cahil moved his grip to my arm.

Onora noticed. "Unless you've decided to branch out on your own?" She waited. "No? Then give her to me. I'll finish my assignment and be on my merry way."

"No."

"Why are you protecting her? She's just going to cause you trouble."

"Go home, Onora. You're outnumbered, and the ladies holding the crossbows have excellent aim."

Onora grinned, showing two rows of straight white teeth. "Are you sure about your math, General?"

"I count fourteen of us and one of you."

Nice of Cahil to include me in his group.

"You forgot to check the ceiling for spiders." Onora dove to the side.

Everyone looked up, but I stared at her, stunned. She had used Valek's words. I broke free of Cahil's grip and hit the floor as gray figures darted from where they'd been hiding between the piles of crates.

Cahil laughed. "There's nothing up—"

Fighting broke out, and I stayed low. I'd been shot by a crossbow bolt before. Once was enough. Because of Onora's spider comment, I didn't know if the gray fighters were my friends or enemies. Had it been a signal to me, or just something she picked up when she'd been training with Valek? Rather than risk joining the wrong side of the fight, I kept away from everyone, ducking behind a pile of crates to wait.

I listened to the sounds of the scuffle—thuds, grunts, steel clanging against steel, cursing, a hiss of pain. Then, without warning, Onora appeared next to me.

"It's safe," she said.

Reacting without thought, I pressed the tip of my switchblade to her throat. "Valek?"

She held her hands wide. "Fighting Cahil, from the sounds of it."

Surprised, I stared at her. Was this a trick?

"No offense, but if I planned to assassinate you, you'd be dead by now."

Right. I lowered my weapon as relief swept through me. "Sorry."

We returned to the main area. Cahil's people littered the floor, and a number of gray-clad figures stood nearby. But what grabbed my attention was the man in black who had his sword aimed at Cahil's neck. Cahil glared. A bloody cut snaked from his hand up to his elbow. His sword lay on the floor at his feet.

"Onora?" Valek asked without moving his gaze from Cahil.

"She's here."

"Watch him," Valek said, tossing her the sword.

She caught it easily and kept it pointed at Cahil.

In two strides, I was wrapped in Valek's arms—my favorite place to be. After a minute, I whispered, "I thought Onora killed you."

"I told you I could handle her."

"But Cahil said…" I shook my head. "Sorry. I should have stayed in HQ." Should have trusted Valek.

"Doesn't matter now. You're safe."

"And she's still mine," Cahil said. "Yelena, tell your husband about our agreement."

8

VALEK

An agreement? Valek leaned back to meet Yelena's gaze and did not like her pained expression. Not at all. He tightened his arms around her for a second, his instinct to protect her flooding him for a moment. Then, with effort, he relaxed and stepped away. "What is he talking about?"

Yelena explained the deal she had worked out with Cahil. As she talked, Valek kept a tight leash on his emotions. After a hellacious night spent healing his injuries and worrying about her, this was the last thing he wanted to hear.

"...we need Cahil on our side. You agreed. He won't listen to reason while under the influence of Theobroma. This is the only way we'll be able to convince him."

Anger shot through him. "No. You can't go to the Featherstone garrison. Bruns will find out, and then you and the baby will be killed." Valek pressed his arms to his sides as the desire to throw her over his shoulder and bolt from the warehouse pulsed through him. She hadn't trusted him to defeat Onora. Didn't believe she'd be rescued. For the first time in years, he was furious at her.

"You can't stop her. She gave her word," Cahil said, holding up a piece of parchment.

The smug superiority of Cahil's tone grated on Valek's already frayed nerves. He pulled his dagger and advanced on the idiot. "I know a quick way to void that."

"Valek, stop," Yelena said.

"Are you that certain he'll see reason?" he demanded.

"Yes."

"What happens if Bruns learns you're there?"

"I'll protect her. It's a provision in our agreement," Cahil said.

The handle of Valek's knife bit into his palm. He'd never regretted killing anyone in his life, but he'd kicked himself for letting certain troublemakers live, because they always returned to cause more problems. Cahil happened to be one of them. However, Valek's plan to stop the Sitian takeover did include Cahil's assistance.

"Can I see the accord?" he asked.

"Of course." Cahil handed him the accursed document.

Valek read through the terms. A red-hot knot squeezed his chest. He sought loopholes. None. After committing it to memory, he returned it. "In ten days, I will be at the Featherstone garrison."

"What if she loses?" Cahil asked.

"I won't," she said with conviction.

But Cahil could lie or break their agreement or brainwash her or...a million things could go wrong. If Cahil failed to switch sides, Valek would kill him. There was no way he'd allow Yelena to remain with the enemy.

"You didn't answer my question." Cahil stared at him.

"If she loses, then we are enemies."

"And she stays with me," Cahil said.

His heart tore in half. "Yes."

"I want your word that you won't try to rescue her or kill me if her plan fails."

Valek met his wife's gaze. Yelena seemed confident. Not much he could do at this point. "I promise not to attempt a rescue or kill you." The words coated his mouth with a foul bile. Valek hated that he'd been forced to say them. Why hadn't Yelena trusted him?

Cahil relaxed.

But Valek wasn't done. "But I *will* be by her side."

The idiot peered at him in confusion. "You just said we'd be enemies."

"Correct. I won't help your efforts or hinder them. But I'll be with Yelena until the war is over. Consider me her personal bodyguard."

"Valek, no." Yelena protested. "They'll kill you or use you to learn about the Commander. Besides, Fisk and the others need you. Sitia needs you."

"I'm not fighting against *you*."

Her face lost all color as she realized that was what she had promised Cahil. To fight against her friends and family. She clasped her hands together. "It won't come to that."

"I hope you're right." Their future happiness depended on it.

Onora stepped away from Cahil. "What's next?"

With all the emotional turmoil, Valek had forgotten about Fisk's people. They stood awkwardly at the edges.

"Back to HQ," he said. They'd have to relocate and change their plans. Yelena had agreed to cooperate during the next ten days. Cahil might claim that meant revealing vital information. Also, if Cahil remained convinced of Bruns's good intentions, then Yelena would be obligated to reveal *all* their plans.

Then it hit him. He couldn't be part of developing the new strategy, or else he might be forced to divulge the intel if he became her bodyguard while she worked for the Cartel. Ah, hell. They were screwed with a capital *S*.

"What about my people?" Cahil asked. "Are they dead?"

"No. Neutralized," Onora said. "They should wake up in a few hours."

"Cahil knows Fisk has people in the garrisons and that the Stormdancers are helping us," Yelena said.

And just when he thought it couldn't get any worse. Unable to speak without growling at her, Valek nodded instead. It was all he could handle at this time.

"Let's go," Valek ordered. The guild members and Onora headed to the door. Before following them, Valek glanced at Cahil's smug expression, and Yelena's pained one. "See you in ten days." He left.

Valek set a quick pace for a few blocks. Then he told everyone to scatter and meet back at HQ. Onora stayed with him as he leaned against a building, the enormity of the situation catching up to him. And the regret. He hadn't hugged or kissed his wife goodbye.

"Can you shadow her?" he asked Onora. "Make sure Cahil doesn't go back on his word not to harm her?"

"Yes. Meet in the town near the Featherstone garrison in nine days?"

"Yes. Thanks."

"Don't worry. She knows what she's doing." Onora gave him a salute and disappeared down the street.

He'd like to believe that, but ever since Yelena lost her magic, she'd been doubting herself. And now this idiotic agreement with Cahil. She must have panicked last night, believed Cahil's lies and, worried that the baby's life was in danger, come up with what she thought was a good solution. If only she'd trusted him.

Nothing to be done about it now. Valek pushed off the wall and headed to HQ.

MARIA V. SNYDER

★ ★ ★

"Please tell me you're kidding," Fisk said.

Valek wished. "No. You need to relocate the Stormdancers, my brother, my sister and Teegan to a secure place. Recall Ari and Janco. Ari is going to be your best bet for strategy and planning. When Leif, Mara and Esau return, have them go into hiding. And get your people out of the garrisons before they're caught."

Fisk sat stunned. "Wow."

"Do you have any null shield pendants?"

"Yes. Leif's learned how to make them using wood."

"Please send one to Cahil with my compliments. And another for Yelena, just in case."

"Got it."

Valek left Fisk to absorb the bombshell he'd just dropped on him. When he arrived at their rooms, Valek paused. The smell of lavender—Yelena's favorite scent—sucked away all his remaining energy. He sat on the edge of the bed and rested his head in his hands as exhaustion swept through him.

Once Onora had returned with Yelena's location, Valek had spent all last night planning her rescue, and that was after he'd used magic to heal his shoulder and hip. Chale hadn't been strong enough to repair such extensive injuries. The fact that Valek managed to mend the damage and didn't flame out and kill himself had been a source of pride.

Summoning the strength to stand, he packed his and Yelena's saddle bags. Then he carried them down the stairs and headed to the hidden stables behind the kitchen.

Fisk chased him. "Where are you going?"

"I need to leave so I don't overhear your new strategies."

"Where do we find you if everything works out?"

Valek considered. "The Cloverleaf Inn in Owl's Hill. Do you know it?"

"Yes."

"Good." He continued past the ovens.

"It'll work out," Fisk called.

But Valek didn't have the energy to reply. Onyx and Kiki greeted him with whickers, and they nosed his pockets for treats. Giving each a milk oat, he stroked their necks and checked their legs for hot spots. All black, Onyx was built for speed. Sleek and quiet, he matched Valek's personality.

Valek saddled both horses and secured Yelena's bags and bo staff to Kiki's saddle. Leading them outside, he turned to Kiki. White coated most of her face, except for a swirl of copper around her left eye. She had white socks, but the rest of her was copper. Her long ears pricked forward.

He relaxed his mental shield, allowing Kiki's thoughts to fill his mind—one of the perks to having magic. As a Sand-seed horse, Kiki used a form of magic to communicate mentally with humans and other non-Sandseed horses like Onyx.

Lavender Lady? she asked, using Yelena's horse name.

With Peppermint Man, he said. *Go find Topaz. He's at the Council's stables. Lavender Lady needs you.*

Needs Ghost No More.

He'd been Ghost, but since he was no longer immune to magic, Kiki had added the "No More" to his name. *Not this time.*

She flicked him with her tail. *Every time.*

He laughed without humor. *Lavender Lady doesn't agree with you.* Besides, he trusted Onora to keep an eye on her.

Smoke Girl part of herd. Kiki approved.

Smoke?

Unable to verbalize, Kiki sent images of Onora sitting quiet and still, blending in with her surroundings and moving with grace, like a wisp of smoke. Kiki hinted at something deeper within the girl. That a fire burned at her core, but she hid it beneath a smoke screen.

A good analogy, Valek thought.

Kiki smart.

Yes, you are.

Come.

I will be there. I just need…time. To cool down? Time to think?

Kiki's blue-eyed gaze peered right through him. He remained still, even though the urge to squirm like a misbehaving child pressed on him.

Come soon. She trotted away.

He wondered how the Citadel's citizens would react to a riderless horse, but then Valek remembered Kiki's ability to stay hidden, despite being so large. Plus, unlike the other breed of horses, Sandseeds refused to wear horseshoes. No clip-clop of hooves on the cobblestones.

Valek mounted Onyx, but he had no idea where to go, except to leave the Citadel. "Let's get out of here, boy."

After they exited through the north gate, Valek let Onyx pick the direction. The steady rhythm of the horse underneath him combined with his exhaustion and it numbed him. His thoughts stilled. His emotions drained. A cool breeze fanned his face. The moist scent of earth and grass filled the air as trees and bushes blurred past, their green buds and blue sky the only colors.

Whenever Onyx stopped, Valek fed and watered his horse. He rested and ate stale travel rations until Onyx indicated it was time to go. The sun set and rose. Twice.

Onyx slowed as the light faded for the third time. Valek roused in preparation to care for his horse. But instead of halting in a clearing, Onyx approached a building. He had his dagger in hand before Valek recognized the cottage he and Yelena had purchased. It was located in the Featherstone lands, near the border with Ixia. Onyx headed to the tiny stable, pushing the door open with his head.

Valek dismounted. "Did Kiki tell you to come here?"

His horse blew a hot breath scented with grain in Valek's face as if to say, *Snap out of it, man!*

Removing Onyx's saddle and tack, Valek groomed, fed and watered his horse before shuffling toward the dark, cold cottage. Horsehair stuck to his sweat-slicked skin and coated his clothes. The warm season should be renamed the shedding season.

He paused in the threshold. It'd been three and a half months since he'd been here with Yelena. This was where their child had been conceived. Memories threatened to push through the fog in his head. Maybe he'd sleep in the stable. No, he was being silly. He entered. The empty rooms held no warmth. A light film of dust coated the furniture. Not bothering to light a fire or heat up the bathwater, Valek washed quickly. The little cottage had been perfect for them. A washroom and kitchen occupied the right side of the ground floor. A large living area filled the left side, and a huge stone hearth sat in the middle, heating all the rooms. The second story loft covered half the building and contained their bedroom.

After trudging up the steps, Valek shook out the blankets on the bed. Yelena's scent slapped him in the face, and he collapsed onto the mattress. All his anger drained away in one gush of misery. Yelena had gone with the enemy, taking all his hopes and dreams with her. Ten days was enough time for Bruns to learn of her presence in the garrison. An intelligent businessman, he'd have informers in all the garrisons. Cahil had been brainwashed like all the rest. There was no way Cahil could protect her, no matter what he promised.

So what the hell was Valek doing here? Pouting. He should

be arranging another rescue. Except he'd given his word to Cahil that he wouldn't do that, and Yelena would never break hers. Until things went sideways with Bruns, Valek's hands were tied.

He breathed in the clean scent of lavender. As he lay on the bed they'd once shared, a realization came to him slowly. He'd been so furious at her for not trusting him that he was doing the same thing—not trusting her. Yelena had been confident of Cahil's ability to see reason, and she'd escaped plenty of tight spots before. And if the null shield pendant was taken from her, the baby created some kind of void, which protected her from magic.

Her comment about Onora finally registered. The idiot had lied to her. Told her Valek was dead. Desperate and upset, she'd made a deal with Cahil to protect the baby. Ah, hell.

He should have picked up on it sooner. Why had he gotten so furious so fast? He could blame his exhaustion on the fight with Onora, the energy needed to heal, and no sleep. But that was just an excuse. No. The Commander had sent Onora after him. Onora, who the Commander had trained and who fought Valek with the clear determination to kill. Considering Owen Moon's influence on the Commander, that betrayal hurt more than it should. Commander Ambrose no longer trusted him after they'd worked together for twenty-four years. When he combined Ambrose's lack of trust with Yelena's, Valek had snapped. However, knowing why he'd been so angry didn't help Valek feel any better now.

Valek pulled the blanket up to his chin. He needed a good night's sleep. And after that? In six days' time, he'd meet up with Onora near the Featherstone garrison. Now that he had time to think about it, a brief amusement flared over Onora's confession that Gerik was her brother. It was one of those things he should have picked up on sooner, but it made perfect sense now that he knew.

But what was he going to do for the next few days? An idea sparked. He dismissed it as too dangerous, but his dreams swirled around the idea, testing it.

In the morning, Valek sat up and knew exactly what to do. Onyx fidgeted while Valek saddled him, turning a twenty-minute task into forty. Then the horse stood rock-still, despite Valek's signal to go.

"I know you were hoping to rest here a few days," Valek said. "We'll be back soon. I promise."

Onyx glanced at the stable with longing. Then he heaved a sigh and broke into a reluctant trot. Valek suppressed a chuckle—no sense upsetting Onyx any further. Valek required his cooperation; walking would take too much time.

Due to the extra time needed to avoid the border guards and keep out of sight, it took them the rest of the daylight to reach their destination—Ixia. Valek found a comfortable spot in the Snake Forest to leave Onyx.

After taking care of the horse, Valek stroked Onyx's long neck and said, "If I'm not back by tomorrow morning, return to the cottage without me. Understand?"

Onyx lifted his head and stared down at Valek.

"I don't like it either, but I need to do this."

The horse snorted. Valek assumed that was an agreement and left. He wanted to be in Castletown before the streets emptied for the night. Due to the small city's proximity to the Commander's castle, Valek was certain there would be extra security officers patrolling the town. If he was spotted, this outing would not end well. His cloak hid most of his advisor's uniform, but he needed to blend in, and there were other uniforms stashed at his safe house in Castletown.

When Valek entered the apartment on Pennwood Street,

MARIA V. SNYDER

he surprised the agents who had been assigned to keep an eye on the city. Adrik and Pasha jumped to attention and saluted. Good to know they remained loyal.

"Report," he ordered.

They glanced at each other. "Uh...there's nothing to report, sir," Adrik said.

Valek raised an eyebrow, inviting them to continue.

"We've been in standby mode, waiting out the storm, sir," Pasha rushed to explain.

"The storm?" Valek asked.

"There's an order for your execution, sir," Adrik said. "All your agents know it's bogus, and we won't work with that... girl because she's with *them*." He spat the word. "We figured we'd lie low until you returned."

"Lie low?"

"We all stopped sending reports to the castle, and all orders coming in have been ignored."

Valek was touched by their rebellion. "You realize that's an act of treason."

"No, it isn't," Pasha said. "The Commander is not in *command* anymore."

"Is it that obvious?"

"As soon as he ordered your execution, we knew. No way you'd do anything against Ixia or the Commander." She flicked a long blond strand of hair from her face.

He wanted to hug them both.

"And there have been a few...inconsistencies with the Commander's orders," Adrik said. "He's never changed his mind before, or given us conflicting orders. It's almost like there are two people in power."

His agents confirmed Valek's suspicions.

"What are your orders, sir?" Pasha asked. "Did you come back to evict the Sitians?"

If only it was that easy. "Not yet. For now, continue to lie low."

Their postures wilted at the order.

"We will evict them at the right time," Valek said. "I need you to spread the word to the rest of my corps that Onora is to be trusted."

Twin surprised expressions.

"Any estimate on a timeline for the eviction, sir?" Adrik asked.

"I suspect things will get hot around the fire festival."

"And if they don't?"

"That means we failed, and they won."

"You didn't train us to fail, sir," Pasha said. "And if we can't fail, neither can you."

Valek laughed. "You're right. Now tell me about the castle complex. What's the word on security?"

"Touch the wall, and you'll have half a dozen guards dropping down on your head," Adrik said.

Owen must have rigged it with a magical alarm. "How about the gates?"

"Only the south gate remains open, and it's tight. All personnel going through it are checked against a list."

Valek considered. "All right. I have a job for you." He explained.

As they headed out with eager grins, Valek rummaged in the supply closet. All his safe houses had the same materials. Soon after the takeover, the Commander had given Valek the freedom to secure these houses and purchase equipment. The addresses hadn't been written down, nor did the Commander know them—the recent orders were probably being sent by Maren. The locations were given to Valek's agents to memorize once they were trusted members of his corps. Each house had its own safe filled with enough money to cover expenses for a year.

It didn't take the agents long to return. They supported a wobbly man between them. He wore a kitchen uniform and muttered nonsense—the effects of goo-goo juice. Best of all, he was about six feet tall with short dark hair.

"His name is Mannix, and he just delivered the castle's meat order to the butcher," Adrik said.

"Good work." Valek dressed in the all-white kitchen uniform with the red diamond shapes on the shirt.

Moving quickly, Valek mixed up putty, matching it to Mannix's skin tone. He then used it to alter his appearance, softening his sharp nose and chin. Tucking his longer hair under his collar, Valek buttoned the shirt up to the top to keep it in place.

"Well?" he asked Adrik and Pasha.

"It should work," Adrik said.

"Should?"

"It's dark. You'll be fine," Pasha said.

He hoped so. If he was caught…

No. Not going to think about it. "Release Mannix in the morning. And stay alert for any news about the castle and the Commander's plans."

"Yes, sir," they said in unison.

"Thanks for the help." Valek left by the back entrance and headed to the castle's south gate.

He strode with confidence and didn't hesitate when approaching the gate. There were six armed guards. Valek recognized them. It was the two others—one man and a woman—standing just inside the gate who he didn't know. The man held a clipboard and the woman stared at him.

"Mannix, cook's aide," she said in a bored voice to the man. Magic brushed his mental shields. Owen had brought in more magicians. Not good. Valek lowered his shield enough for his surface thoughts to be read. At least, that was what he hoped he did. He concentrated on what he needed to do to prep for the morning breakfast rush.

"Mannix, got it," clipboard man said. "Go on."

The gate opened, and Valek headed straight to the castle. His thoughts remained on finishing his work before going to bed. As soon as he entered the castle, he ducked down a little-used corridor. The perks of being in very familiar territory. Valek pulled off the putty and the kitchen uniform, revealing his black skintight sneak suit underneath. While he was tempted to visit his office, he was smart enough to avoid it. Instead, he found a hiding place to wait until the perfect time.

Near midnight, Valek ghosted through the empty hallways. He had written all the security protocols for the castle. As long as they hadn't been changed, he would be able to reach his goal without being spotted. It all depended on Owen's confidence that Valek would never return. Since Owen had easily captured Valek in a null shield and almost killed him the last time they met, the magician had to be feeling pretty confident that Valek would stay far away. And Owen must also believe in Onora's ability to assassinate Valek, or he wouldn't have sent her. Add those together, and Valek was literally betting his life that the protocols had not been changed.

He found a window, drew in a deep breath and then climbed out. He clung to the west wall and braced for shouts of discovery or a crossbow bolt shot through his back. When nothing happened, he scaled the wall.

Avoiding all the booby traps on the roof, Valek reached his target. He opened the window and slipped inside. A bright fire burned in the hearth, and the Commander sat in front of it, sipping his brandy. The other seat was empty. A relief. Valek

MARIA V. SNYDER

had expected to see Owen lounging in Valek's chair, and he had a dart filled with Curare just in case.

"Have you come to assassinate me, Valek?" the Commander asked without even glancing in his direction.

Valek approached the Commander but kept his distance. No doubt the man was armed, and his skills with a knife exceeded Valek's. "No."

He turned his head, and his golden gaze met Valek's. "Why not? I signed your order of execution. I sent Onora after you. Well done, by the way. I didn't think you'd beat her. Pity, though. She had such potential." He paused as if truly grieving. "You know your only chance to leave this room alive is to kill me. If you can."

A big if. "I came to talk."

"Nothing you say to me will change anything." His tone was matter-of-fact, and a bit resigned. The Commander's all-black uniform was pristine as always. Two real diamonds on his collar reflected the firelight, sending sparks of yellow onto the walls.

The faint scent of apples laced the air. "I didn't come to talk to *you*."

"You expected Owen to be here? We're not to that point yet, but he'll be along soon enough."

"Magical alarm?"

"In a way." The Commander tapped his forehead.

"How much time do I have?"

The Commander refused to answer.

Which meant not much. Valek knew the Commander's physical body was female, but Ambrose had always identified as male and lived as a man since puberty. No one else was privy to this information except Yelena. Her Soulfinding abilities detected that the Commander's mother's soul also resided in his body. When Signe had died in childbirth, her magic transferred her soul to her baby. The Commander had trusted Yelena and Valek to keep it a secret.

"I came to talk to your mother," Valek said.

He shrank back in his chair. "She can't talk."

"She can if *you* let her."

"I can't... Owen..." He pressed his fingers into his temples as if enduring a sudden headache.

"Signe's the reason for the inconsistencies. Why you could send me and Yelena away, despite Owen's influence on your mind. Owen doesn't have control of your mother's soul."

"Owen thinks he does, but he can't know...or all is lost."

"I'll be quick so he doesn't find out," Valek promised.

The transformation of Commander Ambrose into his mother, Signe, would have been startling if Valek hadn't seen it before. His features didn't shift, but from one breath to the next, another person peered from his almond-shaped eyes. Even with his bristle-short gray hair, she appeared feminine.

"How did Owen get to Ambrose?" Valek asked her.

"Owen pleaded for his life. He promised my son barrels of Curare for his army in exchange. It appeared to be a standard business deal, but Owen planted a...seed, I think, during that first meeting."

"A seed?"

"A powerful suggestion in Ambrose's mind that Owen was to be trusted."

Ah, hell. That was over four years ago.

"What happened to the null shields in his uniforms?"

"Owen forced Ambrose to lie about them to you so you wouldn't suspect he was being influenced by the magician."

Valek considered. "It worked. Plus, I didn't notice any change in him. Not then."

"No one did. It was subtle. In fact, Ambrose wouldn't be-lieve *me*—he was too focused on getting Curare for his soldiers. Owen kept the connection hidden until he arrived at the castle. By then it was too late."

"When is Owen planning to take over Sitia?"

"Once the Cartel has control of the Sitian military, it's a done deal. They are going to assign military districts and generals to the clans."

"The Sitian people won't accept that." Especially Fisk and his people.

"Owen and the Cartel have a way to change their minds."

"There isn't enough Theobroma for everyone in Sitia."

"They don't need Theobroma. They have something else," Signe said.

A cold wave of fear swept through him. "What is it?"

"I wish I knew. Owen won't tell Ambrose what it is. But it doesn't matter at this point. My son cannot disobey Owen's commands."

"But you can?"

"For now. Owen believes I'm trapped, like Ambrose, and we've been careful to keep up the ruse."

Good to know. Valek focused on the problem at hand. "Do you have any idea what it is?"

"All I know is that Owen learned about it from his ancestor, Master Magician Ellis Moon. It was in the magician's notes."

Valek muttered a curse. "Does Owen have those notes with him?"

"I don't think so. He complained that he could only copy the information, despite being a direct descendant. They're considered vital historical documents and are kept in the Magician's Keep's library. He made an odd comment about how the library wouldn't let him take the files."

Muted voices reached them through the gap under the door. The doorknob jiggled.

"You need to go," Signe said.

9

JANCO

Janco resisted the urge to scratch. No matter what color he dyed his hair, it always caused his scalp to itch something fierce. And the fake ear glued over his scarred one just added to his discomfort. Sweat pooled underneath the putty, driving him crazy. Add in the heat and humidity, and Janco longed for an assignment on the northern ice sheet. At this point, he'd gladly endure frostbite and evade snow cats. Better than dodging deadly Greenblade bees.

The creak of wood and rattle of a harness cut through Janco's misery. From his hiding spot, he craned his neck, peering around a bush. Sure enough, a wagon rode into view, heading west. Two horses pulled it at a fast trot. Janco waited as it slowed. The driver—a tall, impossibly thin Greenblade man Janco had nicknamed Toothpick—must have spotted the tree trunk lying across the road. The tree wasn't big enough to halt the wagon entirely, but in order to continue his journey, the driver would have to roll over it with care or risk a broken wheel.

Janco shifted his weight to the balls of his feet. When the horses stepped over the log, he slipped behind the wagon. As the wheels thumped over the obstruction, Janco climbed in and crawled under the tarp, avoiding the sacks of white coal as he wedged his body between the other supplies.

The wagon increased its speed after it cleared the trunk. Janco grinned and pumped his fist. Toothpick didn't have a clue he'd just picked up a passenger. Not sure how long it would be until they stopped, Janco settled into a more comfortable position.

Janco'd been watching and tracking the deliveries to the Greenblade garrison for two weeks now, trying to identify which wagon brought in the Theobroma for the cook to use in the garrison's food. It had been harder than he expected, since they used a tarp and the schedule was erratic. But once he figured out Toothpick was the delivery man, it didn't take long to plan a way to hop a ride to see just where the Theobroma was coming from.

Janco checked the lump under his tunic, ensuring it remained in place. The null shield pendant kept the Cartel's magicians from brainwashing him and also from detecting him. They'd been rather vigilant about spies, which was why he couldn't simply follow the wagon on horseback.

As the afternoon turned into evening, Janco guessed Toothpick would stop for the night. He remembered General Brazell's Theobroma-producing factory. They had smelled the sweet aroma of the drug miles downwind. He doubted many of the Greenbladers recognized the scent. However, finding an isolated spot to produce the stuff must have been difficult, since the Greenblade forest, which covered two-thirds of their lands, had dozens of tiny settlements all over the place.

When the wagon slowed hours later, Janco prepared to ditch. While certain he could take Toothpick without breaking a sweat, Janco didn't want to ruin the mission. This was an information-gathering endeavor. Ari, his partner, had just about pounded the importance of not being seen into Janco's head.

Slipping out before the horses stopped, Janco dropped onto the road. He ducked into the woods as the wagon continued toward a bright yellow glow. Perhaps Toothpick had decided to overnight in one of the settlements. By the distant brightness, Janco guessed it must be one of the bigger villages.

Janco hurried to catch up, but paused at the edge of the... town? He stared through the trees at the wide array of buildings and factories. People bustled between them even at this late hour. Greenery filled the extra-long glass hothouses lined up like fingers—ten in all. The nutty sweetness of Theobroma fogged the air and mixed with the unmistakable citrus tang of Curare.

Holy snow cats! He'd hit the jackpot.

Or had he? This was blatant, even for Bruns. And judging by the age of the tree stumps and worn paths, this had been here for years. Someone would have noticed it by now. Unless Owen had set it up and scared off the locals?

The answer popped into his head, and Janco almost groaned aloud. Idiot.

He removed the null shield pendant—a gift from Leif—and a dark forest replaced the scene of bright industry. All sounds ceased, and only a moist, earthy scent filled his nose. Pain burned in his right ear.

The town was covered by a massive illusion. Even though Janco hated magic, he had to admit the deception was impressive. The main road curved around the northern edge, so unsuspecting travelers would avoid all the buildings.

Looping the pendant back around his neck, Janco squinted in the sudden light. He spent the next couple hours observing. The activity slowed well after midnight, with only a few people remaining outside. The desire to nose about the complex to learn more pulsed in his chest. Perhaps he'd spot Owen's Master Gardener. The man or woman had to be in charge of

MARIA V. SNYDER

this operation. And Janco even wore the long green tunic and pants that the Greenblade men preferred. His light brown hair and tanned skin matched them as well.

However, Janco remembered the last time he'd pushed his luck. He'd ended up not only getting caught but also causing the rest of his team to be captured. Dax had died, Hale went missing and Leif had almost died.

Being sensible for the first time in his life, Janco left, jogging along the road. He'd report back to Ari and, after they sent the information to Fisk, they'd return and have a good snoop.

Janco arrived in Longleaf late the next morning. Instead of trying to go undercover in the garrison, they'd decided to rent a small house in the nearby town and keep an eye on the flow of traffic going to and from the base.

With a sudden burst of energy, Janco sprinted to the narrow wooden house wedged in the middle of a row. He rushed into the front room and was about to shout his good news, but Ari's tense posture stopped him in his tracks. Ari wore his I-want-to-strangle-someone expression. One that was usually aimed at Janco, but was directed at a young boy. Poor kid.

At six feet four inches tall, Ari loomed over most others. The skinny-mini standing next to him appeared tiny in comparison. Must be one of Fisk's…spies. Hard to call kids under the age of fifteen spies, but the little tykes had come in handy since the Cartel decided to take over Sitia. And the guild members had saved their asses back when Bruns had them. Gotta give them their due.

Sensing trouble, Janco asked, "Something wrong?"

"We're being recalled to the Citadel," Ari said. Frowning, he ran a big, beefy paw—er…hand—over the short curls of his blond hair.

"Who and why?"

"Valek's orders. Tell him," Ari said to the boy.

Janco braced for bad news as Skinny-Mini detailed Yelena's capture and her agreement with Cahil—which explained Ari's murderous glare. Despite the results, using lamplighters for an ambush was a sweet move. He'd never look at them the same way again.

"I need to inform the others. Master Fisk is pulling all agents from the garrisons," Skinny-Mini said.

"Go," Ari said.

"Wait." Janco grabbed his shoulder. "Are you returning to the Citadel after this?"

"Yeah. Why?"

"Tell Fisk we'll be delayed a few days."

"We can't disobey a direct order," Ari said.

"Don't worry, Ari. Valek will forgive us. He'll probably give us a medal."

"Why?" Ari and Skinny-Mini asked in unison.

He told them about the complex. "We can't return without checking it out. It might be the key to stopping the Cartel."

Ever cautious, Ari asked, "How many guards are there?"

"Doesn't matter. We'll be like ghosts—invisible."

"Ghosts aren't... Oh, never mind. We'll check it out, but *I'll* decide if we go into the complex or just watch from a distance."

"Hey, who put you in charge?" Janco asked, outraged.

"Valek."

"Oh, yeah." All his annoyance disappeared. "No problem. I know you'll want to take a closer look. It's irresistible, like candy and babies."

"I know I'm going to regret asking this, but you find candy and babies irresistible?" Ari asked.

"Hell no. They're both sticky."

His partner waited.

"*Some* people find them irresistible. And, you know…" Janco waved his hand. "They're easy to steal…or something like that."

"I was right."

"About what?"

"I regret asking that question."

Janco clapped him on the shoulder. "But you've learned something. Never pick up a sticky baby, 'cause you'll never be able to let go. And I—" he yawned "—am going to catch a couple z's while you go shopping and pack."

As Janco shuffled off to bed, Skinny-Mini said to Ari, "I thought you were in charge."

"Only when it counts."

It was almost sunset by the time they saddled Diamond Whiskey and The Madam. While Janco missed his horse, Beach Bunny—named after a beloved pet rabbit—he had to admit The Madam's calm demeanor was a nice counterpoint to his own fiery personality. Unconcerned, she watched Janco with gray eyes that said nothing could surprise her anymore. He stroked her neck, smoothing the hair on her gray-dappled coat.

Now with Whiskey, Ari had finally found a horse that didn't look like it would collapse under the big, muscular man's weight. The large dark brown horse had a white diamond blaze on his forehead. Strong and quick despite his size, Whiskey shifted, ready to go.

"After you," Ari said, sweeping a hand out.

Janco hopped onto The Madam and retraced the route to the hidden complex. Once the sun set, they'd have to slow down, so he set a fast pace. On horseback, it would take half the time to reach the spot Janco had marked to leave the horses. No doubt there was a magical alarm on the road closer to the facility. He hoped their null shields would prevent them from triggering it.

They set up a base camp deep in the forest. Infiltrating an unfamiliar location took time. While the size of the place was in their favor—an unknown face would not cause alarm—the efficiency with which everyone bustled about was not conducive to blending in. Ari said they would follow the standard three-stage plan.

Stage one—observe. Janco hated this one. For the next twenty-four hours, they took turns watching the facility from different angles, making notes of...well, everything possible. Boring, but necessary. If they planned to go undercover, they'd spend a week or more studying the complex and seeking the perfect place to insert themselves. But for information gathering, this part wasn't that time-consuming—thank fate.

Stage two—forays. More fun than sitting still for hours. Plus, Janco preened because he'd known Ari wouldn't be able to resist. Forays involved making short trips into the complex at different times to clarify their observations. For example, the long rectangular building in the southwest corner could be housing for the workers or a canteen or could contain offices. They wanted to avoid people and find information, so they needed to know where the offices were located.

Since Ari's size tended to draw attention, Janco completed the forays while his partner watched. He strode into buildings as if he belonged there, nosed about the factories, confirming they were indeed producing both Theobroma and Curare, and took a closer look at those huge glass hothouses. Condensation coated the inside of the glass, blurring the contents into an indistinguishable mass of green.

Workers carried long loops of vines from the second hothouse, so Janco headed toward the ones near the end. Checking that no one paid him any attention, Janco ducked into the seventh house and walked into a slice of the jungle. Thick, humid air pressed on his skin with the scent of living green. Insects buzzed around his ears.

A narrow dirt path cut through the plants. He followed it and recognized Curare vines snaked around the trees and hanging from limbs. Underneath the green canopy, pods heavy with beans grew from the trunks of the Theobroma trees. Janco couldn't identify the other plants, so he broke off a few leaves for Leif and shoved them into his pocket.

Knowing Ari was probably having a fit, Janco headed for the exit. The door opened a few feet before he reached it. A middle-age man with dark skin entered. He carried a long pair of pruning shears.

Startled, the man demanded, "What are you doing in here?"

Janco kept calm. "Just looking around."

The gardener peered at him. A shock of recognition zipped through Janco. He'd met this man before, but at the moment, he couldn't recall his name or the place. Bad enough, but if the man recognized *him*, that would be even worse.

Unaware of Janco's turmoil, the man said, "You're not part of the gardening crew or the harvesting crew, so you're not allowed in here."

"Sorry, sir."

"Sorry isn't good enough. Many of these plants are very delicate."

"I didn't touch anything." Janco stepped to go around him.

The gardener held up his shears, pointing the tips at Janco's chest. "Not so fast. You look familiar. What's your name?"

Without hesitating, Janco said, "Yannis Greenblade, sir."

"You'll be docked a week's pay for this little stunt, Yannis. Be glad I don't fire you."

Ah, this man was in charge. Janco lowered his gaze as if in contrition. "Thank you, sir."

"And stay out of *my* hothouses."

"Yes, sir."

The man lowered the shears, and Janco bolted for the door. Holy snow cats, he'd just encountered the Master Gardener. Now if he could only remember the man's name.

10

YELENA

The bang of the door slamming behind Valek echoed in my bones. Shocked and speechless, I stood among the prone forms of Cahil's people in the warehouse. I'd never seen him so angry with me. But he had every right to be. I hadn't believed he'd win in a fight with Onora, or trusted him to rescue me.

Cahil bent to retrieve his sword. "That went better than expected."

I raised an eyebrow. All his people had been neutralized, and a nasty cut snaked up his arm from when Valek had disarmed him.

"When I saw the Commander's new assassin, I thought she'd come to kill us all. And then with Valek… I never thought he'd let you fulfill the terms of our agreement. Although, at the end there, I think he wanted to kill you more than me."

With good reason. I'd ruined all the plans we'd worked so hard to set in motion. The heart-shaped scar on my chest ached. It'd been only two months since we'd exchanged marriage vows and Valek had transformed the Commander's bloody *C* on his chest into a heart, pledging his loyalty to me. In return, I'd cut a heart of my own, vowing to be with him forever.

"Despite your claims, the Commander is not working with Bruns," Cahil said, distracting me from my morose thoughts.

"How did you come up with that?"

"Onora's obviously working with Valek. That fight on the rooftop was probably staged. Her claim that Bruns asked the Commander to send her was just to make me doubt Bruns. Just like you want to do with our accord."

I couldn't argue the point that Valek and Onora were working together. Why hadn't he told me? Perhaps he didn't have time. Did it matter? No. Valek always put my safety first. If he forgave me, I'd never doubt him again. If not...

I shied away from that awful thought.

"Come on," Cahil said, heading to the stairs.

We returned to the basement office. I bandaged Cahil's cut and then sat at one of the desks while Cahil straightened the mess they'd left behind in their hurry to leave. He hummed to himself. The bastard was in a good mood.

"Did you lie about The Mosquito, too?" I asked.

"I didn't lie about Valek. My sources spotted him fighting Onora, and she was seen later. It was a natural conclusion. As for The Mosquito, he is dead. That's been confirmed."

One bright spot in an otherwise miserable day. The sleepless night caught up to me. Exhausted and heartsick, I rested my head on the desk and welcomed sleep.

Voices and movement roused me. Cahil's people had woken, and they filtered into the office area with sheepish expressions. A few sported bruises, and I helped bandage a number of cuts. It could have been worse.

Cahil sent two of them to keep an eye on the door while the rest discussed their next move. A messenger from Bruns

MARIA V. SNYDER

arrived, and I ducked under the desk to avoid being spotted. They went into Cahil's office, but I remained hidden until the man left.

"Good news, Yelena." Cahil smiled. "I've been recalled to the garrison. No need to invent an excuse for our departure."

"Why do you have to go back?"

His grin turned sly. "I'll tell you in ten days."

Bastard.

"We'll leave tomorrow morning for the garrison," Cahil said to his crew. "Hanni, please pick up supper for all of us."

"Not from the Council Hall's dining room," I said. "The Hall's food is laced with Theobroma."

Hanni gave me a wide-eyed stare.

"You don't know that for sure," Cahil said with an annoyed tone.

"How else can you explain the Councilors' willingness to leave and allow the Cartel to take over?"

"They agreed with Bruns's brilliant ideas and strategy."

"Then why not appoint him General and organize the war preparations themselves?" I asked.

"I'm not going to argue with you anymore."

Too bad. It would be a nice distraction from my situation.

"Hanni, buy a bunch of meat pies from the market." Cahil handed her a gold coin.

"Yes, sir." She bolted for the door.

"This place has been compromised. The rest of you pack up all the intel. We'll move the furniture later."

They bustled about, shoving files and various items into boxes and crates. I stayed out of the way.

One of the door guards appeared and gestured Cahil over. "There's a...person at the door. He insists on talking to you and our...guest."

Scowling, Cahil asked, "Valek?"

Excitement swirled in my chest. Did Valek return to say goodbye?

"No, sir. A young man. Says he has a package for you both."

All warmth died.

Cahil belted his sword on and tucked a dagger into the opposite side. He held a hand out to me. "Come on."

Curious and hopeful that maybe Valek had sent me a message instead, I stood. Cahil grasped my wrist tightly.

"I promised to cooperate. You don't need to hold on to me as if I'm going to run away," I said.

He didn't bother to reply. But as he guided me up to the ground floor and through the gloomy warehouse, I remembered he'd done the same thing when Onora appeared. As if the gesture warned her that I belonged to him. Perhaps he worried the young man would attempt to rescue me.

Fisk waited with the other guard by the open door. The fading sunlight lit his light brown eyes. A painful burn shone on his left temple and a raw cut marked his cheek. I shot Cahil a nasty glare. Fisk, though, peered at me in concern. Even though he was seventeen years old, I still saw the small boy that I'd first met over eight years ago superimposed on his tall and lean frame.

"Ah, it's the Beggar King," Cahil said. "Come to check on Yelena, Your Majesty?"

Fisk ignored Cahil. Instead he asked me, "Are you all right?"

"She's fine," Cahil said.

"And she'd better stay that way, or else—"

"What? You'll send your kiddies after me? They're no match for trained soldiers."

Fisk smiled. I marveled that his grin actually lowered the temperature in the room by ten degrees.

"Oh no, General. I wouldn't do something so...overt. There are *so many* ways to make a person's life miserable."

MARIA V. SNYDER

Score one for Fisk.

"Did you just come here to threaten me? I've more important things to attend to."

"I brought you these." Fisk handed a pouch to Cahil and one to me.

Cahil let go of my arm, and I untied the string. Inside was a wooden pendant of a bat hanging on a necklace. Cahil held up an ugly beetle. Leif had been so thrilled when he figured out how to attach a shield to a pendant. His wouldn't stick to glass or metal or stone, but when he tried wood, it had worked. The sudden desire to see my brother pulsed in my chest.

"Null shields, compliments of Valek," Fisk said.

Was this a sign that Valek wasn't angry anymore? I looped it around my neck, even though the baby seemed to be protecting me from magic. When Bruns had captured me, the daily magical brainwashing I endured wore off as the day progressed. And when Rika had used a magical illusion to disguise herself as Valek, I saw through it when she touched my skin. I'd speculated that the baby was stealing the magic, but since I didn't know exactly what was going on or what the fetus was doing with the power, it was a good idea not to rely on the protection it offered.

Cahil gave me a sour look as he tucked the pendant under his tunic, hiding it from sight. "I don't feel any different."

"It's going to take some time for the Theobroma and magic to wear off," I said.

"So you say." He turned to Fisk. "Anything else?"

"I'd like to talk to Yelena in private."

Cahil crossed his arms as if about to refuse, but after a moment he relaxed and motioned for his men to move away. "Stay in sight," he said to me, then strode far enough to give us some privacy if we kept our voices low. But his gaze remained on me.

"Do you have a message from Valek?" I asked before Fisk could even open his mouth.

"Uh…no."

I swallowed my disappointment. It hurt going down and landed in my stomach with a nauseated splash. "How are Lyle, Innis and the scouts doing?"

"Other than pissed about being jumped, they're healing well. I wanted to tell you we're moving HQ and changing all our plans. I'll have the agents out of the garrisons in a few days. If the general doesn't switch to our side in the ten days' time, you can tell him and Bruns what you know and it won't ruin anything."

"But I already ruined everything."

"No. I did. I was supposed to keep you safe. Instead we took you right into that lamplighter ambush."

I shook my head, but his hard expression meant I'd have an easier time convincing Cahil to befriend Valek.

"Is Valek helping you?" I asked.

Fisk creased his brow. "He can't, just in case you get stuck with Cahil."

"Oh." Why hadn't I thought of that sooner? I understood Valek's anger, and now I comprehended the depth of his fury. "Where is Valek?" I held my hands up. "No. Don't tell me."

"I don't know. He left this afternoon." Fisk lowered his voice even more. "I suspect he'll be keeping an eye on you."

A nice thought, but Fisk hadn't seen Valek's reaction.

"Hey." Fisk draped an arm around my shoulder, giving me a half hug. "It's only ten days, and then we'll have another ally. It'll all work out."

I leaned into him. He was as tall as Valek, but he smelled of wood smoke and pine instead of musk. "Thanks."

"Anytime. Stay safe, Lovely Yelena." He gave me another squeeze and then left.

MARIA V. SNYDER

The room's temperature plummeted another ten degrees in Fisk's wake. I hugged my arms and turned toward the stairs. Cahil followed me without saying a word. Thank fate. We returned to the offices and I sat at an empty desk, staring at nothing while I fiddled with the butterfly necklace Valek had carved for me. Would he forgive me?

The smell of beef pies roused me from my dark thoughts. Hanni set one in front of me. Despite my upset stomach, I ate the entire portion. I had to stay strong for the baby. The rest of the evening blurred together. Soldiers returned and left in waves, carrying crates. I noticed that none of the people were familiar. This crew appeared to be close to or younger than Cahil's age of twenty-nine. None of Cahil's old gang—the ones who'd raised him and lied to him about being King Ixia's nephew—were part of this group. Maybe they were stationed at the garrison. Or maybe he no longer trusted them.

Thinking about trust, I almost groaned aloud. Just how loyal were his people? They'd all eaten the spiked food and been brainwashed. What if I managed to wake Cahil, but his agents refused to obey his orders? There was nothing in the contract about his people following the terms of our agreement. I'd have to ask Cahil about it when—or should that be if?—we were alone.

Later that night, Cahil woke me. I'd been dozing with my head on a desk.

"Come on," he said, pulling me to my feet. "Let's go."

"Where?"

"We don't sleep here, and unless you'd rather be chained—"

"No."

"Thought not." He clamped a hand around my arm, escorting me up and out of the warehouse.

Once again, Cahil's crew surrounded us as if they expected an ambush. I pulled the hood of my borrowed cloak up and over my head. No need to tip Bruns off that I was with his general. Few people strolled along the quiet streets. Clouds blocked the moon, but I guessed it was close to midnight. A light breeze blew dead leaves along the road, their rattle the only sound.

"Are you still worried I'll escape?" I asked after a few blocks.

"No. But I'm sure your husband is nearby."

"He promised not to interfere."

"But that won't stop others from trying to get to you. There's still that bounty on your head."

True. We headed toward the southeast quadrant of the Citadel. Before reaching the government's area, Cahil turned right, and we entered one of those old factories that had been converted into apartments.

"You don't live in government housing?" I asked.

"Too many nosy neighbors."

We climbed to the sixth floor, and I waited in the hallway outside number sixty-six with a couple bodyguards while the others checked the apartment and lit the lanterns.

When it was declared safe, Cahil dismissed his crew. "Hanni, Faxon and Sladen, report here at first light. The rest of you, meet us at the stables an hour after dawn."

"And don't eat any of the food at the Council Hall," I added.

Cahil yanked me roughly inside. "*You* don't give my people orders." He locked the door.

"What happens once you know I'm right, but your people are still loyal to Bruns?"

"They're loyal to *me*."

"For now. You and Bruns are on the same page. What happens when you no longer agree?"

"That's not going to happen."

"Use your imagination, then."

He opened his mouth but then closed it.

MARIA V. SNYDER

Not waiting for him to catch up, I said, "They're not bound to our agreement. They can endanger both of us. They should all avoid the Theobroma and wear null shield pendants."

Cahil rubbed a hand along the blond scruff on his jaw. "I'll think about it."

Progress. I glanced around his apartment. Functional and masculine, a deep blue couch and several armchairs occupied the main living area. A few paintings of horses decorated the walls, and I recognized a lifelike portrait of Topaz in one. The small kitchen lined the left wall next to a door to the washroom. Two doors on the right side must lead to bedrooms. The air held a faint stale scent, and I suspected Cahil didn't spend much time here.

Pointing to the furthest door, Cahil said, "That's your room for tonight. I suggest you lock the door, just in case."

"In case an assassin breaks in?" Not a comforting thought.

"Yes, but I highly doubt it. No one followed us from the warehouse."

"I'm not worried about the ones you can spot."

"And I'm certain Valek is ensuring the others won't bother you."

If Valek was actually keeping an eye on my whereabouts. A strange emptiness filled me and I drifted, unconnected and alone. After washing up, I entered the bedroom—a stark, impersonal space meant for guests—and collapsed on the bed.

Cahil woke me the next morning. His people had arrived and brought cheese and bread for breakfast. I longed for a cup of hot tea—more for the warmth and comfort than an actual need. When we left the apartment, I pulled my hood up. Once we exited the building, Cahil grasped my arm again.

The morning bustle filled the streets. Factory workers hurried to report for their shifts and wagons trundled by, delivering goods and supplies. No one appeared to take any interest in us. A gray blanket of clouds sealed the sky, and a chilly, moist wind brushed my cheeks. The prospect of traveling in the rain soured my mood further.

As we walked to the Council's stables, Cahil said, "I thought about your concerns over my unit. And if you're right and Bruns is...brainwashing us, I'd like to have my loyal people free of his influence, as well. Can Fisk get us twelve more null shield pendants?"

I perked up at the good news. "I don't know if he can get that many with such short notice. But you can send someone to the market and ask one of the Helper's Guild members. Make sure your runner mentions my name."

Cahil sent Hanni. If she minded always being the one picked, she didn't give any indication. We continued on to the stables at a slower pace. When we entered the official government district, I scanned faces, seeking anyone I recognized or anyone who paid particular attention to me. I stole glances at Cahil—was he worried about being spotted with me? No. He appeared calm.

We arrived at the stables without any drama. Most of Cahil's unit waited within. I dreaded sharing a saddle with Cahil, but I was looking forward to seeing Topaz again. The familiar sights and smells of the large barn and rows of stalls eased my anxieties. The Council's stables could house over fifty horses—enough room to accommodate each Councilor, his or her aides, and various military personnel's horses. A small army of stable hands kept them all fed and well groomed.

An excited nicker tore right into my heart. Kiki! I broke into a run and found her sharing Topaz's stall. I hugged her, drinking in her earthy scent and soaking in her warmth. Kiki endured my attention for a couple minutes before she nudged me away, snuffling my pockets for treats.

"She showed up yesterday afternoon," one of the stable

MARIA V. SNYDER

hands said. The young boy gestured to the bench next to the stall.

My saddle, bags, bo staff and tack were piled on the wooden seat. Only one person could have sent her. Perhaps Valek wasn't quite as furious with me as I'd thought.

"I recognized her right off," the boy said. "Miss Kiki's not the type to dump and run, so I figured you'd be along sometime."

"Did you tell anyone she's here?" I asked.

The boy gave me a sly smile. "No. I figured it ain't none of their business."

"Thanks." I slipped him a silver coin. "Miss Kiki and I were never here." I added another silver.

He mocked a confused expression. "Who?" He hooked a thumb at Kiki. "Want me to get her ready?"

"No, thank you." Spending time with Kiki was never a chore. Plus I wanted to search my bags. Maybe Valek left me a note inside one of them.

Cahil caught up to me. "I didn't think Valek was the jealous type, but I guess he doesn't like the thought of us sharing a saddle."

I didn't bother to correct him. Valek trusted me. And while he might be overly protective, he was never jealous. Sorting through my bags, I found my travel clothes, personal necessities, cloak, tea bags, three books, weapons and a medical kit, but no note. Disappointment stabbed deep, and pain ringed my scar. I secured the flaps and saddled Kiki. She gave me a wet kiss on the cheek.

"Thanks," I said, wiping hay-scented slobber from my face.

Everyone had their horses saddled and ready to go by the time Hanni returned with a package.

"Report," Cahil ordered.

"As soon as I arrived in the market, Fisk appeared. He had

only seven pendants, but he said one of his members would meet us along the road and give us the rest," Hanni said.

"His kids must be keeping an eye on us," Cahil said, but he stared at me. "It also sounds like they're going to follow us to the garrison." He shrugged. "And thanks to Yelena, I'm sure by the time we arrive, his undercover agents will have left. If not, it won't be hard to find them."

The desire to punch him flowed through me. Would that be a violation of our accord? Probably.

Cahil handed out the pendants to the seven closest to him. A few gave me sour looks as they looped them around their heads, but they all wore them, tucking them underneath their uniforms.

We mounted and left the stables. Fourteen of us on horseback made quite a sight. Even Fisk's newest recruits wouldn't have any trouble following us, not to mention any bounty hunters. I kept my face hidden, and the other horses surrounded Kiki. Hopefully she wouldn't be recognized, even though some of my enemies had gotten up close and personal with her back hooves.

Exiting the Citadel via the north gate, we headed northeast toward the Featherstone garrison. It would take us two days to reach it.

The rain started soon after we left, and it continued for the entire trip. Cahil's crew mostly ignored me, but I enticed Hanni and Kyrie with offers of tea the first morning, and by the second, they joined me without being invited. We encountered few travelers on the road. A handful of Helper's Guild members approached us during the afternoon of the second day and handed Cahil five more pendants without a word. Then they headed southwest, back toward the Citadel.

We neared the garrison that evening. Cahil slowed Topaz so he rode beside me. My stomach knotted. I'd been expect-

MARIA V. SNYDER

ing his lecture about my behavior at the garrison and why I'd spend the next seven days locked in the stockade.

"I'm going to leave you at an inn in Starling's Egg," he said.

Surprised, I gaped at him.

He huffed in amusement. "I've been thinking about it. And no matter what arrangement I come up with, someone is going to recognize you in the garrison. Even if you're locked in a cell, one of the guards will eventually figure it out." He sobered. "Plus, if the cook is using Theobroma, we won't be able to get untainted food without raising suspicions. With you in Starling's Egg, I can join you for all my meals. The town is just outside the garrison."

"A good idea, as long as the chef at the inn isn't using Theobroma, as well," I said.

"You and your sensitive palate will have to let me know. If that's the case, then we'll purchase food from the market stalls."

I glanced at him. He was being very reasonable. A trick? Or was he starting to think for himself? "What about your people?"

"I'm sending the bulk of them on a mission. The rest will stay with you."

"Mission?"

"I'll tell you what it is, if you'd like to exchange information?"

"You already know everything I do, Cahil."

"Oh?"

"Bruns had his magician interrogate me when I couldn't refuse his commands. He relayed it to you when you visited the Krystal garrison over a month ago."

He tightened his grip on Topaz's reins. "Bruns told you about my visit?"

"No. I was in the room next to his office and overheard

everything. And I distinctly remember that you advised him to put a big bow on me and send me to the Commander."

"Bruns should have listened."

"I agree. It would have been a smart move if the Commander planned to attack Sitia."

"Not this again," Cahil muttered.

"But since Bruns knows that there won't be an attack, he knew I'd be more useful to him in Sitia."

Cahil urged Topaz into a canter, pulling ahead. Kiki stayed back. I expected to have that conversation a few times before he was able to accept the logic.

Starling's Egg appeared to be a typical base town with a larger number of taverns and inns for visiting relatives. The market was full of weapon vendors and gear to lure in the soldiers stationed at the garrison. Cahil sent the bulk of his crew to the base, but ordered Hanni, Sladen and Faxon to remain with us.

We avoided the busy downtown district as Cahil led us on a circuitous route to a quieter side street. He stopped at the Lucky Duck Inn. While we settled the horses in the inn's stables, Cahil went inside the four-story wooden building. When he returned, he handed the keys to two adjoining rooms to Hanni. She gave one to Faxon. Guess I was bunking with Hanni.

"Stay out of sight," Cahil said to me. "If you need anything, one of my people will get it for you. Either I'll be here for my meals or I'll eat food purchased from the market. All right?"

"Yes." House arrest was better than being locked in the stockade. Good thing I had a few books with me.

We ordered supper in the common room. Only a few people occupied the other tables and, aside from a few curious glances, they didn't pay us any undue attention. When the server set down five servings of the house pork-and-noodle casserole, everyone waited for me to taste it. Other than a nice medley of spices, the meal was Theobroma-free.

And that began my daily routine. Meals with Cahil and my guards in the common room, and the rest of the time I either read in the room I shared with Hanni, trained or exercised Kiki. I sent Hanni out for a few things, mostly tea bags and more books. I tried to engage her in conversation a few times. Quiet and serious, Hanni avoided divulging any personal details, but she was happy to read my books and discuss the finer points of self-defense and intrigue. Hanni also sparred with me. About twenty-five years old with short brown hair, she handled a knife and a sword with ease but hadn't trained with a bo staff. I showed her a few basic moves.

Faxon and Sladen preferred to remain uninvolved and kept an aloof bodyguard's demeanor whenever near me. However, on a couple occasions, their laughter slipped through the door between our rooms.

On day four of my house arrest and day seven of the agreement, Cahil joined us for a late supper. He strode to our table with stiff movements, and his fierce expression meant trouble. I braced for an outburst, but he kept silent.

After we'd ordered, I was unable to contain my curiosity any longer. "What happened today?"

"Nothing. And don't start with any of your—" he waved a hand "—speeches."

"All right."

Our food arrived, and we ate in a tense silence.

When he finished eating, Cahil leaned back and let out an audible breath. Dark smears of weariness lined his eyes. He asked me, "Did you know that Fisk's people not only infiltrated all the Cartel's garrisons but also were working in many different areas—some quite sensitive?"

Oh, no. "Yes, except I'm surprised by how...deep they managed to get. Were they arrested?" Poor kids.

"No. They all scattered. Fisk must have quite the communication system in place." He scowled. "Better than ours."

I kept my expression neutral, even though I wanted to beam with pride. "Is that why you're so upset?"

"No."

I waited.

"In order to ensure there are no more spies, the Cartel ordered a complete sweep of all the garrisons for null shields." He banged his hand on the table. The empty bowls rattled. "Don't say it."

Swallowing, I refrained from stating the obvious—why would the Cartel be worried about null shields if they weren't using magic to influence their people? It almost killed me. Instead I asked, "Are you worried you'll be caught?"

The idea surprised him. He straightened. "They wouldn't test me."

"Are you sure?"

Cahil surged to his feet. "I'm the General of the Sitian Army."

"And you follow the Council's—or, in this case, the Cartel's—orders. There are a number of magicians in the garrison, including Second Magician Irys Jewelrose." I didn't add that Irys hadn't been brainwashed, but had been biding her time. As a master-level magician, Irys could ingest Theobroma and still resist the influence. "You need to leave the garrison for the next three days to avoid the sweep."

He grabbed my shoulders and hauled me to my feet. "*You* don't give *me* orders."

"She's right," Hanni said. "We need to leave town. All of us."

Cahil turned to her. "Oh?"

MARIA V. SNYDER

She stood. "A week ago, I believed in Bruns and the Cartel and would have given my life to support them. Now I won't." Hanni met my gaze. "I'm thinking clearly for the first time in seasons."

Sladen and Faxon stood on either side of Hanni in a show of support. I suppressed the desire to pump my fist.

Cahil released me and sank into his chair. "I hate—and I mean *loathe*—having to say this, but…you're right. Bruns has been using magic." He held up a hand. "*But*, I still believe he is trying to protect Sitia and is doing an excellent job of training soldiers and magicians on how to work together."

Being an adult, I did not gloat or act smug or do any of the childish actions my emotions urged me to do. Instead, I said, "That's why we need you, Cahil. There is still a slight chance the Commander will attack, and Sitia should be prepared, but Bruns's methods are unconscionable. Our goal is to stop the Cartel and get the Council back into power. We can best meet that goal with you remaining in your position."

"And spying for you?"

"Yes. And perhaps waking others up so they're loyal to the Sitian Council and not the Cartel."

"Which will be difficult if Bruns's magicians do frequent sweeps for null shields. It took us a week."

"One problem at a time," I said. "Right now, you and your people need to avoid that sweep. Perhaps leave for a training exercise?"

"That would work, except…" Cahil rubbed his face. "I can't believe I'm doing this."

"Doing what?" I asked.

"Switching sides. Betraying Bruns. Working with Valek." He waved a hand. "Take your pick."

"It's the right thing to do, and you know it."

Drawing in a deep breath, he said, "Then I should tell you that your father and sister-in-law, Mara, have been captured. They're on their way here, and so is Bruns."

MARIA V. SNYDER

11

VALEK

The door to the Commander's apartment flew open. Owen Moon strode in as if he owned the place. Tyen, another powerful magician, trotted at his heels. Time to go. Valek backed toward the window, but his connection to the power blanket disappeared suddenly. Owen had surrounded Valek with a null shield. Unwilling to let the magician know the shield could no longer trap him, Valek froze as if caught. Signe vanished, and the Commander returned.

"What did you hope to accomplish with this little stunt?" Owen asked Valek. There was more gray in his short dark hair than Valek had remembered, and he looked older than his forty-four years.

Valek didn't respond.

"Still hoping to save your commander?" Owen laughed. "Trust me, it's too late."

Not quite, but Valek wasn't going to correct him and expose Signe.

"So, what do we do with you now?" Owen asked no one in particular. "You are wanted for treason. I say we arrest you and then publicly execute you."

"That won't work," the Commander said. "He'll escape the

dungeon. It's best to take care of him now. We can display his dead body so his loyal corps will understand who is in charge."

Even though Valek knew Owen controlled the Commander, the comment still stabbed right through him like a hot poker. Owen frowned at the suggestion. Probably because the Commander didn't immediately agree with him.

"Tyen, what do you think?" Owen asked.

The broad-shouldered magician was the same age as Owen. They had attended the Magician's Keep together. "I think we should finish what we started two months ago and push him out the window."

Tyen's ability to move objects would make that easy for him to do. And Valek couldn't use his darts to defend himself, because Tyen would knock them aside with his magic. Fear coiled in his stomach.

Owen grinned. "I agree. And this time, he doesn't have any friends to come to his rescue." He straightened his arm, spread his fingers and thrust his palm toward Valek.

Valek reacted as if a force had slammed into him. He shuffled backward until his legs hit the windowsill. Blood slammed in his heart. He met Owen's triumphant gaze.

"Goodbye, Valek," he said, once again extending his arm.

Seeing no other way to escape, Valek fell back through the window. Twisting at the last moment, he hooked a hand on the ledge to slow his momentum and swing his body close to the wall. But his fingers slipped off. Butterflies spun in his stomach as he hung suspended in midair for a fraction of a second before gravity pulled him down.

Air roared in his ears as he fell. Then the unmistakable *thwack* of a crossbow sounded a second before an iron bolt slammed into the stone right next to him. When a second bolt appeared on the opposite side, Valek realized the significance. He grabbed the shaft as he slid past, slowing his de-

MARIA V. SNYDER

scent. Another bolt materialized, and he seized it with both hands. With a jerk that sent a throb of pain through his arms and shoulders, Valek stopped his fall. He dangled two stories above the ground.

A couple more bolts arrived below him, and he quickly used them to reach safety. The guard assigned to watch the wall must have recognized him. Valek waved a thank-you and then dashed away before Owen could retaliate. Valek hoped the man or woman had a believable story to tell Owen about why he or she shot the bolts.

After Valek reached Onyx in the Snake Forest, the day-long trip to the cottage was easy in comparison. As he groomed and cared for Onyx, his mind whirled with the information he'd gained from Signe. Owen had an ace up his sleeve, and it was vital that the resistance discover what it was. Valek needed to check the Keep's library for Ellis Moon's notebooks. Ideally there would be a mention of something that was more powerful than Theobroma.

Valek had two days until his meeting with Onora near the Featherstone garrison. And then… Valek would either be a prisoner, or he and Yelena would be free to rejoin Fisk and the efforts to stop the Cartel. If the worst happened, he'd give the intel about Ellis Moon to Onora before surrendering.

Exhausted from two nights without sleep, Valek trudged up to bed. After a day of rest, he'd travel to the garrison and find out if Yelena's gamble had worked or not.

The morning of the ninth day since Yelena made her deal with Cahil dawned clear and cool. Onyx trotted into the main district of Starling's Egg a few hours after sunrise and headed for the market. Onora was probably hidden among the stalls, waiting for Valek. He slowed Onyx to a walk once they reached the busy heart of the small town. Sure enough, Onora appeared next to them within a few minutes.

"Report," he said.

She scanned the shoppers. "Not here. Meet me at the Lucky Duck Inn on Cherry Street." Onora disappeared.

Dressed in dark brown pants and a light tan tunic to blend in, Valek dismounted and asked a local where Cherry was located. The woman barely glanced at him as she pointed to the northeast. He led Onyx through the streets, letting the horse cool down. He wondered if Onora had been staying at the Lucky Duck while keeping an eye on Yelena. Had his wife spent the last seven days locked in the stockade? Valek hoped not but wouldn't be surprised if she had.

He found the inn on Cherry and approved of its unremarkable appearance and out-of-the-way location. Onyx headed straight to the small stables behind the building. Valek left his horse with the stable boy but instructed him to leave the saddle on, just in case he needed to make a quick exit.

Onora waited for him at one of the tables in the back corner of the common room. It was a typical inn, with a tavern on the ground floor and rooms on the higher stories. He scanned the other occupants—two men and an older woman. The sweet scent of molasses lingered on the air. When he'd left the cottage yesterday, he hadn't had much of an appetite. The prospect of turning himself over to Cahil had soured his stomach.

Valek joined Onora. A young server appeared and he ordered breakfast, despite still having no desire to eat. He'd need energy to deal with the next step. When the girl left, he asked, "Yelena?"

"She's perfectly fine. She was staying here until yesterday," Onora said.

He straightened. "Not what I expected."

"Me, neither, but it was smart." Onora filled him in on

what had happened. "It took Cahil and his crew a week to wake up, but they all came around, just like Yelena predicted."

Yelena had done it. The crushing pressure around his chest eased.

"You owe her an apology," Onora said.

He owed her much more than a mere apology. While Fisk and Onora had faith in her, Valek had believed her agreement with Cahil had been yet another betrayal and bound to fail.

"While you've been off pouting, she's been miserable. You should have seen the stricken look on her face when she found out *I've* been watching over her and not you."

If Onora wished to make him feel worse, she'd succeeded. "You talked to her?"

"Yes. She stood in the small yard behind the inn where she'd been training and signaled that you should join her and all was well. I thought it might be a trick, but she was alone, and they hadn't ever left her alone before. Still, I waited until Cahil left, then visited her room later that night." Onora grinned. "Scared the hell out of her roommate."

"Where is she now?"

"Setting up an ambush."

Clamping down on his surprise, he said, "Explain."

"Her father and sister-in-law were captured and are being escorted here. Yelena plans to rescue them before they reach the garrison."

Not good. "By herself?"

"No. She has three of Cahil's crew with her."

"And Cahil?"

"Taking a hit for the team."

He waited.

"Cahil remained in the garrison. Bruns arrived yesterday, and he's playing host. He's also unprotected. If Bruns's magicians detect a null shield on him, the gig would be up. According to Yelena, Cahil's pretty strong-willed and should be okay for a couple days."

"So, Cahil has agreed to help us?"

"Yes, but he's not happy about it."

That wasn't a surprise. Valek mulled over the information. "Where's Leif?"

"He escaped when they grabbed Mara and Esau. No one's seen him since."

"He's probably following the wagon."

The server arrived with Valek's order. She placed the steaming plate of eggs, bacon and toast in front of him. His stomach growled with hunger, and he realized he hadn't had a decent hot meal since leaving Yelena with Cahil. Valek dug into the food. Between bites, he asked about the ambush.

"They picked a nice little spot about four hours east of the garrison," Onora said. "They figured by that point, the soldiers will have relaxed, thinking they are almost home. Plus it's better than guessing where the group will stop for the night."

"When are they expected to strike?"

"Tomorrow morning."

"Think they'd welcome a couple extra helpers?"

"Oh, yes. I told them I'd be back, but no one was sure about you."

Ah, hell. He had some major apologizing to do.

After he finished eating, he paid and reclaimed Onyx. The horse glanced at a stall with longing. But when Valek mentioned joining Kiki, Onyx's ears perked up. Valek understood the feeling. The desire to see Yelena energized him, as well.

He mounted and headed west at a moderate pace. The number of buildings dwindled, and fields of corn plants stretched out on both sides of the road. Soon the drumming of hooves sounded behind him as Onora caught up. She rode an unfa-

MARIA V. SNYDER

miliar black-and-white piebald mare with a black mane. Janco had borrowed The Madam since he'd lent Beach Bunny to Reema.

"Who is this?" he asked.

"Horse."

"Original."

She grinned. "I figured the name would bug Janco."

It would indeed.

They rode for a while in silence. After two hours of riding, the fields ended and they entered a forest. Valek worried about Yelena and hoped she'd forgive him. The upside to this whole mess was that the people who'd been under Bruns's influence could be woken. The downside was that a person had to be Theobroma-free for a week—a dangerously long time. At least now they had Cahil's cooperation. The General could begin to wake other high-ranking military officials and perhaps even the Sitian Council members. One could dream.

Onora slowed Horse to a walk as they reached the bottom of a small valley. Ahead the dirt road was rutted from a recent washout. A rustle sounded above Valek. He glanced up in time to spot a net of greenery falling toward him. Valek stopped Onyx right before the heavy blanket knocked him to the ground.

Valek landed hard on his left shoulder. He rolled onto his back and reached for his knives just as a person sat on top of him, pinning his arms, while a thin blade pierced the greenery and nicked his neck.

The blade disappeared, and Valek twisted his hips and bucked the person off. He shoved the net aside, jumped to his feet and yanked his knives. Two figures dressed in green camouflage backed away from him. Onora stood with two others—also camouflaged. She wiped dirt off her pants but appeared unhurt and unarmed. Odd.

Then the trees spun around him. The irresistible urge to sleep liquefied his muscles. He staggered and went down on one knee. His heavy knives slipped from his nerveless fingers. Valek touched his neck. A small drop of blood coated his finger. The blade must have been treated with sleeping potion.

Valek toppled. He'd congratulate them on getting the drop on him, but...

Valek woke but kept his eyes closed. Fuzzy memories of being ambushed swirled. His head ached from a sleeping potion hangover. A dull throb pulsed through his left shoulder. He smelled wood smoke. A fire crackled nearby.

"...too slow. We should use Curare instead. It's faster," a woman said.

"But it won't work. Everyone's been eating Theobroma for months. It neutralizes the Curare. And next time, remember to use a dart and not your knife, Hanni," Onora said. "You have more control and can keep your distance. You saw how quickly Valek freed himself from the net. He could have killed you before the sleeping potion kicked in."

Onora? Was she working for the Cartel now?

"I'm sorry. I panicked. Do you think *he's* going to be mad we did a test run on him?" the woman—Hanni—asked.

No answer, but it explained quite a bit.

"Just don't panic tomorrow," Onora said.

"No problem. Tomorrow I won't be jumping *Valek*," Hanni muttered.

"As long as you all remember that the goal is to rescue my sister-in-law and father without killing the guards. Incapacitate only," Yelena said.

Her voice soothed his soul. Valek opened his eyes. He lay on a bedroll with a blanket over him. Nearby, Yelena and Onora sat around a campfire with two men and Hanni. Darkness

MARIA V. SNYDER

surrounded them. He waited. It didn't take long for Yelena's gaze to find his.

She tensed. Even though he deserved it, her reaction stabbed him right in the heart. The others sensed her concern and turned. He sat up. The men and Hanni hopped to their feet. Their hands hovered near weapons. Skittish lot. Valek would have been amused, but Yelena still hadn't relaxed.

"Onyx?" he asked her.

"Fine. He's with Kiki."

Onora poured him a cup of water and brought it over. "Here."

"Thanks." He downed it in one gulp. "Test run?"

"Yeah. They're young and needed the practice," Onora said.

"We're older than you," one of the men said in protest.

"Sorry. They're inexperienced."

That didn't go over any better.

Valek touched his neck. A dart would have left a smaller injury, but the cut had already stopped bleeding. "Were the darts loaded with sleeping potion as well?"

Onora smiled. "Of course. Although I'm surprised you didn't spot the ambush sooner."

He met Yelena's gaze again. "I was distracted."

"Bad form, old man. Don't worry, I won't tell the Commander." Onora refilled his cup.

"Good, because he believes this old man—" Valek tapped his chest "—killed you."

"Oh?" She stilled.

He glanced at the three others. "I'll tell you about it later." He stood. Cahil's crew stepped back and grabbed the hilts of their weapons.

"Relax," he said. "I'm not upset about the ambush. Onora and Yelena know I encourage training and preparation. Kudos to you for a successful test run." He held his hand out to his wife. "Yelena, a word in private?"

Her hesitation hurt worse than his head. But she slipped her hand in his, allowing him to pull her to her feet. Valek led her well away from the others. As his eyes adjusted to the darkness, the shapes of Onyx, Kiki and Horse formed. They grazed in a small clearing. Weak moonlight outlined them in silver.

"Valek, I'm—"

"No." He pulled her into a tight hug. Surprised, she stiffened, then relaxed against him. He breathed in her scent. "I'm so, so sorry. I overreacted. I didn't trust you. And I threw a tantrum and stormed off to sulk like a child. I'm sorry. *Please* forgive me."

"Only if you can forgive me."

"For what?"

She leaned back. "I believed Cahil and thought Onora had killed you, not trusting that you might have worked out an arrangement with her. I should have just trusted you. And I endangered our child."

"You were right about Cahil. Now we have a powerful ally."

"But I should have believed in you."

"All right, you're forgiven."

"So are you."

Relieved, he kissed her long and hard. When they broke apart, they were both panting. He drew her close and wished they were alone. Maybe if they went—

"Why does the Commander think Onora is dead?" Yelena asked.

"I paid him a visit."

"Are you insane?" She broke away and punched him on his sore shoulder.

MARIA V. SNYDER

He grunted in pain, but she failed to look contrite as he rubbed the sore spot.

"Talk," she ordered.

"Like you, I took a gamble." Valek told her about his visit and what he'd learned. "I hope we can find Ellis's notes in the Keep's Library."

"If they're still there." Then she scowled. "And if we're successful tomorrow."

He glanced at the horses. "Speaking of tomorrow, why aren't there more horses?"

"Hanni and Sladen will commandeer a couple from the guards, and Faxon will drive the wagon."

"Any word from Leif?"

"No. We hope he's following the wagon, but Cahil said they were captured near Fulgor."

Valek considered. "He might have gone to Fulgor instead, thinking to get there ahead of them."

"That's what I thought, too. I hope he wasn't arrested." Concern deepened her voice.

"Would Cahil know Leif's status?"

"Eventually."

"How are you going to communicate with him without the Cartel finding out?"

She peered up at him. "One of his loyal crew will get a message to a member of Fisk's guild."

Not the best situation, but there weren't any other options. "Too bad we don't have any glass messengers."

"That might give us away. The Cartel has a group of loyal magicians who have not been ingesting the Theobroma. The drug makes it too hard for them to concentrate. So they're seeking others who are using magic, and they've been using those glass super messengers to communicate between the garrisons."

Another bit of unwelcome news. If the resistance tried anything at one garrison, all the others would be notified right away.

"What else did you have planned for Cahil?" she asked.

"I hoped he could wake the other military leaders and then the Councilors."

"That would be impossible for him to do without tipping the Cartel off." She explained about the frequent null shield sweeps.

He almost growled in frustration. "We need an...anti-Theobroma. A substance that works faster."

"I agree. Something that works as quickly as Curare would be ideal."

"Now you're dreaming, love. I'd be happy with something that shortens the time to mere days instead of a week."

But her brows crinkled in thought, and she was no longer listening to him. He kept quiet, letting her mull over whatever it was that had snagged her attention. Content to hold her close, he relaxed for the first time in ten long days. She had forgiven him, and right now, that was all that mattered.

"My father mentioned that there were a number of hybrid plants in Owen's glass hothouse. One is a Curare that is resistant to Theobroma. And I read through Bavol's notes. He was working with Owen's Master Gardener, and they experimented with crossbreeding a number of different plants. Maybe they discovered something that could help us make an anti-Theobroma." Yelena told him about Bavol's secret glass hothouse in the Avibian Plains. "Fisk and I had stolen the address of the farm where the glassmaker delivered the sheets, but I never made it back to HQ to follow up."

"Once we rescue your father and find Leif, checking that glass house would be the next logical step. Maybe there will be Harman trees there, as well."

MARIA V. SNYDER

"A logical step for them. I need to return to the Citadel and figure out who the Master Gardener is."

He tightened his grip. "*We* need to. There's still the bounty on your head."

She was quiet for a while. "My father will need extra protection. Onora can go with them. You obviously trust her."

"I do, and I need to tell you why."

"Oh?"

"You remember that fight on the rooftop Cahil mentioned?"

"It was real. I know. Onora told me all about it."

"I'm surprised she confided in you."

"Me, too. But she said *friends* shouldn't keep secrets from each other."

"She's making progress."

"She is. And so are you."

"Because I apologized?"

"No. Because you healed your injuries with your magic. You have control of your power. Now you need to learn the extent of your abilities and start using them. We wouldn't have gotten the drop on you today if you had."

She had a point. "All right. When we return to the Citadel, I'll search for a teacher."

"A Master Magician would be ideal, but since Bain and Irys are occupied, Teegan is the next best choice. And he should be back from the coast by now."

"He's fourteen."

"He has master-level powers and has been training with Irys for a year."

"He's fourteen."

"Valek." She used *that* tone. The don't-be-a-bigger-idiot-than-you're-being-right-now tone.

He sighed. "All right."

She rose onto her tiptoes and kissed him. A jolt of desire swept all his other emotions away. He deepened the kiss.

When they broke apart, he said, "Let's find a more private location."

Yelena linked her hands behind his neck. "Because of the horses?"

"No. The assassin in the trees."

She dropped her arms and stepped away. "Is Onora—"

"Not close enough to overhear us, but keeping an eye on us."

"Why?"

"Like all of your friends, she's become protective of you. And I suspect she wanted to ensure I apologized properly."

"Nice of her."

"Uh-huh. Now give her a wave so I can drag you deeper into the woods and ravish you."

A gleam shone in her eyes. "Those that say romance is dead haven't met you."

"That's right. They don't call me Mr. Romance for nothing." He swept her up in his arms and carried her to a nice spot far away from the campsite. Then he proceeded to follow through on his promise.

Morning arrived far too soon. Valek and Yelena had returned to the warmth of the fire after he proved his remorse over his behavior. As the group ate breakfast, Yelena reviewed the plan. She and Faxon would be stationed in the treetops, Hanni and Sladen on the ground right before the washout and Valek and Onora down the road far enough to come in behind the wagon once it had stopped. They expected the wagon to be escorted by eight soldiers, including two scouts traveling ahead of the team. The six of them settled into their spots a few hours before the estimated time, just in case.

MARIA V. SNYDER

★ ★ ★

Valek had never been on a stakeout with Onora before. Fascinated, he watched as she blended in with the colors of the forest. And it wasn't due to her clothing. Yes, she wore earth tones, but if he had glanced away and looked back at her position, he would have thought she'd moved to another location. Janco had mentioned this to him before, but Valek had assumed it was just Janco's tendency to exaggerate.

Had Onora used magic? Without his immunity, he could no longer detect when it was in use, but...

Remembering his conversation with Yelena, Valek lowered his mental shield. The blanket of power pressed down on him. He drew a thin thread and reached for Onora with his senses. Her surface thoughts focused on the ambush. Onora reviewed the plan and listed what could go wrong. For each unexpected contingency, she calculated a way to counter it. Smart.

However, he didn't detect any magic being used. Either he didn't have that ability, or she wasn't using any at this time. Perhaps she used magic to go camouflage and didn't need any more power to sustain it. He pushed his senses further, stretching them toward Yelena's location on the limb above the road. She squirmed into a more comfortable position and hoped the ambush would work. Worry for Esau, Mara and Leif occupied her thoughts. No surprise. It didn't take long for the baby to yank on Valek's power, draining it.

Valek broke the connection. Drawing another strand of power, he aimed it at the road, seeking the scouts. They would be traveling about fifteen to thirty minutes ahead of the wagon. Their job was to flush out any ambushes or spot trouble before the slower and more vulnerable wagon arrived. Nothing.

Saving his strength for the fight, Valek raised his mental

shield, once again blocking the power. He tried to meet Onora's gaze, but without his magic, she'd disappeared.

"What's wrong?" the tree asked in her whisper.

"Do you do that on purpose?" he asked.

"Do what?"

He gestured. "Blend in. Disappear."

"I'm right here. What are you talking about?"

"Your ability to match your surroundings so well that I can't see you anymore."

Silence. She probably thought he was insane.

"Look at your hands," he said.

"They're hands."

So she was immune to her own talent. He changed tactics. "You must have realized by this point just how well you can hide."

"Janco said something about it, but I thought…"

"He was just being Janco, spouting out a plethora of theories, rants and comments, so you have no idea if he's being silly or serious or if the man's a genius?"

"Exactly." A pause. "Wouldn't you have felt me using magic?"

Onora didn't know about his new situation, and he wondered if he should tell her now that he trusted her. Valek decided to wait until she needed to know the information. "Not if you're a One-Trick."

"One-Trick?"

"A magician that can only do one thing. There are a number of them in Sitia, and I suspect in Ixia, as well. They don't consciously pull power. They just have an instinctive ability that has to be magical in origin. For example, Opal used to work with an old glassmaker who could light fires, but he couldn't do anything else."

MARIA V. SNYDER

She was quiet for a while. "It's not conscious. All I do is focus on the mission at hand."

Sounded like a One-Trick, but only a master-level magician would know for sure.

Onora appeared suddenly. She stared at her hands as she laced and unlaced her fingers over and over. "It didn't work when…Captain…Timmer came for me. I couldn't hide…from him…no matter how hard I tried."

"Because you were afraid. Just thinking about him has made you lose your camouflage."

She glanced up in surprise.

"No need to be scared of him. He's locked in the Commander's dungeon and is scheduled for execution in a little over three months."

"Even if I'm not there to kill him?"

"Yes. The Commander might not be in full control of his mind, but one thing he loathes is sexual predators."

"What if Owen releases Timmer or he escapes?"

"Then, when all this is over, we will hunt him down, strip him naked, tenderize him with a few dozen holes and leave him for the snow cats to find."

Onora grinned. "Good plan."

"I thought you'd like that."

They lapsed into silence. After an hour, the familiar thrum of horses reached them. Valek whistled the signal. Soon the two scouts rode into view and passed Valek and Onora's position. The scouts spotted the rutted road and slowed, glancing to the left and right. Smart enough to know this was an ideal spot for an ambush, but not experienced enough to look up.

Yelena and Sladen released the camouflage nets. They fell at a slight angle and swept the riders from the horses. The victims landed with an *oomph*. Using the net ideally avoided any major injuries. If they'd shot darts filled with sleeping potion, the riders might topple, and falling from a moving horse could be lethal.

Hanni and Faxon jumped on the struggling men and poked them with the potion. In thirty seconds, the soldiers stilled. Yelena and Sladen hauled the net back into position while Valek and Onora caught the two horses. Then they helped drag the two sleeping men into the woods. After Valek led the mounts to Kiki, he returned to his position. They reset the trap.

The next part would be a bit harder. About twenty minutes later, a slower beat of horse hooves sounded, along with the creak and rumble of a wagon. Bantering voices floated on the light breeze. Once again, Valek signaled them to be ready.

Two riders led the way. Two others sat on the wagon's bench, and the final two followed the caravan. A tarp had been draped over the cargo area, and Valek hoped Mara and Esau had been hidden underneath it. As the group reduced speed and lumbered past, Valek shifted his weight to the balls of his feet. He held a dart laced with sleeping potion in each hand.

When they reached the washout, the nets were dropped on the leaders, and Onora shot the two on the wagon with darts. The ones in the back froze upon seeing their companions attacked. Valek and Onora snuck up next to them. He stabbed the dart into one man's leg and yanked him from the saddle while Onora did the same to his partner. The soldier hopped up and drew a short sword. Valek stayed just out of reach until the man wobbled and crumpled to the ground.

The ambush was a complete success. Bodies littered the road, but no one appeared to be injured. Yelena and Sladen climbed down from the trees as Valek pulled back the tarp. Mara and Esau had been bound to the wagon and gagged. Esau's face turned red as he struggled to speak.

Hyper-alert, Valek spun and drew his dagger. The soldiers

they had just neutralized sprang to their feet with weapons in hand. Yelena yipped in surprise as one of the scouts lunged from the woods. The scout grabbed her and pressed a knife to her neck. The desire to rip him apart flowed through Valek, and he gauged the distance to the man.

"Drop your weapons or I'll slit her throat," the scout said.

12

HELI

Heli reread the note from Fisk. While glad she didn't have to watch the rather boring comings and goings of the Stormdance garrison any longer, she wondered why Fisk thought it was too dangerous to remain. It had only been a month, but his other operatives...

She grinned at the word *operatives*. The kids working for Fisk were much younger than her own eighteen years. However, they'd fled the garrison like seagulls before a big storm. Something must have happened and, while she had to be on the coast soon to harvest the heating season's storms regardless, she thought Fisk might be overreacting. Especially when she considered his missive.

He believed Zethan, Zohav and Teegan were in danger and needed to relocate to a safer location. As if there were such a thing. Fisk had never been to The Cliffs, so he had no idea just how difficult it would be for an army or even a person to sneak up on them. With four Stormdancers on the beach, there was no way anyone could traverse the narrow path down The Cliffs without one of the Stormdancers blowing them out to sea. Ridiculous.

Oh, well. She shrugged and abandoned her post by the garrison's main entrance. Stopping at the inn where she'd been staying, Heli packed her knapsack and paid her bill. She considered swinging by her parents' house, but that would add two days to her travel time. And there was no way they'd let her leave after only three or four hours. They'd pepper her with a million questions and insist she stay overnight, bringing the total to three extra days. Fisk was probably being overly cautious, but she had to give the guy credit. He had planned and executed a killer rescue.

Remembering that night, Heli straightened with pride. Zethan had called the storm and Heli controlled it, keeping a safe path open for Yelena and Valek and a bunch of their friends to escape the Krystal garrison. It'd been the hardest thing she'd ever done with her Stormdancing magic, and it'd been both terrifying and exhilarating at the same time. And it had been empowering. When Zethan's twin sister, Zohav, started flattening the guards with giant balls of water, she'd believed the three of them could beat the Cartel on their own. Of course, reality arrived the very next day when they hadn't been able to help anyone because it was dry, calm and sunny.

Heli swung by the stables and saddled her horse, Thunder. The gray-and-white stallion twitched with energy. However, like his namesake, he started out strong but soon faded with distance. She'd been working on his endurance, and riding him was still better than walking, but she wished she had a Sandseed horse like Kade. Moonlight could reach The Cliffs in three days, but Thunder would be lucky to make it in four.

The morning of the fifth day on the road, Heli mounted Thunder. Her bedroll did nothing to soften the hard shale of The Flats and made her cot in the main cavern seem like a featherbed in comparison.

They reached the edge of The Cliffs later that afternoon. A

fresh, damp breeze greeted them. Heli breathed in the tangy scent of the sea far below. The strident call of the gulls interrupted the rhythmic shushing of the distant waves. Sunlight painted the water with diamonds.

Home.

Heli soaked in the beauty of the landscape for a moment. The wind had carved a rippling pattern into The Cliffs, leaving behind wings of stone and arches of rocks. Water had drilled holes into them, and the Stormdancers used the caves for living areas, sleeping quarters, storage and housing the glass kiln. The sweet aroma of white coal and molten glass laced the salty air. Helen, the glassmaker, was probably busy making the orbs for the upcoming storm season.

Thunder refused to move when Heli urged him down the narrow trail. No matter how many times he'd been here, he wouldn't descend unless Heli walked beside him.

"You're a big baby," she said, dismounting. "Come on. If we hurry we might be in time for some of Raiden's seafood chowder." Her stomach rumbled just thinking about it.

Halfway down, she spotted dark gray clouds gathering well out to sea. A storm would be here in a few days. Early, but one of the many things she'd learned about storms was that they didn't follow the calendar. Heli glanced down. Kade stood at the end of a rocky outcropping. Waves rushed past but parted before crashing into his favorite perch.

By the time Heli and Thunder reached the sand, Kade had traversed the rocks and was heading in their direction. She waited. He was her boss, after all. Wearing a cautious expression, he strode over the sand with ease. His shoulder-length brown hair blew in the breeze. Heli tucked her own long brown strands behind an ear. The sun and sea had streaked both their hair with blond highlights.

"You're here early," he said once he'd drawn closer.

"Well, hello to you, too."

"What happened?" he asked.

She suppressed a sigh. Kade was always too serious. And she was only five days early—her Stormdancing shift started on the first day of the heating season.

"I received a message from Fisk," she said, then told him about Fisk's concerns.

He huffed. "They're safer here than anywhere else in Sitia."

"I know. Where are they?"

Kade gestured down the beach. "Zethan is surfing...or rather, trying to, while his sister is swimming."

Heli shivered. "The water's freezing."

"Not to them. They say it's warm in comparison to the waters off Ixia's coast."

"And Teegan?"

"Helping Raiden."

"What should we do about Fisk's message?" she asked.

"Let's wait until everyone is together and discuss it over supper."

Heli led Thunder to the small stables on the beach. When the weather turned nasty, as it frequently did during the heating and cooling seasons, they moved the horses up to the storm cave to shelter them from the elements.

Moonlight whickered a greeting. The black horse had a white moon on his forehead. Smoke, another gray horse, poked his head out. Heli didn't recognize the third horse—a cream-colored mare with a blond mane. The new horse matched the sand on the beach. After grooming Thunder and ensuring he had fresh grain and water, Heli trudged up to the main cavern.

The familiar fishy scent of seafood chowder wrapped around her like a soft blanket. A large fire burned inside the cave.

Teegan cracked open clam shells while Raiden stirred a tall pot bubbling on the coals.

Raiden beamed at Heli when he spotted her. All her fatigue was forgotten as she raced in for a hug. Heli had been dancing in the storms since she was twelve, and the forty-five-year-old camp manager was like a surrogate father. Although he tended to father all the Stormdancers whether they wanted it or not, and he was the voice of reason when arguments sprang up. Even Kade deferred to his experience most of the time.

"You're early," Raiden said when she stepped back.

"I missed your cooking."

He huffed. "What happened to, 'If I eat another fish, I'm gonna grow scales'?"

She waved her hand. "That was last year, when all the meat spoiled. You gotta admit that even you were sick of seafood after eating it for thirty days straight."

"That's a lot of clams," Teegan said as he pried open another one and scooped out the insides.

Heli moved closer and inspected his pile of shells. "You're already a pro. What else have you been doing?"

"We've been practicing our magic, learning our limits and abilities, getting ready for the big battle." Teegan kept his tone casual, but she spotted the tension in his shoulders.

While only fourteen years old, he was well on his way to becoming a master-level magician, though he didn't have as much experience wielding magic yet. When they'd rescued Valek and Yelena, Teegan had kept her safe from the enemies' bolts and arrows that whizzed through the air, since she had to be close to the action to see where to focus the calm.

"Do you have any news?" Teegan asked.

"Not much."

"Anything about my parents or family?"

"No, sorry."

MARIA V. SNYDER

He wilted. It had to be hard not knowing what was going on. She squeezed his shoulder before helping him with the rest of the clams.

Soon everyone except Helen had assembled for supper. According to Raiden, she was at a critical point in the orb-making process. Zethan and Zohav had dried off and changed into plain gray tunics and pants. Their black hair dripped water. There was no doubt the two were siblings, and their resemblance to Valek, their older brother, was uncanny. Both had sapphire-blue eyes and angular faces, but Zethan smiled more, so he didn't appear as...intense as his sister.

Zethan gave her a friendly hello, while Zohav's expression darkened with worry. Once everyone settled around the fire with a bowl of chowder in hand, Kade asked Heli to repeat her message from Fisk.

"That's it?" Teegan asked her. "No reason why we need to move?"

"For your safety."

"We're safe here," Zethan said. "I'm not leaving unless they need us to help."

"The only scenario that makes sense is that the Cartel is aware of your location," Kade said.

"So what? I'd like to see them try to attack us," Zethan said with enough enthusiasm to merit a scowl from his twin.

"I can go to the Citadel and gather more information," Teegan said.

"And walk into an ambush?" Zohav asked. "If they know we're here, then they'll be watching for the perfect opportunity."

"It's not like I'm defenseless," Teegan said, stabbing his spoon into the chowder. White drops splattered onto his tunic.

"Where else would we go?" Zohav asked.

No answer.

"I'm not leaving," Zethan said again. "I'm learning so much about my magic here with Kade, and the storm season—"

"—is our concern," Kade said. "The three of you are vital to Valek's plans to stop the Cartel. They might not be able to get to you here, but like Zohav said, they can wait until you're called to the fight and ambush you up on The Flats."

"But we have magic," Zethan said.

"And they have Curare and null shields," Kade countered.

Now it was Zethan's turn to frown. "But I can guide the storms here."

Kade grinned. "You've brought so many already, Zee. We've reached our quota, and the season hasn't even started yet."

Heli glanced at Kade in surprise. "You shouldn't be dancing on your own. It's dangerous."

"Not with Zethan," Kade said. "He brings them just close enough for me to fill a few orbs with their energy, and then he sends them back out to sea."

That was impressive.

"Which is why you need me," Zethan said, sounding like a petulant child.

"Your brother needs you more right now. Sitia needs you," Kade said.

"Then you should come with us," Zethan said. "I need a dancer to keep the storm from hurting the people on our side."

Heli held her breath. If Kade joined them, she'd be in charge of the other Stormdancers for the season—a big responsibility. But a part of her wished to go with them. They'd worked well as a team before. However, Kade was in charge.

As if he read her mind, Kade met her gaze. "I need to stay on the coast. Since we already have so many filled orbs, Heli can accompany you if she wants. If not—"

MARIA V. SNYDER

"I'll go." A mixture of fear and excitement twisted around her heart.

"When do we leave?" Teegan asked.

"At first light," Kade said. "And don't tell us where you're going, but make sure you send a message to Fisk." He stood and filled another bowl with chowder. "Come on, Ray. They need to plan, and Helen must be starving by now."

Heli's mind raced with possible locations for them to lie low. Also, a couple comments from the conversation had snagged in her mind.

Before Kade and Raiden left, Zethan called out, "Who's in charge?"

"If you have to ask, it isn't you." Kade waved good-night.

Before Zethan could respond, Heli said, "I am."

"Why you?" Teegan asked in a tone more curious than combative.

"I'm the oldest. I know Sitia. And I have the most experience." Heli held up three fingers.

"We just turned seventeen," Zethan said. "Plus we were *all* at the Krystal garrison."

"Heli helped my parents free the Bloodrose clan last year," Teegan said.

Heli flipped up her pinky as those random comments connected like lightning in her brain. "And I've a great idea."

13

YELENA

The knife pressed against my throat. Frustration eclipsed my fear. The soldiers we'd ambushed had just ambushed us. They'd pretended to be knocked out by the sleeping potion that had coated our weapons and filled our darts.

"Weapons down, now," the man holding me ordered.

A thin line of pain seared my skin as he emphasized his point.

Valek glanced at Onora, but she'd disappeared. Cahil's crew looked to Valek for guidance. He held a dart, but the drug hadn't worked on the soldiers. No time to wonder why.

"Easy," Valek said. He placed his weapons on the ground with enough flourish to distract the soldiers while he palmed a new set of darts. I hoped those were laced with goo-goo juice, as it appeared nothing else in our arsenal would work. Valek motioned for the others to disarm.

"Let's be reasonable, gentlemen. What do you want?" Valek asked.

"Let's not," the scout behind me said. "Jone and Nusi, secure them."

The two on the wagon hopped down and reached under the seat for manacles. Jone and Nusi approached Valek first.

Valek waited until they were within striking distance. "Now!" He whirled, kicking the manacles from their hands.

I was yanked sideways so hard, I broke free from the man's grasp. In a heartbeat, he flew forward and landed on the ground. He didn't move. Onora appeared next to me and grinned. She drew her knives. Cahil's crew reclaimed their weapons. I turned, and Kiki's copper face peered at me through the greenery. Happy to see her, I grabbed my bo staff and joined the fracas.

Well… I tried. Valek fought Jone and Nusi. They had some skill but lacked experience. Valek slid past their defenses and disarmed them in a few moves. Onora also took down two opponents, and Hanni, Faxon and Sladen proved very capable of handling themselves in a fight. Soon they had manacled all eight of them—five men and three women—to eight trees. The scout who had grabbed me still hadn't regained consciousness.

"What did you hit him with?" Valek asked Onora.

"I didn't. Kiki kicked him with her back hoof. She has excellent aim. I just tugged Yelena out of the way."

Remembering the knife, I touched my throat, smearing blood from a shallow slice along my skin.

Valek pulled a handkerchief from his pocket and wiped the rest off. "Are you okay?"

"I'm fine. I owe Kiki a few milk oats, though." I gazed at the prisoners. "Why didn't the sleeping potion work on you?"

"We're not telling you," Jone said.

Valek held up a dart laced with goo-goo juice. "You won't have a choice."

Unless they were immune to this drug, as well.

"But first…" Valek strode over to the wagon, and I followed right behind him. He cut Mara and Esau loose, then unlocked their manacles.

Bruises marked both their faces, and raw skin ringed their wrists and ankles. Mara ripped her gag off and collapsed in my arms. Alarmed, I hugged her close as she sobbed into my shoulder. Oh, no. Fear bloomed in my chest, squeezing my heart.

Esau rubbed his hands. Dirt and blood stained his tattered clothing. "Thanks for rescuing us."

"Are you all right?" Valek asked him.

"Minor stuff. I'll be fine. Poor Mara had a rougher time of it, though." Esau glared at the group attached to the trees.

Ice filled my veins. Valek and I exchanged a horrified glance. Was she...? Did they...? I couldn't even think the word.

Mara straightened, jerking from my embrace. Tears streaked her face. She wiped them away with an angry swipe. "I..." Pulling in a deep breath, she continued, "It was terrifying to be tied up, utterly helpless and at their mercy." A shudder shook her body.

"Did they...harm you?" Valek asked the question on all our minds.

"No. They threatened to, and their hands..." Another shudder. "But they didn't rape me."

We all breathed a huge sigh of relief.

She clutched my arm. "Where's Leif?"

"We don't know. We'd hoped he was following you."

"He's not. He would have found a way to let me know he was nearby."

I agreed. "In that case, he's probably in Fulgor."

She nodded. "We need to find him."

"We will, but first I need to interrogate the soldiers," Valek said.

"I know why they're immune to the sleeping potion," Esau said. "Those crossbreed plants..." He waved at the wagon, but only a few dead leaves littered the bed. "They've been working

158   MARIA V. SNYDER

on antidotes to sleeping potion, goo-goo juice and a number of poisons. So far, they've discovered one for the sleeping potion. And they also have Theobroma-resistant Curare."

"How close are they to finding an antidote to goo-goo juice?" Valek asked.

"I don't know."

"Then let's see what they know." Valek pricked them with the drug, waited a few minutes and questioned them. Unfortunately, they were just grunts following orders. Their knowledge was limited. The only useful information we gleaned from them was that all soldiers on patrol or those escorting officers or prisoners would get enough of the sleeping potion antidote for the length of their mission.

We would need to find another drug that could incapacitate them. I hoped my father would have an alternative.

When he finished interrogating the soldiers, Valek inclined his head and motioned for us to return to our campsite.

Once we arrived, he said, "It's too dangerous for all of us to search for Leif. Yelena, take Mara, your father and Onora to Owl's Hill. Stay at the Cloverleaf Inn until Fisk's people contact you. They will let you know HQ's new location in the Citadel. Stay together until I return."

Not sure I liked this plan, I asked, "Where are you going?"

"To Fulgor, to find Leif."

Torn, I debated whether I should insist on accompanying him to search for my brother. But I decided that Mara needed me more right now.

"What about us?" Hanni asked. "We can't go back to the garrison. The soldiers saw us helping you."

"Go to the Lucky Duck Inn," I said. "That's our rendezvous location with Cahil. He'll contact you there."

Hanni pressed her lips together but didn't voice her doubts.

"We should get moving," Onora said. "Those guys are visible from the road, and I'm sure Bruns will send a patrol when they fail to arrive."

Kiki had kept all six horses calm during the ambush. Cahil's crew mounted three, and Mara and Esau each took one to ride. The wagon and the last horse would remain behind.

"They dumped all the plants right after we were captured," Esau said, clearly pained by the loss.

His comment reminded me of the picture of the Harman tree. I retrieved it and showed it to my father. "Do you know what this is?"

Esau peered at the picture. "This is a beautiful rendition. Did you draw it?"

"No." I pointed to Onora. "She did."

His good humor returned. "Well done, my girl. You'll have to come on expedition with me. The detail is exquisite."

Embarrassed by the compliment, Onora ducked her head.

"Do you recognize it, Father?" I asked again. "It's called a Harman tree, but we don't know anything else about it."

"It doesn't sound or look familiar. Sorry." He handed it back to me.

Oh well, it was worth a try.

Before Valek mounted Onyx, he pulled me close to say goodbye. "If you're not in Owl's Hill, Leif and I will meet up with you in the Citadel."

I tightened my grip. "What if he's been captured?"

"Then I will rescue him."

"But…" What if Valek was caught or killed? I bit my lip, keeping silent.

He waited.

Trust. I needed to trust him. "Please be careful."

"As long as you promise to do the same."

"Do you think Onora would let me do anything dangerous?"

"As if you'd listen to her. I'm not that naive, love."

I laughed. "All right, I promise to be careful."

He kissed me long and hard. I wished that all this was behind us. That we could just be a regular family, dealing with mundane problems. When he broke off the kiss, his gaze seared into me with a protective fire I recognized.

"Thinking of locking me in that tower again?" I teased.

"Of locking *us* in."

"Now you're talking." I claimed his lips for one more kiss. Then I hopped onto Kiki's saddle and, with a small wave, set off south toward Owl's Hill.

Mara kept quiet during the uneventful two-day trip. I filled my father in on what had been going on with the Cartel and me. He was delighted about his soon-to-be grandchild and new son-in-law, although he warned me that Sitia wouldn't recognize the union until we filed the official papers, which might not happen if the Cartel remained in power.

Memories surged to the surface of my thoughts when we checked into the Cloverleaf Inn, which was one of the only two inns in town. We rented a four-room suite on the top floor so we could stay together. The place had been our headquarters while we'd planned a way to defeat Roze Featherstone and her Warpers six years ago. It'd been a long shot, and it hadn't gone as we'd hoped—Moon Man and many others had died—but we'd won in the end and reinstated the Sitian Council.

With a start, I remembered that I'd been unable to use my magic during that time, as well. If I'd pulled any power, Roze would have learned of my location. The situation with the Cartel was on a grander scale than our problems with the Warpers, but not that different.

I mulled it over. Excitement built as new possibilities bubbled in my mind. I didn't need magic. Yes, I missed it; I've relied on my power for years and helped many people. But I didn't *need* it. I was quite capable of dealing with problems without it.

For the first time since I'd woken up without my magic, I accepted my condition. It was time to move on and stop moping about it. My power would either return when the baby was born, or it wouldn't.

Energized, I strode from my room. Esau sat on the couch, reading a botany book, and Mara was curled up in the armchair with a cup of tea. I called for Onora.

She shot into the living area with her knives in hand.

"Sorry to scare you," I said. "But I'd like to resume our training while we wait for Leif."

Onora glanced out the window. "Now? It's almost dark."

"Don't assassins use the darkness to their advantage?"

"You want to be an assassin?"

"No. But I want to learn all the same skills."

"Me, too," Mara said. Putting her cup down with a clatter, she hopped to her feet. "Can you be an assassin without killing anyone?"

Onora shot her an odd look. "I...don't know. I don't think so."

"Is there a name for people who have those skills?" Mara asked.

"Yes. Dangerous," I said.

Mara rubbed her hands together as a gleam lit her eyes. "Oh, I like that. I want to be *dangerous*."

I exchanged a glance with Onora.

"If she's going to hang out with you and Leif, she should learn how to defend herself," Onora said.

True. "All right, let's get started. Father, would you like to learn how to sneak around in the dark?" I asked Esau.

"I've been sneaking around in the dark since before you

MARIA V. SNYDER

were born," he said. "How do you think I get those notte flowers for your mother's perfume? They only bloom in the dead of night, and any bit of light will make them close up tighter than a...er..." He cleared his throat. "If you can navigate the jungle at night without being eaten by a tree leopard or garroted by a necklace snake, then I'd say you don't need any *assassin* training."

"You know, a simple 'no' would have sufficed," I teased.

"Where's the fun in that?"

"I see where Leif gets his sense of humor," Onora said.

While we waited for Fisk's messenger to arrive, Onora taught Mara and me a number of skills she'd found helpful.

"If you're going to be in a lit room for only a short time, then a way to keep your dark-adapted vision is to close one eye when you reach the light. Then, when you return to the shadows, open that eye and you won't be completely blind," she explained.

Onora also showed us how to read body language and to move without making too much noise.

"It's all in keeping your balance and picking up your feet when you walk. Most people are lazy and shuffle. Rubber soles help, as well, if you're going to wear boots," she said.

"Why don't you wear boots?" Mara asked.

"My toes grip better than any sole, and the bottoms of my feet can feel noisy things such as dried leaves or small twigs before I step on them. To me, wearing shoes is like putting gloves on hands. You lose your sensitivity."

We practiced late at night when there were no other sounds to cover our movements. But we kept our boots on. Onora had been going barefoot for as long as she could remember, and her feet were conditioned to withstand the rough ground and cold air.

"I had to wear boots when I was in the army, but I shucked them whenever possible," she said.

We taught Mara a number of self-defense moves, as well. The training kept me from worrying too much about Valek and Leif or from imagining all the dire reasons Fisk's messenger hadn't arrived yet. After two days of practice, Mara seemed a bit more like her old self. And while the time wasn't nearly long enough to learn everything or to be truly proficient in anything, it was a start in the right direction.

After we ate breakfast in our rooms on the third morning, Onora asked, "How long are we going to wait for Fisk?"

Good question. "He's usually reliable, which means something happened at the Citadel and it might be too dangerous for us to return."

"I can scout ahead and see what's going on," she offered.

"Let's wait another day." Mara had benefited from the down time, and the rest had helped my father. The bruises were fading, and the lines on his face had smoothed. Plus I knew that once we returned to the Citadel, he would immerse himself in research and neglect his health again.

As I dozed on the couch later that afternoon, loud voices woke me. Onora stood at the door with both her knives drawn. I pulled my switchblade and joined her.

"What's going on?" I asked in a whisper.

"An argument. Could be nothing. Wait here." She slipped out the door.

I waited about three heartbeats before following her. Onora crept down the stairs, avoiding all the squeaky spots. She frowned at me when I joined her.

The quarrel grew louder as we descended. By the time we reached the second floor, I recognized the voices. Halfway up the steps to the first-floor landing, the innkeeper stood in front of two men, blocking the way. Impressive, considering one muscular man towered over the slight innkeeper and the other man glowered and fingered the hilt of his sword.

"...not allowed upstairs," the innkeeper insisted.

We had asked him to keep our presence under wraps as much as possible. Of course, the locals saw us arrive, and we had to shop for supplies. But he had promised not to tell strangers and soldiers about us. Fisk's people would have no trouble slipping by him, but these two should have known better.

"Idiots," Onora muttered.

"It's okay, Keyon," I said. "They're friends of ours."

"Friends?" Janco asked, placing a hand on his chest. "You wound me. I consider us family."

So happy to see them both, I rushed past Keyon. Ari swept me up into a hug.

Janco beamed. "Fisk and I called it. We knew you'd be here. Ari's such a worrywart."

Onora sheathed her blades. "And now everyone in a twenty-mile radius knows we're here."

Janco held up his hands. "Not my fault. You know how Ari gets when he's in his protective bull mode. I'm surprised he didn't just toss this little fella out of the way."

"Watch it." Keyon jabbed a finger at Janco. "If you're going to rent a room, this *little* fella might charge you double."

"Sorry, sir," Janco said. "But you have to admit, compared to my partner here, even *I'm* considered a little fella."

The man conceded the point.

"Besides, they can stay with us. Come on up to our rooms," I said. Ari put me down, and I led them up to the fifth floor.

Mara and Esau stood in the center of the suite with weapons in hand when we entered. They relaxed as soon as they spotted Ari and Janco.

Janco immediately flopped into a chair. "We've been traveling all night."

"What happened? We expected one of the guild members a couple days ago," I said.

"That was the plan, but things got hot in the Citadel."

"Hot?" Mara asked.

"Bruns has brought in more soldiers to patrol the streets. He closed all the gates except the east gate and doubled security, checking everyone coming into and leaving the Citadel."

Not good. "How hard is it to get in?"

"For you, impossible."

"Even if I wear a disguise?"

"Yes. They're yanking off hoods, checking for wigs and even have a magician scanning for illusions."

"But you managed to get in," I said.

"No. We didn't even try," Ari said. He sank onto the couch. Exhaustion lined his face. "Fisk has people along the roads to the Citadel. They recognized us and sent us here to rendezvous with you."

"Do you know when the extra security measures started?" Onora asked Ari.

"Four days ago."

"The same day we rescued Mara and Esau," Onora said.

"Rescued?" Janco asked.

We explained about Cahil tipping us off, the ambush and Valek's mission to find Leif.

"Valek will find him. No doubt," Janco said with such confidence, Mara smiled.

It was nice to see her happy. I considered the timing of the security. Bruns's magicians must have used a super messenger to communicate between the garrison and Citadel.

"Fisk thinks it's best for all of us to avoid the Citadel right now," Ari said. "He's going to let everything settle down and

166

MARIA V. SNYDER

then find an HQ outside the Citadel, but still close enough that we can observe who is coming and going. It might take a few weeks."

"But—"

"I have a package for you in my saddle bags from Fisk." Ari inclined his head at Esau. "It's all the notes from Councilor Bavol Zaltana, plus the location of that farmhouse those glass panels were delivered to."

Perfect. Fisk knew me so well.

"And Fisk says that Councilor Zaltana owns the farmhouse."

That was interesting.

Janco jumped to his feet. "And we have news! Humongous news!"

We all waited, but Janco needed more prodding. "And?"

"I found where the Cartel's been producing Theobroma and Curare. And I met the Master Gardener!"

Shocked, I glanced at Ari. "Why didn't you tell me this sooner?"

"He *thinks* the man was the Master Gardener, but we were unable to confirm it."

"Who is it?" Esau asked.

Janco took a deep breath and held it, as if about to make a big announcement. Then he let it all out at once, deflating. "He *looks* familiar, but I can't recall his name. It's been driving me crazy for days!"

"What does he look like?" I asked.

"Like half the men in Sitia," Ari said. "Janco's descriptive skills are as bad as his artistic skills. We were hoping to find a magician who could peer into the chaos that is Janco's mind and identify him."

"Ha. Ha. Not funny."

"Is it Bavol?" Esau asked.

"No. I've met him."

"We can travel to the factory and I can take a look at the guy," I said. "And we could also sabotage it, cutting off the Cartel's supply."

"*If* that's their only facility," Janco said. "It was in the middle of the Greenblade forest and hidden by an illusion."

I wondered if that was generated by Rika Bloodgood. Her strongest magical ability was creating illusions, and she was one of Owen's closest colleagues. Her last known location was the Commander's castle in Ixia.

"Plus the place is huge and well guarded," Ari added. "And doing something big like that will need to be included in our grand plans to stop the Cartel. Fisk's messenger said they've changed, but we don't know what they are."

"Regardless, we need more information," I said.

Janco dug into his pockets and pulled out a handful of leaves. "I took these from one of the hothouses." He handed them to Esau.

Esau's green eyes lit up as if Janco had just given him the perfect present. If only we could get my father into one of those glass hothouses.

"No can do," Janco said when I mentioned it. "After I was caught, they put extra security around them. Then we hightailed it out of there."

I considered our options and remembered the glass hothouse that might be in the Avibian Plains. Explaining the possibility, I said, "We can find that one and see if there's any information of value there before we continue on to the one you found. It'll give us something to do while waiting for Fisk to regroup."

"What about Leif and Valek?" Mara asked. "They'll be caught trying to get into the Citadel."

"Fisk's people can warn them when they get close to the Citadel. Where should we tell them to go?" Ari asked.

MARIA V. SNYDER

"The Stormdance travel shelter across from the plains. Leif knows where it is," I said. "We'll meet them there."

We made plans to leave in the morning. Onora offered her room to Janco and Ari. She moved to the extra bed in my room.

"One of the bounty hunters could have followed them here," she said.

"I heard that." Janco poked his head through our door. "And I'm offended that you think so poorly of our skills."

"After that scene with the innkeeper, I've altered my assessment of your *skills*. Besides, Valek charged me with keeping Yelena safe."

Janco laughed. "Good luck with that."

In order to avoid any more attention directed toward us, we left in shifts the next morning. Esau traveled with Janco, Mara stayed with Ari and Onora kept close to me. No one appeared to take any notice, but a good spy would blend right in with the townspeople.

We met up a few miles east of the Citadel and touched base with Fisk's sentries.

"Is the place still hot?" I asked the young boy.

"Yep. Best to stay well away," he said.

"Can you send a message to Fisk that we're heading to—"

"Is that a good idea?" Onora asked, interrupting me. "It's safer to keep our destination confidential."

"Fisk already knows where we're going," Janco said.

"Then no need to send a message," she replied.

"I'll let him know you passed by," the boy said.

"And if you see Master Leif and Valek…" Ari explained to him where they should meet us.

"I'll inform the others to keep an eye out for them."

"Thank you." I directed Kiki to find us a route heading

southwest. The plan was to ride late into the night. It would be safer to camp near the farmhouse rather than along the road or in a travel shelter.

Kiki set a quick pace, and we arrived a few hours after midnight. We skirted the farmhouse's property and found a small copse of trees wedged between the fields that was perfect for a camp.

"Are you sure no one will see us?" Onora asked. She peered around. "It's not very big or dense."

"The fields around here haven't been planted," Janco said. "I doubt anyone will notice us."

"How do you know?" Ari asked, gesturing beyond the trees. "It's dark out there."

"There's enough moonlight to see there are no fresh grooves in the dirt. And my nose doesn't need light to smell fertilizer. It's the warm season. Any farmer worth his salt would have planted his fields by now."

"Is this from your experience living on your uncle's farm in MD-7?" Onora asked.

"Yeah. How did *you* know about that?" Janco's voice held a suspicious tone.

"From *you*, genius. Am I the only one who listens to you when you talk?" she asked.

"We're *supposed* to listen to his prattle?" I asked. "Who knew?"

"Not funny." Janco mumbled something about checking the area and stalked off.

"Should we light a fire?" Esau asked.

"No," I said. "Just in case there are neighbors."

"I'll take first watch," Onora said.

"I'll take second, and Janco can finish the night," Ari said.

"No." I poked my chest. "*I'll* finish the night. Tell Janco when he returns."

MARIA V. SNYDER

Ari just stared at me.

"Ari," I warned.

"I'll talk to Janco."

A vague response. He could talk to him about the weather and still keep his promise. As I set up my bedroll, I decided to wait for Janco, but once I slipped under the warm blanket, I struggled to keep my eyes open.

Janco woke me at dawn. I growled at him for waiting so long, but he batted his eyelashes at me, trying and failing to look innocent.

"I'm able to stand watch," I grumbled.

"What a coincidence. So am I." He beamed at me, then leaned in closer and lowered his voice. "What I *can't* do is grow a baby inside me. Nor can I hatch an egg by sitting on it. I've the stained trousers to prove it."

"Do you have a point?"

"I thought it was obvious." Janco's expression softened. "Take the rest when you can, Yelena. For the baby. There aren't any guarantees that you'll get a chance later." He gestured to the rising sun. "Besides, it was a short night."

He had a point. I gathered branches and made a small fire. In the daylight, the flames wouldn't attract as much attention. The rest of the group woke and stretched while I heated water for tea.

"I already scouted the farmhouse," Janco said. "It's empty."

"How can you tell?" Esau asked. "It was night, and the occupants could have been asleep."

"No one was in the house, sleeping or otherwise engaged."

Ari shot Janco a look.

"What? I was bored, and now we don't have to tiptoe around."

"Did you find anything?" I asked.

"The place has been abandoned. Not much furniture. Lots of dust and spider webs. Otherwise it was too dark to see."

We ate a quick breakfast before heading to the cluster of buildings in the center of the fields. Weeds and a few small corn plants grew among the leftover brown stubble of last year's harvest. Sunlight glinted off the drops of dew on the leaves. As the air warmed, the earth emitted a fresh scent of grass and dandelions. The heating season started in less than ten days, which meant the baby was about sixteen weeks old. I pressed my hand to the small bulge underneath my tunic. Soon I would start to show, and I'd no longer be able to hide my condition. Not that it mattered at this point. The Cartel found out about the baby when I'd been Bruns's prisoner. And it certainly wouldn't stop them from killing me.

A large porch wrapped around the two-story stone farmhouse. A wooden stable, a barn and two sheds huddled behind it. They all needed repair and a fresh coat of paint.

We split into three teams to search for any information on the glass panels and the location of a glass hothouse. Onora and I tackled the farmhouse. Like Janco had said, it was unoccupied. No squatters had taken up residence while Bavol was gone.

I started in the office while Onora checked the rest of the house. Reading through the files that had been tucked away in the desk's drawers, I only found an invoice for services rendered, made out to Bavol Zaltana. It confirmed Bavol had used this address to send the glass panels. I'd been hoping for more information, but perhaps there would be some when we found the glass hothouse.

Onora shook her head when I asked if she'd discovered anything. Outside, we conferred with the others. Nothing.

"The soil is generative," Esau said when I asked him. "Lots of worms."

"Does this mean we're at a dead end?" Mara asked.

"No. We'll travel into the Avibian Plains and let Kiki sniff out the glass hothouse," I said.

"Why didn't we just do that instead of stopping?"

"There could have been valuable clues or information here. We still don't know who the Master Gardener is or what else the Cartel's been growing." I peered at the horses. None of them except Kiki were Sandseed horses. Would they have trouble with the protective magic in the plains? What about the riders?

"I think I should go into the plains while you wait—"

"No," Ari said. "We stay together."

Janco tapped his chest. "And aren't we immune? Ari and I have null shields, and Mara and Esau are distantly related to the Sandseeds."

"I'm not sure that covers the horses," I said.

"Kiki will take care of the horses," Ari said with conviction.

"What about Onora?" I asked.

"Let her ride Kiki; she'll protect Onora."

I glanced at my horse. She bobbed her head in agreement. Outsmarted, I conceded defeat, and we filled our water skins before mounting and heading south into the plains. It didn't take long to reach the border. The fields with their squat growth ended, and a blanket of long grasses spread over the rolling landscape. The mounds weren't big enough to call hills, but there was nothing flat about the ground under Horse's hooves.

Pulling up beside Kiki, I asked her, "Can you find one of those glass hothouses?" I imagined the structure in my mind, recalling the sweet smell of the white coal.

Unable to use her gust-of-wind gait because of the other horses, Kiki broke into a gallop instead. She set the pace, making wide, curving sweeps over the plains, each one dipping deeper into the interior. After two days of this, she stopped on the crest of a small hillock. In the distance, a glass structure reflected the sunlight.

Janco slid off The Madam's saddle. "Allow me."

"I'll go, too," Onora said.

He crinkled his nose but kept quiet. They melted into the tall grass. I stayed on Horse, straining to track their progress toward the hothouse. The grasses dipped and swayed with the breeze. Time slowed while my impatience increased.

A faint rustle alerted me to Janco's reappearance.

"Well?" I demanded.

"It's full of plants like the ones I've seen in the Greenblade compound. And someone is taking care of them," he said.

Esau leaned forward. "Did you see who?"

"Yes."

"And?" I asked.

"You're not going to like it," he said.

"Tell me."

"It's your cousin, Nutty."

14

VALEK

Yelena's scent lingered on his clothes. Remaining in the middle of the road, Valek watched until she disappeared around a bend. An emptiness ached inside him. Each time they parted, it was harder for him. Instead of giving in to the temptation to chase her, Valek swung up onto Onyx's back. Clicking his tongue, he urged his horse southeast to Fulgor to find Leif.

Four days later, he arrived in the capital of the Moon Clan's lands. Unfortunately, he hadn't encountered Leif, or any sign of him or his horse, during the journey. The afternoon sun warmed his back, reminding him that the heating season would begin in eleven more days.

Valek avoided the busy downtown district. Instead, he rented a small room in a dumpy little inn called Sweet's. After settling Onyx in the dilapidated shed that aspired to be a stable, Valek changed into nondescript clothing and used putty and a bit of makeup to alter his appearance.

His agents stationed in Fulgor had been discovered and sent back to Ixia last season, so Valek spent the rest of the day visiting the places Leif would most likely stay. As the sun crossed the sky, Valek's hopes for quickly finding his brother-in-law faded. Fear stirred in his chest when he spotted guards watching Opal's building. He easily bypassed them and entered. The place was cold and quiet—something he'd never thought he'd equate with the hot glass factory. It was also empty of people. A bad sign.

When he finished checking the obvious locations, he tried to think like Leif. The man was smart and had to know the Fulgor security forces would be keeping an eye out for him. But what about Leif's horse? Valek visited every stable in town, seeking Rusalka. Hours after the sun set, he'd exhausted all his ideas and was starving. Valek entered the Pig Pen for a meal—and to see if Leif was stupid enough to be having supper at his favorite eatery in Fulgor.

The Pig Pen was crowded like usual; however, an undercurrent of tension buzzed through the place. Valek spotted the source of the apprehension. Four soldiers sat at the bar. The stools of Opal's soldier friends, Nic and Eve, were empty, just like their apartments had been. Valek found a table away from the bar and ordered the beef stew and an ale from a server. Despite the name, the tavern was clean. The regulars kept giving Valek the once-over, but he ignored them.

When the server returned with his order, she slipped a note into his hand. Valek glanced up and met Ian's gaze for a brief moment before Nic's twin brother returned to tending the bar.

With a sick tightness ruining his appetite, Valek unfolded the parchment. The note informed him that Leif, Devlen and Reema had been captured and were in the garrison's stockade. And that Nic, Eve and Opal were away on a mission.

Ah, hell.

Since he'd promised to rescue Leif, Valek considered his meager options. Fisk's people had been recalled, and Valek hadn't replaced his own agents. A few of Nic and Eve's colleagues in the security forces might help him, but he doubted

MARIA V. SNYDER

they would without Nic and Eve around to vouch for him. Guess it would a one-man operation for now.

Valek spent the next three days watching the garrison and learning the delivery schedule. Each night, handfuls of soldiers headed to town for a few hours before stumbling back. On the fourth night, Valek donned a stolen uniform and joined the group returning from the taverns. The guards at the gate waved them all through, and the magician stationed there barely scanned their thoughts before returning to sleep.

Since this was a reconnaissance mission, Valek stayed in the shadows and poked around, getting a feel for the place. In the morning, he entered the dining hall. He munched on apples to avoid the foods laced with Theobroma while he listened to the conversations around him. Scanning faces for Devlen or Leif, Valek wondered if they'd been here long enough to have been assimilated, or if they remained in the stockade.

Valek left with a small group of guys, but when they headed to the training yard, he peeled off and made a loop around the stockade. An impressive number of guards watched the single-story building, which meant someone important was inside.

He'd bet a dozen gold coins it was Leif, and that the Cartel planned to use him as bait to lure Yelena and Valek into attempting a rescue. Would they expect one so soon? Valek considered. Getting into the base wouldn't be difficult. It would be leaving with Leif and Devlen, who might be brainwashed and reluctant to go, that would be almost impossible. Valek needed time to think and plan. He searched for a spot to hide for the rest of the day.

While checking out the stables for possible locations to wait, one of the kids running errands paused next to him.

"Your disguise sucks, and you're going to get caught," whispered the girl.

Valek glanced at her. Relief warred with concern. "Reema—"

"Not here. Follow me."

He trailed her through a warren of buildings. She entered one of the smaller buildings. Closing the door, she lit a lantern and scowled at him. "Don't you know they've set a trap for you? You need to leave."

He made a stopping motion. "Slow down. Tell me what's going on. Why are—"

"All right. I guess you can't leave until dark anyway. Sit down." Reema gestured to a couple barrels next to a small table. She pulled her cap off, and her blond corkscrew curls sprang free. Drawing in a breath, she said, "My dad and I were arrested a few days after my mom left. He was locked in the stockade, but they didn't think I—" she held up her hands and curled her fingers in mock quotes "—*posed a threat*. They put me with the other street rats they had 'scripted from Fulgor to run errands."

"Conscripted?"

"Yeah, that. I made friends with Fisk's people and was helping them, but they left right before they dragged Uncle Leif in here."

"Where's your father?"

"Still in the stockade with Uncle Leif. They're bait for you and Aunt Yelena and my mom when she comes home."

"That explains the extra guards."

"Yeah, and there are a couple you don't see."

"But you have?"

"Of course. What do you think I've been doing all this time?" she asked in an annoyed tone, sounding much older than eleven.

"You know this place pretty well?"

MARIA V. SNYDER

"Inside and out." Her blue eyes gleamed. "Do you have a plan for rescuing my dad and uncle?"

Did he? Possibilities raced through his mind. "Where did your mother go?"

"To Tsavorite, in the Jewelrose lands."

An odd destination. "Why?"

"She received a letter from Master Magician Zitora Cowan, asking for help."

Did he dare believe there might be some good news? That they might have another powerful magician on their side? "Is it legit?"

"She seemed to think so. Nic and Eve went with her."

"How long ago did they leave?"

"About six weeks ago. She had to dodge the guards on the way out, and I'm sure they've set up an ambush for her when she returns." Reema's pretty face creased in concern, and she bit her lip.

"I trained your mother. She'll spot that ambush without trouble."

Reema relaxed for about an instant. "What about my dad and uncle?"

Valek considered. "Have you made friends with the street rats still here?"

"Yup."

"Will they be willing to help us?"

"Oh, yeah."

"That's a step in the right direction. Do you have any null shield pendants?"

"Yes, Fisk's people left a couple here for us, but we buried them because of the sweeps."

"You know where they are?"

"Yup."

"Good. Now tell me *everything* you've learned while living here."

"Everything? Even the boring day-to-day stuff?"

"*Especially* the mundane stuff. That's where we'll find the golden opportunity."

In the gray light before dawn, Valek stopped the wagon at the Moon garrison's gate. The officer in charge peered at him in suspicion. He resisted the urge to scratch his fake nose or sweep his now dirty blond hair from his eyes. Would the man notice that Onyx and Devlen's horse, Sunfire, weren't the typical breeds used to pull wagons? It hadn't been hard for Valek to convince the manager at Sunfire's stables that Devlen had approved Valek's request to borrow the horse.

"Where's Phil?" the guard asked.

"Broke his ankle," Valek said in a deep baritone. "I'm just filling in. He'll be back next week."

"And you are?"

"Orrick."

"Got any proof?"

Valek grunted and handed him a paper. "The boss said you'd ask for this." He kept his bored expression even when magic brushed him. Then he thought of Phil and his bloody broken ankle and the damn inconvenience to him. Valek kept up a running litany of gripes until the guard returned the parchment and waved him on. He avoided thinking about how he had arranged Phil's "accident" in order to take over his delivery route. Phil's boss had been thrilled to find a cheaper replacement so quickly.

Once Valek was far enough away from the magician at the gate, he raised his mental shields. He could have borrowed one of Reema's pendants, but if he'd worn a null shield, he would have been spotted at the gate. Good thing he preferred knowing when magic was aimed at him. So far his mental barrier has been effective in keeping other magicians from getting too far into his thoughts.

Valek guided the horses to the kitchen. Not many soldiers stirred at this early hour of the morning. Of those, most headed to prepare breakfast for the garrison. He unloaded the crates of fresh meats and cheeses and carried them down into the cold cellar. Then he piled the burlap bags of garbage waiting to be hauled away onto his wagon. Valek kept a slow pace, despite the risk of discovery, taking as much time as possible. However, no one bothered him or looked at him twice. When he left the garrison, the guard at the gate poked a few of the garbage bags with his sword and checked under the wagon.

Not bad for a dry run. The next day, he repeated the routine. By the end of the week, the gatekeepers waved him through both ways without a second glance.

On day four, Reema appeared while Valek unloaded boxes of bananas. "Did you confirm their location?" he asked without otherwise acknowledging her.

"Yeah."

Her dejected tone drew his attention. "I warned you they might be brainwashed."

"It's not that." She bit her lower lip. "My dad…doesn't look good. He's got bruises and cuts. And there are extra guards hiding inside the stockade."

Valek cursed under his breath. He'd bet all the coins in his pocket the bars had magical alarms. The only thing in their favor was the location of the stockade. Unlike the Krystal garrison, the Moon was a one-story standalone structure, and not in the basement of the administration building.

"Stick close. I need to adjust our plan." He continued carrying the boxes, letting his mind run through various plans and dismissing most of them as too dangerous or a quick way for them to get caught. It took him about four trips to the cold cellar, but he figured out a possible way to rescue them. They'd have to move fast.

"Have you found all the guards, even the ones hiding?" he asked Reema as he heaved the garbage bags onto the wagon.

"Yes."

"Can you scrounge guard uniforms for the older kids?"

"For stand-ins?"

He was impressed by how much she knew about subterfuge. "Yes."

She flashed a grin that Janco would be proud of. "Yes."

Good thing she was on his side. "Okay. The plan with the doppelganger is still a go."

"And then?"

"As Janco would say, 'Hit and git.'"

The horses' hooves sounded loud in the predawn air. Valek approached the gate earlier than normal—they'd need every extra second to pull this off. A long list of things that could go wrong repeated in his head, but he suppressed the worries and focused on the job. The guard yawned as he lifted the gate and Valek clicked his tongue, urging the horses into the garrison. Sweat dampened the reins. He wore two layers of clothing. His plain work coveralls covered a Sitian military uniform.

When he arrived at the kitchen, a man the same shape and size as Valek and wearing the same clothes appeared with Reema. The doppelganger began pulling crates off the wagon.

"Take your time. Move like molasses," Valek said to him before ducking into a shadow and following Reema. She led him to an equipment shed, where he pulled off the coverall.

"How many?" he asked her.

"Twelve guards, nine street rats and one cat."

"I'm the cat?"

MARIA V. SNYDER

"Yup. We thought about calling you the big rat, but I thought you'd be offended."

"I'm sure my ego would have survived." Valek handed her the darts. "Be careful. They're loaded with poison."

Aghast, she held them away from her body. "You're gonna kill them!"

"I hope not. It's diluted My Love and should just render them unconscious. I can't use either Curare or the sleeping potion, as they're now immune to them. And I didn't have enough time to find an alternative." Finding the My Love had taken him much longer than he'd expected as it was. The criminal element in Fulgor was very skittish because the city was under martial law.

She nodded and disappeared. He waited for a few minutes. Then he strode through the buildings, heading toward the stockade. He trusted Reema and her young friends to neutralize the hidden guards. No need to waste energy worrying about something he couldn't control.

When he spotted four rats crouched just out of sight of the stockade's main entrance, he drew in a breath. "Hey!" he shouted.

They sprinted, with Valek a few steps behind them. He rounded the corner, and the four stockade guards stared in their direction.

"Stop them!" he yelled when the kids neared the guards.

They grabbed the rats' arms and shoulders. There was a bit of a scuffle, and two of the soldiers yelped in pain while the other two grunted.

By the time Valek arrived, all four were down on the ground, unconscious. None of the hidden watchers sounded an alarm. Reema and her gang had done their part. Good.

Valek swiped the keys and unlocked the main door. The theory was that only the locks to the cells would be warded with magic. If not... Valek didn't have time for doubts. The rats helped him carry the men inside, and the kids pulled off their outer clothes, exposing guard uniforms.

Valek scanned them. If anyone took a close look, their cover would be blown. "Stand tall and try to make yourselves appear bigger," he said as they hurried outside.

He crossed the guard room to another set of doors. Opening those doors, Valek braced as four figures rushed him. He ducked the first swing and stabbed a dart into one of them. Keeping low, he jabbed another in the leg. In the semidarkness, he caught a glint of steel and blocked the strike, but the blade sliced his skin. Fire raced up his arm. He ignored it.

A thud sounded, followed by another as the two guards succumbed to the poison. The third thrust his knife at Valek's throat. Not wanting to harm the man, Valek sidestepped the strike and sent a dart into the man's neck. The fourth advanced with a sword already wet with Valek's blood. Lovely. Valek backed up and tripped over one of the guys on the floor. As he hit the ground, he yanked another dart from his belt. His opponent leaned over, aiming the blade at his shoulder. Throwing the dart, he hoped it pierced skin as he rolled away from the weapon. The tip of the sword cut along his back. He kept rolling until he hit the wall. The attacker advanced, and Valek palmed his knife, but the man wobbled a bit and then toppled, landing with a loud thump.

Valek didn't have time to celebrate or worry if the noise drew any unwanted attention. He hopped to his feet and checked the cells.

They were empty.

A sick dread coiled in his stomach. They had moved the prisoners. Smart. Valek needed to leave. Now.

Except... He paused. Reema said she'd seen them in here. Valek drew in a deep breath and extended his magic. Con-

MARIA V. SNYDER

centrating on focusing the power, he searched the cells. Power pulsed along the bars. Further in, he sensed the heat from two heartbeats. Leif and Devlen were hidden behind an illusion. Probably gagged.

Valek strode to the entrance.

Reema poked her head in. "What's taking so long?"

"Four guards inside, not two."

"Oops. Sorry."

He gestured her closer. "I need your pendant."

She removed the null shield and handed it to him. "Hurry up."

Valek looped the chain around his neck and returned to the cells. The shield allowed him to see through the illusion. Leif and Devlen slept on metal beds in two different cells. Crouching next to the first one with his lock picks, he hoped the null shield would also keep the magical alarm from tripping, but had no idea if it would work. He popped the lock and swung the door wide.

No audible alarm sounded. Leif wouldn't wake when Valek shook his shoulder. Valek felt his pulse—strong. Probably drugged to keep him quiet. He glanced at Devlen, who hadn't moved despite the noise. This complicated things.

He raced to the entrance. "We need the wagon here. Now!"

One of the boys with Reema said, "That isn't part—"

"New plan. Get the wagon."

"All right." He dashed away.

"What happened?" Reema asked as she followed Valek.

"They're out cold." He opened Devlen's cell, and she raced inside to rouse her father, but the man didn't move.

"Is he—"

"He'll be fine." Valek hoped. By the collection of bruises and cuts on both men's faces, Valek guessed they had resisted.

The clip-clop of hooves and the jingle of the harness announced the wagon's approach. To Valek, a shrill alarm would have been quieter.

"What's next?" Reema asked.

"I need help getting them into the bags."

"Right." Reema dashed off, and soon the stand-in guards and five rats poured into the building. Draping null shields around Leif's and Devlen's necks, the kids wasted no time manhandling the two unconscious men into the burlap bags and loading them onto the wagon with a number of genuine garbage bags.

By the time they finished, the sun threatened to rise. Within minutes, there would be more soldiers up and moving about the garrison.

"Go. Disappear," Reema said to the stand-ins and Valek's doppelganger. They scattered in a heartbeat.

Valek gave her the pendant before she jumped into the wagon and hid in another burlap bag. Valek arranged them so the collection looked like a pile of garbage. He vaulted onto the driver's seat and headed to the gate. Halfway there, he remembered he wore a Sitian uniform rather than his delivery man coveralls. And blood soaked his left sleeve and back.

Valek stopped the horses. He hopped down and, while trying to appear as if he was arranging the bags, he opened Devlen's sack and yanked the man's shirt off.

Glancing around, he noted a few soldiers, but none seemed to be paying attention to him. Valek changed and stashed the torn and bloody uniform shirt under the bags, then closed Devlen's bag.

The sun rose in a burst of color and light. Valek climbed onto the wagon and resumed the journey to the gate. Sweat stung his cuts, and he knew blood would soon stain the green tunic. It felt as if a river of red gushed down his back. Plus his heart seemed determined to pump extra-hard.

MARIA V. SNYDER

The guard didn't move the gate as he had the last few days. Instead, he stood in front of it. Valek kept a neutral expression.

"Took you long enough," the guard said.

"I dropped a damn crate." Valek shook his head as if in exasperation. "Damn apples spilled all over. And then the cook harassed me, yelling that he won't pay for the damaged ones, so I had to count the number that were bruised and write a note."

"Sucks for you."

"Yup. And it's comin' out of my pay, too." Valek spat.

The guard did a loop around the wagon. Then he peered underneath. When he pulled his sword, Valek's heart skipped a beat.

Before he could stab the sword into one of the bags, Valek said, "Hey, can you please not cut into them so deep? Last time one of the damn bags ripped in half when I picked it up. I had a stinkin' mess to clean up, and I stank of rotten fish all day. And I'm already late for my next delivery."

The guard chuckled and sheathed his sword. "Some days are like that." He moved the gate for Valek. "See you tomorrow."

"Thanks," Valek said as the horses crossed through. His back burned as if an archer aimed a crossbow at him, and the feeling didn't dissipate until they were far from the guards' sight. Increasing the horses' pace, Valek guided the wagon to the old warehouse they had rented. It was empty except for Rusalka. She had turned up in a stall next to Onyx one morning, and he'd moved her here as they prepared for the rescue.

"We're here," he said.

Reema squirmed from her bag, jumped down and opened the loading bay door. He drove the wagon inside, and they closed and locked the door behind him. Only then did he allow himself to relax.

He expected Reema to be happy. Instead she frowned at the wagon. Her hands fisted on her hips.

"What's wrong?" he asked her.

"We got away too easy."

Easy? Not according to his burning cuts. But Valek considered. "No one followed us."

"Are you sure? I think—"

"I know how to spot a tail."

"Even one covered by magic?" She rubbed her face with both hands as if suddenly tired. "Ah, I forgot. You're immune and would see right through an illusion." Then she shot him a shrewd look. "But you needed my null shield pendant during the rescue. Why?"

Valek admired her intelligence. Her brother might be the next master-level magician, but she was well on her way to master-level spy. Deciding to trust her, he told her about his new abilities, although he knew that she'd be safer if she didn't know. Plus limiting the amount of people who knew about his magic was a logical strategy, but Leif might have been forced to divulge the information to the Cartel while a prisoner. In that case, all bets were off.

When he finished explaining, she slapped her hand on her thigh. "I thought something was off with you! When we were in the garrison, you didn't spark, but I didn't have time to think about it."

"Spark?"

"Yeah, I see a glow when magic hits a null shield."

Interesting. "Useful."

She shrugged. "Only lets me know who is wearing a null shield. It doesn't really help me."

"But it might help Teegan or Leif or even me."

Reema perked up. "Sweet. Do you like having magic, or do you miss your immunity?"

"Right now I prefer the magic, as I was too easy to capture when I was immune."

"Yeah, I guess my mom has to worry about that, as well." She sobered and climbed onto the wagon to pull back the burlap bags, uncovering her father and uncle.

Remembering her earlier comment about possible followers, Valek relaxed his mental shields and drew a small thread of power. He aimed it at the surrounding area, seeking with his magic. Sure enough, he picked up two watchers cloaked in an illusion. Ah, hell.

Even if he still had his immunity, he wouldn't have picked up on the magic if they kept their distance. Valek needed to be relatively close to a magician to feel its sticky residue. Common knowledge. However, if they knew he was no longer immune, then he needed to rely on his magic more often— something he was reluctant to do. The whole threat of flaming out put a major damper on things. Valek noted the location of the watchers and restored his mental barrier.

"When will they wake up?" Reema asked. She sat cross-legged next to Devlen, clutching his limp hand.

"Depends on how much sleeping potion they ingested."

"Is there a potion that wakes people up?"

"There is something that prevents the effects of the potion." He explained about the ambush to rescue Esau and Mara.

"Too bad we don't have any of that stay-awake medicine," she said. Reema sounded in need of a hug and reassurance.

Valek sat next to her, and she scooted closer to him. He put his arm around her small shoulders and squeezed. Reema leaned against him.

He thought of the watchers outside. "We might be able to learn more about that."

"How?"

"You were right. We were followed."

She jumped to her feet, shaking the wagon. "I knew it!" Then she scrunched up her face. "Did you use your magic?"

"Yup. And I need your help."

Reema readily agreed to the plan. When she left by the main front entrance, Valek slipped out the back. He kept a light magical touch on the watchers. Otherwise he wouldn't be able to see them. He didn't want to risk using the null shields in case one of the men was a magician. They had taken up positions across the street.

As expected, one of them followed Reema, while the other remained in place. Once she and her invisible shadow were gone, Valek circled around. Then he pounced on the watcher who currently resembled a barrel, pressing his knife to the guy's throat before the man could even draw a weapon. The cuts on Valek's arm and back flared to life from the effort.

"Quiet now," Valek whispered into his ear as he guided his captive inside the building, where he slammed his hilt into the man's temple, knocking him unconscious.

Valek yanked off his cloak, revealing a young man. However, the cloak now blended in with the floor. A mirror illusion must have been woven into the fabric. Interesting. Who had the ability to do that? Rika Bloodgood was in Ixia with Owen. Or was she? He'd encountered two well-crafted illusions in one day.

Valek pushed those thoughts aside for now and wrapped the cloak around his shoulders. Valek hurried outside to take up the watcher's position. A couple minutes later, Reema returned with a paper bag. She glanced up and down the street as if seeking a tail before entering the building.

Her shadow joined Valek.

"Candy run," the man said dismissively. "I can't believe the resistance is using *children*. They must be desperate. She had no clue I was following her."

Valek focused on the location of the voice and lunged. The

MARIA V. SNYDER

man fell back with an *oomph*. Sitting on his chest, Valek placed his blade on the man's neck.

"She knows more than you think. Which is very bad luck for you." Valek hauled the man to his feet and escorted him into the building.

Reema crouched next to the prone man on the floor, making a pile of his possessions, including an impressive collection of weapons.

"Hey!" Valek's captive yelled.

She spun toward the noise, wielding a dagger. "Who's there?"

Valek had forgotten about the cloaks. He yanked the one off his captive and shrugged his own off, as well. Reema relaxed, and Valek noted where her knife disappeared—up her sleeve. Smart.

"Find anything useful?" Valek asked her.

Opening her hand, she showed him a dozen darts. "These, but I don't know what they're filled with. They don't smell familiar."

"We can ask his friend."

"I'm not saying a word." The man clamped his lips together.

"In that case, we might as well let you go," Valek said.

"Really?"

He gave the man his humorless smile. "No. But you said a word. The first of many." Valek pricked him with goo-goo juice and hoped it worked.

Within a minute, the man relaxed. At least the Cartel hadn't found a counter to the goo-goo juice yet. A small victory. Valek sat him down so he didn't fall over.

"What's your mission?" he asked.

"Follow you until…" He spread his arms wide as if that explained everything.

"Until what?" he prompted. Dealing with suspects under

the influence of goo-goo juice had its challenges. And every-one reacted differently.

"You go to ground." The man made digging motions with his hands. "Where all the other rats are hiding."

Ah. No surprise the Cartel wished to learn the location of their headquarters. "And then what?"

"Come home, tell the boss, get a big bonus." His grin lasted for a moment before he peered around in confusion.

"Are the soldiers in the garrison going to chase us?" he asked.

"Yeah. Make it big, but let the rats slip away." He leaned forward and put a finger to his lips. "Shh...they don't know we go, too."

Which meant Valek would have to keep these guys under wraps until they escaped Fulgor. He switched topics. "How do you resist the sleeping potion?"

The man shrugged, but his gaze focused on the darts in Reema's hands.

"Is that the antidote?" Valek asked.

"Yeah. But ya gotta take it before."

"Before what?"

"Before ya think you'll need it."

"So if you're pricked with sleeping potion, and you haven't taken it..."

"Won't work after. And if it's been too long since you took it, it won't work."

"How long?"

"About a day. Guys on special missions get enough to last."

Which explained why his partner had so many. "And your mission was so special you also received these illusion cloaks."

"Yeah. Sweet things, blend right on in."

"Who gave them to you?"

MARIA V. SNYDER

"Boss man. 'Cause we are his two best scouts." He pounded on his chest.

"The best, eh? You were spotted by an eleven-year-old," Reema said.

He growled at her and tried to stand up, but Valek pushed him back down. "Where did the boss get the cloaks?"

"From his boss, who got it from his boss...all the way to the top boss."

"Who is?"

"His name is... Top. Boss."

Which meant the man didn't know. When Valek had extracted all the information from the man, he slammed the hilt of his dagger on the man's temple, knocking him unconscious.

Reema placed the darts into a leather pouch. "Now what?" she asked.

"We need to find a place to stash these guys for a few days. Know anyone in Fulgor who can help us?"

"I might," she hedged.

He waited.

"You can't tell my parents. Promise."

"Tell them what?"

She huffed. "I've made a few friends."

"More street rats?"

"Yes."

"Why is that a big secret?"

"They want me to have friends from school."

"I see. Normally that would be ideal."

"Yeah, but when is my life ever gonna be normal?"

True. With her enthusiasm for subterfuge and intrigue, he doubted she'd ever be far from the action.

"Plus those normal friends would have been useless for rescuing my father."

"I agree. However, those normal friends can be useful from time to time."

She cocked her head. "Like when?"

"Like when you need a cover or information. Their families might have skills or resources you could tap into. You should cultivate as many friends as possible, because you never know when that one person might be vital to a mission."

Her blue eyes practically glowed. "That's a good reason."

"Can you find us a couple babysitters for these guys?" he asked.

"No problem." She headed toward the back door but paused next to the man she'd stripped of weapons. "Too bad we couldn't take them on a wild Valmur chase."

"Yes, too bad," Valek said. "Maybe next time."

"That would be fun!"

Oh boy, she'd really caught the bug.

Valek freed Onyx and Sunfire from the harness and groomed them before settling them next to Rusalka in the makeshift stable. Soon after, Reema returned with three grubby street rats—two girls and a boy. Valek explained what he needed them to do and paid them in advance. The older boy stared at the coins in his palm with a sly squint.

"Don't even think about it, Mouse," Reema said to the teen. "I know where you hang."

"So? I ain't gonna do nothin'."

"Good, because I don't want to tell Pickle about—"

"Yeah, I got it. We'll be here every day."

Valek watched in amusement as they glanced back at Reema as they left. "Pickle is scarier than me?"

"To Mouse, yes."

"I do not know whether to be proud of Reema or petrified," Devlen rasped from the wagon.

"Daddy!" Reema flew into his arms, transforming into a little girl.

Devlen hugged his daughter tight. Well aware of the physical aftereffects of being in a drugged sleep, Valek poured Devlen a cup of water.

The big man downed it. He scanned the room before his gaze settled on Valek. "Thanks for the rescue. How—?"

"Reema can explain it to you. I need to check along our escape route and ensure there's not an ambush waiting for us."

Reema toed one of the unconscious men. "They wanted us to escape. Why would they have an ambush?"

"To keep up appearances. Or there might be more watchers waiting."

"Why—? Oh."

"Oh?" Devlen asked.

"In case we spotted these two. They would be the backups," Reema said, as if it was obvious.

"I am leaning toward petrified," Devlen said.

Valek laughed. The motion caused the cut on his back to flare to life. He'd forgotten about his injuries. Blood soaked his right sleeve, and a deep cut showed through the rip in the fabric.

"You will need to change your...or rather, *my* tunic before leaving," Devlen said.

Valek pulled off the shirt with care. Pain burned in his elbow. Showing Devlen his back, he asked, "How bad is it?"

"Bad. It needs to be sealed or stitched up," Devlen said. "Do you have glue or thread with you?"

"No." But he had something better. Magic. Except he couldn't see his back. He needed Devlen's help. "Reema, can you check the route?" Valek held a hand up before her father could protest. "She spotted these guys before I did and can wear one of the mirror illusion cloaks. Even if she's seen, they won't bother her."

Offended, she said, "I won't be seen. And I don't need a cloak."

"Take it, or you cannot go," Devlen said.

Even though she wore an exasperated expression, Reema wisely grabbed one from the floor.

"Go where?" Leif asked in a rough voice. He sat up and rubbed the back of his neck.

"On a mission." Reema gave her uncle a quick hug before slipping through the door.

"Uh...isn't she a little young—"

"Without her help, you and Devlen wouldn't be here." Valek poured another cup of water and handed it to Leif.

"Thanks." Leif surveyed the scene as he gulped the liquid. "Took us out with the garbage, eh? Sweet." Then he straightened in alarm. "Mara and my father—"

"—are safe with Yelena," Valek said.

"But they were—"

"They're safe. I'll explain everything later. I need to heal my wounds first."

"Heal?" Devlen asked.

Valek met Leif's gaze.

"I didn't tell him," Leif said.

"What about the Cartel?" Valek asked Leif.

"No. They wanted to know our plans and where we've been hiding."

No surprise. "And what did you tell them?"

Leif touched a purple bruise on his cheek. "All my best jokes, but they failed to find them humorous."

"I finally have something in common with the Cartel," Devlen said.

"Ha. Ha," Leif deadpanned.

MARIA V. SNYDER

"Are you strong enough to help me?" Valek asked Leif.

"Yes."

Valek turned his back on Leif and relaxed his mental barrier. He pulled a thread of magic and connected with his brother-in-law. "Let me see through your eyes."

Leif focused on Valek's injury. The slash started along his left shoulder blade and crossed over to his right side, ending at the waistband of his pants. Gathering another thread of power, Valek used it to repair the damage, sewing the muscles and skin back together. Then he healed the smaller and deeper wound on his right arm. Exhausted from the effort, Valek leaned on the wagon.

"That is new," Devlen said.

"Leif—" Valek began.

"I'll tell him. Go lie down before you fall over."

Valek shuffled to his pack and spread his bedroll. He collapsed onto it. Leif's voice lulled him to sleep.

Reema was back by the time Valek woke a few hours later. The three of them had made a camp of sorts on the floor of the warehouse.

"No one lying in wait," she said when he asked her about their planned route.

"What's next?" Leif asked.

Color had returned to both men's faces, and they seemed more alert. "We'll leave Fulgor when the workers are going home. The extra traffic on the streets should help us blend in. Then we'll rendezvous with Yelena and the others."

"Opal is due home soon. I am not leaving without her," Devlen said.

"How soon?"

The big Sandseed stiffened as if preparing for a fight. "Any day."

Which meant she was overdue. Valek considered his options. They could remain here and wait, risking capture. He could leave Opal a note explaining their whereabouts. But it might be picked up and deciphered by the Cartel's soldiers. A third option popped into his mind. Yelena wouldn't like it, but it was the safest course of action.

"The three of you will travel to the Citadel and catch up with the others. I'll stay and wait for Opal."

Devlen tried to protest, but the need to protect his daughter overruled his desire to be reunited with his wife. And Reema argued that she'd been just fine on her own, thank you very much, and could gather intel while they waited for her mother. Leif, though, was happy to leave.

In the end, Valek won. When they left the warehouse, he wore one of the mirror cloaks and trailed them, ensuring no one followed them. Reema kept the other cloak.

The cloak came in handy over the next couple days. Guards lay in wait at the glass factory for Opal's return. He figured Opal would dodge the watchers and check inside before leaving. And that was exactly how it played out when Valek spotted her on the first day of the heating season.

Her panicked expression fueled his desire to chase her. But he waited to see if anyone besides him had picked up on her location. Once he confirmed no one had any interest in her, Valek intercepted Opal near Nic's apartment.

"Oh, thank fate!" She grasped his arms. "Do you know where Devlen and Reema are? Are they safe?"

"Yes."

"Where—"

"Not here," he said.

"Right."

Opal stayed quiet as she shadowed him to the warehouse. But she pounced with more questions the second after he closed the door.

MARIA V. SNYDER

He explained what had happened to her family in her absence and why. Guilt, relief and concern crossed her face.

"So this Cartel has control of the Citadel?" Her brown eyes widened in alarm. "What about Teegan?"

"He's safe, too." Another hour passed as he filled her in on their efforts to thwart the Cartel and Teegan's role. "We need to figure a few things out first, but I hope we can stop them before they take over all of Sitia."

"We need to warn Nic and Eve and—" She gasped. "Zitora!"

His heart banged against his chest. "Did you find Zitora?"

"Yes, and she's on her way to the Citadel. We had no clue what's been going on with this Cartel. If we don't stop her, she'll be caught by them!"

15

JANCO

Yelena jerked as if slapped. "My cousin Nutty? Are you sure?"

Janco hated to be the bearer of bad news. He swallowed the sour taste in his mouth. "Yeah. I never forget a face."

"Except the guy you saw in the Greenblade forest," Ari muttered.

Esau leaned forward in his saddle. "Why is that bad news? Nutty is more than capable of caring for the plants."

"It's bad because she might be working for the Cartel or for the Master Gardener," Yelena said.

"She's not working for them," Esau said with conviction.

"We can ask her," Onora said. "She's alone, and there are six of us."

True. Although they only needed two of them. He and Onora would have no trouble sneaking up on her. The tall grass of the Avibian Plains made an effective camouflage.

"What if there are others hiding behind an illusion?" Ari asked.

Janco brandished his null shield pendant. "No chance."

"How about hiding inside the glass hothouse?"

"It's too small for more than a couple. And we can handle more than a couple."

"How small?" Esau asked, sounding disappointed.

Janco opened his mouth to reply, but Yelena said, "All right. Let's go ask."

Janco mounted The Madam and guided her to the clearing in the plains. A small hut sat next to the glass hothouse. The door to the hut creaked open. He rested his hand on the hilt of his sword. Both Onora and Ari also braced for action.

Nutty glanced out. Her maple-colored hair had been pulled back into a ponytail. She scanned the riders, and with a whoop of joy, she sprinted straight for them.

"Yelena! Uncle Esau! I'm *so glad* to see you." Nutty beamed at them. She skidded to a stop next to Yelena and bounced on the balls of her bare feet. "I've been so homesick."

"What are you doing here?" Yelena asked.

Confusion dimmed her smile. "Helping Bavol. Didn't he tell you?"

"No."

"Didn't he send you? He said he would send someone…but that was a while ago."

"No. He's been…preoccupied. Why don't you fill us in?"

She bit her lip and gazed at Onora and then Ari and Janco. The girl—well, not technically a girl, as she was about twenty-three years old—had freckles sprinkled over a small nose, which she crinkled as she peered at Yelena. "Um…they're from Ixia."

Considering both he and Ari had been in Sitia for a while and had tanned in the southern sun, she was rather observant. Janco approved.

"They're trustworthy," Yelena said.

But she still appeared uncertain. Janco didn't blame her.

They all sat on their horses, staring down at her. If it'd been him, he'd have barricaded himself in that hut by now.

As if reading his thoughts, Esau dismounted. "Come on, Nut. Show me what's growing in that fabulous glass hothouse of yours."

Nutty perked right up. "Isn't it grand?"

"Whose idea was it to build it with glass?"

"Bavol's, I think." She shrugged her thin shoulders. "It was already built when I came here to help." Nutty led him to the hothouse and they disappeared inside.

"Should we follow them?" Onora asked Yelena.

"No. Esau will find out as much as possible. Let's take care of the horses."

Esau and Nutty remained in the hothouse while they groomed horses and set up camp. The late afternoon sunlight reflected off the glass, and Janco strained to see any movement inside.

"Do you think she jumped him?" he asked Onora in a whisper. "Should we go in there?"

"Leave them be," Mara said, talking for the first time since they'd arrived. "Esau gets distracted when surrounded by plants."

"And you're not getting out of your turn to cook supper," Onora added.

Janco suppressed a sigh over the lack of action. Filling a pot with water, he set it on a few hot embers to boil for Yelena's tea. He knew how to make one meal—rabbit stew. He sorted through their meager travel rations. Ugh. Nothing even resembling meat. His stomach growled just thinking about fresh, juicy—

"Here." Ari handed him a bow and a small quiver full of arrows. "Make yourself useful."

Janco sprang to his feet. "You know me so well."

MARIA V. SNYDER

"I'll help," Onora said, joining him.

"I'm quite capable of hunting on my own." He slung the quiver onto his back.

"I'll flush prey into the open. It'll go faster."

"The prey in this case are rabbits, not *humans*. Do you even know how to hunt animals?"

Her expression turned flat. "The Commander isn't the only person who has killed a snow cat. I'm sure I can handle a couple rabbits." She strode into the tall grasses without looking back.

Janco met Ari's gaze. "She's kidding. Right?"

Ari shrugged his massive shoulders. "You were rude. Go apologize."

But when Janco tried to catch up, Onora had disappeared. Probably sitting right next to him, blending in with the gold-and-brown stalks that radiated in every direction. The null shield didn't seem to help him spot her when she turned camo.

"Sorry," he said to the clump on his left, feeling silly. "I'm not used to having company when I hunt. It's..." Janco pulled in a breath. "It's one of the rare times I'm alone. I really appreciate your help, though, so if you could—"

"Are you always this noisy when you hunt?" she asked from the right. "You're scaring away supper."

Apology accepted. The strength of his relief surprised him. "Did you really kill—"

"Hush," she ordered.

Soon after, the first of many rabbits bolted across his path. With Onora's assistance, he shot four rabbits by the time it was too dark to see. Much faster than on his own. Not that he'd admit that to her. He'd already apologized. His male ego couldn't handle another confession.

When they returned to camp, Ari had already prepped a couple skewers. Onora and Janco skinned the rabbits, and soon the enticing smell of roasting meat filled the air. Esau and Nutty finally emerged from the hothouse. Dirt stained Esau's knees and elbows and caked the undersides of his nails.

Since everyone was starving, they ate first. Then Yelena turned to her father and invited him to share what he'd learned.

He ran a hand through his thick gray hair. "The plants are all similar to what was growing in Owen's hothouse. Theobroma, Curare and a collection of medicinals. No sign of that crossbreed to produce Theobroma-resistant Curare. But there are a few experimental Theobroma varieties and crossbreeds. Looks like Bavol was trying to figure out a way to counter Theobroma's effects."

Yelena leaned forward as hope gleamed in her eyes. "Did he succeed?"

"Too soon to tell. Damn tree takes years to grow."

"What about that grafting technique? The one that speeds up the growth?" Mara asked.

"That only works when you have a mature tree," Nutty said. "Since none of them have matured, we don't know if it'll work. Once we determine if it will, then we can grow more."

Not the best news. But not the worst, either.

"How long until they've matured?" Ari asked.

"About two years or so."

Janco groaned. By then they'd be reporting to Commander Owen.

Yelena pulled the drawing of the Harman tree from her pack and handed it to Nutty. "Do you recognize this?"

She studied the picture. "No, sorry."

Yelena hid her disappointment, but Janco knew discovering why those Harman trees were so important to Owen and the Cartel was vital to their success.

"How long have you been involved?" Yelena asked Nutty.

MARIA V. SNYDER

"Bavol asked me to help him with some crossbreeding a few years ago, but he said it was a matter of high security and it would be treason if I told anyone." She glanced around as if expecting him to jump from the nearby grasses and yell at her for divulging the information. "Then a couple seasons ago, he asked me come to the plains. He'd built this hothouse as a prototype. He was working with two others, but he wouldn't tell me who they are. Said it was safer for me to not know. The last time I saw him, Bavol suspected he was in danger and told me to stay here and that he would send someone."

"See? I told you she wasn't working for the Master Gardener," Esau said.

Nutty pulled at her ponytail. "Is Bavol all right?"

"As far as we know," Yelena said. "The Cartel moved all the Councilors to the Greenblade garrison."

"The Cartel?"

"I'll explain in a bit, but first, did you discover who was working with Bavol?"

"I saw them. They came for a brief visit soon after I arrived. Bavol told me to hide in the hothouse. I peeked out. I recognized one of them." She hunched down as if afraid of getting caught.

"Who is it?" Yelena asked.

Nutty bit her lower lip.

"We need to know." Yelena's tone held patience.

Janco, in contrast, had to suppress the desire to shake the name from the girl.

"Will he get in trouble?" Nutty asked.

"It depends on whether he knowingly helped the Cartel, or if he was tricked."

"It's Oran," she blurted. "One of our clan's elders."

Yelena clutched her tunic in distress. There could be more

members of her clan involved with the Master Gardener, and that would throw suspicion on her entire family.

"Shouldn't be too big a surprise," Esau said. "He has the knowledge and could arrange the transport of the plants without trouble. Hell, even I've discussed these plants with him many times."

Nutty pressed her hands over her heart. "Have I done something wrong?"

"No," Yelena said. "You were helping Bavol. You had no idea what he was doing with the information."

Nutty didn't relax. "What about Oran? Should I have reported him?"

"To who?" Janco asked, but he didn't wait for an answer, "Bavol's your clan leader, and the Council is under the Cartel's influence. If you said something to them, you could have been arrested or conscripted or killed."

"And Oran could just be helping Bavol, as well," Mara offered. "We're jumping to conclusions. He might not be the Master Gardener. Esau, didn't you think it might be someone from the Greenblade Clan?"

"Yes. They have a few experts with the knowledge and skills, as well," Esau said.

"Have you met Oran Cinchona Zaltana?" Yelena asked Janco.

"Not that I can recall," he said.

"Hold on," Esau said. He pulled a notebook and a thin piece of charcoal from his pack. Drawing a quick sketch of an older man, Esau turned the page to face Janco. "Is this the man you saw in the Greenblade hothouse?"

"Yes! But why does he look so familiar?"

"You've met Bavol, correct?"

"Yes…" Janco wasn't sure where this was going.

MARIA V. SNYDER

Esau drew a picture of Bavol next to Oran. "They are half brothers."

Ah! Finally, they had a name and a face for the Master Gardener. Except the Ixians were the only ones who looked happy about it. Nutty wilted, and Yelena fidgeted with the fabric of her tunic.

"What about the other person with Oran?" Onora asked Nutty.

"Can you describe him?" Esau asked.

"Her," she corrected him. Then, sounding doubtful, she said, "I can try."

"It's just like when you're clinging to the very top of a tree when on expedition with me," he said. "Just describe the parts, and I'll work on putting it together."

"Okay."

As she worked with Esau, Ari leaned close to Janco. "I hope she's better at description than you are."

Janco made a rude noise. "Forgive me for not being perfect at *everything*."

When they finished, Esau showed them the picture. The woman had blond hair and large oval eyes. Pretty and pale like an Ixian, she appeared to be in her late thirties. Janco didn't recognize her.

Yelena cursed. "That's Selene Moon."

"Who's Selene?" Janco asked.

"Owen's wife. She was born in the Greenblade Clan but took his clan's name when they married. I don't remember her file saying anything about her being good with plants," Yelena mused.

Oh. "Hasn't she been incarcerated in Dawnwood prison for her role in Leif's kidnapping a few years ago?"

"Obviously not anymore." Yelena fisted her hands and pressed them into her lap. "She's a powerful magician. That's bad enough, but now I'm wondering who else Owen rescued from prison."

Janco groaned at the prospect of dozens of murderers and criminals helping Bruns and company. Bad enough that they had magicians on their side. Oh, yeah. This just kept getting better and better.

16

YELENA

My heart twisted at the thought of Owen rescuing his wife, Selene, and other criminals from the Sitian prisons. With close to four years to pick and choose who to release, and with Loris's and Cilly's magic to help alter the correctional officers' memories and implant new false ones, he could have recruited a small army of professional delinquents. If Owen hadn't rescued his brother from Wirral's maximum security wing, we might never have discovered he was still alive. Good thing Owen made mistakes. Those would, hopefully, lead to his defeat.

We all sat around the campfire, lost in our own thoughts. The logs snapped and crackled as the flames licked at them with greedy orange tongues.

"Now we know that either Oran or Selene is the Master Gardener. How does that help us?" Janco asked.

I considered. "We could kidnap Oran and find out where all the other glass hothouses are located. Cutting off the Cartel's supply of Theobroma would be a major blow."

"Would he tell us?" Onora asked.

"Unless he's immune to goo-goo juice, he should."

Onora crinkled her nose at the mention of the juice.

Janco rubbed the scar where the lower half of his ear used to be. "Wouldn't that tip the Cartel off to what we're doing? If it was me, and one of my expert green thumbs disappeared, I'd triple the guards around all those hothouses and Theobroma factories."

He had a point. I borrowed one of Valek's tactics. "What do you suggest?"

"I found that complex by following the delivery wagon from the garrison. We could send teams to all the garrisons and locate all the hothouses and factories."

We already knew who supplied the Greenblade garrison, so that left ten garrisons, requiring twenty people. Fisk could probably provide the manpower. Could we locate and destroy them in time? We had guessed the Cartel and the Commander would complete the takeover of Sitia by the middle of the hot season. The Theobroma took at least seven days to wear off. To be on the safe side, all the Theobroma would need to be destroyed by the beginning of the hot season, which was sixty-six days away. It should be enough time, but what if we missed one of the factories?

I voiced my concerns to the others.

"Fisk's kids are good for surveillance, but I wouldn't ask them to attack professional soldiers," Ari said. "Plus, as soon as we hit one compound, all the others will be alerted. We don't have enough people to strike all the hothouses at one time."

Another good point.

Esau squirmed in his seat and ran a hand through his gray hair. He had a pained expression that I'd learned to recognize. "Do you have a suggestion, Father?" I asked.

Unhappy, he dragged his gaze to mine. "I might have a way we can kill off the Theobroma trees without tipping off the Cartel."

MARIA V. SNYDER

Janco glanced at him in surprise. "Why do you look so glum? That's fantastic news!"

"There's a strong chance it would destroy *all* the Theobroma trees in Sitia. Every one."

I understood his reluctance. To Esau, plants, trees and flowers were almost as precious as people.

"Good riddance," Janco said. "It has brought nothing but trouble. In my mind, it's just as bad as magic."

"It counters the effects of Curare," Esau said.

"Until the Theobroma-resistant Curare is ready," Janco shot back.

"That won't be for another three or four years."

"That's based on the plants in this hothouse and the one in Broken Bridge," I said. "Owen's people had more time. There's a possibility that it's ready now." A sobering thought. "What's your idea, Father?"

He stared at his hands, then picked up a twig from the ground. Using the broken end, he cleaned the dirt from under his nails.

"Father?"

Esau sighed. "There's a fungus that grows in the Illiais Jungle. It's called Frosty Pod because it resembles snow. It causes the pods on the Theobroma trees to rot. I've isolated it to one part of the jungle and have been working on a fungicide. But if we were to harvest the spores and spread them, then it would damage all the pods and appear natural."

"Spread them how?" Ari asked.

"With the wind. We'd need to be upwind on a windy day."

"And be in the perfect spot," Janco said. "And hope the wind is strong enough to carry the spores throughout Sitia."

Undeterred, Esau said, "We can travel from city to city, starting at the Illiais Market, then to Booruby and farther north."

"What about through the glass walls of the hothouses?" Janco's good mood soured and he stabbed a stick into the fire. "Besides, we can't control the weather."

Excitement shot through me. "No. But Zethan and the Stormdancers can. Would seeding rain clouds with the spores work as well?" I asked Esau.

"Fungus loves moisture."

"Can the spores get inside the hothouses?" Ari asked.

"There are small holes in the glass panels in the ceiling that allow the smoke from the burning coals to escape," Esau said. "Plus those spores will stick to boots and clothing, so when a worker enters the house, he'll drag them in with him."

"How long until the pods rot?" Ari leaned forward.

"I don't know for sure, as I'm never there right when they're infected, but it's aggressive. The pods shouldn't last more than ten days. Eventually the fungus kills the tree as well, but that takes longer. However, the tree won't produce any more pods."

I glanced at Ari. Judging by the contemplative gleam in his eyes, he was probably thinking the same thing as me. The fungus just might work. I calculated the timing. Ten days for die-off, then probably another twenty before the Cartel ran out of Theobroma—maybe sooner, but it was better to over-estimate—then add ten for the effects to wear off. Forty total. That meant we would have to *finish* spreading the spores by day fifty of the heating season if we wanted to attack the garrisons in the middle of the hot season. So with at least ten days for travel time, our start date would need to be day forty of the heating season, which was forty-six days away. Of course, starting sooner would be even better. I explained my math to the others.

"Father, can you collect enough spores by then?" I asked.

"There are not enough right now for your plan to work. I'll need time to find a dark, moist location to grow more of

MARIA V. SNYDER

the Frosty Pod. Given enough nutrients, heat and moisture, the Frosty Pod should multiply like rabbits."

"Then we have to start as soon as possible," Ari said.

I agreed. "After we rendezvous with Valek and Leif, we'll break into two teams—one to go with my father to help with the spores, and the other to arrange for Zethan and a Stormdancer to meet Esau at the Illiais Market on day forty."

The next morning, we packed up our small camp. The plan was to head for the Stormdance travel shelter. I avoided considering the possibility that Leif and Valek wouldn't be there and instead focused on my stubborn father.

"I need to return home and get started right away," he argued. "We don't have much time."

He had a point. Except… "It's not safe for you to travel alone. The Cartel will be searching for you."

"I'm going with him," Nutty said. "I'm not staying here."

Aghast, Esau asked, "But what about the plants?"

"We'll take a few of them with us, but we *do* have an *entire* jungle full of plants."

He ignored her jab. "It's a shame we can't take the glass hothouse."

I interrupted his musings. "Promise me you'll travel through the plains as long as you can."

"Of course," Esau said.

"All right. Mara, would you like to go with them? I'll send Leif to you as soon as he arrives."

"No, thanks. I'd rather not wait any longer than I have to. Besides, I'm still in training," she said, glancing at Onora.

Janco perked up at that comment. "I can show you this sweet little self-defense move."

"I hope it's not the one you used to fight off Svend," Ari

said drily. "'Cause you ended up in a mud puddle with broken ribs after you tried that one."

"Svend doesn't feel pain," Janco protested. "It would have worked if—"

"Time to saddle the horses," I said, stopping the impending argument.

After everyone was ready to go, I kissed my father goodbye. We arrived at the travel shelter two days later, near sunset. The shelter was located in the Stormdance lands just to the west of the main north-south road. The road hugged the western border of the plains and extended from the Citadel all the way south to Booruby, the capital of the Cowan Clan's lands.

The disappointment and concern was universal when neither Leif nor Valek waited for us inside the small wooden structure. All that greeted us were two rows of uninhabited bunk beds, a cold stone hearth and an empty stable. If all had gone well in Fulgor, they should have beaten us here by two or three days. Perhaps it took Valek longer to find Leif than expected.

Keeping positive despite the heavy weight of worry pulling at my heart, I decided that since we were safer in the plains, we would camp out of sight of the road and check the shelter at random intervals.

Janco looked at the bunk beds with longing before we left.

"The ground in the plains is softer than that thin straw mattress," Ari said to his partner.

"I know. It's just the *idea* of sleeping in an actual bed."

"You can stay. Just remember to scream really loud so we can hear you in the plains and escape," Onora said.

"Ha. You'd miss me. It'd be way too quiet," he said.

"Nothing wrong with quiet," she said. "Unlike—"

"Watch it. Or I'll…"

MARIA V. SNYDER

Onora waited, but when the threat failed to be voiced, she asked, "You'll what?"

"I'll sing every campfire song I know—loudly and off-key."

"So? You sing everything loudly and off-key."

I ignored them as I directed Horse back into the plains and asked Kiki to find us an ideal spot before full dark. Onora teasing Janco was a good sign. Each day she spent with us, she'd relaxed just a little bit more. Soon she'd be a true member of our herd.

Once we set up camp and ate supper, we created a schedule to check the shelter. I planned for the four of us to take turns, but Mara insisted she be included in the rotation.

"I need to practice being dangerous," she said.

"All right, but you'll have to go with Onora a couple times first to learn how to best approach the structure without being seen," I said.

"Okay."

"What about the Sandseed protection?" Ari asked. "Won't that mess up Onora's sense of direction?"

"We're close enough to the border that it shouldn't be a problem. And if they're not back by a certain time, I'll send Kiki to find them."

"Rescued by a horse." Janco snarked. "I can't decide if that's humiliating or just plain sad."

Kiki snorted and whacked Janco on the head with her tail.

"Ow! That stings."

"Be glad she didn't kick you," Onora said.

We soon settled into a routine, taking turns cooking, hunting and checking the shelter. One day turned into two.

Then three. The first day of the heating season dawned bright and clear. Not a cloud stained the sky, and the scent of living green floated on the air. Too bad the mood at our camp wasn't as pleasant. A fog of worry tainted all our actions and the few comments.

Four days without a sign of them. Fear and panic mixed and simmered in my stomach. No way it would have taken Valek more than a couple days to find Leif. Unless my brother had gotten captured by the Cartel. To keep Mara occupied and, if I was being honest, to distract myself, we kept training with Onora. Ari and Janco also took turns teaching Mara self-defense as I practiced the skills they'd taught me over nine years ago.

Onora asked me how long we were going to wait.

I clamped my mouth shut before I could snap at her that we'd stay until they arrived. "Fisk knows we're here," I said. "He'll send word if he hears anything."

She drew a picture in the soft ground with a stick.

Drawing in a breath to calm my nerves—an impossible feat, but at least I could say I tried. "If they don't appear by tomorrow night, I'll send Ari, Janco and Mara to catch up with my father and Nutty."

Onora met my gaze. "And us?"

"We'll travel to Fulgor."

"The boys won't like that."

"No, they won't. But my father needs help with the spores. And he'll need protection." I frowned, hating to admit that he might not be safe in the Zaltana homestead. "There could be a few clan members working for the Cartel who might try to stop Esau or sabotage his efforts."

On the fifth day, I couldn't keep still as the desire to move, to do something, *anything* pulsed through my body with a mind of its own. I kept checking on Kiki at various times throughout the day.

This time, she nuzzled my neck in comfort, then glanced at her back, stepping close to me.

MARIA V. SNYDER

"You want to get some exercise?" I asked.

A nod.

I called over to Onora. "I'm going for a ride. Be back soon." I grabbed Kiki's mane and mounted. It'd been a while since I rode bareback.

Onora appeared next to Kiki. "Is this wise?"

"We'll stay in the plains. No one can catch a Sandseed horse in the plains," I said.

"Unless they're riding another Sandseed."

Insulted, Kiki snorted.

"Sandseed horses are good judges of character." I patted her neck. "They wouldn't let a dishonorable person ride them."

Onora's posture remained rigid.

"Do you really think Kiki would let anything happen to me?" I asked.

She blew out a breath. "All right, but don't be gone long."

"Yes, Mother."

"*You* can joke. *I'm* the one who will be in trouble if you're hurt."

I looked at her.

"Yeah, I know. No one would blame me. Ari and Janco keep telling me I'll have more success herding snow cats than protecting you, but that doesn't mean I shouldn't try."

That was actually sweet. Kiki gave her the horse equivalent of a kiss on her cheek. Surprised, Onora touched the wet spot.

"Thank you," I said. "We won't be long." I nudged Kiki with my knees.

Kiki broke into a gallop. Holding on to her copper mane, I enjoyed the fresh air blowing in my face as she raced over the rolling terrain. Without warning, she switched to her gust-of-wind gait. The ground beneath us blurred as her stride smoothed. We flew in a river of wind.

I doubted she sensed danger. Perhaps Kiki had just missed

the speed. She couldn't use the gait when we traveled with the others. And the plains were the only place she could truly fly.

Eventually she reverted back to a canter, then slowed to a walk. Her sides heaved as sweat darkened her coat. We remained in the plains, but I didn't recognize the area until I spotted a familiar clump of stunted pines.

Alarmed, I stopped her and dismounted. "Why did we come so far? Did someone chase us?"

She turned her head to the right. I squinted into the sunlight and spotted a distant brown cloud of dust that meant riders. My first thought was of danger. We needed to hide. Except if they had followed us, why would Kiki stop here? Kiki didn't wait for me to make up my mind. She walked in their direction. I hurried to catch up.

When we crested a mound, all worries melted. Two horses headed our way. I recognized Rusalka and Leif in front, but when I focused on the unfamiliar second horse, my apprehension reappeared in a heartbeat. Not Valek, but Devlen and Reema.

A thousand awful scenarios played through my mind about why Valek wasn't with them. By the time they drew closer, I was all but convinced he'd been captured. Or killed.

Leif shot me a wide grin when he stopped Rusalka next to Kiki. Faint bruises darkened his face. Dirt and blood stained his travel clothes, and he appeared tired.

"I'm so glad to see you." Leif hopped off the saddle and pulled me into a hug. "When Fisk's people said you'd passed by over ten days ago, I worried you wouldn't wait for us." He released me and peered around. "Wait. We're far from the shelter. What happened? Where's Mara?"

"She's fine. She's back at camp with the others." I gestured to Kiki. "We went for a ride, and she must have sensed Rusalka and decided to intercept you."

MARIA V. SNYDER

"Where's the camp?"

Unable to hold it in any longer, I asked, "Where's Valek?"

"He's fine." Leif grabbed my arm to steady me. "He stayed behind to wait for Opal."

"Why?" I glanced at Devlen and Reema. Both looked equally exhausted, although Reema waved and smiled at me.

"Long story. I'll tell you later. How far is the camp?"

"Another day at least."

He frowned. "That must have been some ride."

"We've all been so worried about you. And I would stay with you, but Onora will have a fit if I don't return." Probably too late. We'd been gone most of the afternoon.

"Onora?"

"Valek didn't tell you about Cahil?"

"No, but we were together for only a few hours."

"It's a long story, as well. At least we'll have lots to talk about while we wait for Valek and Opal." And that reminded me. Mara. She needed Leif. "On second thought, maybe you should go on ahead, and I'll stay with Reema and Devlen."

Leif stilled. "Why?"

I led him away from young ears and told him about her terrifying experience.

A cold, hard fury blazed in his gaze. "I'll kill them."

"She might beat you to it."

He grabbed my arms. "What are you talking about?"

I explained how she was training to be "dangerous."

He released his painful grip on my biceps. "Oh, no, she's not. I'm not allowing her to get involved in any more danger."

Remembering Mara's where-you-go-I-go declaration, I asked, "Does that mean you'll stay away from danger, as well?"

He growled at me. "Of course not."

"Then good luck with that."

He huffed with annoyance, then strode back to Rusalka. "Where's the camp?"

"I'm sure Kiki has told Rusalka the location. Please tell Onora where I am."

"All right." Leif mounted and urged his horse into a gallop. They soon disappeared.

"Are we stopping for the night?" Devlen asked.

Kiki grazed nearby. She needed more time to recover. "Yes. You both look like you could use the rest."

"Leif's been setting a fast pace." Devlen dismounted stiffly, then helped Reema down. "Reema, please go find some branches to start a fire."

She ran her hands through her curls, dislodging a few clumps of dried mud. "You know I'll find out what happened to Aunt Mara eventually. No need to send me off so the adults can talk."

"Reema." His warning tone did nothing to discourage her.

She shrugged but did as he asked.

"She is very perceptive," Devlen said. "Although in this case, it does not take a genius to guess Mara is the reason for Leif's dismay."

I filled him in as I helped him take care of his horse, who was introduced to me as Sunfire.

His reaction to Mara's rough treatment matched Leif's. "I shall be happy to assist them both in ensuring those men are punished."

That evening, Reema told me an elaborate campfire tale. I listened without interrupting. By the end, when she finished with how she'd helped Valek rescue her father and Leif, I'd learned quite a bit about Reema. She would be a force to be reckoned with in the future. The very near future, if she had any say in the matter.

"Why is Valek waiting for Opal?" I asked Devlen.

MARIA V. SNYDER

Lines of worry etched his face, but he tried to keep his tone light as he explained her trip to find Master Magician Zitora. While he talked, Reema snuggled closer to her father.

I remained sitting, despite my heart urging me to jump up and down at the possible good news. Instead, in an effort not to get my hopes up regarding Zitora, I asked, "Was Opal successful?"

"I have not received any word from her, but I was incarcerated for most of the time she has been gone. The Cartel may have intercepted a message from her."

That would be bad. Really bad. The Cartel knew enough tricks to capture Zitora, and when the Theobroma didn't work on her, they'd realize it hadn't worked on Bain and Irys, either. I considered. Opal left on her mission when Valek and I were still Bruns's prisoners. Once we escaped, we sent a message warning them, but by then it was too late.

The best-case scenario would be Opal helping Zitora and convincing her to return as an active Master Magician. Since Opal was unaware of the Cartel's existence, Zitora would probably travel to the Citadel. In that case, we would need to stop her. Nothing I could do about it at the moment. Instead of rushing off, I chatted until they tried to hide their fatigue. Then I ordered them to go to sleep. Plus, if we left at dawn, we might reach the camp without having to stop for the night.

As the flames burned low, I stared at the darkening sky. Stars popped into view. More and more of them, until points of white fire glittered from every inch. A strange sensation in my abdomen distracted me from the spectacle. Just a light stroke, as if a fingertip traced a line on my skin. But the touch came from the inside of my body. Odd. After it happened the second time, I had an inkling of the cause. To confirm my suspicions, I reached underneath my tunic and rested my hands on my lower stomach. When it occurred again, I felt the gentle flutter from both sides.

The baby had grown big enough for me to feel its movements. Excited and amazed by the truly unique experience, I kept my fingers splayed over the bulge. The baby was about eighteen weeks along, and I wondered when I'd be unable to hide the telltale bump.

The light touches continued, and I wished Valek's hand rested next to mine. A pang of loneliness and worry gnawed on my heart. I hoped we'd be together soon.

The next day, we arrived at camp late. Everyone was asleep except Onora. She materialized from the darkness as soon as Kiki stopped.

"We need to work on our communication," she said.

"Oh?" I dismounted and stretched. "I told Leif—"

"Your definition of 'not gone long' and mine are completely different."

"Talk to Kiki. She's the one who changed the plan." Unless… I wondered if she had sensed Rusalka before we even left. I'd have to remember to ask her if I ever recovered my magic. Funny how that uncertainty no longer squeezed my heart with anxiety.

Onora frowned.

I chuckled. "It's all part of that 'herding snow cats' Ari and Janco warned you about. You'll get used to it."

"I doubt it," she muttered, but she helped us take care of the horses.

Reema peered at her in between yawns. "Are you the assassin who wants Uncle Valek's job?"

"Eventually, yes." Onora considered the young girl. "Are you thinking of challenging me for it?"

"Oh, no. I'm not skilled enough," Reema demurred.

MARIA V. SNYDER

But Onora was too smart to fall for it. "Uh-huh. From what I've been hearing, you could put the sass into as*sass*in."

Reema's grin erased all signs of innocence. "Ooh, I like! But don't worry, I wouldn't want to limit myself by working for the Commander."

"Free agent?"

"Something like that."

"Reema, it is time for bed," Devlen said. "You can finish your conversation later. Like, ten years later."

In the morning, we gathered around the campfire and exchanged information. Mara leaned on Leif, who sat behind her with his arms wrapped around her torso.

"Time is not on our side," I said. "Leif and Mara, you'll join up with Esau and Nutty in the jungle. I need you to protect him while he cultivates the Frosty Pod. If the Cartel discovers what he's doing, they'll come after him. The rendezvous is at the Illiais Market on day forty."

Leif nodded, then said, "Since we can't use Valek's sleeping potion anymore, I'll brew up my own recipe. It takes longer to kick in and doesn't last as long, but it's better than nothing."

"Thanks." I glanced around. "Ari and Janco, once we learn where Teegan and the twins have relocated, you'll need to join them and escort them to the Illiais Market, along with a Stormdancer. Doesn't matter which one."

"How do we deduce their new location?" Janco asked.

"One of Fisk's people will know."

"What about you?" Ari asked.

"Onora and I will stay at the Citadel—or rather, outside the Citadel—to keep an eye out for Zitora, Valek and Opal."

Ari crossed his arms. "It's not safe for you to be that close. One of Fisk's kids can watch for them, and you can come with us."

"Zitora won't listen to a strange kid. I need to talk to her myself."

"What if you miss Valek? He'll be upset if you're not here."

Janco huffed in amusement. "*Upset* is too mild a word. Try *furious*."

I ignored him. "Kiki can sense other Sandseed horses. If Opal is with him, then Kiki will pick up on Quartz, and if he's alone, then Valek'll skirt the plains. We'll ride close to the western border in case we see him or Zitora."

"That's risking a lot for a long shot," Ari said. "Opal's trip could have been for nothing." He glanced at Devlen. "No offense."

"None taken. There is a chance you are right."

I used a firm tone. "Either way, I need to update Fisk and learn where we are regarding stopping the Cartel." No one argued. This time. "Devlen, you can either wait here for Opal or come with us to the Citadel."

His gaze lingered on Reema before he spoke. "Leif is on the Cartel's most wanted list. They will have watchers on all the roads, and he and Mara might be intercepted before he reaches the jungle."

"Hey, I'm not that easy to catch," Leif protested.

"Oh? What about Fulgor?"

"I..." Leif snapped his mouth closed.

"Devlen, there's not much we can do about that," I said. "The spores are our best chance to cut off their supply of Theobroma."

"I understand. Which is why Reema and I will travel with Leif and Mara. Reema can stay with her grandparents in Booruby, and I will help protect Esau."

"No," Reema said, scrambling to her feet. "I should go with Aunt Yelena and Onora."

I shook my head. "You're—"

"You're gonna need me."

"We are?"

"Yup. You're gonna need to sneak into the Citadel at some point, and *I* can get you in."

"Fisk has an entire network of guild members who can help us," I said. "They know the Citadel inside and out."

"Yeah, but they don't know *people* like I do. And that helper kid we talked to said even they are having a hard time getting through the gate."

"I'm okay with it," Onora said.

"I am not," Devlen said with force. "Reema, you are coming with me."

She sulked, but it was the right decision. Bad enough Devlen and everyone here were risking their lives. I wouldn't be able to live with myself if anything happened to Reema.

Energized by our prospective tasks, we prepared to depart. While Leif mixed some leaves into a pot of boiling water for his sleeping potion, I promised Devlen to inform Opal of his plans.

"How long will Valek wait for her?" he asked me in a low voice.

"Until she returns."

"But what if she..." He swallowed hard, clearly unable to utter the dire words.

I touched his arm. "Does he know where she was headed?"

"Yes."

"Then he will track her down and bring her home."

"But the Cartel—"

"One problem at a time. Right now, we're lying low until we determine how best to attack them. By then, Valek will be back."

He smiled his thanks and strode over to help Reema saddle Sunfire. I fingered Valek's butterfly pendant, or rather, the lump it made underneath my tunic. My confident comment to Devlen left a bitter taste in my mouth. Everyone looked to me for leadership, but I had no idea if anything we were planning would even work. All I knew was that we couldn't give up.

Leif finished concocting his sleeping draft. He distributed vials to everyone, warning us about its limits again.

"How long does it take?" I asked him.

"About a minute or two, depending on how big the person is. For Ari and Devlen, it would take even longer. Oh, and it doesn't affect some people at all, which is why we don't use it for critical situations."

Lovely. "Is there a way to know *who* it will work on?"

"Nope."

I rubbed my forehead. Best to focus on the positive.

Right before Leif and his group left, Reema rushed over to me. She thrust a folded cloak into my arms. "You're gonna need this."

"What is it?"

"A mirror illusion is woven into the fabric. When you wear it, you'll blend into your surroundings."

Amazed, I struggled to find an appropriate response. "How—?"

"The guys who followed us from the rescue had them. I forgot to tell you, sorry!"

Considering all that had happened to her, I wasn't surprised she'd missed a few details. But the implications that the Cartel had these threatened to overwhelm me. I concentrated on Reema instead. "You should hold on to it. It'll keep you safe."

She waved it off. "I'm not gonna need it to hide at my grandparents'. Besides, even if I used it, my grandma would find me anyway. I swear the woman always knows when Teegan and I are doing something we…er… Gotta go. Bye!" She dashed back to Sunfire.

Sitting on Rusalka, Leif laughed. "May I make a suggestion?"

"Of course," I said.

"Don't hire her to babysit."

Two days later, I waited with Ari and the horses while Janco and Onora scouted for an ideal location to make camp. It had to be close enough to the Citadel to keep an eye on traffic flowing to and from the city, but far enough away that we wouldn't be spotted by the Cartel's patrols.

Ari burned off his excess energy by grooming Whiskey. The horse groaned in pleasure over the extra-hard rub. I wondered if Ari would rather be out scouting than babysitting me.

"What's wrong?" Ari asked.

"Nothing, why?"

"That's the third time you've glanced at me with your concerned face. That usually means bad news."

"No. I was just thinking."

"About?"

"Why didn't you go with Janco instead of Onora?"

"She's better." His tone was matter-of-fact.

"Does that bother you?"

"Well, there's always that bit of jealousy when some young recruit is faster or stronger or smarter, but she's part of our herd. And, you know…" He gestured with the curry comb. "Best man for the job, and all that."

"No bruised ego?"

He laughed. "I don't have an ego. Janco has enough for both of us."

True. I fed all the horses a peppermint. Kiki thanked me with a sticky lick. An hour later, Janco and Onora returned.

"We found this sweet little spot at the base of a hill," Janco said. "We can climb the hill and see the Citadel's eastern gate, clear as day."

"So why do you look so glum?" I asked.

He rubbed his right ear. "You know all those rug rats of Fisk's—the ones who've been keeping watch on the roads?"

An uneasiness rolled through me. "Yes."

"They're all gone."

"What do you mean, gone?" Ari asked.

"They've disappeared."

"Are you sure?"

Janco gave Ari a give-me-a-break look. "A couple locals heard rumors that a patrol picked them all up."

"A random sweep, or with intent?" Ari asked.

"They wouldn't arrest kids unless the Cartel had information," Onora said. "The Sitians wouldn't stand for their children being taken, but the guild members don't have families."

They might not have parents and relatives, but they had Fisk. Which meant…

I closed my eyes as the awful news sank heavily in my stomach. "The Cartel has captured Fisk." The words were barely a whisper.

No one corrected me.

"Now what?" Janco asked.

"We have to get into the Citadel," I said, opening my eyes. Reema's comment about needing her help repeated in my mind, but I shoved it down. At least we had the illusion cloak. "Once inside, we'll need to determine what's going on, and then rescue Fisk."

"That's a tall order," Janco said.

"I'm aware of that," I snapped, but regretted my harshness immediately. In a softer tone, I asked Janco to show us the spot they'd found to make camp.

He led us to a small clearing in the forest northeast of the

Citadel, nestled between the road to Fulgor and the road to Owl's Hill. At the base of a hill, the ground was damper than ideal for bedrolls, but as he'd claimed, the view from the top was worth the extra chilly nights and weaker fires.

It didn't take us long to set up and cook supper. Sitting around the sputtering flames that hissed from the moisture in the branches, I outlined the plan. "We'll break into two teams and take turns watching the gate and the road from Owl's Hill. Valek said he'd check the Cloverleaf Inn before traveling to the Citadel. We need to intercept him and Opal before they arrive at the gate. And the same goes if we spot Zitora." That road also led to the Featherstone garrison. If Bruns decided to move Fisk, that would be the closest garrison. "Ideally we'll discover a gap in their security so we can enter the Citadel undetected."

"What if Valek and Opal are already in the Citadel?" Ari asked.

"Then we'll rendezvous with them there."

"Or rescue them, along with Fisk," Janco muttered.

Ari punched him in the arm.

"Ow! Come on. We were *all* thinking it."

"What are the teams?" Onora asked.

"The boys and the girls."

"I suddenly feel like I'm in elementary school again," Janco said.

Onora opened her mouth, but I shook my head. "Too easy. We *all* know Janco didn't graduate from elementary school."

Janco hunkered down. "I'm not feeling the love."

"We'll take the first shift," Ari said, bringing us back to business.

I agreed. "We'll do three shifts a day, alternating teams. Also alternating positions each shift. This way, everyone has a chance to study the gate at different times of the day."

"Smart. What about at camp?" Ari asked me. "Do you want one person to stand watch?"

"No. Kiki will alert us of any intruders. Even asleep, she'd hear or smell them before they can get close. Plus, the person on the hill should be able to hear if there are any problems below, and vice versa."

"What about the person watching the road?" Onora asked.

Good question. "He or she can wear the illusion cloak for extra protection."

"But how do we know if he or she is in trouble?"

"The old-fashioned way," Janco said.

We all waited.

"You don't know?" He acted smug.

"Janco," Ari warned.

"Fine. A high-pitched whistle. Or in the case of the *girls*, a girly scream will do."

This time Onora smacked him on the shoulder.

He rubbed the sore spot and glowered at her. "Definitely *not* feeling the love."

Ari woke us at dawn. Or rather, he woke me. Onora was already making breakfast, and she set a pot of water on the fire for tea. Ahh...the small comforts of life.

I stretched like a cat and then sat up. "Any trouble?"

"No. There were only a few people on the road." Ari rolled his shoulders and neck.

"Janco?"

"They closed the gate for the night. No one in or out." He plopped onto his bedroll. "I did a little exploring to keep awake." He shooed away our protests over the added danger. "There's magic at the gate."

Not a surprise, but it would have been nice for something to go our way. "We have null shield pendants."

"Which may or may not work," Janco said. "If there's a magician stationed there and he can't read us because of the shields, we're caught. And if it's not a magician but one of those magical alarms, we don't know if a null shield will trigger it."

"What about the other gates?" Onora asked. "The Helper's Guild kid said they were closed, but—"

"They're barricaded, with no way through," Janco said. "And they have these nasty-looking spikes."

We all stared at him.

"What? I saved you some time. Sheesh."

We ate a quick breakfast before Onora and I set off for our shift. She volunteered to watch the road.

"Zitora's twenty-eight years old with honey-brown hair and pale yellow eyes. Pretty, with a heart-shaped face," I said. Although it had been almost four years since I last saw the Master Magician. I hoped she hadn't changed her looks too drastically.

Ari tried to hand Onora the illusion cloak, but she waved it off. "I blend in, remember? Give it to Yelena."

But when I donned it, nothing happened.

Janco cocked his head like a puppy. "You look the same. Ari resembled a big fat bush when he wore it."

"That's because I was *standing* near a bush... Oh, never mind. Is it the baby siphoning the magic?"

"Probably." At least, that was the theory—the baby siphoned magic when it was touching me or directed at me. What I couldn't determine was what it was *doing* with the magic. I changed back into my own cloak, which had a number of hidden pockets with nasty surprises, giving me a sense of security. Probably a false sense, but better than being completely vulnerable.

Onora trudged up the hill with me, then headed toward the road. I found a comfortable spot to watch the gate. A few people already waited in a line to enter. The guards allowed only one person through at a time. They alternated sides. One into the Citadel, and then one out. The person stood at the threshold for a few minutes before he or she was allowed to pass. As the day wore on, the line grew longer, but the routine didn't vary.

Halfway though my shift, there was a commotion at the gate. A few shouts reached me as two guards grabbed the man being inspected. They ripped off his cloak and yanked something from around his neck. Forced to the ground, the man was manacled and escorted away. That answered the question of the null shield pendant. It would be a bad idea.

By the end of my shift, I hadn't witnessed any gaps in the security or noticed any way that we could sneak inside. Dejected, I returned to the camp by midafternoon. Onora joined us with nothing to report. Ari and Janco left soon after for the evening shift. I tried to sleep, but my mind whirled.

What if we couldn't get inside? We could rush the entrance, but that would just tip everyone off that we were in the Citadel, and Bruns would probably triple the guards around Fisk. In that case, we'd have to abandon plans to rescue Fisk for now. Instead, we'd endeavor to recruit a Stormdancer and locate Teegan and Valek's siblings. Then what? I mulled over our lack of resources and personnel.

If our plan to kill off the Theobroma pods worked, the soldiers loyal to the Cartel would no longer be under the influence of the drug. They would need trusted leaders to follow.

The Sitian Council. The Council members had to be rescued from the Greenblade garrison before the soldiers woke so they would be ready and able to lead. A good plan. Except it would be Onora and me storming the castle, so to speak. Unless Valek magically appeared with Opal and Zitora. A girl could hope.

MARIA V. SNYDER

The next two…four…six shifts netted the same results. No ideas on how to sneak through the gate and no familiar faces on the road. Then again, would Valek be in disguise? He, too, was on the Cartel's most wanted list.

On the morning of our third day of fruitless spying, it was my turn to watch the road. As I hunkered down in the underbrush, I planned our next move. We'd travel to the Cliffs. Hopefully Kade would know where Teegan and the others were hiding. Not the best strategy, but better than wasting more time. In fact, the more I thought about it, the stronger my desire to leave. It was already midafternoon. I stood and froze.

Walking along the road were two people I recognized— Cahil's scouts, Hanni and Faxon. Which might mean that Cahil and the rest of his men were not far behind.

If that was the case, then we had a possible way into the Citadel. As long as they were still free of the Theobroma. Only one way to find out. Taking a risk, I strode from the woods and hailed them.

"No," Ari said when I explained my plan. "It's insane."

"I gotta agree with the big guy on this one," Janco said.

"It's brilliant," Onora said. "I'm in."

Ari fisted his hands but kept them pressed to his sides. "No. Two of you can't rescue Fisk. You'll get captured."

Onora snorted. I put my hand on her shoulder, stopping her retort before this turned ugly. "This would be an information-gathering mission only."

"Still no." Now Ari crossed his arms, trying to appear more massive and intimidating.

It worked on Hanni, who glanced at me with worry. "If you're going to do it, you should leave soon. General Cahil and the rest of the team are departing Owl's Hill in the morning."

"Then we'll *all* go," Ari said.

"No. Too many unfamiliar faces will trigger suspicion. You and Janco have to go to The Cliffs and recruit a Stormdancer. You only have thirty days to get to the rendezvous point." I outlined what I needed them to do as I rolled up my bedding.

"No."

I sighed. "Ari, I don't need your permission."

"*If* you get into the Citadel, and that's a *huge* if, how are you going to leave?" he asked.

"The same way. We'll get papers from Cahil."

"And the magician at the gate?" Janco asked.

"If we keep our thoughts on our duties for the General, we shouldn't raise any alarms."

"Sounds like your plan might just work," a welcome voice said from the trees.

Everyone except me yanked weapons as they spun toward the sound. Our argument had put them all on edge.

Valek stood at the border of the clearing with his hands wide. "One change, though. *I'm* going with Yelena into the Citadel."

17

VALEK

Yelena stepped into his arms, and he pulled her close. He hadn't realized how much of the painful tightness in his chest had been due to worry. Having her by his side filled a void inside him.

Over her shoulder, Valek studied the expressions of the people gathered in the small clearing. Ari set his jaw and Janco stiffened, clearly preparing to continue to object to Yelena's plan. Onora, too, appeared displeased with the change. Too bad. In the last five days, he and Opal hadn't seen any other way into the Citadel. This was their only chance.

Breaking apart, he kept one arm around his wife's waist. "We need to figure out where they're holding Zitora and Fisk. See if there's any hope for a rescue."

"I knew Opal would find her," Yelena said.

"Except I lost her." Opal emerged from the greenery.

Yelena, Ari and Janco took a moment to greet their friend. However, they didn't have time for lengthy explanations.

"We arrived just as Zitora entered the Citadel," Opal said.

"Was she arrested?" Yelena asked.

"No, but a few of the guards followed her. Bruns is smart

enough to try to recruit her to his cause before using strong-arm methods," Valek said.

"And just how are you and Yelena going to rescue them?" Ari demanded.

"*If* we attempt a rescue, it will depend on a number of factors." Valek used his flat tone, warning Ari.

But Ari was in protective bull mode. Nothing to do but let him say his piece.

"And how are you going to escape the Citadel?" he demanded. "They'll have doubled the guard at the gate."

"I don't plan on taking any unnecessary risks. You should know that better than most." He gazed at his friend. "Besides, Onora will be helping, as well."

"I will?"

"How is she going to get inside?" Janco asked, more curious than combative.

"By doing what she does best—blending in."

Onora's gaze turned distant as she worked it out. The matching sour expressions on the power twins' faces meant they had accepted the inevitable.

"Yelena, where are Devlen and Reema?" Opal asked.

Valek was surprised she'd waited this long to ask.

"On the way to Booruby." Yelena filled them in on the hothouse, Nutty and about Theobroma-killing spores while she packed her bags and saddled Kiki. She also mentioned that Ari and Janco needed to find Valek's siblings, Teegan and a Stormdancer to help spread those same spores.

Opal played with the ring on her finger as she listened. When Yelena finished, Opal glanced at Ari and Janco. "Kade would never let Teegan, Zethan and Zohav leave the safety of The Cliffs alone. He'd either go with them or send Heli."

"That's good to know," Ari said. "Do you know where they might go?"

MARIA V. SNYDER

"Yes. To my parents' house in Booruby."

"Are you sure? We have no time to be wrong."

"Yes. Teegan knows it's a safe place. The Avibian Plains are right next to the glass factory. The Sandseed protection recognizes my family, so they can hide in there if trouble arrives. Which it probably will, because if they messaged Fisk with their new location, the Cartel might already be on the way to intercept them."

Although he'd just learned about the existence of his younger brother and sister a season ago, a protective instinct flared under Valek's ribs at the thought of them being in danger. Plus his mother would kill him if anything happened to them. Valek suddenly understood why Janco feared his own mother.

"Then we'd better get moving," Ari said.

They packed in record time. Opal whistled for Quartz. They had left her and Onyx a quarter mile away, just in case.

"Where do we rendezvous with you once the spores are airborne?" Ari asked.

"Longleaf. It's a town near the Greenblade garrison," Yelena said.

"Why?" Valek asked.

She sketched out her thoughts about the Councilors. "They need to be freed first regardless."

He agreed.

"What if you're not there?" Ari asked.

"If we're not there by…" She drummed her fingers on her pants. "By the first day of the hot season, then you're in charge of stopping the Sitian takeover. Assume the Cartel knows everything Valek and I do when you're formulating a strategy."

Janco glanced at her, then at Valek, then at Ari. "Holy snow cats, she's serious!"

"Of course she's serious," Ari said. "If they're caught, Bruns won't let them escape, and he has the magicians to—" he spun a finger around the side of his head "—steal their thoughts."

Or, in Valek's case, they'd just need to threaten Yelena or the baby, and he would cooperate.

"I know that, but I was hoping for a more upbeat send-off," Janco grumbled.

"We'll always be with you in spirit," Yelena said. "Is that more upbeat?"

"That you'll haunt me? No. That's creepy."

The goodbyes were quick after that, although Ari and Janco paused long enough to obtain a promise from Yelena to not do anything stupid.

"You mean don't do anything Janco would do?" she teased.

"Exactly." Ari nodded.

"Hey! Who's the one who agreed with Ari that it's too dangerous to go into the Citadel?" Janco asked with a wounded lilt to his voice. "Avoiding that place is the smart thing to do."

"It is smart," Yelena said. "I guess there really is a first time for everything."

He pressed a hand to his chest. "You wound me."

She pecked Janco on the cheek. "Be careful. *All* of you."

Quartz and Onyx arrived in the clearing. The horses all rubbed heads in greeting before Opal, Ari and Janco mounted and headed south, planning to ride in the plains to avoid being spotted. Hanni and Faxon returned to the road. They had orders to rendezvous with Cahil and his team before they entered the Citadel tomorrow.

"How does blending in get me through the gate?" Onora asked Valek.

"An hour before dawn, go lean on the Citadel's wall. You'll blend in with the white marble streaked with green. Then move closer to the entrance and wait. Let a few people cross through, then empty your mind of all thoughts and slip in-

MARIA V. SNYDER

side with the next person going in. The magician at the gate shouldn't pick up on your presence."

"How do you know?"

"You're pretty hard to read." He held up a hand, stopping her. "When I saw Yelena earlier, I scanned the area with my magic. I sensed Ari and Janco and the horses, but not you. It's only when I focused on you that I could hone in on your thoughts."

Onora stared at him. "You have magic?"

He met Yelena's gaze. "You didn't tell her?"

"It's *your* secret to share."

Valek turned to Onora. "Here's the short version—I lost my immunity and gained magic. I can heal and read other people's thoughts. I may be able to do more, but haven't had the time or the instruction to find out. But trust me when I say you'll get into the Citadel."

True to form, Onora took the news in stride. "All right. Where should I meet you once I'm inside?"

"The Unity Fountain," Yelena said. "Do you know where it is?"

"No, but I'll find it. What if you can't get through?"

"Then collect as much information as you can about what's going on and leave the same way you arrived," Valek said. "We'll meet you back here in two days. If we're caught, then catch up to Ari and Janco. They'll need your help."

"Yes, sir."

"What about Horse?" Yelena asked.

Onora smiled. "I'll stable her nearby."

"Be careful. See you later." Yelena gave her a quick hug.

Valek clamped down on a laugh. The girl could handle Valek's new magical powers without missing a beat, but a hug from a friend left her a bit shocked. Her hand trembled just a bit as she swiped a strand of hair from her face.

Yelena and Valek mounted their horses and headed to Owl's Hill. They stayed in the forest, letting the horses pick the best path through the underbrush. Only a few hours remained before the sun set, and the warm air held a hint of moisture.

"How did you find us?" Yelena asked him.

He ducked under a low-hanging branch. "By doing the same thing you were, love—watching the road from Owl's Hill." When Yelena had stepped from the woods to talk to Cahil's scouts, Valek thought she was an illusion or a hallucination, as he hadn't slept much since he'd seen the new security measures at the Citadel's gate. He feared the worst after he'd gotten a closer look and knew there was no way to enter without getting caught.

Not at that time. However, if Cahil remained Theobroma-free and was still willing to help, by this time tomorrow they'd be in the Citadel. If not... Best to worry about that later.

Cahil had rented the top story of the Cloverleaf Inn. Watching the windows of the inn, Valek waited in the shadows near the stable. Yelena had stayed with their horses just outside the small town. Not without protesting, but Valek needed to ensure Cahil remained an ally before he risked her and the baby. Besides, scaling walls and sneaking into rooms late at night was his forte.

Once all the lanterns in the suite had been extinguished for a couple hours, Valek climbed the side of the building until he reached a window to one of the bedrooms. He unlocked it and slid it open. As he eased into the room, light from the half moon shone through a layer of thin clouds, giving him just enough illumination to see Cahil wasn't one of the two sleeping men. Two more people slept on the couches in the living area. No one stood watch. Good for Valek, but a misstep for Cahil. Valek checked the next room. Cahil was alone—

MARIA V. SNYDER

another blunder. Too bad they were allies, or he'd give in to the temptation to permanently take care of a big problem called Cahil.

Instead, he stood next to the bed and cleared his throat. Cahil surged awake with a knife in his hand. Impressive.

"Relax," Valek whispered as Cahil scrambled to his feet.

"Who's there?" Cahil demanded, thrusting the blade forward.

Valek sidestepped and pulled the hood of his sneak suit down. But he kept his weight on the balls of his feet, just in case. If Cahil had reverted back to being Bruns's lackey, the young man would likely yell for help.

Cahil kept his guard up. "What are you doing here?"

"No hello for your comrade-in-arms?"

"Let's not pretend we like each other. What do you want?"

"Why are you returning to the Citadel?" Valek asked.

"Orders from Bruns. He didn't specify a reason."

"Does he suspect you're involved with us?"

"Not that I can tell. But with Bruns, you never know for sure." Cahil shrugged, trying to maintain a relaxed attitude about Bruns discovering his deception, but the stiff line of his shoulders said otherwise.

"Tomorrow, when you arrive at the Citadel's gate, will the guards inspect each of the members of your crew or just let you in as a group?"

Cahil lowered his weapon. "Unless they have a reason to be suspicious, they'll just wave us through."

"Will they notice if you have two more?"

"Two? You and...?"

"Yelena."

Cahil cursed. "If they recognize either of you—"

"They won't."

"Why do you want to get inside? You no longer have allies

there. The Beggar King and his minions have been arrested. You can't free them."

"No?" Valek kept his expression neutral, despite the confirmation that Fisk had been captured. He wondered who'd tipped the Cartel off.

"All right, you and Yelena probably can. I've seen you two do some impossible things. In fact, it's better if I don't know your plans. But if you get caught, my involvement will be exposed, and I'll no longer be able to help you or myself."

"We know the risks."

"Fine. What do you need from me?"

"A couple uniforms for me and Yelena. And tell your men that we'll be joining you."

"Done." Cahil strode into the living area and woke his crew.

Valek tolerated a number of sour looks and low grumbles. It wasn't his fault that they didn't have the training to detect an assassin slipping into their rooms late at night. Despite their mood, they dug into their packs for tunics and pants that would fit Valek and Yelena.

Valek dropped the bundle of clothing out the window before he straddled the sill. "Cahil, may I make a suggestion?"

An instant wariness touched his pale blue eyes. "Go ahead."

"Set a watch schedule. Have two guards awake at all times, and don't sleep alone."

"Why? I'm allied with both sides."

"But you're not friends with the Commander. He has other assassins working for him."

"You said it would be a subtle takeover. No war."

"The Commander took over Ixia by assassinating *key* people in power. In other words, those people who might object to the new regime and had the resources to cause problems.

MARIA V. SNYDER

People like the Sitian Councilors and the general of the Sitian army. Besides, it never hurts to be extra-vigilant."

"Noted."

Valek gave him a mock salute and climbed out the window. He doubted Cahil's security would stop a trained assassin, but at least it might slow the person down. Scooping up the bundle, Valek hurried back to where Yelena waited.

She had built a small fire. His comments to Cahil about being prudent rose to mind, but not many assassins could slip past Kiki. Valek paused before his wife noticed him. Over the twenty-five days since they'd been apart, the angles of her beautiful face had softened, while her skin and hair shone. All due to her pregnancy. She might not be showing yet, but to a careful observer, the signs were there.

"Stop skulking about in the woods and come tell me what Cahil said," Yelena called.

He strode into the firelight. "How did you know?"

"Kiki. She raised her head as if she heard something, then relaxed." Yelena pointed to the clothing. "I take it you were successful."

Valek filled her in. "We only have a couple hours to get ready. I'll do your disguise first, and then you can nap while I work on mine." He pulled supplies from his saddle bags. Holding up a pair of scissors, Valek tested the edge of the blades for sharpness.

Yelena made a small *huh* sound and crinkled her nose.

"Sorry, love—the women in Cahil's group all have shorter hair. But with some artful braiding, I can make it appear even shorter without having to cut off as much."

"Not that." She grabbed his hand, pulled up the bottom of her tunic and pressed his palm to her stomach.

"What—"

"Just wait."

The warmth from her body soaked into his skin. He wished they had time for a proper reacquaintance. Perhaps just a nibble on her earlobe. Valek leaned closer, but without warning, a sensation brushed along his fingers. He drew back and met Yelena's gaze. Tender delight shone in her eyes. The light touch repeated, and understanding hit him. Hard. His lungs constricted as if he'd been sucker-punched.

"The baby?" he asked the obvious in a whisper. All he could manage.

"No. Bad indigestion from Janco's cooking," she teased. "Of course it's the baby."

He knew that, so why did the ground soften beneath his feet and the world tilt and spin around him? Because now the baby was tangible. Not just a concept or a belief. Real. Excitement mixed with fear, and the desire to protect crashed through him like a burning hot wave. He staggered to his knees under the weight.

Confused, Yelena held his hand. "What's wrong?"

"You can't go," he said.

She stilled. "What do you mean?"

"Tomorrow. It's too dangerous. Let me and Onora—"

Yelena knelt next to him. "You're overreacting. Besides, *you* argued for it. Remember?"

"Our baby changed my mind."

She grasped both his hands in hers. "You need me. If any of Fisk's members escaped, they won't talk to you or Onora. Zitora also won't trust either of you. And the library in the Keep may not allow you to view Master Magician Ellis Moon's notes."

Her words were all logical. Once inside the Citadel, the risk of capture diminished. Yet the sick fear gripping his insides with its sharp claws refused to let go.

In a softer tone, she said, "There will be no family for us if Bruns wins."

Another valid point.

"And fate might smile on us, and we'll find a weakness that we can exploit, or better yet, that you can use to assassinate Bruns."

Valek's calm detachment returned, cooling his inner turmoil and solidifying his determination to see this through to the bitter end. "You'd let me assassinate Bruns?"

"Oh, yes."

"What about the rest of the Cartel?"

"No. They're pawns."

Pity. "Owen?"

"Yes with a capital Y."

Something to look forward to. "How about Cahil?"

"No."

"What if I say please?"

"Still no."

"How about pretty please?"

"Valek." Her tone warned him to stop. She picked up the scissors he'd dropped, wiped off the dirt and handed them to him. "Time to get to work."

In the early morning half light, they waited in the woods along the road to the Citadel. Both wore the uniforms Cahil had provided. Valek's nose itched under the putty that hadn't had time to harden completely. He'd finished Yelena's first, then worked on his own before tending to the horses. After covering Kiki's white patch with a copper color that matched her coat, Valek had darkened her mane and tail. For Onyx, he'd scrubbed off the black dye on his legs, revealing the white socks underneath.

When Cahil's group rode past, Yelena and Valek joined

them. He stayed close to the front, while Kiki merged with those near the back. Cahil nodded in acknowledgment but said nothing. No one spoke much during the rest of the trip.

Hanni and Faxon waited for them a few miles from the Citadel.

Cahil pulled Topaz to a stop. "Any trouble?"

"No. All's quiet," Hanni said. She scanned the riders and, at first, bypassed Valek. "Didn't Yelena— Oh!"

"Hop aboard." Cahil jerked a thumb behind him. "Faxon, share Yelena's mount." At Valek's questioning stare, he added, "The guards at the gate are used to seeing a few doubles, since I like my scouts to remain on foot."

Valek nodded. It was a good strategy.

Cahil urged Topaz into a gallop, and they followed close behind. Valek kept a firm hold on his emotions as they approached the gate. He lowered his mental shield and focused on being happy to return to the Citadel and perhaps having a chance to visit his family.

Riding past the long line waiting to enter, Cahil slowed. The guards scrambled to clear the entrance, and soon the group crossed into the Citadel. A light touch of magic brushed his thoughts. Valek concentrated on his duties for the general and what he needed to purchase at the market. He didn't breathe easy until they were far away. Valek raised his mental barrier again, protecting his thoughts from magic.

They stopped so Faxon could change horses. Before they parted ways, Valek asked Cahil how long he planned to be in town.

"I don't know. It depends on Bruns."

"Will you be using your headquarters?" Valek asked.

"When we can. Why?"

"We'll check in from time to time for updates."

"All right." Cahil frowned. "What happens if you're caught?"

"I suggest you and your crew leave before they have a chance to question us." Valek kept his voice flat, but his heart thudded against his chest at the thought of Yelena being Bruns's prisoner.

"And go where?" Cahil asked.

"South, to Booruby," Yelena said.

Cahil opened his mouth but then pressed his lips together. He gestured for his group to follow him. Yelena and Valek found an empty alley and switched back into their nondescript Sitian clothes before heading to the Unity Fountain.

"We need to keep our disguises on while we're in public," he said.

"What about lodging?"

He gave her a sidelong glance.

"You've got to be kidding." Her tone implied she was far from amused.

"It's secure." Or at least, it *was*.

"That's not the point. I've tolerated all the others, but having an Ixian safe house *inside* the Citadel is..."

Valek waited for her to find the words. Although *smart* was the word he'd use.

Instead she sighed. "It doesn't matter anymore. I'm no longer the Liaison. Why should I care if Ixia is spying on Sitia?"

"Because you want peace between the two countries. Although I think having safe houses helps keep the peace."

"We're not going to argue about this again."

"I wouldn't call it an argument. More of a discussion."

She ignored his comment. "Why didn't you tell Onora to meet us there, then?"

"It's better if we take a more circuitous route, just in case anyone follows us from the gate."

"But the guards—"

"There are still assassins and bounty hunters after you. They're not going to raise the alarm because they want their money."

They reached the Unity Fountain. Eleven waterspouts ringed the huge jade sphere that was the heart of the fountain. Large holes had been carved into the twenty-foot diameter sphere and another smaller sphere, which was nestled inside could be seen through the openings. The holes in the second showed a third and then a fourth. A total of eleven spheres had been chiseled from this stone. One for each of the Sitian clans.

A few people milled about, and a couple kids dashed through the sprays of water, shrieking with delight. Yelena dismounted and removed her cloak. The sun was at its highest point. Sweat dampened her collar. She walked toward the fountain. Valek hurried to catch up with her.

"What are you doing?" he asked.

"It's good luck to drink the water."

"But bad luck to wash off your makeup."

"Good point." She returned for her water skin and filled it with fountain water.

Valek did the same. They could use the luck. The mist from the waterspouts cooled his brow. Glancing around, he searched for Onora. She should have beaten them here. He considered using his magic to locate her. Would it work in the crowded Citadel? And, more importantly, would it alert another magician that he was here?

The sphere chuckled. "Broad daylight. I can't believe you didn't notice me."

Onora hopped down from her perch in one of the outer holes. Her tunic was wet from the spray.

"Wow. You weren't kidding. She's *really* good at blending in," Yelena said to him with a touch of awe.

MARIA V. SNYDER

"I take it you had no trouble at the gate?" Valek asked Onora.

"I kept expecting people to give me odd looks or to point to me and alert the guards. 'Look at that strange Ixian girl standing by the wall!' But no one did." Onora shrugged. "And here I thought my ability to go undetected was due to my mad assassin skills."

Valek kept a straight face. Nice to see her relaxed and joking. "Anyone follow you here?"

"No. But you have an admirer," Onora said.

"The brown-haired boy?" He'd noticed him when they first arrived.

"Yup. Friend of yours?" she asked Yelena.

"Perhaps he's one of Fisk's."

"But would he recognize us?" Valek asked. If a kid could spot them, then they were in trouble.

"Fisk's been training them," Yelena said. "Besides, if they're on the lookout for a couple on horseback, we fit the description."

A good point. "Let's get the horses stabled and see if our friend follows us. Onora, we'll meet you at the Ninth Street stables."

They took a circuitous route to the stables located near the market and the safe house. The boy kept his distance, but also kept them in sight. At the stable, Yelena asked the groom not to get Kiki's face wet, remembering the horse wore makeup as well.

"She hates that and will kick you," she said.

"Thank you for the warning," the young woman said. "Where would you like me to deliver your bags?"

"I'll take them," Valek said. "We're not far."

When the groom removed Kiki's saddle, the horse looked at Valek.

He opened his mind to her.

Home? she thought with longing as an image of the Magician's Keep filled his mind.

Not yet, he answered.

Onora arrived after the horses were settled.

"Anyone else interested in us?" he asked her.

"No."

"Good. Let's have a chat with our new friend. There's a narrow side street a few blocks up. When we enter it, find a spot to blend in and get behind the boy," he instructed her.

"Yes, sir."

Valek hefted their saddle bags, but Yelena kept her knapsack slung over her shoulder. The three of them sauntered along the sidewalk, then turned right. As soon as they were out of sight, Valek and Yelena hurried to the other end, while Onora disappeared. Too focused on them, the boy didn't notice her absence. When they reached the end of the street, they retraced their steps.

Caught in the open, the boy froze for a second before whirling around and running into Onora. He tried to dodge past her, but she tripped him, following him down with a blade pressed to his neck. He immediately ceased struggling.

"Why are you following us?" Onora asked.

"I…thought you were…someone else."

"Lame, boy. Try again."

He sagged as if in defeat. "I thought you might need some help."

Yelena stepped closer. "This is a strange place to offer help."

The boy craned his neck to see her. "Circumstances aren't important when lending a helping hand."

She smiled. "He's one of Fisk's. Let him up."

Onora pulled him to his unsteady feet. "Why didn't you say so?"

MARIA V. SNYDER

He wiped off his pants. "Because it was just as likely that you would arrest me."

"Then why follow us?"

A shrug. "A hunch. I thought you might be part of the resistance, but I wasn't sure since I didn't recognize you."

"How about now?" Valek asked. "Do you recognize us?"

"Not really, but I know Master Fisk was working with a number of adults, and when I saw you two…well, there's not many adults who visit the Unity Fountain in the middle of the day without kids."

Valek had heard enough. It would only be a matter of time before they drew unwanted attention. "Let's continue this discussion at the safe house. Actually, it's the apartment above Alethea's bookshop. Onora, take…"

"Phelan."

"…Phelan, and meet us there."

"Yes, sir."

"Um… I'm not sure…" Phelan tucked his hands into his pockets. "I don't even know who you are."

"It's safer for you if you don't," Yelena said. "But we are friends of Fisk's. And we're hoping to free him if possible."

"Yeah?" He glanced around. "Where did you hide your army?"

Sarcasm, or a sardonic assessment? Valek would discover that eventually. Onora led the boy back the way they'd come.

Valek linked his arm in Yelena's as they headed in the opposite direction.

"Is there food at the apartment?" she asked.

"Probably not."

"Then we should stop at the market and purchase some supplies."

"Hungry?"

She laughed. "Always. Or so it seems. I think that must be Leif's problem, too."

"I doubt he's pregnant, love."

"Ha. No. He must be always starving. Lately all I can think about is Ian's beef stew and the raspberry pie Opal's mom bakes and the sweet cakes Sammy cooks and—"

"I get it. You're hungry."

"Famished."

"Let's get to safety first. I'd like to learn from Phelan how dangerous a visit to the market would be."

"Probably not as dangerous as having a hungry pregnant wife."

Valek hoped she was joking.

A layer of dust coated all the furniture in the cramped two-bedroom apartment above Alethea's bookshop. The agents who had been assigned to this safe house had aided in Valek's rescue from the Krystal garrison and then returned to Ixia. Though small, this was one of Valek's favorite locations. The windows overlooked the busy market. Lots of interesting things happened there. He'd neglected to mention the second safe house to Yelena. That one was near the Council Hall. And while it would be an ideal place to watch Bruns and his minions as they scurried to and fro, it would also be perilous to be that close.

While Yelena checked the cupboards for food, Valek built a small fire in the hearth. A cup of tea would soothe his wife for a while. Onora and Phelan arrived soon after he'd poured her a mug of her favorite blend. She chewed on a piece of beef jerky she'd found in her bags. Valek guessed Ari and Janco had taken the bulk of their travel rations with them to Booruby.

Phelan sat on the edge of one of the armchairs. Onora settled in the other while Valek and Yelena occupied the couch.

MARIA V. SNYDER

Since she was the least intimidating of the three, Valek had asked Yelena to take point on the questioning.

"How did Fisk get caught?" Yelena asked.

The boy gripped the armrests. "Do you know about the Problem Gang?"

"No."

"They are a rival group that formed a couple years after Master Fisk founded our Helper's Guild."

"I didn't know they had a name."

"They dubbed themselves the Problem Gang because they cause problems. It's all the kids who would rather bribe, cheat and steal from people than help them. They also sell illegal goods and services." He rubbed a hand on his leg. "They managed to get a spy inside our guild, and he or she learned we did more than just help and ratted us out to the Cartel." He flashed a scornful grin. "For a price, of course."

Yelena's grip on her cup tightened, but her voice remained steady when she asked, "Was anyone hurt or...killed?"

"Right before the soldiers raided our headquarters, Master Fisk told us all to scatter and disappear. A few of the guild were hurt resisting arrest, but no one was killed. Lots of us escaped, but after Master Fisk was in custody for a few days, the soldiers invaded all our hideouts and dragged in our field agents from outside the Citadel."

Valek hoped the Cartel had used goo-goo juice on Fisk to extract the information. He didn't wish to consider the alternative, but Yelena's rigid posture and clamped jaw meant she'd already envisioned poor Fisk being tortured.

"How did you escape?" he asked Phelan to distract her from her morbid thoughts.

"Luck. I was on a food run when the soldiers attacked our hidey-hole. Ever since then, I've been on the move, living on the streets."

"Where are they keeping everyone?" Yelena asked.

"They sent most of the guild members to the garrisons. Bruns Jewelrose's been telling everyone that he's cleaning up the streets, and instead of begging and taking from the good people of the Citadel, these criminals will be rehabilitated so they can give back by protecting Sitia from the Ixians."

Interesting strategy. Who could argue with that? "And the Problem Gang?" he asked.

"Lying low. I think the Cartel is paying them to keep up the ruse."

"And Fisk?" Yelena asked.

"In the cells under the Council Hall. We tried to get to him, but no one goes into the Council Hall without being questioned. Even the kitchen and housekeeping staff are being searched when they enter. None of our usual methods will work to bypass security."

Onora met his gaze. She raised her eyebrows as if to say, *Challenge accepted*.

"Do you know where Master Magician Zitora Cowan is?" Yelena asked.

"Rumors have been flying that she's back. We haven't seen her, but many of us wouldn't recognize her," Phelan answered.

"She has to be with Bruns," Valek said. "She would head straight to the Keep, and when she saw it was closed, her next stop would be the Council Hall." He considered. "Are there still watchers at the Keep?"

"A few. Not as many as there were before the other gates were closed."

Good to know. "How many guild members are still free?"

"No. We're not going to endanger them any further," Yelena said. "They've risked their lives for us already. Phelan, you and your friends are to find a safe spot to hide in until this is all over."

He glanced at Valek, then Yelena, and recognition shone in his gaze. "Lovely Yelena, we are not going to hide. There are only a dozen of us, but we already have shifts of people watching the gate, the market and the Council Hall. How can we help?"

Yelena huffed in frustration. Valek understood her desire to keep them safe, but if they were determined to help, then he wouldn't pass up the opportunity.

Unable to remain seated, he stood. "How's the market? We need provisions."

"Let us shop for you. There are too many soldiers in the market, and they are all looking for new faces."

"All right." Valek paced. It helped him think. "What is the status of the Council Hall?"

"Guards inside and outside all entrances. Shift changes every four hours around the clock."

"Where does Bruns sleep at night?"

"The Council Hall."

Valek clamped down on a curse. So much for targeting the man between locations. He mulled over the information from Phelan and developed a plan for the next couple of days. Giving the boy a few coins, Valek listed the items and food they needed.

After Phelan left, Valek sent Onora to observe the Council Hall. "I'll relieve you later tonight. While there, watch for Zitora."

"Yes, sir." Onora prepared to leave.

"Aren't you going to eat first?" Yelena asked.

"I'll get something on the way."

"But Phelan said—"

"No one will see me. Queen of blending in, remember?" She swept her arms wide in a dramatic fashion.

Yelena laughed—one of Valek's favorite sounds. "Just wait until I tell that to Janco."

"Go ahead. He'll just argue with you that *he's* the queen," Onora shot back.

"Don't you mean king?"

"Janco doesn't worry about the details."

"True. He'll just wave it off and say it's all royalty."

The girls shared a smile.

When Onora left, Yelena asked, "What's my task?"

He hesitated, knowing if he ordered her to eat and rest, she'd probably punch him. "I need you to go to the Keep's library to search for information about those Harman trees and find Ellis Moon's notes. But..."

She leaned forward. "But what?" Her tone held an edge.

"I'd like to check the security at the Keep first." No response. "Please," he added. "You can go in the morning."

Yelena relaxed back on the couch. "On one condition."

His heart paused in mid-beat. "And that is?"

"That you tuck me into bed properly before you leave tonight." Heat burned in her gaze.

Desire shot through him. "As my lady wishes." He bowed. "Perhaps you'd like to retire early? Like right now?"

"Nice try, but food first."

Undaunted, he settled next to her on the couch. "Phelan will be a while." Valek cupped her cheek, turning her face toward him. He ran his thumb over her lips. "Let me distract you from your hunger."

"When you put it *that way*, how can I resist?" she teased.

He pulled her close and kissed her with the full depth of his love. It was a long time before he broke away. "Still hungry?"

A pink flush spread over her skin as she gasped for air. "Oh, yes. But not for food." Yelena laced her fingers behind his head and claimed his lips.

They never made it to the bedroom.

Yelena was curled up asleep on the couch when Phelan returned with the supplies late that afternoon. However, the spicy scent of the still-warm meat pies woke her.

She wolfed down two while Valek questioned the boy. "Do you know where General Cahil's headquarters is located?"

"No. Why?"

"I want you to assign a few people to keep an eye on it and let me know when the general is there."

"All right."

Valek told him the address of Cahil's safe house. After Phelan left, Valek ate and then tucked Yelena into bed. The lack of sleep caught up to him, and he curled around his wife and slept for a few hours.

It was full dark by the time he reached the Council Hall. Onora signaled him with a faint whistle. Blending in a hidden corner, she was impossible to see. The lamplighters had finished their duties, and the air smelled of lantern oil. Heat pulsed from the buildings as the air cooled.

"What do you think of their security?" he asked, staring at the Hall's front entrance. The large square structure had multiple tiers and resembled a wedding cake. Constructed from the same green-streaked white marble as the city walls, it also sported jade columns at the grand entrance on the first floor. No windows or doors had been installed on the ground floor, and steps led up to the well-guarded double doors.

"It's tight."

"Can you get in?"

"Yes, but I couldn't get anyone out."

"Have you seen anyone significant?"

"There's a fair amount of traffic, but I haven't recognized anyone."

"All right. Go get some sleep. Tomorrow night we'll take a peek inside."

She grinned. "I'll let you tell Yelena."

"Chicken."

Onora gave him a wave before ducking out of sight. Valek remained in place for another hour, but it appeared as if the Hall was closed for the night. Ghosting north to the Magician's Keep, he checked for watchers and found a couple stationed near the main entrance, which was the only way in if you weren't aware of the underground passage. A wall also surrounded the Keep, and four towers, one at each corner, rose high into the air.

Satisfied that no one else lurked nearby, he traveled to the west side of the Keep. He slipped down a narrow alley and counted doors. The third one on the left was unremarkable. Valek pulled his lock picks from their hidden pocket and opened the door. Bracing for an attack, he entered the darkness.

Nothing. All remained quiet. He drew in a breath. The dry scent of dust tickled his nose. Closing the door, Valek then groped for the torches and flint that had been set on a nearby table. With a quick strike, a spark flew, igniting the torch. The light burned his vision for a moment. When his eyes adjusted, he descended the stairs and used the tunnel to cross under the Keep's wall. The passage ended in the basement of Second Magician Irys Jewelrose's tower.

Once Valek ensured the tower remained empty, he left the torch in a holder near the tunnel and did a sweep of the campus. It had been abandoned only about three months ago, but a cold, lifeless feeling permeated the air. After the Cartel had managed to position their cook in the Keep's dining

MARIA V. SNYDER

room, they laced most of the food with Theobroma. When all the students, staff and magicians had ingested enough of the drug, Bruns's loyal magicians brainwashed everyone into believing that Ixia was going to invade Sitia. Determined to stop the Commander, the Keep's personnel traveled to the garrisons and joined the Cartel. Valek had to admit it was a brilliant plan.

Valek stopped in the library. It appeared as deserted as the rest of campus, but he searched for an ambush just in case. Happy to see it remained as desolate as the rest, Valek hurried to the exit tunnel.

Back at the quiet Council Hall, Valek considered his options. Built to withstand invaders, the building had few places to enter. The tall, narrow glass windows of the great hall stretched three stories high but didn't open. Valek wondered if a magical alarm had been attached to the slick marble walls. Only one way to find out.

Looping around to the back, Valek stood close to the hall and lowered his mental barrier. No magic buzzed, other than from the power blanket around him. He pressed his palm to the cool stone.

Nothing. Or so he thought. A…consciousness sought him, as if drawn by his magic. Valek quickly raised his shield, but distant shouts cut through the quiet night, and the unmistakable sound of drumming boots echoed. He cursed.

18

HELI

When they arrived at the gate, Heli halted Thunder. "Are you sure your grandparents won't mind?" she asked Teegan, who stopped beside her. "There are four of us."

"For the twenty-third time, no. My grandparents will be thrilled." Teegan dismounted to unlock the gate.

"Until you tell them we're being hunted by the Cartel," Zohav muttered darkly.

Everyone ignored her. Zohav had an annoying tendency to exaggerate the direness of every situation, and Heli was too hot and tired to correct her. Yes, the Cartel sought them, but the Cartel had no idea where they were—unless they'd intercepted the message to Fisk, informing him of their new location. Which she doubted, since Fisk's people were ignored by most adults. No, the missive would have reached Fisk by now.

It had taken them *forever* to reach Teegan's grandparents' home in Booruby. They had traveled a circuitous route to ensure no one followed them, which added more time to the trip, so they reached the city on the fourth day of the heating season. And it was confirmed that Thunder was the slowest horse in Sitia. The cream-colored horse in the Stormdancer's stable turned out to be Teegan's mount—a sweet mare named

Caramel. Plus Smoke showed no signs of fatigue, even with the twins riding together. Meanwhile, Heli could have walked behind and pushed her horse faster.

The hinges squealed as Teegan swung the gate wide. He led them up to the large stone farmhouse. Instead of a farm, there was a glass factory, a few sheds and a small stable that looked new. Puffs of light gray smoke blew from a chimney atop the factory. The Avibian Plains surrounded the small complex on three sides, leaving only one direction open for an attack. Heli approved.

A short woman with graying hair opened the door to the house. She put her hand up to block the sun from her eyes.

"Hi, Grandmom!" Teegan gave her a quick hug. She peered at them over his shoulder. If she was surprised by their arrival, she hid it well.

"What are you doing here?" she asked him. "Aren't you supposed to be in school?"

"Oh, yeah, she sounds *thrilled*," Zohav said in a low voice.

"Hush," Zethan scolded her.

"The Magician's Keep is closed. Haven't you heard?" Teegan asked.

"No. Why didn't you go home, if that's the case?"

"Uh, Grandmom, can we discuss this inside?"

Her demeanor changed in an instant. "Of course! Where are my manners? Your friends must be thirsty." She gestured to the stables. "Please feel free to use our facilities. There's grain and hay, but I'm not sure how fresh it is. It's been a while since we had equine visitors."

Teegan trotted over to Caramel, but Heli waved him off. "Go explain things to your grandmother. We'll take care of the horses."

Not wishing to intrude, the three of them took their time grooming and settling the horses. When they finished, Heli grabbed her saddle bags and headed to the house with the twins. The door opened before they arrived. Teegan stepped to the side to allow them into a large, comfortable kitchen. A fire burned in the vast hearth. Pots of delicious-smelling edibles bubbled on the coals. Heli's stomach growled but, unsure of their welcome, they remained by the door, standing awkwardly. The older woman finished stirring one of the pots and wiped her hands on her apron.

"Grandmom, this is Heli, Zethan and his sister, Zohav," Teegan said.

"You're welcome to stay here with us until you're needed." She gripped the stained fabric of her skirt in a tight fist.

"Thank you, Mrs. Cowan," Heli said.

"Please, call me Vyncenza. Teegan will show you to your rooms. Supper will be ready soon."

Teegan led them through a living area and up a set of stairs. The air smelled of anise and cinnamon.

"What did you tell her?" Zethan asked.

"She'd already heard rumors about the Cartel but didn't know what was really going on."

"No, I mean about *us*?"

"Oh, that." Teegan shrugged. "I told her we were helping Aunt Yelena and Uncle Valek, and they told us to lie low until they needed us."

Which explained why the woman fretted with her skirt. Yes, Teegan was a powerful magician, but he was only fourteen and her grandchild.

"Does she know that we're Valek's...you know," Zethan said.

He flashed a grin. "Didn't have to. She's quick, but she thought you were his children and was worried about Aunt Yelena's reaction."

Zohav choked. "Bad enough being his sister—"

MARIA V. SNYDER

"I wish I had a sister," Heli said to distract her. "Being an only child, I didn't have anyone else to play with, and I had my parents' attention *all* the time. It would have been nice to share that pressure with another sibling."

"I always wanted an older brother," Teegan said in a quiet voice. "Especially when we were living on the streets and I had to take care of my sister."

Heli felt foolish for complaining. Even Zohav remained quiet.

On the second floor, Teegan pointed to a room down the hall. "That's my mom's old room. Heli and Zohav can sleep there. Zethan and I can share my Uncle Ahir's room." He jerked a thumb at the door behind him.

"Will he mind?" Zethan asked.

"Nope. He grew up with *three* older sisters."

Zethan made sympathetic noises. Zohav swatted him on the arm.

Teegan grinned. "Yeah, he says he needs his *man time* when I visit."

Having heard enough, Heli hefted her bags and entered Opal's childhood room. She dumped her stuff on one of the two twin beds. A couple of colorful pictures hung on the walls, but it was the collection of glass animals on the shelves that drew her attention. Some of the statues glowed with an inner fire. Beautiful.

Soon after they unpacked a few things, Vyncenza called them downstairs for supper. Teegan had regaled them with stories about his grandmother's cooking while they traveled. Heli had considered it a form a torture, but now...now, she practically drooled with anticipation. The heady scents of roasted beef and garlic made her almost dizzy with hunger.

An older man with short gray hair and dark brown eyes was already seated at the long table. He introduced himself as

Jaymes, Teegan's grandfather. Heli noted his resemblance to Opal—tall and thin, while her mother shared the same heart-shaped face as her other daughter, Mara.

The small talk ceased when a young man—probably Ahir—blew into the room. Around her age, he was as tall as his father with the same eye color, but a mop of black hair flowed to his shoulders.

Ahir whooped when he spotted Teegan. "How's my favorite nephew?" He high-fived the boy, who beamed at him.

"I'm your *only* nephew."

"For now. Wait until Mara and Leif start popping out the babies." He puckered his lips and used his hand to make popping sounds.

"Ahir, manners," Vyncenza scolded. "We have guests."

"Ah, so we do. Tee's friends from the Keep?" Ahir sat down next to his nephew.

"Close," Teegan said. He explained their adventures over the last couple months.

Judging by the increasingly alarmed expression on Vyncenza's face, Teegan must be giving him more details than he'd given his grandmother earlier. Heli hoped the woman didn't insist they go hide in the plains or hire bodyguards.

When Teegan described the big rescue at the Krystal garrison, all color leaked form Vyncenza's face. Ahir, though, peered at Heli with a contemplative purse.

"Do your parents know what you've been doing?" Vyncenza asked in a strained voice.

Teegan hesitated. "I'm sure Aunt Yelena or Uncle Valek sent them a message."

"You don't know?" Color returned to his grandmother's face in a flush of red.

Oh, no. Heli came to his aid. "Because Teegan's been safe at The Cliffs, we haven't gotten much news."

"And Reema's safe in Ixia," Teegan added.

Even Heli knew that was the wrong thing to say. Vyncenza exploded. Heli understood her reaction—no one appreciated being kept in the dark about the status of their loved ones. Poor Opal would have a lot of explaining to do once this was over.

Ahir interrupted her tirade. "Relax, Mother. It's obvious they can handle themselves." He poked his fork in Heli's direction. "She's the other Stormdancer who helped free Opal and her friends from that Bloodrose cult."

Heli was surprised Opal had told him, and that he remembered her name.

"And," Ahir continued, "Tee might be younger than them, but I'd bet he's more powerful. Right, Tee?"

"Uh…" He glanced at his grandmother, who still seethed, then at his grandfather, who hadn't said a word. "Master Jewelrose did say I should be able to pass the master-level test. But I'm—"

"—helping to stop the Cartel right now, along with the other Master Magicians," Heli said. While that comment wasn't well received, it was better than informing his grandparents he was still learning how to control and use his magic.

It took a while, but his grandmother settled down, and they finished supper. The twins cleared the table without being asked. Heli suspected it must have been their job at home. She wondered if they missed their parents. Heli had grown used to being away from home for months at a time once her Stormdancer powers developed at the age of twelve. However, the other Stormdancers filled in for her family.

Vyncenza refused to let Heli wash the dishes but allowed her to dry them. After she left the kitchen, Heli slowed down, enjoying a moment of solitude. It didn't last long. Ahir arrived to put everything away.

"Was Kade at The Cliffs?" he asked as he shoved a stack of plates into a cupboard.

"Yes. He was working with the twins." Although she doubted that was the reason for Ahir's interest.

"Why didn't he come here with you?"

"It's the beginning of the heating season. Lots of storms are expected, and he's the strongest." Not that there were many dancers left. Heli hoped more Stormdance children would develop the power. When Ahir didn't respond, she added, "Our priority is to our clan. Those storms can kill, and we rely on their energy to fuel our factories."

Ahir scooped up the utensils and sorted them. "Is he... okay?"

Confused, Heli said, "He's fine."

"I mean...about Opal. I...really liked him. I like Devlen, too, but..."

It had been a shock to Heli when Opal chose Devlen over Kade after they had almost died at the Bloodrose compound rescuing her. "He sulked and was grumpy for a few months, which isn't that big of a change in his personality, trust me. He was happier when he was with Opal, but lately he's been better." She lowered her voice and said in a conspiratorial whisper, "I think he's starting to like Helen, our new glassmaker. She's a real sweetheart."

Ahir smiled. "Good."

Heli agreed. They worked in companionable silence for several minutes. She dried the pots and handed them to Ahir, who hung them above the hearth.

"What about you?" he asked. "Do you have a boyfriend back home?"

Her heart thudded. She focused on the towel in her hands. "No."

"That's a surprise. Unless you and Zethan..."

MARIA V. SNYDER

"No." Heli met his gaze. "He's not my type."

"Really? He's a good-looking guy—a young Valek." A pause. "What is your type?"

Heli considered. No one had ever asked her before. Everyone just assumed she'd eventually get married and have Stormdancer babies. Was he just making conversation, or was he interested in the answer? Her pulse sped up. "Zohav would be more my type if she wasn't so sour all the time." She held her breath, waiting for his reaction.

"Oh." Ahir clutched the pot to his chest. He blinked a few times, as if it helped him sort her comment into its proper pile, like the silverware. "She's pretty, but you're right. She's far too serious."

Heli relaxed. She knew of a few other same-sex couples, and most people were accepting, but there were always a handful who found the idea to be objectionable, so she'd never told anyone before. Not like she had any time to date anyway.

"You want me to keep it between us?" Ahir asked.

"I'd rather you didn't gossip about me. But if someone asks, don't lie. It's not a secret."

"All right." Then he laughed. "I advise patience with my mother. She thinks she's a matchmaker and will try to hook you up. If you want her to find you a match, just tell her your type, and she'll try to find you a heart mate."

Heli grinned. "Did she send you in here?"

"No. I volunteered." He held up a pot. "Don't worry. I wanted to ask you about Kade in private. However, my mother thinks otherwise, so when she starts singing my praises to you, just know that they're all true."

"Your modesty is staggering."

He mock-bowed. "That's me. Actually, I'm looking forward to hearing what she says. I haven't done anything remarkable. Not like Opal and Mara."

She wished to reassure him, but she didn't know him well enough to do so. They finished putting away the pots and joined the others in the living area.

Zethan sprawled on the couch with a hand pressed to his stomach. He groaned. "That was the best meal ever. I'm stuffed to the gills and will never eat again."

Vyncenza leaned forward. "There's still a slice of cherry pie left."

Zethan hopped to his feet. "Mine."

After two days of eating, resting and more eating, Heli grew bored. Teegan had given them a tour of the glass factory. Helen's little kiln at the coast looked like a toy compared to the massive machinery and quantity of equipment needed to run eight kilns. Not to mention the number of workers scurrying about. Intrigued by the scale of the operation, Heli followed Ahir and Jaymes into the building on the third morning, hoping she could lend a hand.

The hot air pressed against her like a physical force as the kilns roared in her ears. Without thinking, she used her magic and pulled the moisture from the heat. It condensed into tiny water droplets, which she blew out the door with a light wind. The temperature in the factory dropped twenty degrees.

All the workers paused and stared at her. Oops. "Sorry, I…"

"That was amazing," Jaymes said. "Will it last?"

"Until the heat from the kilns builds up again." Glass melted at twenty-one hundred degrees, so it wouldn't take long.

"Too bad."

"What are you doing during the hot season?" Ahir joked.

Jaymes showed Heli how to gather a slug of molten glass from the kiln, spinning it onto a metal rod called a pontil iron so she could help the glassmakers who sat at their gaffers' benches crafting bowls, vases, goblets and decorative statues.

MARIA V. SNYDER

It was hot, tiring work, but she enjoyed being useful. At the end of the day, Ahir taught her how to shape a ball of glass into a flower by using a pair of large metal tweezers.

He inspected her daisy. "Not bad for a first effort."

"How do you get it off the iron?" she asked. Helen usually had all the glass orbs ready by the time Heli arrived.

"You put in a jack line, like so." He spun the pontil iron on the bench as he pressed another metal tool into the soft glass, carving a groove. Ahir then carried the rod over to a box filled with sponges. Tapping the pontil with the end of the tool, the daisy cracked off right at the line and fell into the box. "Now we have to wait until it cools."

"I can cool it." The air was unstable and easy to push with her magic. A breeze sprang to life.

"No, don't." Ahir made a stopping motion. "If it cools too fast, it will crack. Instead, we'll put it in an annealing oven to cool slowly." He donned a pair of heat-resistant gloves and carried the daisy to a metal cabinet. A few other pieces were already inside. "It'll be ready tomorrow."

"Working with glass takes a lot of patience."

"And skill. These glassmakers—" he gestured at the empty benches "—they make it look easy, but they've spent thousands of hours to get to that point."

It was difficult to imagine working that hard. Her ability to connect with the weather and harvest storms had always been a natural extension of her. Sure, it took some practice to funnel the energy into the glass orbs, but no longer than a couple hours.

A brisk wind blew the next morning, and a sheet of dark clouds threatened rain. Jaymes muttered about the weather at breakfast.

"What's wrong with the wind?" Zethan asked him, digging into his pile of bacon.

"It blows the sand around, making the glass gritty."

"And it cools the kilns, so more coal is needed to keep them at temperature," Ahir added.

"I can move the storm for you," Zethan offered. "It won't be hard."

"That might attract the wrong kind of attention," Zohav said.

Heli hated to agree with her. "I can keep a bubble of calm around your factory, Jaymes."

"No need to exhaust yourself for us. It's a minor inconvenience."

"It doesn't take that much energy. I do it all the time when I'm dancing in a storm."

Ahir stroked his chin. "You know, having a Stormdancer around is handy. When everything is resolved with the Cartel, you should consider going into business."

Surprised, she asked, "Doing what?"

"Weather stuff. Couples could hire you to ensure they have a sunny day for their wedding. Kade gave us beautiful weather for Leif and Mara's day. Or farmers could engage your services to water their fields when it gets too dry." Ahir sat up straighter. "You and Zee could work together when you're not needed on the coast. You'd be rich in no time."

"I never thought of it that way," Heli said.

Vyncenza beamed. "That's my smart boy. Always thinking." She tapped her temple with a finger.

"Yeah, always thinking of ways to avoid work." Jaymes stood. "Come on, Mop Top, the glass doesn't gather itself."

Their days fell into a routine. During the day, Heli helped in the factory while Zethan and Teegan practiced their magic.

Zohav preferred to stay with Vyncenza, learning how to bake pies, crochet and cook, which had surprised everyone, including Zohav. At night, Zethan sprawled on the couch, groaning about eating too much, Zohav read a book next to the lantern, and Heli, Ahir and Teegan played cards or dice.

Heli should have recognized it for what it was—the calm before a storm—but she was having too much fun. When Ahir woke her a few hours before dawn on the ninth morning, she shouldn't have been startled.

"What's wrong?" she asked, sitting up in bed.

"Dad says we have company. And it's not our distant cousins coming for a visit."

Alarmed, she scrambled to her feet. "Are they in the house?"

"No. He spotted them outside the gate. Looks like they're waiting for something…or someone."

Her first impulse was to run and hide in the plains.

Zohav pushed her covers back. "How many are there?"

"Dad says six or seven, maybe more."

"What do they want?" Heli asked.

Ahir shrugged. "I don't know. But Tee might. He's downstairs."

Heli almost smacked her forehead. Of course. They rushed to join Zethan, Teegan and Jaymes in the dark living area.

"Mom's asleep. It's better if we don't wake her unless we absolutely have to," Ahir whispered.

Teegan peered into the night.

"Robbers?" Heli hoped.

"No," Teegan said. "The Cartel. They know we're here."

"All of us, or just me?" Heli asked. Bruns had learned that one of the Stormdancers had helped with Yelena and Valek's escape, but he shouldn't know about the twins or Teegan.

"All of us."

Damn. Something must have happened at the Citadel. "Are we surrounded? Can we slip out the back?"

Zethan turned to her. "There are only seven—"

"Ten," Teegan corrected him.

"—only *ten* of them. Between the four of us, we can easily blow them away."

"Yes, we could, but they'll just come back with reinforcements." Heli mulled it over. "What are they planning?"

"A sneak attack while we're still sleeping." Teegan flashed a grin. "Good thing they didn't know Grandpop checks the kilns at night." Then he sobered. "They have Curare and null shield nets with them. No magicians, though."

"They won't be able to use their weapons because they'll be too busy flying through the air, and so will their reinforcements," Zethan said.

Heli touched his arm. "We still can't stay here. We're putting Teegan's family in danger. We need to leave. Jaymes, you and your family also need to find a safe place to go. The Cartel won't be happy when we escape, and they'll question you or use you to get to Teegan."

"*When* we escape?" Zohav asked. "You're that confident?"

Heli resisted snapping at the girl. Instead, she glanced at Zethan and Teegan. "Escaping won't be the hard part."

"What's the hard part?" Teegan asked.

"Making them *think* they have a chance to catch us."

Except for Zohav, there were answering grins all around. Heli explained her plan, and the four of them slipped through the back door to their positions. There wasn't much light, so they moved with care. The twins hid behind the well while she and Teegan sidled up to the stables. All three horses were awake, with ears pricked forward and nostrils flared.

Since Heli needed to know where the soldiers were, Teegan updated her on their positions.

MARIA V. SNYDER

"There are twelve of them now," he whispered. "They're climbing over the gate. Huh. Someone must have told them it squeaks." A few long seconds passed. "They're moving to surround the house. Two of them know how to pick locks."

Heli gathered her power. "Let me know when they're close." Aiming a powerful and narrow wind gust took a great deal of concentration and energy. She hoped to loop it around the house and strike them all with one mighty gust.

"Almost there..."

The gate squealed open.

Teegan gasped. "Father. Reema."

19

YELENA

The bright mid-morning sunlight woke me from a dreamless sleep. I yawned and reached for Valek, but his side of the bed was empty. Alarmed, I sat up. It was a few hours past dawn; he should have returned by now. Shoving the blankets off, I dressed quickly and hurried to the small living room.

Onora stood by the window, staring down at the busy market. A pot of water steamed on the stone hearth.

"Has Valek reported in?" I asked her.

She turned. "Not yet."

"Shouldn't he be back by now?"

"It depends." Onora didn't appear to be worried. "He might be following a lead." She strode to the hearth and nudged the pot closer to the burning coals with the toe of her boot. She must have been out early, because she only wore her boots when pretending to be a normal citizen.

Her lack of concern only increased mine. "What if he was caught?"

"Not much we can do about it right now. If he's not back by this afternoon, I'll visit the Council Hall and see if I can learn what happened."

I'd planned to go to the Keep today, but I'd promised Valek

to wait until he checked it out. Perhaps he ran into trouble there. Too many possibilities. I strode to the window, hoping to spot him among the shoppers.

"Have some tea." Onora poured a cup. "Sit down. I'll make you something to eat."

"Are you bribing me?"

"Would you rather fret until you're sick?"

"Yes," I said peevishly.

"And will that change anything?" She answered for me. "No. And it isn't good for the baby."

Fine. I flopped down on an armchair like an adolescent and dust puffed up, making me sneeze. My emotions had been erratic lately. I'd accused Valek of overreacting, but I guessed he wasn't the only one. "Sorry," I said when she handed me the tea.

"No problem. Besides, you're doing better than my aunt."

Strange comment. "What do you mean?"

"My aunt sobbed through her entire pregnancy. Or so it seemed. She'd cry when she couldn't find matching socks or when a bird flew into the window pane."

"So I can blame the baby for my mood swings?"

"Yup. And she was absentminded and really goofy at times. She called it baby brain."

That explained quite a bit.

"And swollen ankles. Hers blew up like melons." She spread her hands to demonstrate the size.

Lovely. I wondered what other effects the baby would cause. "You know more than I do about this. Were you close to your aunt?"

"I..." Onora focused on slicing an apple. "She raised us after our mother died."

I realized I didn't know much about Onora's past. I knew that she'd trained as an assassin, and she'd been abused by her commanding officer. Valek's news that Sergeant Gerik was her brother had been a complete surprise. "Do you have other siblings?"

"No. Just the two of us." She paused. "When my aunt and the baby both died in childbirth, my uncle kicked us out, so we joined the military." She shrugged. "You know the rest."

"Sorry to hear that."

"It's all in the past." Her tone remained flat.

She wasn't fooling me. I'd spent a couple years running from my traumatic past, and I recognized the signs. It would catch up to her eventually. I just hoped I'd be there to help her get through it once it did.

Onora set a plate full of ham and apple slices for us to share on the table between the armchairs. The table had been wiped down.

"You dusted. Thanks."

She bit into a piece of ham. "I was bored."

We ate the rest of the meal in silence. I kept glancing at the door, as if my will alone would cause Valek to appear.

"My aunt also had strange cravings for food," Onora said. "One time, she sent me to the market for eggs—dozens of eggs. We ate omelets and scrambled eggs for a week straight." She laughed at the memory.

"How long did you live with her?" All humor fled her face, and I wished I hadn't asked the question.

"About six years. My dad left us a year before my mom died. She sickened with a lung infection, and by the time the medic determined the source, it was too late." Onora stared into the past. "Same with my aunt. We lived too far from help, and my uncle wouldn't let her travel to town when the baby was due. He said the midwife would do fine, even though both the midwife and my aunt thought the baby was breech." Her shoulders stiffened, but then she drew in a quick breath as if

MARIA V. SNYDER

she'd realized something. "Not that it will happen to you! Valek will have you surrounded by healers and medics. You don't have to worry."

I hadn't thought that far ahead. Right now my priority was for Valek and me to survive the Cartel's takeover. Once that happened, then I could focus on our future.

I checked the door. Still closed.

When Valek failed to show up by midafternoon, I decided I wasn't waiting any longer. I touched up my disguise.

"Where do you think you're going?" Onora asked.

"While you check the Council Hall, I'm going to visit Cahil's headquarters. Maybe he has some information on Valek."

"No. It's too dangerous."

"I'm not asking permission." No way I'd sit here another minute.

"Cahil might not even be there."

"Then I'll find Phelen, see if he's seen or heard anything."

"What if Valek shows up before one of us returns? You know he'll panic when no one's here."

"Nice try. We can leave him a 'be back soon' note."

Onora muttered under her breath, but then said, "I'm coming with you."

Not like I could stop her. "Fine."

We looped around the Council Hall just in case Valek had stayed there to watch the traffic.

"Do you want me to go inside?" Onora asked. "See if they've caught him?"

I considered. Valek wasn't easy to catch. "Not yet. If there's no sign of him, that'll be plan B."

Our next stop was Cahil's headquarters. A shudder rumbled through me when I stepped inside the abandoned warehouse. The time I'd spent here hadn't been pleasant.

No one guarded the entrance. I followed the dust-free path through the stacks of dirty crates that littered the floor. The place smelled of grease, rusted metal and mold. When we arrived at the top of the stairs that led down to Cahil's underground offices, we spotted a faint yellow glow. At least one person was here, probably more.

Onora pulled her daggers and slid off her boots before signaling me to follow her down the stairs. I grabbed my switchblade but didn't trigger the blade.

The light brightened, and the murmur of a distant conversation floated on the air. By the time we reached the bottom, I recognized Hanni's and Faxon's voices. Onora eased into the room so quietly, they didn't hear her.

"...going to be hard keeping silent when—" Hanni jerked to her feet with her sword in hand when I entered. Faxon followed a second after.

Guess I wasn't as stealthy as Onora. No one moved. They blinked at us for a moment before relaxing.

Hanni sheathed her weapon. "No need to sneak up on us. We're on the same side."

Onora shrugged. "Habit." She scanned the area. The room was filled with desks, and a door in the back led to Cahil's office. "Are you alone?"

"Yes. I guess you heard about Valek."

My pulse jumped. "No. What happened?" My tone was sharp and squeaked in panic.

"Then why—"

"What happened?" Must. Not. Shake. Her.

"Master Magician Zitora Cowan detected him near the Council Hall, and they've been hunting him all morning."

I sank into a nearby chair. They didn't have him. Yet. "Hunting?"

"Yes. General Cahil was summoned to the Hall an hour

MARIA V. SNYDER

ago to help with the efforts. Master Zitora can track Valek within a few blocks, so they are setting up an ambush and plan to steer him into it."

"Where?" Onora asked.

"The messenger said they spotted him on the roof of the third ring."

Onora glanced at me. "Third ring?"

"It's one of the business and factory rings that are located around the market," I said. "Hanni, do you know his position on that ring?" Otherwise, it'd be miles of ground to cover.

"Northeast."

Still a rather large area, but it was better than nothing. I thanked her. We dashed up the stairs. Onora snagged her boots as we crossed the warehouse.

"The intel's an hour old," Onora said, pausing at the door to put on her boots. No need for stealth. Not yet.

"I know, but it's a place to start."

When we exited the building, I took a few seconds to get my bearings. Cahil's headquarters was in the southeast section of the fifth ring. Heading north at a quick pace—not fast enough for me, but if we were seen running, it would draw unwanted attention—we scanned the streets, alleys and rooftops as we cut through to the third ring. Once we reached the northeast section, we slowed, seeking any signs of an ambush. Trying to appear as if I wasn't frantically searching for my husband, I resisted the urge to yell his name.

At one point, Onora leaned close to me and said, "Have you ever heard the term 'looking for a snowflake in a blizzard'?"

"No, but there are millions of snowflakes in a blizzard."

"Exactly."

"That makes no sense. It'd be easy to find a—"

Onora touched my shoulder. She drew me into a side street.

"There are a number of soldiers ahead. Stay here while I go check it out."

My protest died in my throat. Valek was more important than my ego. I nodded. She left her boots with me and then disappeared. It took all my self-control not to poke my head around the corner to see where she was going.

Instead, I inventoried my weapons just in case I needed them. Then I compared my boots to Onora's—hers were two sizes bigger. I paced while trying to ignore the various horrible scenarios that threatened to play out in my mind. Counting the buildings on both sides of the narrow street—there were eight—I tried to guess what type of industry went on inside them. One had to be a garment factory, judging by a delivery wagon outside full of bolts of colorful cloth. Although they could also be manufacturing bedding.

Without warning, Onora appeared at my elbow. I jumped a foot into the air. "Well?" I demanded.

"They know he's nearby, but not exactly where. Soldiers are blocking the streets and alleys, and a group of eight is searching buildings. I think Zitora is with that group."

Not good. I mulled it over. "Where?"

"A few blocks north of here."

"Can you show me?"

She scrunched up her face. "Why?"

"I'm not sure."

"Okay." She said the word as if placating a crazy person. "Stay right behind me."

The deserted streets felt strange in the middle of the day. Onora stayed in the shadows and slowed once we'd crossed two streets. She stopped next to a wagon that had been abandoned. The soldiers must have chased the driver off while they searched for Valek.

"They're another block north," Onora said.

I scanned the area. It was familiar, but I couldn't remember why. If I was Valek, where would I hide? Onora might know. She'd had the same training. But this was the Citadel. Fisk would know best. Fisk!

"Come on!" I said. Turning around, I hurried a block south, then found the alley that led to Fisk's first headquarters. I hadn't been there in years, but I remembered the deceptive entrance. Unlike the other doors in that alley, this one only appeared if you stood in a certain location. I hoped Valek also recalled this little quirk. It took me a few minutes to find it. Being with a jittery assassin who thought we were too exposed didn't help.

Finally I popped the lock, and we entered the semidarkness. Dust motes floated in a beam of sunlight from the single window. A thick coat of dust painted the broken furniture. Cobwebs filled the corners. Empty, but another chamber was further inside. It had beds for the Helper's Guild members. Keeping my disappointment at bay, I moved deeper into the shadows.

"Yelena," Valek said behind me. It was Onora's turn to jump.

I turned and stifled a gasp. Dark smudges lined his eyes. Already sharp-featured, Valek now appeared almost skeletal. I opened my arms for a hug, but he grabbed my hands, lacing his fingers in mine instead.

"Ahh." Valek sank to the floor. "I hoped you'd find me here."

Alarmed, I knelt next to him. "What's wrong? What happened?"

"When I was checking the Council Hall with my magic, she picked up on me and latched on with her incredibly strong powers. My barrier is barely keeping her from discovering my location. Otherwise, she would have found me by now."

"Why is she chasing you?"

"Because she doesn't believe me about Bruns. I tried to explain, but Bruns has already convinced her that the Commander is planning to invade Sitia. She thinks I assassinated the Councilors, Irys and Bain, and that I'm coming for Bruns next."

I sat back on my heels. "Does she know about your magic?" That would be bad.

"No, she thinks it was only because I was so close that she was able to reach me. And that my immunity allows me to lie to her." He gave me an exhausted grin. "She and a contingent of soldiers are hunting me."

"They also set up an ambush for you," Onora said.

"I figured they would try to flush me into a trap."

"Why didn't you return to the apartment right away?" I asked. "I could have talked to her."

"I couldn't risk Bruns discovering our location."

"What about now?" Onora asked. "Can Zitora find us while you're holding Yelena's hand?"

Valek's strained face was grim. "Yes. It's just a matter of time."

"I thought the baby blocked magic," Onora said.

"The baby drains it," I said. "Are you using your magic?" I asked Valek.

"No. I stopped using mine to block her as soon as I held your hands, but the baby is siphoning her power through me. Being the second most powerful magician in Sitia, *she* can follow that drain of magic."

Which explained his exhaustion.

"Is she close?" Onora asked him.

"Yes. They're a block away and heading for the mouth of the alley."

"How many are with her?" She pulled her daggers.

MARIA V. SNYDER

"Eight. Best to ambush them. Do you have any darts with sleeping potion?"

"Yes."

"Good. Find a hiding spot in the alley. When they come, hit as many as you can."

"What if they're resistant, like the ones who were guarding my father?" I asked.

Valek cursed.

"Wait," Onora said. "We have that new draft Leif cooked up for us."

So much had happened, I'd forgotten about that. Or was it baby brain?

"Thank fate," Valek said. "Give some of them to Yelena and then get into position."

"Yes, sir." Keeping ten, Onora handed me six darts. Then she disappeared through the door.

"Yelena, do you have your blowpipe with you?" he asked.

"Always." I loved that weapon. Stolen from Bruns's armory, it had a rifling pattern on the inside to improve even my terrible aim.

"Stay here and hit anyone who comes through that door."

"And you?"

He pushed to his feet, pulling me up with him. "I'm the bait." He let go of my hands.

I clamped down on my protest. "What is she planning to do once she catches you?"

"Take me to Bruns for interrogation. I considered letting her so I could see where they're holding Fisk, but..." He rubbed his ribs, probably remembering the last time he was Bruns's prisoner and had almost been beaten to death.

"Better to get Zitora on our side first. You need to convince her, love." He sat down on the floor next to the door. If anyone entered, the open door would hide him from view.

I moved to the deepest shadow that had a clear shot to the entrance. Careful not to prick myself with the sharp tips, I laced the darts in my tunic for easy access. Then I loaded a dart into the pipe and waited. My stomach did flips—or was that the baby, energized by all the magic? Easier to blame him or her than my nerves.

After a moment, Valek said, "They're in the alley." He closed his eyes. "Onora has engaged."

A few shouts and sounds of a scuffle reached us.

"Right outside." Valek's voice strained with the effort to speak.

I raised my blowpipe and aimed. The door flew wide. Spotting the guard's neck, I puffed, then loaded another dart. People tumbled into the room. I shot at anyone I didn't recognize until I ran out of darts. However, many of the guards remained on their feet, and while I managed to hold my own with my switchblade for a minute or so, the small confines of the room limited my maneuverability. Two guards disarmed me and grabbed my arms, pinning me between them.

"Yelena! Figures I'd find you here." Zitora's tone turned deadly. "Traitor, where's that killer Valek?"

Flabbergasted by her anger and hatred, I stared at her. Words refused to move past my lips.

"Behind you." Valek pressed a knife against her throat. She didn't make a sound or move, but he tightened his grip on her and said, "Don't."

Zitora glowered at me. Finally the sleeping draft kicked in, and the men holding me swayed and collapsed. Wow. Leif hadn't been kidding when he'd said it would take longer. Onora entered and, in a few quick moves, disarmed the other two before they also succumbed to the drug.

"Is that all of them?" Valek asked Onora.

MARIA V. SNYDER

"For now. When they don't return, the others will come investigate."

"Yelena." Valek met my gaze. Lines of strain showed on his face.

Oh, right. I approached and grabbed Zitora's hand.

She cried, "You? You're the one draining my power?"

"Not me. The baby."

She glanced at my abdomen, and for the first time, I wished I had a baby bump.

"It's hard to explain, but if you stop aiming your magic at me, it won't...er...collect it. At this point, we don't really know what it's doing with the magic."

"You're not making any sense," she said.

I figured she might be distracted by the deadly weapon at her throat. "Valek, put the knife away. Why don't you and Onora go guard the door?"

"Are you sure?" he asked.

No. "Yes."

He stepped away from Zitora, and I released her hand. When she didn't move, he titled his head at Onora, and they left the building.

She crossed her arms. "My magic might not affect you, but I still can escape at any time. All I have to do is set this place on fire."

"You can, but you won't. There are innocent people living on the upper floors." Before she could respond, I held up both my hands. "Give me five minutes of your time. Please."

"And what if I don't agree with what you have to say, Traitor?"

Oh, boy. "Then you can go."

"Just like that?"

"Yes. I'm not the enemy."

She glanced at the prone forms scattered on the floor.

"Those men are asleep. Not dead."

"Fine."

Where to start? "The Councilors, Bain and Irys are not dead either. And you don't have to take my word for it. Try contacting Irys or Bain."

"How? There are no more super messengers. Your Commander had them all destroyed."

One thing about Bruns—the man was smart and a smooth liar, which Zitora should have picked up on. Unless… "Bruns wears a null shield pendant, doesn't he?"

"Of course, or you'd attack him with your Soulfinding magic."

"I can't access my power right now. The baby is blocking it." I hoped.

"That's ridiculous."

"Read my thoughts. See that I'm not lying."

She scrunched up her face as if smelling a rotten egg. "I can't."

Shoot. Valek had been able to read my thoughts a month ago. The baby's ability must be getting stronger as he or she grows. "That's the baby."

Zitora failed to appear convinced.

I tried another tactic. The truth. "Bruns has lied to you. His Cartel is planning a takeover of Sitia and is working with the Commander, who is under Owen Moon's control."

"He said you might try to twist things around. Besides, Opal never said a word about this Cartel to me."

"That's because when Opal left to help you, we didn't know the extent of their reach. They've been feeding everyone Theobroma and using magic to brainwash everyone. At least tell me you noticed the taste in the food at the Hall."

"I did, but Bruns said the new chef likes to use it as seasoning, and it's harmless in small quantities."

Bruns had an answer for everything. I needed to try yet another angle. "You don't even know Bruns. But you know me and what I've done to keep Sitia safe. Do you really think I would do anything to harm it?"

"You're married to Valek and are having his child. You could have been sent here as a spy."

She had a point. Although it'd been years since anyone had accused me of being an Ixian spy. Which reminded me of Cahil. "Do you trust General Cahil?"

"Yes."

"Talk to Cahil before you report this to Bruns. Ask him about Bruns. He'll say the man's a genius and is going to save Sitia, but use your magic and you'll sense he's lying."

"Why would he lie?"

Time to take a gigantic risk. My heart fluttered. "Because he's working with us. And you know how much Cahil hates me. So if he's helping us, that's because he understands Bruns is dangerous and must be stopped."

Her expression softened just a bit. "If you're telling the truth...am I in danger?"

"Not if Bruns thinks you still believe him. He's waiting for the Theobroma to build up in your system so he can brainwash you, too. He hasn't learned that it doesn't work on the Master Magicians. Both Irys and Bain have been playing along until we're ready to fight back." I took a deep breath to steady my voice—I'd just dug us in deeper. "If you tell Bruns what I just said, he will kill them, and you, as well as Cahil. And then it's only a matter of time before the rest of us are all dead." I rested my hand on my stomach. "When you believe me, tell Cahil. He'll get a message to us and we can arrange for you to escape."

"And if I don't believe you?"

"*That* message won't be hard to miss." I called for Valek and Onora.

They returned and we hurried into the back room. A grimy window let in enough light for us to find the exit. Fisk always ensured there was a back door in his headquarters, just in case. Once we stepped outside, I grasped their hands so it would be harder for Zitora to track us to our apartment.

"Did you convince her?" he asked.

"I don't know."

He slowed. "We need to leave the Citadel right away."

"Bruns already knows we're here. And I may have doomed us all anyway, so there will be no point in trying to leave. It will only delay the inevitable."

It was a sign of his exhaustion that he just squeezed my hand.

After a few blocks, Onora said, "I'm gonna swing by the Council Hall. If I'm not back by midafternoon tomorrow, worry. Otherwise, don't." She aimed that comment at me as she released my hand.

"Sorry, but I'm *gonna* worry anyway. Get used to it."

"Yes, sir."

"That's nice, but it would be better without the sarcasm."

She flashed a rare smile and ducked down a narrow side street. Valek and I took a winding path back to the apartment. He towed me to the bedroom.

"Is the Keep safe?" I asked, thinking I might have a couple hours to check the library.

"Yes, but I need you, love. Zitora could find me again, and I don't have any energy to block her."

He released my hand long enough to strip off his shirt and pants. The heart-shaped wound on the center of his chest had healed, but the scar hadn't faded. I traced it with a fingertip.

MARIA V. SNYDER

The mark on my chest matched his—symbols of our marriage vows.

He caught my hand and kissed my knuckles. Then he swayed with fatigue, so I pushed him down on the bed. "Sleep." I shucked off my boots and tunic before joining him. Although he pressed against my bare back, he reclaimed my hand just before falling asleep.

Onora woke us...later. Outlined by the lantern's yellow glow, Onora stood at the threshold. Valek was already sitting up and clutching a knife—where did that come from? Darkness streaked with lamplight flickered against the windows. My stomach roared with hunger. We must have slept for hours.

"I've news," Onora said a bit awkwardly.

"We'll be out," Valek said.

She nodded and closed the door. We disentangled, reaching for clothes. Once we were dressed, Valek claimed my hand as we joined Onora in the living area.

She sat in one of the armchairs with her bare feet propped up on the table. I wondered what she'd been climbing—the walls of the Council Hall were too slick. Valek and I sat on the couch opposite her.

"Report," he said.

"It was pretty quiet at the Hall," she said. "If Zitora had informed Bruns about us, there would have been lots more commotion."

So far so good. "Fisk?" I asked.

"Down in the cells, with layers of security around him." She flexed her fingers as if stretching the joints. "I didn't know you'd taught him the hand signals."

Valek tensed next to me. "You talked to him?"

"Yup. I scared the crap out of him. Poor kid."

"Is he...healthy?" I asked, bracing myself for the answer.

"Yes. He was mostly pissed off and upset about being caught, but when I explained you were safe for now, that calmed him down. He says he's sorry that Bruns knows everything."

Poor kid, indeed. The desire to hug and comfort him pulsed through my chest.

"Have they been feeding him Theobroma?" Valek asked.

"No, but they used magic to extract all the information from his mind."

Oh, no. That was a horrible experience. Now tears threatened, and Valek rubbed his thumb on my hand.

"Can you free him?" Valek asked.

Onora pursed her lips in thought. "If there was a major distraction in the Hall, I could rescue him from the cells. Not sure if we'd escape the Hall, though."

I tightened my grip on Valek's hand.

He squeezed back. "What about Bruns? Did you see him or Cahil?"

"I did a sweep and found where he set up his office. He's staying in one of the guest suites on the third floor. Cahil wasn't around."

"Are there layers of security around him, as well?"

"Yes. Not as many, but I think a few are magicians. I recognized Cilly Cloud Mist." She frowned, probably remembering when Cilly tried to erase her memory.

No surprise Bruns was keeping Cilly close.

"Can you reach Bruns?" Valek asked.

Onora sat up, setting her feet on the floor with a thump. "You mean...?"

"Yes. Assassinate the bastard."

Her already pale face whitened as she pressed her arms on her lap. "I..." Onora stared out the window.

When she didn't say anything, Valek asked, "Could I reach him?"

"No. You'd never get inside the Hall without blending in. But if he leaves…"

"I'd rather we target him while he's asleep. That would give us more time to get away. And I doubt he'll venture outside knowing I'm in the Citadel. Ideally, we'd kill him at the same time we make our move in the hot season, but this might be our only chance to reach him. You'll have to do the honors."

She dragged her gaze to him. "I…"

"Never killed anyone?" he asked, but it sounded more like a statement than a question.

"Yes."

20

VALEK

Onora confirmed what he'd suspected for a while now. She'd never assassinated anyone. Talk about bad timing for this revelation.

"How can you call yourself an assassin, then?" Yelena asked in surprise.

"I have all the training and skills. I just haven't...couldn't... can't..."

Yelena reached over and grabbed the girl's hand. "That's not a weakness. That's a strength."

Onora gave her a grateful smile.

"What about with the Commander?" Valek asked. "Do you hide your full fighting abilities like you have with me?"

"No. But like you, he stopped me by doing something unexpectedly desperate. And I was glad, because I already knew I couldn't finish him."

That explained why the Commander had been so freaked. She'd gotten closer than Valek, and it had terrified him. "What about now?"

She quirked her lips in an ironic half smile. "We've sparred a few times, and I've identified his weakness."

So had Valek, or so he'd thought. Ambrose liked to dangle

the bait and see if you'd bite. But if he'd been forced to do something desperate, then maybe she truly could beat him. Not like any of this helped them now. He considered their meager options.

Rescue Fisk, or assassinate Bruns. There was no way they could do both. Either would bring instant attention to them. Plus there was Zitora to consider. She could expose everything. A bone-deep ache of exhaustion throbbed through him. He hadn't had nearly enough sleep.

"Now what?" Yelena asked.

"Tomorrow we'll go to the Keep's library and touch base with Cahil. After that…" He shrugged.

"We rescue Fisk," Yelena said in a tone that dared anyone to argue with her.

He glanced at her. "You have a plan?"

"Onora said she needed a distraction. So we're going to provide one for her."

"Go big or go home?"

"No."

"No?" he asked.

"Go big *and* go home."

They woke late the next morning. Onora returned from her mission while they ate breakfast.

"How did it go?" Yelena asked.

"After I did a reconnaissance of the Hall, I met with the Helper's Guild and explained our plans to them." She huffed in amusement. "Bets are already being made. We're not favored to win, but I put a silver coin on us."

"Only silver?" Yelena raised an eyebrow.

"No need to break the bank."

Yelena laughed. "As Janco would say, 'Gotta love the confidence.'"

Onora smiled, but it failed to reach her eyes. Valek wondered if she worried about Janco's reaction to her not being quite the Little Miss Assassin he'd always believed her to be. It hadn't changed Valek's opinion of her. She hadn't lied. Everyone had just assumed and never asked her directly. Killing a person was not easy in any situation. Some people couldn't do it even to save their own lives. Valek, on the other hand, recognized the need to eliminate certain people to ensure the safety of others, but he'd never done it lightly or for no reason. Which was why he had no regrets.

Focusing on the problem at hand, Valek asked Onora if she'd talked to Phelan.

"Yes. The General visited his headquarters late last night. He might be there again tonight."

"Good. Any signs of trouble?"

"None so far, but Bruns might be biding his time, hoping to draw us out."

In that case, Bruns would succeed.

When they finished eating, Valek escorted Yelena to the Keep, despite her protests that he was being overprotective.

He was, but this time he had a legitimate reason to tag along. "While you're checking the library, I'll search Bain's office. He might have had the same idea as us, and since he's the First Magician, the library might have allowed him to borrow Master Magician Ellis Moon's notes."

"That's a good idea."

"Don't sound so surprised, love. I might start to think you're only interested in me for my body."

"Did you say something? I was too busy staring at your muscular chest."

"Nice."

They crossed the tunnel into the Keep without trouble. Yelena clutched her hands together while she scanned the

MARIA V. SNYDER

empty campus. Valek squeezed her shoulder in support before she headed to the library. Without her touch, he needed to reinforce his mental barrier. Zitora might not be searching for him, but he wasn't going to risk opening his mind at this point.

He looped around to the back entrance of the administration building that housed the Master Magician's offices, along with the Keep's clerical staff. Valek ghosted down the hallway to Bain's office. Halfway there, a muffled cry sounded. Drawing his knives, he paused to listen. A bang and a thud echoed. Valek tracked the noise to Irys's office. The door stood ajar. He peered inside and cursed his rotten luck.

Zitora faced the back wall, but before he could retreat, she said, "I know you're there. I shouldn't, because of your immunity." She turned. "But you're no longer immune. Are you?"

"No." Valek eased into the room.

She held up a hand. "Stop right there."

He did as instructed and slid his daggers back into their pockets. They wouldn't help him in this situation. Nothing would. Her power could rip through his barrier like tissue paper. The only reason she hadn't done it before was because he'd surprised her. Now she'd had time to think about it.

"You have magic. How did it happen?" she asked.

No sense lying. His and Yelena's future rested in what happened next. "I made peace with my brothers' murders. Seems that released the null shield I'd unknowingly grafted onto my soul when I'd witnessed their murders. Once the shield was gone, my magical powers were freed." That was Yelena's theory, and the timing confirmed it.

"Did you come here to kill me?" she asked.

"Do you think I can?"

"No. You're strong, but not as strong as me."

"Then why are you worried?"

"I wouldn't call it worry. More like curiosity. Indulge me."

"You have nothing to fear. You fall under the category of a Sitian who has been duped or brainwashed, and therefore are not to be killed or harmed if possible. Yelena's orders."

"Then what are you doing here?"

"Investigating. I hope Bain has some information to help us counter the Cartel." He was growing tired of her suspicion. "Have you talked to Cahil yet?"

"No. We haven't been able to talk privately. In fact, unless I'm in my room, I'm never alone. That magician, Cilly, is always hovering nearby. Bruns says it's for my protection from you." She frowned. "She's tested my defenses a number of times, trying to get a sense of my loyalties. Don't worry, she doesn't have the power to get through. And I haven't told Bruns what Yelena said or that she's here."

One good thing. "You're alone now."

"Master Magician, remember? I'm done with being *protected*."

He approved. "This is a good place to hide."

"I'm not hiding." Zitora hooked her thumb toward the wall behind her. She stood in front of a large safe. The painting that had covered it rested on the floor. "Can you open it?"

Janco was the expert, but Valek had some experience. "Maybe. It depends on the model."

"Will you open it for me?"

Ah, there was the right question. "If I can."

She stepped aside. Moving slowly so he didn't startle her, he crossed the room. He inspected the safe. Made of thick steel and with a complex lock, it would be difficult to crack. He spun the cylinder, feeling for that subtle vibration. It took him multiple tries, but finally the door opened.

He backed away. "What are you looking for?"

She dug into the contents, pulling various things out and

MARIA V. SNYDER

setting them onto Irys's desk. "Ahh." Zitora removed a glass super messenger. "I thought she'd have one in case of an emergency."

Smart. "Now you can contact Bain and confirm our story."

"That's the idea." Yet she hesitated.

She still didn't trust him.

"I'm going to Bain's now. If you have time, ask him if he has any of Master Magician's Ellis Moon's papers." He left.

Bain's office was only a few doors down from Irys's. Unlike Irys's neat organization, a mess sprawled on every surface. Valek would have thought someone had searched the place if he hadn't known Bain so well. The most powerful magician in the world loved researching little-known historical details when he had time. But as a member of the Sitian Council, he rarely had time.

Valek started with his desk and scanned the various piles of parchment. He found a list of missing magicians, and Valek wondered how many of them remained alive. Then he remembered Fisk had helped hide a few, which meant Bruns likely knew their locations. The desk drawers were crammed with...well, everything. Valek slid them shut without digging deeper. If Bain had gotten the notes, they would be on top somewhere. He strode over to the table. Flipping through the files, he searched for anything that appeared old.

"They're in Bain's tower," Zitora said.

Valek spun around.

She cradled the messenger like a baby. Her eyes shone with unshed tears. "They're both alive!"

A relief. While the intel on the status of both the masters was fairly recent, there had been no guarantee that they remained alive.

"You were right," she said. "I'm so sor—"

"Don't apologize. Otherwise I'd have to apologize for not

getting to the Citadel in time to stop you from entering in the first place, and a whole list of other transgressions."

She laughed. It was a light, sweet sound.

Bain's tower was located in the northeast corner of the Keep. As they trudged up four flights of stairs to the living quarters, he asked Zitora what she'd told Bruns about the chase.

"I told him I'd lost you. That it was pure luck that I'd sensed you in the first place. He has watchers stationed all around the Citadel now, but they aren't aware that you're wearing a disguise."

Good to know, especially considering their plans for tomorrow night. They retrieved the thick file of Ellis's notes from Bain's night table. Then they crossed the campus to the Keep's library.

Yelena sat at a table in the middle of the reading room. Sunlight streamed in from the skylight above, illuminating the open book before her. Two piles of tomes were stacked on both sides of her.

She glanced up when they entered and shot to her feet. "What—"

"Relax," he said. "She contacted Bain."

She blew out a breath. "How?"

He filled her in, then pointed to her book. "What are you reading?"

"When I didn't find Ellis's journals, I pulled books that mentioned plants, hoping to find a reference to the Harman trees." She swept her hand over the piles to her left. "Nothing so far."

"Keep looking while I read through the journals." He placed the file on the table. They were safer here than in the apartment. Valek turned to Zitora. "You can stay in the Keep until the big rescue. We're going—"

"I'm not leaving."

"Why not?" Yelena asked.

"I'm going to stay with Bruns and play along, like Bain and Irys. I'll be in the perfect position to help you when you stop the Cartel."

Such confidence.

"How will we contact you?" Valek asked.

"Here." She gave him the super messenger.

Magic pulsed inside, and the vibrations traveled up his arm.

"You can contact us all," she said.

"I don't—"

"It's not hard to use. I can teach you." She took back the glass cube. "Let down your mental barrier and reach out to me with your magic."

He did as instructed. At first, he hit a solid brick wall. *Zitora?* he thought.

An opening appeared. *Welcome to my mind,* she thought. *Sorry about the mess. I've had an interesting couple of days.*

Same here.

She smiled. *All right, now you know how to knock on another magician's shield. Now I want you to reach out to Irys and tell me when you've hit your limit.*

He sent his awareness to the northeast, toward Irys in the Featherstone garrison. A few people traveled on the road outside the Citadel. Then he picked up on the thoughts of those living in Owl's Hill before he was unable to go farther—although he was shocked he had managed to even reach that far. *I'm at the end.*

Zitora placed the messenger in his hands. *Use the magic inside to propel you further.*

It was like a concentrated piece of the power blanket. As the extra magic infused him, he flew over the miles, seeking Irys. Then he slammed into a stone barrier. Dazed, he needed a moment to collect his wits before knocking. *Irys?*

Valek? What are you *doing here?*

Long story, but I can access the power blanket now, and Zitora's teaching me how to use your super messenger.

A pause. *Ah, good. Contact me again when I'm needed. Remember those messengers have a limited amount of magic. Once used up, it can only be recharged by Quinn.*

How can I tell how much has been used?

I could send a dozen messages before it's depleted. Since you aren't as strong, it would be less for you. Maybe eight total.

He calculated. It'd been used three times—twice by Zitora, who was stronger than Irys. *Six left?*

Yes. That's probably right. Good luck. Give Yelena my love.

He retreated, returning to the Keep's library. Not that he'd ever left. Odd. Both Yelena and Zitora stared at him expectantly.

"Irys sends her love," he said.

They both grinned.

Yelena gestured to the messenger. "That's a game-changer for our side. I told you your magic would come in handy."

"Yes, love, you were right."

Zitora slapped him on the back. "If you keep using those words, you're going to have a long, happy marriage." Then she sobered. "I'd better head back before Bruns gets too suspicious. Good luck with the big breakout." She turned, then stopped. "Oh, I almost forgot." She pulled a locked wooden box from her pocket. It was about six inches long and two inches wide. Zitora handed it to Yelena. "Give this to Opal when you see her."

"What is it?" Yelena asked.

"Opal will know what to do with it."

They spent the rest of the daylight hours reading. Valek quickly realized that his knowledge of magic and all things magical was rather limited, despite his years countering it, so they swapped tasks. Now he scanned pages of text and botanical drawings, seeking any sign of the Harman tree.

At one point, Yelena glanced up and said, "Ellis was a genius, but he had a warped way of thinking. Now I know where Owen Moon gets his crazy ideas. Owen must have read through these when he was a student at the Keep." She tapped a page with her fingernail. "Ellis believed that only the very strong and master-level magicians should be able to keep their powers. He thought all the others were just a danger to themselves and others. He wanted to start a magicians' guild to keep track of everyone."

"That sounds like Bruns's philosophy." And Bruns was close to Owen's age. "I wonder if Owen and Bruns knew each other before—" A thought popped into his head. While the Commander had financed most of Owen's glass hothouses in order for the man to produce Curare, Owen would have needed funds prior to that endeavor. Money to pay for his failed effort to recover the Ice Moon from the Commander. Had Owen and Bruns been planning this takeover all along?

"Before?" Yelena prompted.

He explained his theory. "The Ice Moon would have accomplished their goal of limiting who has access to magic." Once activated, the huge blue diamond could have stored the entire power blanket within its depths. But that would be too much power for one person to wield, so the Master Magicians sent the Ice Moon to the Commander for safekeeping. Believing it was a dangerous weapon, he had sliced it into thin sheets and incorporated them into the stained glass windows of his war room. Had he known what it had been capable of, the Commander might have been tempted to use it. He'd never trusted magicians and would have been happy to strip them of their powers.

Yelena fingered the edges of a book as her forehead crinkled in thought. "When the attempt to retrieve the Ice Moon failed, they came up with a plan B to control the magicians."

"For now. The Theobroma is just a short-term solution. Eventually they will need to weed out the magicians who are not dedicated to their cause."

"By killing them all?" she asked with a horrified tone.

"I doubt they would risk upsetting Sitians with such an extreme action. They need another way to neutralize them."

"Like me?"

He considered. "If they had succeeded in blocking your magic, I'd think they would have used that substance on the other magicians by now. Perhaps they're experimenting with null shields. They can be attached to objects. Maybe they found a way to inject a shield into a person's body or bloodstream."

Color leaked from her face. "Do you really think...?"

"I've no idea if it's possible. But I'm pretty certain they're working on something. Bruns and Owen want control of who keeps their powers and who doesn't. Since the magicians are all in Sitia, the Cartel must be leading the efforts. Maybe the answer is in Ellis Moon's notes."

They kept working.

Yelena finished before Valek. "Is this everything you found?"

"Yes. Why?"

She pushed the file away. "It's missing a few journals. Ellis mentions experimenting with various substances, but he keeps referring to a lab book for more details."

"It might have been passed down through the family. Owen is Ellis's great-great-grandson."

"Or it could be shelved under a different topic."

They searched through the rows and rows of bookshelves

for the lab notes but found nothing. Then Yelena helped him look through the rest of the botany books that she had collected earlier. Nothing. And the last of the light was fading. He hefted half the stack to return to the shelves while Yelena grabbed the rest. They all belonged in the same section of the library. When he slid in the last volume, another book title caught his eye. *Ixian Horticulture.* The image of the trees in the castle flashed. Could it be?

He grabbed it and brought it to the brightest spot in the library. Yelena followed him and leaned over his shoulder as he flipped through the pages. Unlike all the other books, he recognized many of the plants and trees. Funny how he'd never known most of their names.

Valek paused at a drawing of a familiar circular leaf.

"The Cheeko tree," Yelena said with a laugh. "The leaves are good for camouflage. Remember?"

"That is one of my favorite memories." When they'd first met, he'd suspected she was intelligent, but when she had glued them onto her bright red uniform in order to blend in with the forest, it confirmed his assessment. Plus she'd looked adorable, even with mud on her face and her hair covered with leaves.

Valek continued to turn pages, scanning each one as the light dimmed.

"There!" Yelena stabbed a page with her finger.

Excitement pulsed as he spotted the Harman tree with its distinctive leaves. He read through the description, but it focused on planting the tree for shade and listed the ideal growing conditions.

"Why can't anything be easy?" he asked.

"Were you hoping for a footnote that tells us why Owen is so interested in it?"

"Yes."

She patted his shoulder. "At least we know it's grown in

Ixia. That's more than a few minutes ago. And maybe there's something here that my father will find useful."

He gripped the page to rip it free from the book.

Yelena stopped his hand. "The library won't like that."

Since so many student magicians had spent long hours in here researching over many years' time, magic had infused every inch of this place—the library was very protective of the books.

"Will it let us take the book?"

"I don't know."

Feeling silly, he addressed the walls. "This book might help us solve a problem, and if we do, then the students will return and study here again."

Yelena covered her mouth with a hand and her eyes shone, but she didn't laugh.

"Come on," he said, tucking the book under his arm. "We need to check in with Onora."

They left the building without any shelves crashing down on them—a good sign. Crossing under the Keep's wall, they ascended and slipped into the alley. No one appeared to notice as they joined the flow of day shift workers hurrying home. The streets buzzed with conversation. The sun had just set, leaving behind a flat gray twilight that would soon turn black. Valek held Yelena's hand, keeping her close. Zitora had warned that watchers sought him. They would be on the lookout for a lone man versus a couple. He hoped.

They talked on the way back. Yelena said she was craving sweet cakes.

"You're always in the mood for sweet cakes, love."

"But this time it's because of the baby." She told him about Onora's aunt.

"Anything else you plan to blame on the baby?" he teased.

"Actually..." Yelena explained about baby brain. "So it

MARIA V. SNYDER

wasn't my fault that I forgot about my disguise when I was going to drink from the Unity Fountain's water spout."

"It was due to baby brain?"

"Exactly!"

He laughed. "I thought I'd heard every excuse possible, but that's a new one."

She glared at him. Oops.

"However, since I have *very* limited experience with pregnant women, I'll defer to your expertise in these matters from now on." He brought their clasped hands up and kissed her knuckles.

"Was that an apology? Am I supposed to swoon now?"

"Yes it was. And I believe swooning is required. Don't worry, I will catch you."

"Men," she muttered, shaking her head.

Onora waited for them in the apartment. She had purchased supplies for the rescue and bought half a dozen meat pies. Yelena groaned in pleasure as she devoured the warm, spicy beef. So much for sweet cakes. Onora and Valek shared an amused glance.

"Everything should be good to go," Onora said after they finished eating. "However, the timing of your distraction is going to be crucial. So far, most of the activity in the Council Hall occurs in the late afternoon, when everyone is leaving for the day."

"When do the guards change shifts?"

"About an hour before."

Smart. They'd still be alert during the afternoon rush. "What about the mornings? When do the guards switch?"

"An hour before dawn. But I can't get in until there's activity. Unless I go in the afternoon before."

"No need. We'll stage the distraction in the middle of the

rush. But if Yelena doesn't get in, abort the rescue. The rest of the plan will remain the same."

"Yes, sir."

"I'll get in," Yelena said with confidence.

And that was half the battle. Most often, if you acted like you belonged, no one questioned you. However, the magician at the door would be their biggest obstacle. They were already on high alert for Valek, so Yelena was their best bet. But that didn't stop the anxiety from gnawing on his stomach. His ability to shut down all his emotions has been shot to hell since he lost his immunity. Or had it been since Yelena confirmed her pregnancy?

Phelan arrived with a few more supplies and an update. "General Cahil's in his headquarters."

They reviewed the plan with Phelen before Yelena and Valek left to visit Cahil. His headquarters was located in a warehouse that was no longer in use to store goods. Instead, the large piles of crates served as obstacles for anyone trying to sneak in. Cahil had converted the basement into an office space for his crew of loyal people. Similar to Valek's corps, but on a much smaller scale.

The guards at the entrance allowed them to pass, but their sour expressions deepened. Yelena led the way through the crates to the stairway. Cahil was hunched over a table in his office, discussing tactics with two of his men. He scowled when they entered, but he ended the meeting.

Cahil closed the door and turned around. "You do realize every soldier in the Citadel is hunting for you. Right?"

"Do they suspect Yelena is here, as well?"

"No. Master Zitora said she scanned the entire Citadel and didn't sense her." He glanced at Yelena. "Are you using a null shield pendant? Because she fell hard for Bruns's lies and is looking for blood. At least there is no need to worry she'll expose the other Masters."

Valek decided not to enlighten Cahil about Zitora. Not just yet. "Why did Bruns summon you here?"

"To escort Master Zitora to the Moon garrison. He wants her trained and ready. Bruns is certain the Commander will invade right after the Ixian fire festival."

"We know that's a sham. What happens when his soldiers don't show?" Yelena asked.

"I don't know. He's making plans for all the northern garrisons to march to the Ixian border and be in position by midseason. He's transferred Master Bain to Krystal so each garrison has a Master Magician in the lead, and all our magicians will be accompanying our army."

Valek kept his expression neutral, but his mind whirled. They had guessed wrong. The Commander's forces would invade, and there would be a battle. There would be casualties on both sides. In the chaos of the battle, no one would realize who had specifically targeted the magicians to neutralize them, but they would all know who to blame.

The Commander.

21

JANCO

Janco sensed the ambush before he reached the edge of the Avibian Plains. Which was kind of amazing, considering the house wasn't even in sight. He'd left Ari and a very reluctant Opal behind so he could scout the premises. Smart move. As he crept from the tall grasses, he counted at least four crouched figures in the dim moonlight.

With Opal's horse setting a break-neck pace—he now understood why they called it break-neck, 'cause if you fell off at that speed, you'd break your neck for sure—they'd arrived at Opal's parents' place in just four days.

Once this was over, he planned to sleep for a week.

Janco looped around the house and, sure enough, ambushers covered all the doors and windows. Twelve total. Shoot. Too many for them to fight. And he doubted he could fetch his partner and Opal in time. It appeared things were about to go down. The air felt...unsettled. Then he remembered. A Stormdancer might be sleeping inside. If he could wake—

The gate squealed. The noise sliced through the heavy silence like a sharp blade through flesh and had the same effect. The figures whipped around to advance on the poor sod.

Janco cursed. What the hell were Devlen and Reema doing here now?

No matter. Janco straightened from his crouch and drew his sword. A high-pitched wail sounded, followed by a whoosh. One after the other, the ambushers were slammed to the ground. And for once, Janco wasn't exaggerating—an invisible force had literally picked them up and slammed each one into the ground so hard that they didn't get back up.

A smaller figure darted from the shadows of the stable and launched at Devlen. The big man caught him in midair and hugged him. Ah, sweet. Janco sheathed his sword. Another person also materialized from the shadows, but she moved at a much slower pace. After that display of power, Janco was surprised Heli still had the energy to stand.

All four of them whirled around when he approached. A knife flashed in Reema's hand. Nice.

"It's me. Janco." He spread his hands wide.

Teegan peered at him, but his forehead creased with suspicion. "Null shield. That's why I didn't sense him. Can you take it off?"

About to ask why, he answered his own question. He could have been brainwashed by the Cartel and turned into a spy. Janco pulled the pendant off. "Hope you're not too traumatized by my thoughts." A prickly, unpleasant sensation invaded his mind as his ear tweaked with pain. It disappeared just as fast.

Teegan grinned. "Tell my mom we'll be joining you in the plains as soon as we pack up."

Good. "Are Zohav and—"

"We're here," Zethan said. "Just enjoying the show. Since Heli hogged all the fun."

"Next time you can do the honors," Heli said in a tired voice.

"Sweet."

Zohav frowned.

"Don't worry, Zo," her brother said. "I'll let you in on the action."

Which just caused her expression to deepen. But Zethan laughed, clearly not discouraged by her reaction. Janco approved. The boy had potential.

While they gathered their things and saddled the horses, Janco returned to Ari and Opal.

"Well?" Opal asked immediately.

"Relax, Mama Bunny, your family is safe. They'll be here soon."

"Here? What happened?"

He explained how Heli had stopped the ambush. "...that air blast of hers was a thing of beauty. If I was the Cartel, I'd be shaking in my boots right now."

"It's better if they underestimate us," Ari said. "And don't you mean Mama *Bear*?"

"Nah, female bears got nothin' on bunnies when it comes to protecting their young. I once saw this—"

"I should have known better than to ask." Ari walked away.

"Do you want to hear my story?" Janco asked Opal.

"No."

"Fine. But the next time you get bitten by an overprotective mama rabbit, don't come crying to me." He pouted, but no one paid any attention to him, so he checked The Madam's legs for hot spots. After all that hard riding, he hoped to give her a couple days' rest, but they would need to travel further into the plains to avoid the Cartel's next attempt. 'Cause they certainly weren't going to stop, and it appeared that they'd upped the stakes.

He grinned. *We scare them.*

Within the hour, a group of nine people and four horses

MARIA V. SNYDER

trudged into view. Opal whooped and raced to meet them. She scooped up her kids and hugged them both to her as if they weighed nothing. Devlen wrapped his arms around them. A hollow pang of longing ricocheted in Janco's equally hollow chest, surprising him. He'd never considered settling down before. All this drama with the Cartel was getting to him. Pah. Janco looked away.

Ari interrupted the family reunion. They needed to put a few miles between them and Booruby.

"Where are we going?" Opal's dad asked.

"South. We'll find a medium-size town where you can stay," Ari said.

They had a total of twelve people and seven horses, so most had to double up. Janco shared The Madam's saddle with Opal's father. Ahir joined Teegan on Caramel. Opal rode with her mother on Quartz, the twins shared Smoke, and Devlen and Reema stayed on Sunfire. Ari and Heli each rode alone, but Whiskey and Thunder carried additional bags.

Quite the posse. With all the extra weight and baggage, they moved slower than Janco's grandmother—and he'd seen snails lap her.

Traveling through the plains as long as possible, they stopped near the Daviian Plateau's border to make camp. There were still a few hours until sunset, but everyone drooped with fatigue. While they made camp, Janco hunted for a few rabbits. The fresh meat would help revive everyone. When he returned, Opal's mother took the skinned rabbits and turned them into the best campfire meal he'd ever eaten.

Zethan brandished a forkful of meat. "This is why I gained ten pounds in the last week. Ahir, it's a wonder you don't weigh five hundred pounds."

"I sweat it all off in the factory." Ahir glanced at his dad. "Did you warn our employees about the Cartel?"

"No. I just left a note for my assistant saying we had a family emergency. She'll take care of filling orders while we're gone," Jaymes said.

"Uh, what about the ambushers lying on the ground?" Janco asked. "They're not going to be happy when they wake up." Considering how hard they'd hit, they might still be out cold.

Teegan grinned. "No worries. We cleaned up the mess."

"How— No, never mind," Opal said. "I don't need to know. I'm just glad we're all together and safe." She put her arm around Reema, who leaned into her.

Which reminded Janco. "Devlen, did something happen to Leif and Mara? You should have dropped Reema off a while ago."

"They reached the Illiais Market without any trouble. Reema stayed with us because..." He glanced at Opal.

Janco straightened. This ought to be interesting.

"I'm good at spotting places to avoid," Reema said.

"What do you mean?" Ari asked.

She shrugged. "We didn't want to draw attention. And I know where to travel so we didn't get noticed." Then she crossed her arms. "Which is why we should have stayed with Uncle Leif and not wasted time coming up here. You're gonna need me."

Devlen ignored that comment. "Once the others continued into the jungle, we returned to Booruby. I wanted to arrive before dawn, just in case there were watchers on the house."

"I was asleep, or else I would have warned him about the ambush," Reema said. Then she beamed at her brother. "But Tee took care of it!"

"Heli did all the work," Teegan said. "I just directed traffic."

Janco glanced at Heli, but the poor girl was curled up, fast

MARIA V. SNYDER

asleep. It wasn't long before the other kids joined her. Ari, Janco, Opal and Devlen took shifts guarding the camp.

Two days later, they entered the town limits of Kerrylee. It was smaller than desired and hugged the western edge of the Daviian Plateau. But according to Reema, the place had no watchers working for the Cartel. How the girl knew this, Janco hadn't a clue, but he'd learned to trust the little scamp. They found a nice inn for Opal's parents and brother to stay at, and for the rest of them to spend the night. Devlen and Opal were having a family discussion about Reema's future.

Janco caught a few words as he passed their room on the way down to the common room. He smiled as Opal kept repeating, "She's only eleven," with Devlen reminding his wife how Reema had aided in his and Leif's rescue. Should be an interesting conversation, but Janco wasn't about to listen at the door. No need to spy on his friends.

The warmth and bright lights of the common room wrapped around him like an embrace. He scanned the occupants. Banished from the discussion upstairs, Reema played cards with Teegan, Zethan and Heli, but she shot dark looks at the stairs, as if her unhappiness could travel up to her parents' room. Ari sat nearby, drinking ale. Janco joined him and ordered a pint.

When the drink arrived, he took a long pull. It wasn't half-bad.

"What do you think?" Ari asked him.

"It's a little sour, but I like the lemony flavors."

"Not the ale. Our next move."

Oh. He scratched his ear. "I think the others will be safe traveling to the Illiais Market without us."

"You think they'll take Reema with them?"

"They'd be stupid not to."

"Thank you," Reema said.

"Hey, it's rude to eavesdrop on people's conversations," Janco said.

"Oh, sorry. I wouldn't want to be *rude*. Is it rude to talk about someone when she's sitting right here?"

Janco opened his mouth to reply, but Ari shook his head. Instead, they moved a few more tables away. However, due to her sly smile, Janco suspected the scamp had rabbit ears.

"I agree that there will be enough people and magicians to spread the spores," Ari said. "We can leave for the Green-blade garrison tomorrow. I want to gather as much intel about the place as possible before we rescue the Councilors. Do you think Opal will let Teegan come with us?"

"Do you think Teegan will listen to his mother if she says no?"

"Some kids actually listen to their mothers."

"Really?" Janco blinked at Ari. "What a concept."

"Your poor mother. She should get a medal for not killing you."

"Oh, she tried. Many times. That's how I learned the fine art of duck and cover."

Devlen and Opal joined them four ales later. From the shine in Opal's eyes, he guessed they'd done more than discuss their daughter. Understandable, considering they'd been apart for months. Reema showed remarkable restraint by not pouncing on her parents right away. It also helped that the scamp was soundly beating her brother at cards. Good. It would keep the boy humble.

Ari told Opal and Devlen their plans and asked them about Teegan. "I think you'll have enough protection. Plus a bigger group of people will draw more attention."

"I agree," Opal said. She glanced at her children. "As much as I want to keep them safe from harm, I know we won't be safe until this is over. Teegan can decide."

"What about Reema?" Janco asked.

"She coming with us."

"Woo-hoo!" Reema said. When they all looked over at her, she slapped a card down. "I win!"

Smooth recovery. Janco'd been right. Rabbit ears.

Teegan chose to accompany Ari and Janco. They picked a rendezvous location near the Greenblade garrison.

"When you're done spreading the spores, meet us there," Ari said. "I think Yelena and Valek are planning the big counterattack to commence during the first month of the hot season."

"And if they don't escape the Citadel?" Janco asked.

"Then we'll implement the other counterattack."

"Oh, the *other* attack. I feel so much better now."

The next morning, as they were saying goodbye and eliciting promises to be careful, Heli pulled Janco aside.

"You're going to rescue the Councilors?" she asked.

"We're going to try."

"I have something that might help you. Come on."

Surprised, he followed her. She opened her bulging saddle bag. He had wondered what she'd packed in there. Heli pulled out a wrapped bundle and handed it to Janco. It was shaped like a small watermelon and about as heavy.

"What's in here?"

"A glass orb. Be careful. It's filled. And you do *not* want it to break."

Confused and alarmed, he asked, "You mean there's a storm inside it?"

"Not quite. The energy from a storm is trapped inside. And if you shatter the orb on…let's say, the garrison's wall…the energy released will bring that wall crashing down."

"Holy snow cats! That's…" Janco couldn't find the proper words for just how awesome it was.

"I couldn't carry more than two, but Kade and Zethan have filled lots of extras. They're storing them at The Cliffs. Just make sure you're a safe distance away before you use them. Maybe they'll come in handy for the big counterattack." She grinned.

"Sweetheart, there's no *maybe* about it."

MARIA V. SNYDER

22

YELENA

I paused halfway up the steps to the Council Hall. Leaning slightly forward, I pretended to huff from the effort of the climb, resting a hand on my huge fake belly. My five "children" bounced up the stairs. Then, when they realized "mom" wasn't keeping up, they hopped back down. The two oldest supported me as I waddled up to the landing.

"Thanks, ducklings." I patted my "sons" on their shoulders.

The guards at the entrance watched us with amusement. I kept my thoughts on the task at hand, suppressing the doubts and million worries about what could go wrong deep into my subconscious. Free Fisk first. Then I'd fret over the next task.

There were a few other people entering the building, and I followed them with my children in tow. "Sir, can you direct me to where I obtain permission to leave the Citadel?" I asked one of them.

"Second floor. Can't miss it. There's a line."

"Thank you." Out of the corner of my eye, I spotted the magician turning her attention to me. I signaled my children. They started bickering and it escalated into fighting. Then they knocked into the magician as they wrestled. I swooped in and scolded them, apologized and made them say they were sorry before we all trundled off.

As I waddled, I kept expecting her to call after me or sound the alarm, but nothing happened. The stairs to the upper floors were visible from the open lobby. According to Onora, the queue for the permits stayed long all day, and it trailed down the steps. I joined the line with a sigh, rubbing my lower back. My ducklings pretended to get bored and wandered off. The magician at the entrance scanned the people exiting and didn't appear to be interested in me.

Onora had left the safe house earlier this afternoon. I assumed she'd entered without trouble. Now it was just a matter of waiting for the signal. I rubbed my back with a little groan.

"Maybe you should sit down, dear," the lady next to me said.

"It's worse when I sit. This duck is just being difficult." I patted my stomach.

She nodded knowingly. "I had one like that. Are you due soon?"

"Not for a week, at least."

"Not a good time to travel."

"Oh, no, I'm not leaving yet. Once the new duck is born, I'm going to visit my mother. Let her wrangle the others while I rest."

"That's a good idea."

We stood in companionable silence as the line inched along. I scanned the flow of people crossing the lobby and using the other set of stairs. Valek's theory about Bruns's plans to target all the magicians tried to sabotage my thoughts. We needed to stop that battle and find a way to protect them. How we would accomplish this monumental task had so far failed to materialize.

Instead of worrying about it, I switched my concern to

MARIA V. SNYDER

Valek. His part of the plan was just as dangerous as ours, but he'd downplayed it with his usual bravado. Then, out of the corner of my eye, I spotted Onora on the far end of the lobby. She nodded at me—our agreed-upon signal—before disappearing.

"Oh, my!" I clutched my bulging stomach.

"Is it the baby, dear?" the lady asked, her voice shrill with alarm.

"It's just a cramp—oooohhh! I'd better…" I waddled down the stairs. "Ducks, come on, we're—aaaahhh!"

The kids joined me in the middle of the lobby, which had grown quiet. Everyone stared at the pregnant lady making noises. Good. I took a few steps toward the exit. "We need to get ho—oooohhh, no!" I gasped, stopping and bending over as if in extreme pain. "The baby is coming!" Squeezing my stomach, I ruptured the seal on the water skin that was hidden under my tunic. Except it wasn't water that splashed onto the floor.

The people closest to me jumped back, but the guards at the door stepped forward to render aid. However, it was the guards streaming up from the cells under the building that scared me.

"Now!" I covered my nose and mouth with a cloth just as my ducklings threw small glass spheres onto the liquid. They shattered on impact.

An angry fog hissed and spread. My kids swarmed out of the way of its gray tentacles, making a beeline for the exit. Breathing shallowly through the fabric, I remained in place as the people around me stumbled to the ground. Then I, too, bolted for the door.

Outside, the kids had already disappeared. Kiki waited at the bottom of the steps. I mounted, and she took off for the Citadel's gate, weaving through the government quarter. Once we were safe, she slowed so I could remove the deflated water skin and allow the others to catch up.

Time for part two. We rendezvoused with Onyx and the guild members a couple blocks away from the gate. Valek's horse was saddled and ready.

"Is everyone here?" I asked. We would leave no one behind.

"Yeah, except for Master Fisk," Phelan said with a worried frown.

"He's not on horseback," I said. "Fisk and Onora should be here soon." Along with Valek, unless he was unable to ditch his pursuers.

Kiki pricked her ears back and turned. Onora and Fisk raced into view. She waved us on. "Go, go! The guards are right behind us."

Damn. I hesitated. Valek hadn't appeared. Where was he? I glanced at the kids and at Fisk's pale face. We couldn't wait.

"Fisk, mount Onyx. You take Valek's role."

Onora helped him into the saddle.

"All right, let's go," I ordered. The words sizzled on my tongue and seared down my throat.

The kids raced ahead of us. Just before we turned the last corner and would be in full view of the gate's guards, we all paused. I hooked my right foot through the stirrup and swung my left leg over. I dropped the reins so they dragged on the ground and shifted until I clung to the side of the saddle, as if I was about to fall.

I signaled. Showtime. The guild members ran straight at the armed soldiers, screaming about a runaway horse just before Kiki burst into view. Onyx followed close behind, with Fisk bravely trying to grab Kiki's reins and save the damsel in distress. I played my part by screaming for help and carrying on.

There were only a few guards at the gate. Valek had suc-

MARIA V. SNYDER

cessfully drawn off the extras who had been stationed there. Did they catch him?

The men and women dove to the side when it became obvious they would be trampled by the horses if they didn't. I tightened my hold and braced as Kiki broke through the gate in one powerful stride. A loud crack split the air, and splinters flew in all directions. Pinpricks of pain peppered my hands and face. I glanced back. Onyx and the kids poured from the Citadel like water breaking through a mud dam. The plan was to scatter once we were free and meet up later. Kiki slowed, and I pulled myself back into the saddle.

While elated that we'd rescued Fisk and the guild members, my heart burned for Valek. I tried not to get too upset. He might still be free but unable to leave the Citadel. Once I rendezvoused with Fisk and the others, I could wait for when Cahil and his group left to escort Zitora. He would have information on Valek's whereabouts. Or Valek might even be hidden in his posse. A girl could hope.

The trip to Bavol's farmhouse seemed to take an eternity. Since it was close to the plains, it would be an ideal hideout for a couple of days. Fisk and his people would need to move on in case Valek had been captured. The bitter taste of ashes coated my mouth at the thought.

It was dark by the time we reached the farm. Fisk and Onyx had beaten us there. Since the kids were on foot, it would take them longer to arrive. In the meantime, I lit one of the stable's lanterns and tended to Kiki's injuries. Cuts crisscrossed her chest, and thick wooden splinters protruded from her neck and legs. Blood ran down her front legs. Poor girl.

I rubbed a little of the watered-down medical Curare into her wounds first. Finding a pair of tweezers, I carefully tugged the pieces free from the cuts. Fisk groomed and settled Onyx before he joined me.

Limping slightly, he leaned against a beam. Lines of exhaustion etched his young face. Purple bruises stained his skin. His defeated posture said more than his haunted gaze.

"I'm sorry," he said.

"Don't be. It's not your fault."

"It is. I should have—"

"Stop right there. Should haves are a complete waste of time and energy. They can't change the past. It happened. You learned a lesson. Now you know what not to do. That's what you focus on for the future."

He didn't reply. After a while, I glanced at him. He rubbed his arm but stared into the night as if deep in thought.

I pulled the last splinter from Kiki's copper coat, then washed her wounds before smearing on one of Leif's healing salves. Thinking of Leif, I calculated the timing of his trip. My brother should have reached the jungle by now. Had our father started cultivating the spores?

The pain in my chest, which had died down to a smolder while I'd been distracted, flared to life once more. Would Valek divulge that information to the Cartel? He was resistant to goo-goo juice, but not to magic. And Cilly would take great delight in scrambling Valek's brains as she searched for information. Revenge for killing her brother.

"Thank you." Fisk interrupted my morose thoughts. "For…" He swept a hand wide. "Rescuing me, and getting my kids to safety. Despite the danger."

"You're welcome. Besides, it was my turn." I touched his shoulder. "Tag, you're it."

That surprised a laugh from him. "I don't know if I can top today. When I saw you hunched over, screaming about the baby, for a moment I actually worried you were going to squat down and pop the kid out right there in the lobby."

Pop the kid out? If only it would be that easy. "Don't worry. I've about two seasons to go."

We shared a look as we both acknowledged the unspoken—if I survived that long. If any of us did.

Fisk wrapped his arms around his stomach. "I'm sorry about Valek."

"Me, too, but he knew the risks. And he's escaped worse situations. The man doesn't know how to quit. And we shouldn't, either." Energized, I grabbed my saddle bags and headed for the house. "Come on. Your people are going to be hungry and thirsty when they arrive."

The place was just as dark and empty as it had been the last time I'd visited. Just to be safe, I did a sweep of all the rooms. When I returned, Fisk was building a lattice of branches for a fire. I moved to help him, but he waved me off.

"Go get cleaned up or you're gonna scare my kids." He pointed to his cheek.

I touched mine. Ow. My fingers came away sticky with blood. So worried about everyone else, I'd forgotten about my own injuries. In the washroom, I plucked splinters from my face, neck, hand and arm. Just like with Kiki, I cleaned the wounds and rubbed a healing ointment into the stinging cuts. By that point, my disguise was ruined. I scraped off the putty and untangled my black hair. At least Valek had left the strands long enough for me to collect them into a single braid. It reached just past my shoulders.

A fire roared in the hearth. Fisk huddled next to it, soaking in its heat.

I sat next to him. "Bad enough to be locked in a cell, but then the cold dampness seeps into your bones until you believe you'll never be warm again."

"Yeah, I hadn't experienced it before." He watched the flames as they danced. "I've been hungry, poor, homeless, alone and afraid, but I've never been so helpless and terrified. So…"

"Exposed?"

"Ripped apart." He rubbed a hand over his short beard. "All my thoughts and memories laid bare. All my secrets. My kids who depend on me…taken. Nothing I did made a bit of difference."

"I know. It's rough, and it leaves you feeling raw. But you walked away with your personality and memories intact. You're still Fisk. They could have taken that, as well."

"So, I should be grateful?" His tone was bitter.

"Not at all. Just think about it. As bad as it feels right now, and when all you want to do is curl up in a ball and ignore the world, remember—you are alive, both body and soul. You didn't die, so don't act like it. There are a lot of others who can't say the same thing."

"Is that your idea of a pep talk?"

"Yup. Mind you, it's just plain old Yelena's words of wisdom from her own experiences, and not the Soulfinder talking."

"That's okay. I've heard the Soulfinder is a bit of a drama queen anyway," he teased—a good sign for his recovery.

"Tell me about it. Plus, she's always in the middle of trouble."

His small smile widened suddenly. "Cilly didn't get everything."

It took me a moment to follow his shift in topic. "No?"

"No. She doesn't know about your deal with Cahil, thank fate!"

"Why not?"

"She didn't know to ask or to look. Bruns is confident that his people are loyal."

Thank fate, indeed.

As Fisk warmed up, an unpleasant odor emanated from

MARIA V. SNYDER

him. Unfortunately, I was well-acquainted with the reek of dungeon. I sent him to get cleaned up before his kids arrived.

Around midnight, they started trickling in, either alone or in pairs. All were tired and hungry, but still had enough energy to give their leader a hug or a high-five. We fed them and sent them to bed. The farmhouse had plenty of bedrooms.

"Not many helpers left," Fisk said in a dejected tone.

"Phelan said none of your guild were killed. They've been sent to the other garrisons, which is a good thing for us."

"They've been brainwashed and forced to work for the Cartel. How is that a good thing?"

I'd forgotten that he didn't know about the spores. Without telling him all the details, I said, "There will come a time when they'll recover their senses, and then they'll be in the perfect position to help us stop the Cartel."

Fisk shook his head. "My guild has gone in well over our heads. It's too dangerous for them."

"I agree it's dangerous. I didn't want them involved in your rescue, but they refused to lie low. Even with the Cartel rounding them up, they still gathered intel."

"Are you saying that even if I order them to stay uninvolved, they'll ignore me?"

"Yes." I patted his arm. "You did a good job raising them."

He huffed.

A few more members arrived by dawn. Fisk refused to go to sleep, even though I promised to man the door. Instead, he dozed on the couch.

Phelan showed up in the morning. Mud coated his pants, and rips marked his sleeves. "I picked up a tail and couldn't shake him. Tenacious bastard. I hid in the briars for a few hours until he gave up."

"Is anyone else coming?" Fisk asked him.

"How many have arrived so far?"

"You make thirteen," Fisk said.

"That's everyone."

A sad relief shone on Fisk's face, but the comment sliced through me. Onora was still missing. I didn't panic right away. Knowing her, she was probably waiting for everyone to be safe inside before joining us. But just to be sure, I asked Phelan if he'd seen her.

"No."

"She told me she was staying in the Citadel," Fisk said.

"What? Why didn't you tell me?" I demanded.

"I thought you knew. She made it sound like it was part of the plan."

A sick dread swirled in my stomach. "What did she say?"

"That she needed to stay behind and keep an eye on Bruns."

Oh, no. She planned to assassinate Bruns.

I couldn't sleep. I paced around the living area while Fisk and his guild slept. The midafternoon sun painted a sheen of brightness on the trees and grasses. Yet to me, the colors resembled mud.

Onora and Valek remained in the Citadel. Perhaps they would team up and Valek would kill Bruns to save Onora from doing it. But what should I do? Should I assume they wouldn't reveal our plans to the Cartel and proceed as arranged, or should I change everything? There were forty-five days left in the heating season. I needed to be at the Greenblade garrison before the start of the hot season.

Kiki whinnied. I froze for a moment. She repeated the sound. Distressed, and definitely trying to get my attention, I yanked my switchblade and triggered the blade. Peering through the windows, I studied the land between the house and stables. Nothing. Kiki jumped the stall door and ran to the house.

I bolted outside. "What's wrong?"

She spun and returned to the stables. I followed her. Onyx thumped at the walls. Was he injured? Perhaps one of the splinters from the gate had struck him and festered. I ducked inside and stopped. Valek slumped over a bale of hay. A knife jutted from his back.

An ice-cold lance of fear shot right through me, pinning me in place. He looked...

Dead.

Racing to his side, I paused. His magic might be able to heal him, but not if I touched him. I crouched next to him and called his name. His eyelids fluttered, as if he needed every ounce of energy to open his eyes, but he didn't wake.

Alive. For now.

I ran into the house and woke Fisk and Phelan. They carried Valek into the house and lay him on his stomach in the master bedroom downstairs. Valek moaned.

"Should we pull the knife out?" Fisk asked.

"No. He might bleed to death if it pierced his heart." My thoughts jumbled into a swirl of panic. No healer. No magic. No way he'd live without one or both.

"One of us could fetch a healer from... Where's the closest town?" Phelan asked.

"No time," I said. The words repeated in my mind. No time. No healer. No magic. Think! There was magic in the Avibian Plains, but could Valek access it? No. Kiki had magic. Who else had magic? No one. What else?

Holy snow cats! I sprinted to the stables and into the tack room. Valek's saddle and bags rested on a pile of straw bales. I yanked open the pouch and dug deep, flinging items left and right. It was down deep at the bottom, rolled in one of his tunics. Racing back to house, I dashed into Valek's room, gasping for breath.

Fisk and Phelan hovered near him.

"What's that?" Phelan asked.

Wrong question. No time to explain.

"What do you need us to do?" Fisk asked.

Right question.

I handed the bundle to Fisk. "Unwrap it." Then I instructed Phelan to move Valek's arms until his hands were over Valek's head. Pointing to the knife, I said, "Phelan, when I say three, you yank the knife free in one quick motion."

With an "ah" of understanding, Fisk dropped Valek's tunic on the bed.

I picked it up and folded into a square. "Press this to the wound right after you remove the knife," I instructed Phelan.

When he gave me an odd look, Fisk said, "She can't touch him."

"You know what to do?" I asked Fisk.

"Yes."

"Be quick."

"I know."

"On three. One. Two. Three."

Phelan yanked. Valek jerked awake, gasping in pain. Fisk thrust the glass super messenger into Valek's hands while Phelan staunched the wound.

It was a gamble. A long shot. If Valek wasn't conscious enough to tap into the magic stored inside... I hovered nearby, completely useless.

Fisk pressed Valek's hands to the glass. Valek's head dropped back onto the mattress. His eyes drifted shut.

MARIA V. SNYDER

23

VALEK

A hot poker of pain speared him with unbelievable agony. His eyes watered, and sweet oblivion beckoned as his body shut down to protect against the onslaught.

"No, you don't!" Yelena yelled. Her voice was distant, but the panic and fear were clear. "Come on, Valek. Use your magic."

Magic? He'd tried. Before. It worked. For a while. But… not strong enough.

"Come on, you bastard."

The bastard was the guy who'd stabbed him in the back. Except he couldn't remember which of the five did the deed.

"Heal yourself. Use the super messenger."

Messenger? His hands tingled and pulsed with magic. But he couldn't see his injury. It hurt to think. It hurt to breathe. It hurt.

As if reading his mind, Yelena said, "Reach inside. Like when you reach out with your magic, but this time, reach inside instead."

Black-and-white spots swirled as energy drained from his limbs.

"Do it now. That's an order!"

Conditioned to following orders, Valek gathered the magic and concentrated on the pulsing fury of pain in his chest, projecting his awareness into his body, sensing the injury. His heart struggled to beat as blood spurted from an inch-long tear. Fear gripped him. The injury was too severe to repair.

"Valek, do it for your child."

The memory of the baby's movements caressed his mind as gently as the baby inside her had caressed his fingers. Using the magic in the messenger to strengthen him, Valek pulled a thread of power and stitched the tear in his heart.

Lightheaded with the effort, he drew in a deep breath. He wasn't done. Blood had pooled in his chest. Too much. He guided it back through the cut arteries in his back before working on repairing the muscles and tissues, looping tiny, neat stitches. He rested for a moment. Yelena's voice roused him again, goading him into action.

Feeling a bit stronger, he drew more power from the blanket, since a part of him knew to avoid draining the messenger. By the time he finished knitting the skin together, he shook with fatigue. The temptation to pull in more power throbbed.

Resisting the lure of unlimited energy, Valek let go. He hoped he'd done enough to quiet that insistent voice, so he could rest in peace.

He woke in snatches. Faces came and went. Fisk. Phelan. Yelena. Valek reached for his wife, but she wouldn't touch his skin. Liquids burned down his throat, and he shivered under a thousand pounds of blankets until fire raced over his skin and he flung them off. Pulling in a breath became a struggle. Oblivion was far easier.

But the voice returned. "You missed something. Look again," it ordered. He tried ignoring that voice. It demanded too much. However, it refused to give up and it sawed into his mind, cleaving its way into his core. "Fight or die," it challenged him.

And that voice saved him. Again. He'd never backed down from a fight. Valek connected to the blanket of power and sought the injury with his awareness, seeking what he'd missed. A sliver of metal was lodged in his rib. Red inflammation and green pus hovered around it. A hole in his right lung leaked air. Sewing the hole was second nature. Once completed, his breathing returned to normal.

The shard, however, would have to be removed. He needed help and another pair of hands. When he built up enough strength, he asked for a volunteer who wouldn't faint at the sight of blood. And who would allow Valek to invade his or her mind.

Fisk volunteered. Yelena's strained face softened with surprise. Valek wondered why, until he encountered the damage in Fisk's thoughts. Another had invaded, and she had a heavy touch. Like a bully, she had taken what she wanted and left a mess behind.

Valek kept a light connection with Fisk, being a mindful guest. He showed the young man what Valek needed him to do.

Fisk cursed. "I've gotten some strange requests from clients before, but this one beats them all." He glanced at Yelena. "He wants me to cut into his back."

"Why?"

"Metal shard left behind."

"Oh. No need, Valek. Push it from your body. It will cut through muscles and skin, but you can repair the tears as it travels. That will cause much less damage." She frowned at him. "Why didn't you just ask me?"

He gave her an apologetic smile. "Baby brain."

She relaxed. "No. I'm sorry. I'm just not used to you

being…" Yelena drew in a breath. "Let me do the thinking for you until you're recovered. Okay?"

"Yes, love." He rolled onto his stomach and worked on evicting the unwelcome visitor. Pain once again sliced through his back, but he managed to wiggle it out. Blood and pus poured from the new wound. He let the pus drain before stitching up the cut. Yelena wiped the fluids up with a towel, being careful not to touch his skin with her own.

Too exhausted to move, Valek closed his eyes, but he vowed to get better just so he could hold his wife again.

The days passed in blurs of activity. Waking, eating, talking and sleeping. He explained to Yelena and Fisk how he'd drawn the bulk of the guards away from the gate. A smile at the memory. Janco would be proud of the taunt he'd used to goad them into action. Valek had led them on a merry chase throughout the Citadel and well away from the distraction at the Council Hall.

Then the smile faded. They'd been harder to shake than expected. A magician had accompanied them, and she'd tracked him with her magic. By the time he looped back to the gate, the soldiers had recovered from their surprise. And behind him, the Council Hall guards had arrived, charging toward the exit, trapping him between the two.

He'd faced ten. Nothing left to do but surrender. Fear was a pale shadow compared to the regret that pulsed in his heart for failing to rejoin Yelena. Except Onora had appeared from nowhere. She ambushed a couple guards, and Valek couldn't let her have all the fun.

He ignored Yelena's squawk of protest and continued the story. It hadn't taken long to realize five armed opponents exceeded his fighting skills. "A blow to my ego."

When the knife had sliced into his back, he'd yanked power,

MARIA V. SNYDER

flinging his magic away from him in a blind panic and flattening the guards to the ground.

"A mini flameout?" Yelena asked him.

"No idea, love. By the time I came to my senses, Onora was gone. I clutched magic to my chest and ran until I couldn't." He reached for her. And since he no longer relied on his magic to heal, she laced her fingers through his. "Then the nagging started."

She huffed and tried to yank her hand from his grip.

He tightened his hold. "It saved my life. Thank you." Valek kissed her knuckles.

Fisk laughed. "Power nagging. I love it." He paused. "Don't tell my mother."

"Where's Onora?" Valek asked. "I need to thank her, too."

Both Yelena and Fisk sobered. He braced for bad news, but Fisk's report wasn't all doom.

"She's quite capable of avoiding capture," Valek said.

"What if she tries to assassinate Bruns?" Yelena asked.

"She'll probably succeed. Why are you upset? It would derail the Cartel's plans."

Yelena sat on the edge of his bed. "I'm worried about her soul." She looked down at their clasped hands. "Killing another changes a person."

He squeezed her fingers. "I know. Onora will have to decide what to do. If she kills Bruns and manages to escape, then it's a good thing most of her friends understand exactly what she sacrificed in order to save others."

Yelena's expression grew thoughtful. He wondered what she mulled over. Before he could ask, she released his hand and stood.

"You need to rest." Yelena pulled the blankets up to his chest. "You have to regain your strength."

"I sleep better when you're with me, love." He patted the bed beside him.

"And that's my signal to go." Fisk paused in the threshold. "My kids are bored and want to help. What should I tell them?"

Valek exchanged a glance with Yelena. She nodded.

"Send them to the three northern garrisons. When the Theobroma starts to wear off, they'll be in position to help spread the word," Valek said.

"Spread the word about what?"

"To listen to the Master Magicians and follow their orders."

"What will be their orders?"

Valek tried to shrug, but it still hurt too much. "I don't know. We haven't figured that out yet. Let me know if you have any ideas."

Fisk just muttered as he left.

"Can you contact the Masters?" Yelena asked.

He touched the super messenger. It sat on the bedside table, just in case he needed it. Magic hummed inside, but how much was left? "I hope so." Valek considered. "Bruns told Zitora that all these had been destroyed, but we know he's been using them—and he has Quinn, who can recharge them."

"You want to steal one?"

"Or two or three or—"

"I get it." She perched on the edge of the bed and pulled off her boots. "We can see if there are any in the Greenblade garrison when we free the Councilors."

That reminded him. "How long have I been out of it?"

She stripped down to her underclothes. "It's close to the middle of the heating season. We've been here for ten days."

Shocked, he sat up. "Ten…" But his head spun, and his muscles shook.

Yelena tsked and pushed him back down. "You almost died.

MARIA V. SNYDER

Even with using magic, you can't recover that fast." Sliding into bed with him, she snuggled close.

"We need to leave soon." There wasn't much time left.

"When you're healthy." Her tone implied it was not up for discussion.

He lay there, staring at the ceiling. A few dusty cobwebs hung in the corners. Depending on how well-guarded they were, it could take days or weeks to plan and then execute the Councilors' rescue. Then they would need at least a week for the Councilors to recover their free will.

"Stop fretting," Yelena said. "Rest."

When he didn't relax, she took his hand and placed it on her slightly bulging belly. Even through her undershirt, he felt the baby's movements. Amazing.

"A little over halfway," she said.

That scared him. So much to do before they were safe. He tensed again.

"What do you think? Boy or girl?" she asked.

Ah. A classic distraction technique, but he played along. "Girl."

"Why?"

"Because she already takes after you, love."

"How's that?"

"From the very beginning, she's been in the middle of the action, causing trouble."

"Ha. I think it's a boy, because of all your brothers. Your parents had six boys and one girl. The odds are good for a boy."

"And for twins," he said.

She pushed up on her elbow, looking a bit panicked. "No. Teegan said 'two healthy heartbeats.'"

"Are you sure he wasn't referring to two babies?"

"I…" Yelena swallowed. "I thought he meant me and the baby. Can you see?"

"I can try."

She lay back down, and Valek slid his hand under her shirt, resting it on her warm stomach. Reaching with his magic, he sought the baby...or babies. But his power was taken from him before he could sense anything. The more he tried, the greater the drain. He stopped. "Sorry, love. Guess we'll have to find out the old-fashioned way."

"Easy for you to say," she muttered.

"If it helps, the baby has grown in strength as well as size. You're even more protected from—" Struck by an idea, he mulled it over.

"Magic?"

He chased the logic. Excited, he turned to her. "Do you think you could wake those under Bruns's influence with a touch? The Cartel uses magic to manipulate their loyalties, so if you drain that magic away, wouldn't they wake up?"

Yelena gaped at him. "I'm... But Loris was able to control me."

"That was three months ago. And even then, you said you were able to shake off his magic after a few hours."

"What about Cahil?"

"What about him? Did you touch him skin to skin? Or his crew?"

"No." Her face lit up. "It might work."

And if it did, that might just be the break they needed. Valek snaked his hand up her stomach. "This calls for a celebration." Desire purred in his voice.

She grabbed his wrist and plucked his hand from her body. "No. You are to rest, recuperate and recover."

Right. "If I follow your orders, will I get a reward?"

"Yes."

The future had just brightened even more.

MARIA V. SNYDER

* * *

Five days later, Valek was finally declared healthy enough for travel. He received his reward the night before they left.

Breathless, and with their heartbeats in sync, they lay together. Valek wondered aloud if their bedroom exertions endangered the baby.

"No. Medic Mommy said we can have relations—those are her words, by the way, not mine—up until the last couple of weeks. However, I'll be huge by then and probably resemble a turnip with legs. I doubt that you'd even want to have relations."

He cupped her cheek. "You are more beautiful to me today than yesterday. Each day, when I think I can't possibly love you any more than I already do, you prove me wrong. So I'm very confident that even if you turn into a turnip with legs, I will love and desire you."

She turned and kissed him on the palm. "I love you, too."

He nuzzled her neck, then nibbled on her ear. "Besides, turnips are my favorite vegetable."

"Am I supposed to melt in your arms after *that* comment?"

He pretended to be confused. "Turnips don't melt." Which earned him a hard smack on his arm. "Ow." He rubbed his bicep.

"Any other comments?"

"You're even beautiful when you're annoyed."

"Nice save."

"The truth is easy, love." He pulled her closer and breathed in her scent. Contentment filled him as he drifted to sleep.

Morning came too soon, but Valek refrained from complaining as Yelena studied his face for signs of fatigue. They said goodbye to Fisk. He'd reluctantly declared the farmhouse his new headquarters until the Cartel was gone.

"It's too quiet. It smells weird. And it's dead boring," Fisk said. "How do people survive out here?"

"Some people like dead boring," Yelena said, smiling at him.

"Well, I don't. Better hurry up and evict those bastards."

"Glad you're feeling better," she said.

He grinned back at her. "Me, too."

Carrying their bags to the stable, Valek and Yelena saddled their horses. When Valek mounted Onyx, the big black horse pranced underneath him, energetic and ready to go.

Fisk followed them. Before they left, he asked, "How will I know if you rescue the Councilors?"

"When we knock on your door," Yelena said.

"Oh."

"If we're not back by the beginning of the hot season, we failed."

"And you're in charge of taking down the Cartel," Valek added.

"Lovely."

"You're the best man for the job," Valek said.

"Yeah, yeah. I'm the *only* man for the job. Better not get caught, or I'm gonna be stuck here and might have to…gasp… farm."

"Well, if that's not incentive to survive, I don't know what is," Valek teased. "Thanks for the pep talk."

"Yeah, yeah." Fisk headed back to the house.

As soon as Valek tapped his heels, Onyx exploded into motion. Kiki ran right beside him. Even with a few detours to avoid patrols and using extra caution when entering Longleaf, they arrived near the Greenblade garrison in three days.

The town was mid-size and had a number of inns. Ari and Janco had a safe house nearby, but Bruns had probably plucked that location from Fisk. Valek doubted the Cartel would be actively searching for them here, but he ensured they wore disguises when then rented a room at the Thermal Blue Inn for one night. Since they couldn't plan a rescue in a public establishment, Valek would find another dwelling tomorrow while Yelena chatted with the locals. The horses remained in the forest surrounding the town.

They ate a late supper in their room, but they joined the other guests for breakfast the next day. The common room was about half-full. Conversation buzzed and the smell of bacon filled the air. Yelena dug into a huge pile of steaming eggs, but he picked at his, pushing the yellow clumps around his plate. The trip had worn him out more than he'd expected. He'd thought getting pushed from a window by Owen twice was the closest he'd ever come to death. That crystal-clear moment when gravity tugged was forever etched into his mind. The first time, Ari's strong hands had snatched him from that fate, and the second, an unknown rescuer provided handholds. Escaping death a third time had been much harder. He doubted he'd survive a fourth.

A man and his son entered the common room. They strode over to their table. Valek reached for his dagger, but then he recognized the man's swagger.

Janco and Teegan joined them. They both wore disguises.

"You gonna finish that?" Janco asked, sitting next to him.

"Here." Valek slid his plate over.

Janco flashed him a surprised grin before he grabbed a spoon.

"How did you find us?" Valek asked.

"I've been doing daily sweeps since we arrived," Teegan said, tapping his head.

Interesting. Valek hadn't felt any magic. "I didn't pick up on it."

"You're not supposed to." Teegan smirked.

"Can you teach me that?"

The question startled the smirk from Teegan's face. "I don't know."

"Can you try?"

"Yeah, sure."

"Good. I need to keep working on my control and learn what I can and can't do before we take the next step." The boy's presence meant Ari and Janco had caught up to the twins and a Stormdancer. Valek glanced at Janco. "How long have you been here?"

Talking around a mouthful of eggs, Janco said, "Two weeks."

"What about my father?" Yelena asked in alarm. "Did something happen?"

"No. He's fine." He waved his spoon. "Opal, Devlen, Reema and the twins are all fine." Janco lowered his voice. "I'm sure they're making heaps of spores by now. There were just too many rabbits in the stew, and we thought we'd get a head start on things."

"Does that include securing a safe place for all of us?" Valek asked.

"Of course."

"Then we'll finish our discussion there."

After breakfast, Valek and Yelena grabbed their bags from the room they'd rented. They followed Janco and Teegan to a small building a few blocks over. The place had once been a tailor shop. Bolts of moth-eaten cloth, cloudy mirrors and dusty mannequins decorated the first floor. Black curtains covered the large display windows in the front.

Alerted by the noise, Ari came downstairs. After the hellos, he carried Yelena's bag to the second floor, despite her protests, and showed them the living quarters. Teegan and Janco followed them.

"There are three bedrooms," Ari said as he deposited her pack in the unoccupied room. "Janco and I are in there, and Teegan has the little one." He gestured to a door on the left.

Valek set his bag next to Yelena's. There was a living area with a couple couches and armchairs. A few bolts of cloth and parts of a sewing machine littered the floor. The tailor must have lived here.

Janco picked up the top half of a broken mannequin. "This place went bust."

Everyone groaned at the bad joke.

"Come on, guys. That's a classic."

No one agreed.

Ari turned to Valek. "Please tell me you need Janco to travel far away from here for a dangerous undercover mission."

"Let me guess," Yelena said. "He's been driving you crazy."

"Janco and boredom don't mix well."

"That's 'cause the boy genius here has taken all the fun out of everything." Janco pressed his fingertips to his temples. Talking in a falsetto, he said, "They're doing another sweep in town. We'd better hide."

"I do *not* sound like that," Teegan protested.

"Report," Valek ordered before they started to bicker. He settled on the couch next to Yelena. The others sat, or in Janco's case, plopped.

Janco gestured to Teegan. "I'll let the boy genius fill you in."

Teegan gave Janco an indulgent look, as if Teegan was the adult and Janco the child. "I've been spying on the garrison with my magic. I know where the guards are stationed, where the Councilors are housed and, most important, who the magicians are and what they can do."

"That's impressive," Yelena said.

He shrugged off the compliment. "Most of them have been

eating Theobroma, so their thoughts are dripping from their heads."

"Are the Councilors together?" Valek asked.

"Yeah. They're all staying on the second floor of the barracks. Although Master Magician Bain is not there."

"He was moved to the Krystal garrison." Valek considered. "Can you reach Bain from this distance?"

"It's probably too far for us to connect. Why?"

"We're going to need to coordinate with the Masters."

"With your help, we might reach him," Teegan said.

Good to know. "What's the status at the gate?"

"No need to worry about the gate," Janco said. "We have another way into the garrison."

The man appeared mighty pleased with himself. Valek took the bait. "Oh?"

"Heli gave us a storm orb. When you're ready, we'll blast a hole into one of the walls. Ka-boom!" Janco threw his arms wide.

Smart. With that much energy at their disposal, the possible uses were endless. If they had more—

"Way ahead of you, Boss. While Boy Genius and I were scoping out the garrison, Ari paid Kade a visit on the coast and picked up a few more."

Yelena jumped up and hugged Ari. "That's fantastic!"

The big man actually blushed.

"But once we set one of those babies off, there's no more sneaking around," Janco said. "We're committed, big time."

"Hit and git," Yelena said.

He grinned. "Exactly."

"We need to find a location that will limit casualties but is close to the barracks," Valek said.

"Done," Teegan said with a flourish reminiscent of Janco.

"What we don't know is what happens after all hell breaks loose."

Yelena frowned at Janco.

"He didn't learn that from me!"

"Uh-huh."

"The next part is easy. We round up the Councilors and escort them to the farmhouse," Valek said.

"How are you going to convince them to leave?" Teegan asked. "There are eleven of them. I can only influence three or four people at a time."

Impressive. "We'll wear uniforms to blend in and tell them we're taking them to safety."

"And when they realize we're not Bruns's minions?" Janco asked.

"Yelena will convince them to stay with us." Valek explained his theory.

"I thought babies only sucked their thumbs," Janco mumbled.

"Our child is exceptional," Valek said, daring Janco to disagree.

He held up his hands. "Easy there, Papa Bear."

Yelena laughed. "If it doesn't work, we'll fall back on plan B."

"Plan B?" This was new.

"They're sure to drink water that first day, so we'll tell them they've been poisoned. They'll have a week to live unless they get the antidote, which is at the farmhouse. By the time they arrive there, the Theobroma will have worn off."

"Brilliant plan," Valek said with a smile. "Wherever did you get that excellent idea from?"

"Shut up."

"I love you, too."

Janco glanced at Teegan. "I think we're missing something."

"It's probably one of those lovey-dovey things," Teegan said. "My parents do it all the time, and it's gross."

Laughing, Janco said, "Give it a few years, puppy dog."

Valek considered. Once they rescued the Councilors, the Cartel would step up their attempts to find them. They would surround the garrisons with soldiers and be extra-vigilant. Therefore, they couldn't move too soon, or else they'd give the Cartel more time to prepare. If all went well, they needed to rendezvous with the rest of the team by day fifty of the heating season, which was sixteen days away. It would take them at least six days to escort the Councilors back to the farmhouse. What to do in the next ten days?

"Are you up for a field trip?" Valek asked the power twins.

"Always," Janco immediately replied.

"Yes, sir," Ari said.

"Good. I think it's time to have a talk with the Cartel's Master Gardener." He listed a number of questions they'd need to ask. "Think you can handle it?"

"Is sand the most horrid stuff in the world?" Janco asked.

Ari swatted his partner on the shoulder. "He means yes. We can. What's our timeline?"

"Be back here in nine days."

"Got it."

"Am I going with them?" Teegan asked.

"No." Valek glanced at Yelena. "You're going to work with me."

The next day, Ari and Janco set off for their mission. Valek and Teegan rode Onyx and Kiki through the woods north of Longleaf while Yelena remained in town. The scent of pine increased as the air warmed. Birds darted between limbs, cutting through the shafts of sunlight that speared the tree canopy.

When Teegan thought they were far enough away from the magicians at the garrison, they stopped and dismounted.

"What can you do?" Teegan asked.

"I can heal and communicate with other magicians." He described what had happened with the soldiers.

"Not a flameout," Teegan said. "You would have been unconscious for longer than a few minutes. Remember when you healed Leif? You were asleep for days afterward."

True. "Then what was that?"

"You probably overloaded their minds, and they passed out. If you'd knocked them down, they would have been conscious. But we'll soon discover the extent of your abilities. What do you want to start with first?"

"It doesn't matter."

"All right." The boy searched the ground and picked up a thin branch. "Let's see if you can start a fire." He held it up. "Concentrate and direct your magic at this. Think heat and fire. I have to get a little angry at it for it to work for me." Teegan furrowed his brow. Flames erupted on the end of the stick. He extinguished it. "Your turn."

Valek dropped his mental shields. Gathering a thread of power, he aimed it at the branch as Teegan instructed. Nothing happened.

"Try again. It took me a couple times. Think of Bruns. That might help to *inflame* you." Teegan chuckled.

Fueling his magic with rage, he hurled the power. Nothing. Not even a wisp of smoke. A third, fourth and fifth effort had the same results.

"That's a no for fire. Let's see if you can move the branch. Using magic is all the same, really. It's an invisible force that you can manipulate... Well, that's how I imagine it, anyway. To move an object, I picture the magic in the shape of a hand

and reach out and—" the stick flew from Valek's fingers to Teegan's "—take what I want." He grinned. "Your turn."

Valek envisioned a hand, a spoon, shovel, pitchfork and a strong wind, all to no avail. The branch stayed put, but a wave of weakness crashed into him. He leaned against a tree to keep from falling over.

"And that's a no for moving objects." Teegan dug into his pocket, withdrew a small paper bag and tipped a piece of hard candy onto his palm. "Here, this will help."

The sweet taste of strawberries filled Valek's mouth as he sucked on it. After a few minutes, he felt better.

"Okay. Let's see if you can influence me." He gave Valek a cocky grin. "I'll let my defenses down. It's similar to reading a person's thoughts, except you're taking over, giving the orders, and they have to follow them. Just don't have me jumping around like an idiot."

Connecting with Teegan's mind was almost second nature for Valek—a scary prospect. The boy's curiosity dominated.

You're sending too much magic, Teegan thought. *Use the same touch as if you were sneaking into someone's room to assassinate him.*

Valek adjusted the flow.

Better. Now, let's see what you've got, Teegan challenged.

One thing Valek excelled at was giving orders. *Sit down.*

The boy plopped onto his butt, surprising them both.

Keep going, Teegan encouraged him.

Hands up.

Stand.

Come here.

Teegan obeyed each command.

Now I'm going to resist. Let's see how strong you are.

Jump around like an idiot.

The boy grinned but didn't move.

Valek increased the pressure, but Teegan's feet stayed on

MARIA V. SNYDER

the ground. Valek ramped it up a bit more. Still no response, but the boy's cheeky demeanor disappeared as he concentrated on countering the order. With a final burst of energy, Valek threw everything he had at Teegan. Nothing.

Sagging with exhaustion, Valek sank to the ground.

Teegan breathed in deep, wiping sweat from his brow. "That was impressive. Not master-level strength, but I doubt there are many magicians who could withstand that." He pulled a water skin off Onyx's saddle, gulped down a few mouthfuls and handed it to Valek.

"Thanks." The cold water soothed his throat.

"Most magicians have one skill that dominates and maybe a couple others, but those aren't as strong. Like Aunt Yelena has…had…the Soulfinding thing. If she told me to jump, I couldn't resist her. Not even Master Bain can. And then she can heal…in a strange way, but it works. But that's it. I'm guessing your major thing is going to be influencing others, but we'll see." Teegan studied Valek. "I think that's enough for today. We can try again tomorrow."

"I just need a few more minutes, and I'll be ready for more."

"Oh, no. I've strict orders."

Ah. He had Yelena to thank for that. But she was right to limit their session, because by the time they returned to the tailor shop, it took every bit of his energy just to climb the stairs and collapse onto the bed.

The next morning, Yelena wouldn't let him work with Teegan. He had to promise to eat a hearty breakfast, or she would have refused to let him get out of bed. Not that he minded a day in bed as long as Yelena joined him, but her stubborn gaze froze all his desire.

"You're whiter than the Citadel's walls," she said in *that* tone. "You're rushing your recovery and will wind up having a relapse if you're not careful."

He pouted until she agreed to at least snuggle with him. A small but crucial victory—he always slept better with her in his arms.

Finally allowed to do more experiments, Valek and Teegan traveled to the clearing the next day. They worked for a few hours but were unable to discover any more of Valek's talents.

"Try calling the wind," Teegan said. "You might be half Stormdancer, like Zee and Zo."

An interesting thought. Valek reached for the…air. Unlike with living creatures, he couldn't make a connection. Water, too, proved to be unresponsive.

"What about null shields?" he asked.

Valek stilled. "What about them?"

Most of Valek's friends would have recognized the warning tone, but Teegan failed to heed it. "You obviously created one when you became immune to magic. I can teach you how—"

"No." Just the thought of them turned Valek's blood to ice.

"But it could—"

"We have plenty of other people who can create them." Valek stared at the boy. The subject was closed.

Teegan, however, refused to drop it. "We do. To me, magical abilities are like weapons. The more talents you have, the bigger your arsenal." He gestured at Valek. "As an assassin, you have quite the variety of weapons at your disposal. But I'm sure you wouldn't refuse to add another just in case you need it."

Boy genius indeed. "What if I end up…stabbing myself?" And grafting the blasted thing onto his soul again.

"You won't. You have control of your magic now." Sensing a change in Valek's opinion, Teegan continued, "I'll link with you to ensure you don't."

"You're going to make a heck of a Master Magician," Valek said.

MARIA V. SNYDER

Teegan's face lit up at the compliment. "Does that mean you'll try?"

"Yes, but I'm not happy about it."

"An understatement," Teegan muttered. "All right." He explained how to build the shield.

The steps reminded Valek of the fishing nets he'd helped repair on the coast of MD-1. First he wove a web of magic threads coated with…oil was the only way he could describe it. The oil repelled magic. Then he tightened the strands until they formed a sheet, which could be shaped into anything. Valek's napkin-folding skills transferred over to creating shields. By the end of the afternoon, Valek had it down and even managed to impress the boy genius.

"That's all for today, or Aunt Yelena is gonna kill me."

An exaggeration, but Yelena did insist Valek take another day off, which became a pattern—one day of rest, followed by a work day.

On the sixth day, Teegan said, "I think we've explored all the magic talents that *I* know. We could test the extent of your skills with mental communication. You might be a Story Weaver."

Doubtful. "Will that help me when I'm fighting Owen?"

"Not unless you want to heal his mental anguish."

"I'm pretty sure I'll be *causing* him anguish." And pain and death. His fingers twitched at the thought. "We can determine that later." Valek mulled over his plans for stopping the Cartel. "Let's see if the two of us can reach Bain from here."

"All right." Teegan grasped his hand.

The boy's power surged northwest, seeking Bain. His ability to bypass all the other people along the route impressed Valek. He would have skimmed their thoughts, looking for the master magician.

Reading his thoughts, Teegan said, "Master Bain and I have

linked before. It's super easy to find someone once you've done that. It's like spotting a yellow dandelion in a grassy field."

However, even with their combined strength, they were unable to reach Bain. Disappointed but not surprised, Valek strode to Onyx, who napped in the mid-afternoon sunlight, and retrieved the super messenger. "Do you know how much magic is left in this?"

Teegan touched it with his finger. "Not much."

"Do I have enough to contact all the Masters?"

"Not you, but I might be able to, if I keep the conversations short."

Valek guessed that would have to do.

On the ride back to town, Teegan grabbed Valek's arm, stopping him when they were a couple blocks away from the tailor shop.

Instantly alert, Valek scanned the surroundings. "Trouble?"

"Yes."

24

JANCO

All this creeping around could wear a man down. Good thing Janco loved sitting still for hours and pretending to be a bush.

Not.

The compound in the middle of the Greenblade forest hadn't changed too much since Ari and Janco's last visit, when he'd run into Oran Zaltana, who might or might not be the Master Gardener. Ten glass hothouses remained lined up in a row, the sweet aroma of Theobroma mixed with the sharp tang of Curare was still polluting the air as the factories pumped the stuff out by the barrel…or so it seemed.

Yup, if he didn't count the ring of soldiers guarding the place, he'd swear nothing had changed.

They'd crept as close as they dared and had been observing the place for days. Ari and Janco were dressed in green tunic and pants to blend in with the Greenblade workers who buzzed about the site with far more energy than Janco had ever had in his life. Pah.

The best time to approach Oran was when he was alone in his room at night. Otherwise, the man spent all his time inside the hothouses. They'd identified which building he slept in, but not which room. For that to happen, Janco needed to get past the ring of guards.

The soldiers stood within sight distance of each other. If one of them were to suddenly collapse or disappear, his neighbors would know right away. Even if Ari and Janco neutralized half a dozen, there would still be soldiers left standing to raise the alarm.

Well away from the compound, Ari and Janco discussed their pitiful options as the sun set.

"Why can't we use that fancy cloak?" Janco asked.

Ari arranged the kindling into a lattice. "If you had bothered to listen, Teegan explained that since the compound is already covered by an illusion, the mirror illusion would cancel them both out. As soon as we stepped through the barrier, we would be visible."

"Great, just when I was thinking magic might be good for once," Janco muttered.

"At least you're thinking." Ari patted Janco on the head as if praising a well-behaved dog.

Janco growled.

Ari ignored him. "What else can we do?"

"We can create a distraction," Janco said.

"Only if you can create a distraction that won't alert them that something *else* is going on. As soon as the ruckus dies down, you know they'll search the place," Ari said.

"We can start a fire. That'll keep them busy for a while."

"And risk it getting out of control and harming innocent people? No."

Janco flopped onto his bedroll. They'd set up a small temporary camp that could be quickly abandoned without too many tears.

Ari settled next to him. He dug a piece of jerky from his pack and chewed on it. "Let's face it. We can't complete this

MARIA V. SNYDER

mission. The risk of getting caught is too high, and even if we did manage to escape, we might tip our hand, ruining Valek's plans."

Janco disliked failing. Very much. He lay back and stared up at the darkness. However, he agreed with his partner. They lacked recourses. Nothing here but dirt, leaves, bushes, trees—

An idea popped into his heat. What an idiot!

He jumped to his feet. "Ari, do you still have that rope?"

"Yes. Why?"

"'Cause I have a plan."

"The guards—"

"Won't suspect a thing."

"Why not?"

"'Cause I'm not gonna try to go through them. I'm gonna go over their heads." He pointed up to the tree canopy.

"Nice."

The plan was simple and easy, which should have clued Janco in that it wouldn't be as simple or as easy as he'd thought. First, using a rope to climb a tree required a lot of upper body strength. The darkness complicated things as well. Hard to find handholds when you couldn't see your hands.

Once he reached the upper limbs, he didn't need as much muscle. He wound the rope around his waist. However, in order to keep the noise of his passage from tree to tree as quiet as possible, he inched along the branches, which meant he probably sounded like a fat, out-of-shape Valmur. At one point, he imagined the soldiers below having a great laugh as they took bets on how far he'd get before plummeting to his death.

Good thing he wasn't afraid of heights. Or was he? A limb dipped with his weight. He clutched another while his heart swung from rib to rib. Easy there. When his pulse returned to—well, not normal, but not thumping as if his life depended on it—he transferred his feet to a thicker perch. Whew.

When he'd moved far enough away from the ring of protection, Janco unwound the rope and tied it to a sturdy trunk. Going down was easier on his arms but burned his palms. Once on solid ground, Janco paused, listening for sounds that he'd been discovered. All quiet.

Ghosting through the forest, Janco kept to the shadows as he aimed for the building they'd suspected housed the officers and other important people. Not many windows had been installed, probably for security purposes. A few people hustled between the structures even this late at night. Since he was dressed for the part, Janco strolled into the open as if he belonged there.

No one even glanced at him. Janco entered the building and paused. Lanterns lit the corridors, illuminating closed doors. Now what? He couldn't knock on each one and inquire where he might find the Master Gardener...or could he? Maybe pretend there was an emergency?

No. Too risky. He'd just have to do it the old-fashioned way. Once he'd checked all three stories—same design as the ground floor—Janco retreated outside. A few hours remained until dawn. Ari knew not to expect Janco back until the next evening. Janco snooped around a bit but, finding nothing interesting, he returned to Oran's building. Locating a hidden spot with a view of the entrance, he settled into a comfortable position to wait.

Good thing Oran was one of the first to leave, which confirmed he resided there. Now Janco just needed to occupy himself for the rest of the day. He followed a few people to a canteen. He stole a couple apples and a banana. Then he joined a team hauling vines from the hothouses to a factory.

MARIA V. SNYDER

No one questioned him. Everyone looked stressed and harried, so he fit right in.

He kept an eye on Oran as the day turned into night. The man worked inside the hothouses almost nonstop. Late that night, he swung by the canteen, ate supper and headed to his quarters. When Oran reached the door, Janco was a few steps behind him. Oran climbed to the third floor without realizing he had a tail. Only when Janco followed him down the corridor did the man become suspicious.

"What are—"

Janco placed the tip of his knife on Oran's throat. "Quiet. I don't want you to wake your neighbors."

Oran swallowed.

"Your room," Janco ordered. When he didn't move, Janco pressed a little harder. "Now."

The man led him to the last door on the left. Fumbling for a key, Oran finally managed to unlock it. The light from the hallway illuminated a spartan room. Janco pushed him inside.

Oran stumbled a few steps, then spun to face him. "I recognize you."

"Good, that'll save time on the introductions, Oran Zaltana."

Alarmed, the man straightened.

"It took us a while to discover that you're the Cartel's Master Gardener."

"I'm not—"

Janco held up a hand. "Save it." He pointed to the lantern on the night table. "Light that, and then sit down."

Oran hesitated until Janco stepped closer. Then he hurried to strike a spark. Once yellow glowed from the element, Oran settled on the unmade bed. Janco closed the door. The man fisted the blanket in fear when Janco advanced.

"You'll never—"

Janco didn't wait for the rest of the warning. He jabbed Oran with a dart filled with goo-goo juice. Many people had tried telling him he'd never get away with it or that he'd never leave the place alive. And those same people were always wrong. Just once, Janco would love to hear a truly unique threat.

Oran slapped a hand over the tiny wound. "What the hell was that?"

"A truth serum."

"That's..." He gazed around the room as if confused about why it had started to spin.

"Cheating?"

"Yes."

"Who says I have to play fair? The Cartel certainly isn't. Now tell me about your work as the Master Gardener."

"Not me. Nope. I'm...going to be sick." Oran heaved, vomiting onto the floor.

Janco jumped back just in time. Great, a puker. It happened from time to time. A nasty smell invaded the small room. Lovely.

"Who is the Master Gardener?" he asked.

"Bavol doesn't know."

Talking to a person under the influence of goo-goo juice required a certain level of patience. "Know what?"

"He's working for us." Oran giggled. "Shh. Mr. High and Mighty is really a traitor."

"Who's us?"

"The Cartel. Although I suggested *Alliance*...it's a stronger..." He swept a hand out. "You know."

"Word?"

"Yep."

Janco tried again. "Who's your boss?"

"Uptight know-it-all."

MARIA V. SNYDER

"Really? I heard…"

"Don't listen. She thinks she knows it all, but really…nothing."

Ah. "But she's Owen's wife."

"So she says."

"Were the hothouses Selene's idea?"

"No. Bavol's. He built…little bitty one." Oran spread his thumb and index finger about an inch apart. "Clueless to the potential."

"What about the Harman trees? What do they do?"

"Oh…that." He made a dismissive sound. "Uptight know-it-all's pet project."

"But it must be important."

"Not to me. It's a weed."

"You don't know."

"It's Ixian. Not my area of expertise."

He was getting closer. "It's Selene's area of expertise."

"It's unnecessary. I provide plenty of Theobroma."

"Always good to have a backup plan."

"She's killing people." Oran stood up.

Holy snow cats. Janco kept his expression neutral, although his heart danced a jig in his chest. "That's to be expected."

The man wobbled on his feet. "Bavol and I…we…never, not…ever experimented on people. She…" He sank onto the bed. "She's gone now. Took her poison and left."

"Where's she been doing this?" Janco asked.

"Plot behind…" He gestured to the window.

It took Janco a while, but he learned the location of Selene's lab. He pricked Oran with Leif's new sleeping draft and waited for Oran to succumb.

With his time running out, Janco sought the garden plot Oran described. He found rows of young trees stripped of their bark. A small building next to it appeared to be empty. Janco picked the lock and slipped inside.

The smell almost knocked him off his feet. No mistaking the acrid stench of death mixed with bodily fluids. He held his breath and lit a small lantern, planning to do a quick search of the room. Cages filled with dead bodies lined the back wall. Their open, lifeless eyes didn't reflect the light.

The place had all the paraphernalia of a laboratory—beakers, burners, containers and hoses. Nothing else remained that might help them discover what exactly Selene had been doing. Would it be too much to ask for a journal filled with notes?

Sick to his stomach, he turned to leave and spotted another door. Also locked, but he fixed that in seconds. More cages, but this time, people stirred awake inside them. He froze.

"Isn't it a bit early for breakfast?" asked a woman, pushing up on her elbow as she squinted in the light.

Janco debated. There were four of them. He should bolt, but he couldn't. What would Yelena do?

"I'm not with them," he said.

All four scrambled to their feet.

"Are you here to rescue us?" asked an older man. The skin clung to his skeletal face and gaunt arms.

"I…can't," Janco admitted. "I'll be lucky to escape myself. Please tell me what's going on."

"Why should we?" spat the woman. "You're not going to help us."

"Not now. But I promise I will do everything I can to return and free you."

They appeared doubtful. Given their circumstances, Janco didn't blame them. "Look, I'm working with Yelena, the Soulfinder, and we need to know what Selene's been doing so we can stop her. We've been doing everything we can to upset the Cartel's plans."

"I doubt you'll be able to stop them, young man, but if you piss them off, I'd die a happy man." The older man gestured to his companions. "We're the survivors. Selene's been injecting people with sap from the Harman trees. With each batch, she adjusts the concentration. By the time it was our turn to test the sap, she had determined the right dose, and it didn't kill us."

"It did something worse," the woman said bitterly. "We can't use magic anymore. It's all dead air."

Holy snow cats just didn't seem strong enough for this news. Janco stared at her, speechless for the first time in his life. His mind processed the information, turning it over. A small part of him thought magic had caused nothing but trouble, and he'd be happy to see it gone for good. But one thing his friendship with Yelena had taught him was that it wasn't the magic that was evil, but the person who used it to do evil. He finally found his voice. "Do you know if there is a cure?"

"No."

Yikes. "How long have you been here?"

"We *volunteered* a year ago." The woman gave him a humorless smile. "Bought into the entire 'save Sitia' propaganda, until it was too late. Now they don't even bother to feed us the Theobroma or waste magic on us."

"No offense, but why are you still alive?" Janco asked.

"Just in case the poison wears off," the older man said.

That would ruin Bruns's plans. "Has it?"

"Not yet, but I'm hopeful."

"It's been a season, Rurik. It's not coming back," the woman said.

"How long has Selene been gone?" Janco asked.

"Once she found the right concentration, she produced gallons of the stuff. I think she finished with the last batch a couple weeks ago and left soon after," Rurik said.

"Thanks."

When he turned to go, Rurik said, "Remember your promise."

"I will." But right now, he needed to deliver this information to Yelena and Valek.

25

YELENA

The market hummed with activity. Late afternoon was a busy time for the merchants as workers stopped for supplies before heading home for the evening. Dressed in a light green tunic and tan pants, I blended in with the crowd of mostly locals. A few soldiers from the garrison shopped, but they were more interested in the vendors selling roasted pork than in me. I kept an eye on them, though, just in case their focus shifted.

The enticing aroma of fresh baked bread drew me to a popular stand. I was on a mission. We needed more food. Not a surprise. Valek expended a great deal of energy practicing his magic, Teegan was a teenage eating machine and I was pregnant. Mass quantities of bread, meat and cheese were being consumed on a daily basis.

As I lugged my bags toward our hideout, the nape of my neck tingled. I turned right at the next street and glanced back. Two soldiers strode down the street at a brisk clip. They weren't carrying packages, and their gazes were trained on me. I hurried to the next intersection and turned left. Sure enough, they followed me. Unease churned, ruining my appetite. Had someone recognized me at the market? Or had a magician used magic to find me? Either way, I needed to shake the tail.

Recalling my lessons from Valek, I found a short street. I turned down it, and, as soon as I was out of their sight, I dropped my bags, sprinted to the end, bolted left, crossed the road, ducked down an alley and hid behind a row of trash cans. My heart banged against my chest, urging me to keep going. Instead, I pulled out my blowpipe, loaded a dart while palming another and waited.

Boots drummed on the cobblestones.

"This way," one man yelled.

Shadows crossed the mouth of the alley. I counted to ten, then crept deeper into the alley, hoping there was an exit. Avoiding the piles of rotting leaves and puddles of a foul-smelling muck, I encountered a locked gate at the end. Swapping my blowpipe for my lock picks, I popped the lock and eased into the street. A few people lingered near a fruit stand and a horse pulling a cart trotted by, but there were no soldiers in sight.

I drew in a deep breath and took a long, circuitous route back to our hideout. We would need to leave Longleaf right away and camp in the woods until Ari and Janco returned.

Circling the tailor shop, I sought watchers before entering through the back door. The sun hung low in the sky. Valek and Teegan should—

Large shadows broke from the walls and rushed me. I reached for my switchblade, but it was knocked from my hand before I could trigger the blade. Fear shot through me, increasing my pulse to triple time. A sword flashed just as my arms were pinned. I braced for the thrust, but the tip hovered mere inches from my neck. This explained why I'd lost my tail so easily, but not why I'd had one in the first place.

"Search her," a female voice ordered.

MARIA V. SNYDER

The four goons closed in, hands searching and removing most of my weapons.

"She's clean," one goon said.

"Put her in the chair," the lady said.

I was shoved into the old armchair. Dust puffed up in a cloud. The goons moved, making a tight semicircle around me, revealing Selene Moon, Owen's wife. Her long blond hair shone almost white in the sunlight. Normally as pale as Valek, she appeared as if she'd been spending time in the sun. Worry for Ari and Janco flared to life. Had she captured them while they tried to sneak into the compound and learned our location from them? If so, all was lost.

"I see prison's been good to you," I said.

"I wouldn't think you'd be so smug, considering you walked right into our trap." She gestured to the corner. My bags of food were slumped against the wall. "You thought you were safe once you'd ditched the tail." Selene tsked. She had me there. I refrained from commenting. Instead, I dropped my gaze as if dejected, but I scanned the floor for my switchblade and spotted it near her left boot.

One of Selene's goons came down the stairs, increasing the total to five. "Nobody is up there, but there's evidence of at least three others living here," he said.

Selene turned her silver-eyed gaze on me. "Who are they?"

I considered giving her the silent treatment, but I needed to stall for time. Once they dragged me into the garrison—if they didn't just kill me here—it'd be harder to escape. "My Ixian friends. The people who helped stop you and Owen from getting the Ice Moon." Ah, the good old days. Reminding her of the past had the desired effect.

A flush of red painted her cheeks. "Where are they now?"

"Gone on a mission."

"What mission?"

I smiled. "To hunt you down, of course. We know what you've been up to, Selene," I bluffed.

"Is that so?" Her icy tone promised pain.

I ignored it. "Yup."

"Are you having fun?"

Not at all. I gripped the armrests to keep my distress from showing on my face. "Yup."

"Not for long. You have no powers, Yelena. You're not even wearing a null shield. There is nothing to stop me from taking the information from your mind."

Except the baby. But I wasn't going to tell her that. "So why bother with all these questions?"

"I thought I'd give you the option to cooperate."

"How nice, but would you believe anything I told you?" I paused long enough to see her doubtful expression. "No. So why go through all this? Unless…"

Selene arched a nearly invisible eyebrow.

When she failed to take the bait, I continued. "Unless you're still terrified of me."

"Don't be ridiculous. You're no longer the Soulfinder."

Had she done something to ensure my fate? We'd thought it was the baby blocking my magic, but it was just a theory. I could have been targeted around the time of conception. Swallowing my alarm, I bluffed, "How do you know my powers haven't returned?"

"In my experience, once they're gone, they are gone." She smiled, showing a row of straight white teeth. "But just in case, I'll make sure you're never the Soulfinder again."

I lunged, grabbing her wrist. "Too late."

Her goons rushed to her aid, and multiple hands seized me. When I spotted the terror in her eyes, I knew she'd tried to use her magic against me and failed. They broke my grip and shoved me down into the chair.

She rubbed her wrist and stepped back, but then stopped. A cold calculation slid into her gaze. Oh, no.

"That was...interesting. But if you truly had your powers, you wouldn't need to touch me." Selene dropped her hands. "Something else is going on. Care to tell me?"

"No."

"That's okay. We'll find out soon enough. Let's go." She gestured to the goons bookending me.

They seized my upper arms and hauled me to my feet. I struggled and managed to break free for a second before goon number three stepped in. Pinned between all three of them, I gasped for breath from my exertions.

"Don't be ridiculous, Yelena. That baby in your belly won't prevent me from hurting you."

"That's because *I* will prevent you," Valek said from behind her as his knife appeared at her throat.

Everyone jerked with surprise. I silently cheered. My delay tactics had worked.

"Tell your thugs to unhand my wife," Valek ordered.

"Do it," Selene hissed as blood welled under the blade's sharp edge.

They released me. I smoothed my garments, making a show of it as I scanned the room for Teegan. No sign of him. Good.

"Now tell them to return to the garrison."

An odd command. The goons looked at each other in confusion. I met Valek's gaze. He winked at me. Ah.

"Go." Selene waved them off. "Bring reinforcements."

"Please do," Valek said.

Now I was confused, but I trusted my husband.

After the goons left, Valek pushed Selene away. "Let's talk."

She touched the cut on her neck, then glanced at her hand. Blood coated her fingertips. "Big mistake."

"Oh?"

"Owen isn't the only one who knows how to build a null shield."

Valek froze with his hands and knife pressed to his side, acting as if trapped. Not sure of my role in this, I dove for my switchblade. Sweeping it up from the floor, I triggered the weapon. The blade shot out with a distinctive *snick*. Selene faced me.

"I can squeeze the life from him," she said.

"Not before I stab you." I advanced.

Fury and frustration creased her beautiful face. She bolted for the door. I moved to give chase, but Valek caught my arm.

"No. Let her go."

"Why?"

"Because if she and her men went missing, there would be a manhunt."

"But there's still going to be a manhunt once they all return to the garrison and report they've seen us."

"Yes, but the Cartel won't think we've gotten information from Selene and change their plans."

Oh. That was a good point. "It still would have been nice to discover what she knows."

"Who said we didn't?" Teegan asked. He stepped from the back room with a huge grin on his face.

"What if she sensed you in her mind?" I asked in alarm.

"Uncle Valek had her quite distracted. Besides, I'm smooth." He swiped his hand through the air.

Teegan has been spending too much time in Janco's company. Before I could move, Valek wrapped me in his arms. "Thanks," I said into his neck. He smelled of the forest.

"Anytime." He released me and we shared a smile.

"Enough with the kissy face," Teegan said. "They'll be back soon."

Right. "Okay, Mr. Smooth, time to pack up."

MARIA V. SNYDER

We rushed around and grabbed our belongings and the food. Dashing through the streets of Longleaf, we made quite the sight. Eyewitnesses would report that we'd fled town and disappeared into the forest, heading northwest. In reality, we looped around to the south side of the garrison, but far enough away from the reach of their magicians. We hoped.

"What about Ari and Janco?" I asked as we set up camp. "Were they captured at the complex?"

"No," Teegan said.

"How did Selene find me, then?"

"She received a tip from one of the merchants."

So much for my disguise. "We need to warn Ari and Janco not to return to town."

"We're pretty close to their return route. The horses will alert us when they're close," Valek said.

"Are we still going to rescue the Councilors?" Teegan asked.

"Yes. In fact, tonight would be ideal. The garrison commander will send extra patrols into town to search for us, which means not as many guards in the garrison."

"Yeah, but there will be more chance of us running into all those extra patrols," Teegan said.

"And they might find Ari and Janco instead." I paced.

"Don't worry, love. Those two know how to avoid patrols. But you're right. As Janco would say, 'There are too many rabbits in the stew.' We'll hang tight until everything settles down."

Valek spread his bedroll, even though it wasn't full dark yet. Although he tried to hide it, I recognized his fatigue. Normally so graceful and fluid, his movements jerked, as if every action required a great effort.

I sat next to him, and he draped an arm around my shoulders, pulling me closer. "What did you learn at your magic lesson today?" I asked him.

"That he can make an *awesome* null shield," Teegan answered, pumping a fist in the air.

"And how to recognize them." He smiled. "Selene was so pleased with herself, thinking she'd trapped me."

Which reminded me. "And what did you learn from Selene?"

Teegan's humor faded. "She confirmed that the Cartel plans to target all the magicians during the Firestorm—her words, not mine."

"Firestorm?" Valek stared off into the distance. "Which matches our guess that the Commander plans to attack around the time of the fire festival."

"It does. But I don't think they intend to kill the magicians. She took great pleasure in the fact that we were going to be hit with some kind of substance."

"Do you know what the substance does?" I asked, hoping we'd finally learn what exactly the Cartel was planning.

"No, sorry. I only had time for a brief glance into her rotten thoughts. But—" Teegan glanced at the forest.

Both Valek and I reached for weapons.

Teegan shook his head. "It's Ari and Janco. Kiki's leading them here."

Sure enough, two men and four horses appeared from the forest. Dirt and mud splattered their clothing, and their stiff dismounts indicated they'd spent too much time in the saddle.

Janco pulled a leaf from his hair. "I was really looking forward to sleeping in a bed tonight."

"Look on the bright side—if we'd stayed in the tailor shop, you'd be sleeping in the garrison tonight," I said.

He grunted. "So I gathered."

We filled them in on Selene's visit. Ari and Janco exchanged a glance.

"What did you discover?" Valek asked.

MARIA V. SNYDER

"That substance she mentioned is called Harman sap. And it can block a magician's magic."

We all stared at Janco in shock.

"Are you sure?" Valek asked.

"Unfortunately."

"Is there a cure?" My voice was barely a whisper. Perhaps that was what had happened to me. If that was the case, at least it hadn't affected the baby. It was no longer a theory that he or she had some form of magic.

"No one knows," Janco said.

"You haven't been hit with it, Yelena," Ari said.

I clamped down on my emotions. "How do you know?"

"Selene didn't discover the correct concentration until a season ago."

A rush of relief swept through me. I grabbed Valek's arm to steady my wobbly legs. However, the good feelings died when I considered that the Cartel could still target me with the sap, and perhaps block the baby's powers, as well. And the rest of our herd was at risk, too.

"Does it wear off?" Teegan stood as if rooted to the ground.

"They don't know." Janco explained what had happened to the volunteers.

Valek was the first to recover. "It doesn't change anything. We assumed the Cartel planned to target the magicians. This is...kinder, and they can still blame the Commander."

"No wonder the Commander invited Owen in with open arms," Ari said. "He'd jump at the chance to get rid of *all* the magicians."

Janco was the only one not horrified by the prospect. "Maybe we can snag a few vials and use it on Selene, Owen and their sycophants."

We all stared at him.

"What? If they use it on us, then we'll be able to level the playing field. No magicians on either side." He shrugged. "Seems fair to me."

"Fair?" Teegan choked, truly appalled by the prospect of losing his magic forever. "It's—"

"An issue to be discussed later," Valek said, ending the discussion.

Two nights later, we prepared to rescue the Councilors. As the strongest of us, Ari volunteered to throw the storm orb at the wall, but Teegan thought he'd still be too close and might be killed.

"I've watched the Stormdancers. Those things are packed with energy," Teegan said. "I can use my magic to deliver the orb."

Janco shook his head. "According to Heli, it's gotta hit with some force or the glass won't break."

We rigged a slingshot instead, with Valek aiming and Teegan on hand to nudge the orb in case it went off course. Not like we could practice.

I crouched with Ari and Janco about two hundred yards away from Valek. Teegan promised he'd be able to protect the two of them from flying debris, and there was no reason for the rest of us to be with them.

The faint twang of the slingshot reached me a few seconds before a roar of sound dominated all my senses. Wind and pressure flattened me to the ground. Leaves, dirt, branches and a fine white powder blasted over me. My skin felt rubbed raw. The cacophony ended as suddenly as it began. Unless I'd gone deaf.

Janco pushed up to his knees. "Holy snow cats!" His voice sounded very far away.

Glad my hearing still worked, I turned to see what he gaped at. The storm's energy had cleared a path in the forest. And in

MARIA V. SNYDER

the distance, a huge hole replaced the garrison's wall. Then it hit me. There was no sign of Valek or Teegan. Panicked, I jumped to my feet. Ari was right behind me as we waded through the debris, calling their names.

A small hand poked up from a pile of leaves. Ari and I cleared the branches and bits of the wall from the mound. Underneath, Valek covered Teegan's body. His shirt was streaked with bloody rips, but he rolled off the boy with a groan.

Teegan sat up. "Wow. That was...incredible!"

"What happened to protecting the both of you with your magic?" I asked Teegan. My voice was sharper than I'd intended.

He jerked as if slapped. "Didn't expect...so much...power."

I touched his shoulder. "Sorry."

"Not his fault," Valek said. He struggled to stand.

Ari pulled him to his feet as if he weighed nothing. "Let's go before they regroup."

We trudged through the rubble and climbed over the broken edge of the wall. Soldiers milled about in shock, some of them sporting bloody cuts and gashes. A few helped others who lay on the ground. Cutting through the chaos, Teegan led us to the nearby barracks. Chunks of the wall were embedded in the sides of the building, and the glass had shattered in all the facing windows. People streamed from the building, gaping at the damage. A number of them milled about, unable to act, while others looked as if they were waiting for orders.

I pointed to a group of people. "There's Councilor Cowan."

Teegan nodded, then called the Councilors to him with his magic. They shuffled toward us as if sleepwalking.

Ari, Janco, Valek and I guided them to the wall and encouraged them to climb over. All the while, we assured them they would be safe as long as they kept moving away before the rest of the garrison collapsed. When we entered the forest, Councilor Tama Moon resisted.

I clasped her hand and murmured comfort and reassurance in her ear. After a minute, she met my gaze.

Confusion swirled in her eyes, but also recognition. "Yelena, you're here."

"Yes, I am."

"For us?"

"Yes."

"Good."

I hoped that was a sign that the baby had drained the magic brainwashing her, but I didn't know for certain. When she steadied, I moved on to Councilor Bloodgood. I made sure to touch them all during the long trek through the forest. It lasted until dawn, when it became obvious we all needed a break.

"Do you think we're far enough away?" Janco asked. He gulped a mouthful of water before handing the skin to Ari.

"Teegan?" Valek asked.

Valek's injuries looked worse in the daylight. But he wouldn't let me tend to them or use his magic to heal them, claiming they were minor.

"We have a good lead on them. Plus those tracks Janco made earlier have led half of them in the opposite direction," Teegan said.

"Good." Valek studied our traveling companions.

The Councilors huddled in pairs. Their expressions still remained a bit stunned. But none complained or demanded to be returned to the garrison. They thanked Ari as he shared a water skin and strips of jerky. However, I suspected the questions would soon start.

"We need to split up," Valek said.

No one appeared to be happy about this—quite the opposite. And while I trusted Valek had our best interests in mind, the Councilors still believed he worked for the Commander.

"Why?" I asked him.

"We're too big a group. It will slow us down and attract unwanted attention."

"Shouldn't we be *seeking* help?" Councilor Greenblade asked. She spread her hands wide, indicating the trees around them. "My clan will be more than happy to render all of us aid and shelter."

"We can't endanger your clan," I said.

"Endanger them, how? The Commander is our enemy, not our own people," Bavol said, speaking for the first time.

Hostile glares focused on Valek. He met my gaze. "Time for plan B?"

I shook my head. Not yet. Instead, I explained to the Councilors about the Cartel, Bruns, Owen and the Commander.

"No, you're wrong," Councilor Cloud Mist said. "The Cartel is *helping* us defeat the Commander."

"Then why are you in the garrison and Bruns is at the Citadel?" I asked.

"To protect us from assassination." Councilor Cowan pointed at Valek. "To protect us from him."

"If I'd been sent to kill you, you'd be dead by now," Valek said in a flat tone.

Not helping. I held up my hands. "Trust me, please. You need time for your heads to clear. Look beyond what you've been told and form your own opinion. You all know me. I've helped you with various problems in the past. Just give me seven days. After that, if you wish to rejoin Bruns and the Cartel, we won't stop you. I give you my word."

As the silence lengthened, Janco jiggled the water skin, reminding me of plan B.

"I'm willing to wait," Bavol said. "Yelena's risked her life for Sitia many times. She deserves our trust."

Tama Moon said, "Without Yelena, my soul would be forever trapped in another body."

"She saved my wife and your children from the Daviian Warpers," Councilor Stormdance reminded everyone. "We can give her seven days."

Only Janco appeared disappointed that we didn't need to resort to plan B. Relieved that they had decided to trust me, I shook each of their hands to thank them, and to draw off any magical influence that might remain. I wasn't sure if it had worked, another touch certainly couldn't hurt.

Valek split the Councilors into two groups. "Teegan, Ari and Janco will lead Councilor Moon's group. Yelena and I will escort the rest." Valek gathered the five of us together for some instructions. "Teegan, keep scanning for trouble. Head east and then north to the farmhouse. Yelena and I will go north, then east. We'll meet you there."

The trip back to the farmhouse took us longer than expected. Many patrols swept the forests and the roads heading north. It didn't take a genius to guess we'd be traveling toward the Citadel. I hoped no one had discovered Fisk's new headquarters, or else we'd be finished. In order to defeat the Cartel, we needed everyone, including the Councilors, who had finally shaken off the effects of the Theobroma. By the time we neared the end of the journey, our group fully supported us and I hoped Teegan's group felt the same. Bavol and Valek even walked together, debating various courses of action and devising ways to counter the Cartel.

We drew close to the farm on the afternoon of the eighth day, which was also day fifty-two of the heating season. Valek scouted ahead while we waited. He returned with good news.

MARIA V. SNYDER

The place was still safe from the Cartel, and we had visitors. Lots and lots of visitors.

Leif met us at the stables. "Teegan and his group showed up late last night," he said, helping me remove Kiki's saddle.

"How did your mission go?" I asked as I combed the nettles from Kiki's tail.

"We encountered some troubles. At first, the spores wouldn't reproduce, and then Father almost killed the ones we had, but the spores are all blowing in the wind now. Heli, Zohav and Zethan made an effective team. It was kinda scary, actually."

"Did you run into any difficulties returning to the farmhouse?" Valek asked. He groomed Onyx in the next stall.

"The number of patrols has increased the last couple days, but Reema kept us from having any unfortunate encounters with them."

"Reema? What's she doing here?" I asked in alarm.

"Same as us. She's good. We're going to need her." Leif set his jaw. Clearly not happy about the necessity of endangering a child, but determined to defend the decision.

"Does Opal—"

"Yes. She's in the house with Devlen." Leif frowned. "Father's here, too. He won't go home where it's safe *either*."

"Must run in the family," Valek muttered.

We ignored him. I sensed the tension rolling off Leif's stiff shoulders, and his emphasis on the word *either* was a big giveaway. "How's Mara doing?"

He crossed his arms. "She's mad at me. I tried to get her to stay with Mother in the jungle."

Even I knew that wouldn't work.

"What am I supposed to do?" he demanded. "She's been dragged into the middle of all this. She's been captured, beaten and terrorized. I can't *not* try to stop her."

"But you can trust her," Valek said. "She understands the danger and chooses to be here. Respect her wishes, even when it feels like your insides are on fire." His gaze burned into me.

And I'd increased his pain by endangering our baby. But to me, there was no other option. There would be no happily-ever-after for any of us unless we defeated the Cartel. We needed every able-bodied person. And if that meant including a magic-sucking unborn baby, then so be it.

Leif sighed and relaxed. "You're right. I know that. It's just hard. And at times, she's like a stranger to me. She's changed so much."

I touched his arm. "Patience, Leif. Just be there for her. It takes time. But she'll never return to the same woman you married. She can't. None of us can. No matter if our experiences are good, bad or in-between, we all change and grow as the years build up."

He rested his hand on mine. "Thanks. But I'm not going to apologize for wanting to keep her safe."

"You don't have to," Valek said. "You need to apologize for not trusting her."

Again I felt his gaze on me, and I wondered if he was thinking about our problems with trust when I'd been captured by Cahil.

"Apologizing can be quite enjoyable if you do it right," Valek said.

And that would be a yes. Heat swept through me as I remembered just how he had sought my forgiveness.

"I'll take that into consideration," Leif said.

When we finished settling the horses, Leif hefted my saddle bags to carry them into the house.

"Careful. There's a storm orb in there." I tried to tug them away from him. "I can carry them."

"I *trust* that you can." He shot Valek a smug smile as if to

MARIA V. SNYDER

say, *See? I learned something.* "But it would put undue strain on your body. Which is bigger than the last time I saw you."

"Did he just call me fat?" I asked Valek.

"Oh, no. I'm not getting in the middle of this."

I huffed. "I'm six months along, and think I look pretty damn good."

They both rushed to assure me.

The house was stuffed full of people. I counted twenty-six total, including the Councilors. It was a bit overwhelming when Valek and I first entered. Everyone was talking and hugging and laughing, and Leif wasn't the only one to notice my baby bump. Opal and Mara took turns feeling the baby kick, both squealing like two teenage girls when the baby obliged. Eventually we focused on the reason that had brought us all together, and the mood turned serious.

Councilor Bavol Zaltana stood in the middle of the living area. He'd been appointed the spokesperson for the Sitian Council. "I'm glad you all made yourselves at home. I had bought this property in the hopes of developing a way to increase our Theobroma and Curare production. I built the first glass hothouse here four years ago, and it was a success. Worried that it was too visible to Ixian spies—" he smiled at Valek "—I moved it into the Avibian Plains." Then a sadness pulled at his face. "I believed I was helping Sitia. That everything I did would help keep us safe from the Commander. I trusted Oran and had no idea he was giving all my information to Selene. The Cartel played me like the fool I am."

"You can't blame yourself," Tama Moon said. "They played us all using the Theobroma."

"And their plans were brilliant," Valek said. "Even the Commander was caught in their trap."

"How do we stop them?" Councilor Stormdance asked.

He gestured at the people sprawled around him. "This is it, right? The resistance."

Fisk stood up. "We have a few other helpers in the garrisons."

"Onora is in the Citadel, and we have General Cahil's support," I said.

"And don't forget the Master Magicians," Valek said.

"But they have the army," Tama said.

"We hope that won't be for long," I said, and explained our efforts to destroy the Theobroma pods.

"Sorry, Bavol," Esau said, responding to Bavol's horrified gasp. "There was no other way to reach all the hothouses."

"The soldiers will follow the Cartel's orders, even if they're no longer brainwashed," Councilor Bloodgood said. "The threat of an Ixian invasion has always been very real. It's the reason for their very existence."

"But the magicians and those in charge will be able to think for themselves," I said. "That will help."

The mood lightened considerably.

"There is a new problem, though," Valek said.

He explained about the Harman sap, which destroyed the optimistic feelings in the room. Silence followed. Then came the questions.

"The best we can do is warn the magicians," Valek said, cutting through the buzz of alarmed voices. "They can wear extra layers of clothing to keep the darts from reaching their skin and can guard against an attack from both sides."

Bavol gestured to Valek. "We've been discussing the situation on the trip here. Valek has a plan that I believe will work. It'll be dangerous, and we're going to need everyone's full cooperation. If you're not willing to help, please leave now so that if you're apprehended, you won't endanger the rest of us."

No one moved.

Bavol nodded. "Good. Valek, you're in charge."

He stood and gazed at us. I marveled at the situation. The Sitian Council had appointed Valek, who had once been the most feared man in Sitia, to lead them. And he'd accepted it without a moment's hesitation. If he pulled this off, he would save both Sitia and Ixia. And if he failed... I clamped down on that line of thought and listened to my husband with pride swelling in my chest.

"We're going to form four teams," Valek said. He held an open notebook. "The first team is assigned to the Krystal garrison and includes Ari, Janco, Zohav and Zethan, as well as Councilors Krystal, Stormdance and Bloodgood. Second team is stationed at the Featherstone garrison and includes Leif, Mara and Esau, plus Councilors Featherstone, Cowan and Jewelrose. The third team consists of Opal, Devlen, Teegan and Reema, and Councilors Moon, Cloud Mist and Sand-seed. They are assigned to the Moon garrison." He looked at me. "The Citadel team will include Yelena, Fisk and Heli, plus Councilors Zaltana and Greenblade."

Valek then explained what he needed all of us to do. "Timing is vital. You must strike at the exact same time on day twenty of the hot season. I want to attack before they march to the Ixian border."

Silence once again dominated the room. I calculated. That was twenty-eight days away. If the spores did their job, then there would be just enough time for the effects of the Theobroma to wear off. Conversations started as people discussed logistics. Most wanted to leave soon so they could be in position well before the date. I considered my part of the plan to breach the Citadel and realized there was one name Valek hadn't included in any of his teams.

I pulled my husband into the room we shared with Leif,

Mara and Esau for a private chat. As soon as he closed the door, I asked, "What are *you* going to be doing?"

"I'm going after Owen."

No surprise. "By yourself?"

"No, love. I'll have help."

"Who? There's no one left!"

"Not in Sitia," he agreed.

Oh. "You still have loyal people in Ixia."

"That's the hope. It's been a while, though. The Commander might have gained their trust." He reached up and rubbed my forehead with a thumb, smoothing my crinkled brow. "Don't worry, love. I'll be in familiar territory, and Owen doesn't know I have magic."

"He might be stronger than you."

"That's possible." Valek grinned. "But I have better aim."

"That cocky attitude is going to get you into trouble."

"*Get* me? I think it's safe to say it's *already* gotten me into trouble more times than I can count."

"Don't look so proud of that." I swatted him lightly on the arm.

He grabbed my wrist and pulled me close. His touch sent spikes of heat through my body.

"Do I need to apologize?" he asked in a husky whisper.

I glanced at the door. There were twenty-four others in the house.

"It locks, and this will be our last chance for a while."

He had me at *it locks*.

The next day, I sorted through my saddle bags. Each of the garrison teams would be armed with one storm orb, and the Citadel team would take the other two. My team would remain at the farmhouse longer than the others, since we were only a few days south of our destination. My knapsack was a complete mess, so I dumped the contents onto the bed. Weapons, vials, darts and travel clothes in desperate need of a wash tumbled out, along with the box Zitora had given me for Opal.

I'd completely forgotten about it. Picking it up, I searched for her. She sat with her family in the living area. When I caught her attention, I gestured for her to join me in the kitchen.

"That girl is going to be the death of me," Opal said.

"Valek is quite impressed with her." I set a pot full of water near the fire. With so many people in the farmhouse, we kept the hearth burning so there was enough hot food for everyone.

"Reema's proved herself, but I worry she's too confident."

Laughing, I put a tea bag into a mug. "That's always my concern with Valek." I considered. "But it's that confidence that makes them so successful."

"I know. Did you want something?"

I'd forgotten again. Was this another symptom of baby brain? Pulling the box from my pocket, I handed it to Opal. "Zitora said you'd know what to do with this."

Opal stared at the box in shock.

Not the reaction I'd expected. "What's wrong?"

"This is..." Her hand tightened around it.

"It's locked, but you shouldn't have a problem with that." And if she did, there were at least seven of us who could open it in no time. Eight, if I included Reema, who I suspected probably had lock-picking skills by now.

"That's not it." She drew in a deep breath. Her brow creased as if she was conflicted. "I need to talk to Devlen."

"I'm sorry, Opal, I didn't mean—"

"Not your fault. You didn't know."

I waited.

She pressed it to her chest. "There's a syringe full of my blood inside the box."

Of all the things that could have been inside, I'd never thought that would be it. "That's...well, kinda gross, but... why is it significant?"

"You remember the whole nasty business with the blood magic and the Bloodrose cult?"

"Yes." Blood magic was illegal. Those who used it became addicted to the magic and did terrible things in order to increase their power.

"What isn't well known is that after all was said and done, there was still one syringe full of my blood left. The blood was drawn *before* I lost my magic. Basically, if I inject this blood into my bloodstream, my siphoning magic should return."

Now it was my turn to stare in shock. Opal's magic was very powerful. She could siphon other magicians' magic into a glass orb, forever robbing them of their powers. "Who else knows about this?"

"Devlen, Irys and Zitora. But Yelena..." Opal's voice broke. "I don't know if I can... I have no desire to reclaim my powers. But my family is in danger. I should..."

I clasped her hand. "It's your decision. I will support you either way. And I won't say anything, so no one will pressure you."

She nodded, looking a bit more relieved.

Then I remembered the blood Roze Featherstone had injected into her skin to increase her powers. When I'd drained the blood from her, it'd turned black and rancid. "Besides, it might not be...potent anymore. Blood spoils."

"Magic is keeping it fresh. I can feel it through the box," Opal said.

"Oh." Then it hit me. "Oh! I'm glad the baby didn't take it." That would have been terrible. However, it appeared the baby only siphoned the magic aimed at us.

Opal shrugged. "Then I wouldn't have to make a decision."

MARIA V. SNYDER

She peered through the window, deep in thought. "You've lost your magic, too. What would you do in my place?"

"Reclaim my power. No doubt." If only I had filled a syringe with...

I gasped.

"What's wrong?" she asked.

"Opal, you just saved all the magicians in Sitia!"

26

VALEK

"Slow down, love. You're not making any sense," Valek said to his excited wife. Opal stood next to Yelena with a wide grin on her face. They had pulled him away from a meeting with the Councilors for a private chat.

"We have a way to protect the magicians," Yelena said.

"I understood that part. It's the next bit I'm having trouble following. How does extracting a syringe full of blood save a magician's power?"

Yelena glanced at Opal. "I'll let Opal explain. She has more experience."

"Unfortunately," Opal said dryly. "Don't you remember what happened at the Bloodrose cult? With me and Galen?"

"I thought that was specific to you two because you shared blood."

"That was part of it. But in essence, a person's ability to use magic is in the blood. I don't know why, but it's been proven. This magic ability remains in the blood even when it's drawn into a syringe. The power can be transferred to another magician by injecting it into his or her bloodstream, or it can enhance a magician's power by tattooing it into the skin." She rubbed her arms. "But it can also be used if something happens to a magician's magic. As long as it was drawn *before* the ability to wield magic is lost."

It didn't take him long to make the leap in logic. "So, basically, if all the magicians draw a vial of blood and then are hit with the Harman sap, they could theoretically reclaim their powers?"

"Yes!" Opal said.

No wonder they'd been so enthusiastic. He thought through the logistics. "When I contact the Master Magicians, I'll warn them about the sap. They'll have to find enough syringes for everyone and someone who isn't squeamish to draw the blood."

"They only need a few syringes," Opal said. "The blood can be stored in glass vials."

"How do they preserve the samples?" he asked.

"The masters can do it," Opal said. "And I believe Teegan will be able to do it for you and the others who are here."

Valek hadn't even considered his own magic. It was so new, and he hadn't had time to come to terms with it. The thought of being hit by the Harman sap didn't upset him, but he would take the steps needed to preserve the ability, just in case.

When news about the Harman countermeasure circulated, the mood in the farmhouse was positively buoyant. Valek spent the next few days reviewing the plan with his team leaders in the small office. Since Teegan and Leif had the ability to mentally communicate with the Master Magicians, they'd been assigned as the principals. Even though Zethan could only receive a mental communication, he was also picked to be a lead.

"Don't try to contact the masters when you first arrive," Valek instructed them. "There are other magicians in the garrisons who are seeking magic, and we don't want to tip them off that you're nearby."

"Shouldn't the magicians be on our side by then?" Teegan asked.

"Assume they aren't until it's *confirmed* that they are no longer under the Cartel's influence. There are also messengers who are Theobroma-free, so don't take any unnecessary risks. Contact them right before all hell breaks loose."

Smiles all around. Although Zethan's didn't last.

"Zee, Bain will reach out to you," Valek said. "He will know you are coming, and of all the masters, he can bypass anyone who is trying to snoop."

"Just don't be offended when he calls you 'child,'" Leif said. "He calls everyone that, even the Keep's bursar, and that man is only a few years younger than Bain."

When they finished the meeting, Valek asked Teegan to stay. He uncovered the super messenger and handed it to the boy. "Time to contact the masters and let them in on our plans. Start with Bain, then Irys. If there's enough power left, reach out for Zitora. If not, you'll be close enough when you arrive near the garrison."

"And I have a light touch," Teegan bragged.

"There's that."

Then the boy sobered. "I don't know Master Zitora. She might not let me in."

A valid point. Valek considered. "She knows me."

Teegan tapped on the glass. "We should do this together. We'll have more power, and you can answer any of her questions that I don't know."

"Good idea."

"Boy genius, remember?"

"How could I ever forget?" Valek's voice dripped with sarcasm.

Teegan grinned. "Baby brain."

He mock-growled at the boy but couldn't keep a stern ex-

MARIA V. SNYDER

pression. Now that everyone had heard it, the phrase was quickly becoming the excuse for everything. Teegan grabbed his hand, and they contacted Bain, Irys and then Zitora. The magic in the messenger died before they finished their session with Zitora, but Teegan now had a connection to her.

Tired from the effort, Valek considered resting—perhaps Yelena needed a nap—but Ari and Janco entered the office soon after Teegan left. They stood in front of the desk.

"We're not happy about you facing Owen alone," Ari said.

"I don't expect to go toe-to-toe with the man," Valek said.

"What do you expect? 'Cause there are three of them and one of you," Janco said.

"I expect to assassinate them. If I do it correctly, they will have no idea what hit them."

Janco grinned. "Way to go, Boss."

Ari elbowed him. "We still think you should take—"

"There's no one *to* take. And you know it." Valek understood their concern, but there was nothing he could do about it.

"Little Miss Assassin would have been perfect to act as your backup." Janco's expression turned somber.

"Don't worry about her," Valek said. "She's more than capable of taking care of herself."

He brightened a bit. "Yeah. I bet she's driving Brunsie crazy."

"Hanging out with Janco, she certainly had enough experience with the fine art of pestering someone to distraction," Ari said.

"Hey!"

Valek studied his two friends as they bickered. They had saved his life, protected Yelena, and done so much for him over the years, including committing treason by being here instead of with the Commander in Ixia.

And now, he needed to ask them to do one more thing.

Interrupting them, Valek said, "When you breach the garrison, please keep an eye on the twins. They're powerful, but they're still young, and my mother would be upset if anything happened to them." He already had more of an understanding of this parent-child bond, and his own baby wasn't even born yet. Valek could only imagine how much worse it would be once the child joined the world and faced all the dangers and hazards associated with living.

"Will do, Boss," Janco said. "I understand all about keeping mothers happy."

"You do?" Ari asked with a doubtful tone.

"Yes. Just because I *ignore* it doesn't mean I don't *understand* it."

After Valek ensured everyone understood what they needed to do, he planned to leave the next morning. Having the most experience with syringes, Devlen drew a vial of Valek's blood, which Teegan preserved. Valek would find a safe place to hide it on his way to the castle. Each magician would decide where to hide his or her own blood. This ensured that the vials weren't stored in one location and would protect them from being sabotaged by the Cartel.

When he joined Yelena in their room, the desire to lecture his wife about being extra careful and staying alive boiled up his throat with searing bubbles, but he kept it in check. She understood. And he was sure she was biting back on her worries as well.

Instead, they locked the door and spent the evening being together. When they'd exhausted their bodies, they lay intertwined and talked about everything but the upcoming Firestorm.

"If it's a boy, we could name him Valek," Yelena said.

MARIA V. SNYDER

"Then we'd both respond when you called," he said. "No. Too confusing."

"What do you suggest?"

He decided to have some fun. "Rock. That's a strong name."

"It's also an inanimate object. Try again."

"Steel. Another powerful name."

"That's not a name."

"Storm?"

"Valek." She'd had enough.

He considered. "How about Vincent? After my brother." Grief bloomed in his chest for a moment. Valek and Vincent had gotten into a lot of trouble as boys.

Yelena squeezed his hand. "It's perfect."

"But we both know the baby's a girl," he said.

"We do?"

"Yes, we do. What should we name her? Sweetie Pie?"

She elbowed him. "How about Daddy's Little Girl?"

"I like that."

"Figures."

He chuckled, but then thought of their future daughter. She'd be beautiful and strong and smart and stubborn, just like her mother. No doubt about that. "How about Liana?" It was Yelena's middle name, but it also meant *vine*. "She's already wrapped around both our hearts."

"That's lovely."

Morning arrived far too soon. The garrison teams prepared to leave, and the Citadel team gave them a hand with packing. After saying goodbye and good luck to everyone, Valek kissed Yelena.

He refused to say goodbye to his wife. Instead he said, "I will see you in a few weeks."

"You'd better."

Swooping in for another kiss, he cupped her cheek. "Yes, sir."

Valek mounted Onyx. They headed northwest. The Commander's castle was about a three-day ride north, but Valek planned to approach it from the west. He found a stable for Onyx a few miles south of the Ixian border. The horse would draw too much attention and be hard to hide from the Ixian patrols. Realizing that the vial of his blood would likely be safer here than with him in Ixia, Valek hid it in Onyx's saddle. He then packed a small bag and slung it over his shoulders.

When he reached the border, he expected an increase in the number of patrols guarding the edge of the Snake Forest. What he didn't expect was the sheer number of soldiers in the forest. He suspected the Commander—or rather, Owen—planned to have the army in position well before the fire festival. But did that mean they would strike sooner? He hoped not, or all their plans would be ruined.

With so many bodies to avoid, Valek needed to use his magic to enter Ixia undetected and to steal a patrolman uniform. He arrived in Castletown late on the fourth night. Ghosting along the quiet streets, he kept to the shadows. When he neared the safe house on Pennwood Street, he slowed. The place appeared empty, but he extended his magic to search the rooms, just in case. The good news—no ambush waited for him. The bad news—no one else was inside.

Valek waited until late, hoping his agents would return. When it was obvious they weren't coming back, he debated his next move. His agents might have left a message for him, explaining their whereabouts. Or there could be a magical alarm set to go off if he entered the building. Not willing to take any chances, Valek searched for another place to lie low.

He found an empty house that had seen better days. Wedged between two others, the narrow three-story building was one strong windstorm away from collapse. Cracks scarred the stone foundation, and the wooden beams sagged. The smell of mold permeated every empty room, and a hole in the roof allowed entrance to a variety of birds that nested on the top floor. Valek set up his bedroll in the only dry corner on the ground floor.

The next day, Valek poked around the town, hoping to get a sense of what had been going on in his absence. He noticed the population of the town had dwindled, and the mood was glum, despite the warm sunshine. Also, it was the first day of the hot season, which meant the fire festival was only a month away. There were only two festivals celebrated in Ixia, and both were always highly anticipated.

Valek widened his explorations and discovered the source of their…discomfort. Soldiers filled the festival field outside Castletown. Instead of brightly colored tents, rows of camouflaged military bivouacs lined the ground. He worried that this meant they planned to march sooner. Valek needed a way to confirm their intentions. Perhaps he could mingle with the soldiers in the mess tent? Too risky. What else?

He almost groaned aloud. He could target an officer and read the person's thoughts. Valek wondered when using his magic would become second nature.

He watched the activity from a hidden location for the rest of the day. A few people looked promising, but Valek didn't want to rush it, nor did he wish to rip the information from someone's mind. He'd rather coax it out, so the person would have no idea Valek was ever there. But he doubted he had that light a touch. After a couple days of observation, he found a potential mark—a male captain. The man wasn't ranked high enough to be making decisions but should be aware of the details of the attack.

A few hours after the captain retired to bed, Valek crept to the man's tent—which was rather easy, since no one had bothered to station guards around the encampment. He crouched behind the shelter. Since he wasn't sure of his magical range with this many people around, he preferred to err on the side of caution. Valek hoped the captain would explain Valek's presence in his mind as strange dreams.

Lowering his shield, Valek extended his awareness. The captain was alone. And awake. Damn. Valek floated on the very surface of the man's thoughts. Captain Campbell reviewed all the tasks he needed to do on the morrow. The list was quite long—probably why Campbell couldn't sleep. Most of the items could be taken care of by a lower-ranking officer in the captain's unit, but this man liked to be in control and refused to delegate. Good for Valek, because he sensed the man housed a deep well of information.

Valek used his magic to encourage the man to fall asleep. Once Campbell drifted into a deeper slumber, Valek nudged the captain toward considering the future. Campbell longed for the festival, especially the pit beef and cream cakes.

No sweets once it's over, Valek thought.

No, but something important. Images of soldiers fighting with swords flashed in Campbell's mind. *So much training…better pay off.*

Valek picked up on the man's worry. *Sitia'll be ready for us.*

Yeah. Columns of soldiers formed. They marched right into rows of Sitian ranks. Sadness darkened Campbell's thoughts over the imagined battle. *Casualties can't be avoided in the initial attack.*

Picking up on the word *initial,* Valek gently prodded.

Second attack from the rear. Surprise, surprise, Sitia.

An icy chill ripped through him, but he kept his emotions in check. *How?*

Slow leak over the last couple of seasons. Use the tunnel.

MARIA V. SNYDER

Valek stifled a curse. Owen had been using the smugglers' route under the border to sneak soldiers into Sitia. While the Sitian army fought off the Ixians, another Ixian force would move in behind them. The Sitians would be trapped between the two and forced to surrender. At least the Commander wasn't planning a slaughter.

Hard to hide so many, Valek thought.

Best of the best. Kept out of sight. Assassins in first, to target the leaders.

Even the Cartel?

All *leaders*.

No surprise Owen planned to double-cross Bruns. Good riddance. It was the others that concerned Valek. Without any leaders, Sitia would be easy pickings.

When?

After the Sitian army leaves the garrisons.

That made sense. They'd no longer be protected. Valek needed to warn them, just in case his mission failed.

Before breaking his connection with Campbell, Valek pulled on a bunch of random thoughts so the captain wouldn't suspect he'd been interrogated. The man might, regardless. It was hard to tell. A few sessions with Teegan hadn't given Valek enough experience. He suspected it would take years to fine-tune his skills.

Tired from the exertion needed to read Campbell's mind, Valek returned to his hideout. He lay on his bedroll and pondered the information. At least the timing of the attack remained the same. However, he wasn't sure how to get a message to the resistance. Perhaps he could reach Irys. The Featherstone garrison was the closest to Castletown. But would his fumbling efforts do more harm than good? Another magician could pick up on his attempt, exposing Irys or bringing unwanted attention to his whereabouts.

He decided to wait. If his mission appeared to be headed toward failure, he would endeavor to warn Irys and the others.

Once he'd rested, Valek spent the next three days monitoring the traffic through the castle's gate. The security personnel just about tripped over each other in the narrow opening. And he counted at least three magicians—they stood out due to their lack of visible weapons. Plus Valek recognized Tyen, Owen's chief minion, who spent most of the day glaring at everyone. Probably upset about being assigned to guard duty.

Not a single person touched the compound's walls, which meant the magical alarm remained. And without his agents to help, Valek's chances of getting inside undetected dwindled to zero. If he had a storm orb, he'd be able to breach the castle without any trouble, but that would certainly alert them.

There was only one way to get inside—as a prisoner. But he had to do it right. If he was spotted in Castletown or caught trying to sneak through the gate, Owen would suspect Valek had done it on purpose. Basically he needed Owen to believe he'd outsmarted Valek. That line of thought led to the safe house. It had to be rigged with a magical alarm. Owen would know exactly when Valek entered.

Valek spent the rest of the day and evening preparing for his capture. After midnight, he packed up his things and headed to the safe house. No one lurked inside. Before unlocking the door, he paused. Once he touched the knob, there would be no turning back. If Yelena knew what he was about to do, she'd be very upset. But she'd understand. No one was safe until this was done.

The door swung open without a sound. The dark interior appeared the same. Valek closed the heavy black curtains and then lit a small lantern. He lowered his mental shield but didn't sense any magic. If he'd triggered an alarm, it was beyond his ability to detect. He checked all the rooms and found nothing of note, except for a faint layer of dust. Back in the main living area, he scanned the table. Files had been left behind, and he wondered what Adrik and Pasha had been working on.

When he opened the top file, a pop sounded. The ever-present weight of magic around him disappeared. A single small piece of paper had been tucked inside. It read, Gotcha.

Valek laughed. Owen had set a booby trap for him. There was a null shield around him, which would have effectively trapped him here until they arrived to collect him. Nice. He tested the boundaries of the shield. It circled the table, allowing him some room to move, but not much. He wondered how long it would be before they arrived. Just in case there were other booby traps in the apartment, Valek stayed close to the table. If he set off another one, Owen would think someone else was here. Playing the part of ambushed victim, Valek sat on the table and waited.

They took their sweet time. Probably to rub it in. Fine. Valek's assassin training included patience.

The rasp of a key in the lock roused Valek from a light doze. He pulled his daggers. As soon as the door swung wide, he threw his knife. It thunked into a wooden shield. They'd come prepared. He waited for a clean shot, but as the shielded man advanced, Valek spotted Tyen behind him. To keep up appearances, he tried to hit Tyen with his second throw. But it veered off course as Tyen's magic deflected the blade. The darts Valek had lined up along the table flew off with a single gesture from Tyen.

"Do you have anything else?" Tyen asked with a bored tone.

Valek gave him his cold killer gaze. He spread his arms wide. "Why don't you check my pockets?"

"Cute. Boys." Tyen stepped aside as four thugs fanned to the sides.

They held a net. Ah. He'd wondered how they would contain him without Owen to adjust the null shield. He assumed a null shield had been woven into the rope. Once the net was around him, it would allow them to move him without a struggle. Not about to make this easy for anyone, Valek circled behind the table, keeping it between him and the advancing men. All he could do with only a small space to maneuver.

A needle of pain pricked his neck. Focused on the thugs, Valek hadn't kept an eye on Tyen.

The magician shrugged. "You were screwed either way."

True. Valek pulled the dart from his skin. A heaviness flowed through his body, pressing him toward the ground. His arms felt as if they'd turned to stone. The thugs threw the net over him, and the weight of the ropes knocked him down as the sleeping potion knocked him out.

Dry-mouthed and with a killer headache, Valek woke in one of the cells in the dungeon underneath the castle. Lying on a pallet covered with vile-smelling straw, he rubbed his forehead as he took stock of his situation. No magic surrounded him. Valek concentrated, sensing that the shield had been woven around all the bars of his cell.

His uniform had been replaced with a standard-issue jumpsuit. A faint glow of lantern light flickered on the damp stone outside the bars. He wasn't in one of the deeper levels, which meant he'd probably get visitors. He was alone in his cell for the moment, but multiple forms occupied the cells next to him. When he pushed to a sitting position, the others stood and shuffled close to the bars separating them. Valek recognized all of them—his agents.

"Are you okay?" Adrik asked. Faded purple bruises marked the man's face.

"Yes," Valek's voice rasped. There wasn't any water in the cell.

MARIA V. SNYDER

A shuffle sounded, and then Qamra's hand appeared between the bars. She held a metal cup of water. Valek took the water and downed it, despite the unidentifiable bits floating on the surface.

"Thanks," he said. He scanned the people. A few had cuts and bruises in varying stages of healing. Most were grim-faced, but a couple smiled in anticipation. "Report."

Adrik gestured. "We refused to follow orders and are here awaiting execution. They plan to…burn us alive…during the fire festival." His voice hitched.

Valek didn't blame him. Burning someone to death was cruel and horrific. "The Commander prefers hangings."

"Well, we all know *he's* not making the decisions anymore. That magician thought fire was a more fitting execution."

"And my other agents?"

"Are following the Commander's orders." He pointed to his ear, then signaled. *We have a friend in high places.*

Advisor Maren?

Yes.

Smart, but dangerous. If Owen and the Commander discovered she was only pretending to be loyal, they'd milk her for information before killing her.

We're hoping you have a brilliant plan, Adrik motioned.

He wasn't sure of its brilliance. And he couldn't tell them, either. If a magician read their thoughts, Valek's plan had no chance. *No, sorry, I don't.*

His agents reacted with dismay. Worried, strained expressions replaced the smiles. He hated lying to them, but he hoped they'd forgive him later, once they'd managed to escape.

"That magician, Owen, did something to your bars with his magic," Adrik said, then signed, *He's under the impression that will keep you contained.*

"Then I'm stuck here like the rest of you," Valek said in a defeated tone.

Really? Adrik gestured, still hopeful.

Really.

The mood turned downright ugly.

Valek's expected visitors arrived a few hours later. Owen, Tyen and Maren stood on the opposite side of the bars. The Commander was smart enough to avoid endangering himself by entering the dungeon. The Commander also wasn't the type to gloat—unlike Owen, who looked mighty pleased with himself. Maren kept her expression neutral, though, even when she met his gaze. Standing, Valek moved closer to the door and sized up the enemy. A short sword hung from Owen's waist. Tyen had Valek's daggers tucked into his belt—a nice little dig at besting Valek. Maren was unarmed, as far as Valek could tell, which said quite a bit. Owen might not fully trust her yet.

"I knew you wouldn't be able to resist returning to Ixia," Owen said. "Did you like my trap at your safe house?"

Valek considered keeping quiet, but the man had an ego that Valek planned to manipulate. "It was clever."

Owen preened. "I've been two steps ahead of you this entire time. In fact, I'm quite happy that your resistance is going to use those storm orbs on the garrisons. It'll help me tremendously."

Valek acted surprised, but it just confirmed what Campbell had told him about the attack from the rear.

"No sarcastic comeback?" Owen asked.

Now was the time for silence.

"I guess you've realized you're out of luck and options. You're up first for execution."

"Is it scheduled for tomorrow?" Valek asked.

"No. You'll be going up in flames as part of the grand opening ceremonies for the fire festival. It'll be quite the show."

"Too bad I'm going to miss it," Valek said.

Owen tapped the bars with his finger. "A null shield will be around you at all times. And *I* control that shield. Right now, it's as big as your cell. But all I have to do…" Owen held his hands wide and then brought them slowly together.

Valek stared at the magician, but he kept his senses open to determine the exact location of the shield. If he didn't react properly, it was the end of the road. Owen's lips quirked just a bit as the shield closed around his body. Valek stiffened, pretending his arms were pinned to his sides. A glint of cruelty shone in Owen's eyes, and Valek held his breath as if his lungs were being squeezed. Valek's gaze promised pain and death, but Owen merely laughed at Valek as he held the shield for a very long minute before spreading his hands apart again. Valek sucked in deep breaths, trying not to gasp, which just amused Owen even more. Good.

"Face it, Valek. You can't escape," Owen said.

"I've heard that before. And it wasn't true then, either."

"Is that so?" Owen jerked the door to Valek's cell open. "It's not even locked. Go on, then. Escape."

Unbelievable. Owen had just given him an unexpected gift. Valek strode up to the opening but jerked to a stop just shy of breaking the threshold. While Owen and Tyen delighted in the action, Valek signaled Maren. If she wasn't on board, Valek was done. Maren, however, didn't react at all.

"You're a relic," Owen said. "Your weakness is well known, and any magician who can erect a null shield can beat you. Considering your immunity served you so well all these years, it's ironic, isn't it?"

Valek dropped his shoulders a bit. "I'm well aware of the irony."

"Good. You have lots to think about before I return to escort you to the pyre."

Owen turned to leave.

"I do have one question," Valek said.

The magician paused. "Yes?"

"Any last words?" Valek moved. He stepped through the door, grabbed Owen's short sword and stabbed it deep into the man's stomach. Hot blood gushed over his hands, adding to the satisfaction of seeing the shocked expression on Owen's face.

Maren had a knife on Tyen, but she yelled as the man's magic slammed her into a wall. She crumpled to the ground in a heap as the weapon clattered to the floor. Tyen gestured, and the knife flew at Valek.

Valek dodged the blade, but soon both daggers were sailing through the air and there wasn't enough room to maneuver. He put his back against the wall and waited to grab the weapons when they came close, risking a nasty slice. However, once Tyen caught on to his plan, the man just pinned Valek in place with his magic. Shit.

Pulling power, Valek projected into Tyen's mind. A strong barrier prevented Valek from getting inside.

Tyen stared at him. "Never thought you'd stoop to using blood magic, but that's the only way to explain your magic."

Valek didn't bother to correct him.

"You can't be as strong or as skilled as I am." Tyen spun the knives in the air until their tips aimed at Valek's throat.

"If you stop now, I'll let you live," Valek said.

"I'm a dead man regardless. You know that. Least I can do is take you with me." The blades shot toward Valek.

Desperate, Valek yanked a big chunk of magic. With no time to knit a null shield, he shaped it into a spear and drove it into Tyen's mental barrier with all his strength. It punched a hole right though, flooding Tyen's mind with Valek's magic.

Stop! Valek commanded. *Sleep!*

The man and knives dropped to the ground. Valek peeled away from the wall. The dungeon reeled under his feet as his muscles turned to goo. Collapsing to his knees, Valek scraped his remaining energy together to fumble underneath the jumpsuit. He clawed the flesh-colored putty away from a set of lock picks. He managed to toss them to Adrik before the world spun around him, sending him into a whirlwind of blackness.

Valek woke up in the infirmary. His wrists were cuffed to the metal bars of the bed's headboard, and his ankles were cuffed to the footboard. He would have laughed at how utterly ridiculous it was to secure him, but he didn't have the strength to even produce a sound. At least he wasn't in the dungeon. Small mercies. The next time he woke, Medic Mommy tsked over him. Every single muscle in his body ached, and just the thought of moving sent him back into oblivion.

The third time he roused, he wondered if this was how a newborn felt—unable to do anything but suck liquids. He stopped counting after that. His moments of wakefulness blurred together. Maren's visit eased his worries for her. She reported that both Tyen and Owen were dead. He wished to know how Tyen had died, but that required too much effort.

Instead, he asked, "Rika?" in a whisper.

Maren frowned. "You need to rest. As near as the medic can tell, you're suffering from a complete, full-body exhaustion." She stood to leave. "Was all that about the null shield just a ruse this entire time? If so, it was a pretty damn good one."

So why did she act so unhappy? Was she upset to be left behind when everyone else had gone to Sitia?

Summoning the strength to talk, he said, "No."

She huffed as if she didn't believe him, then strode from the room without answering his question about Rika. Maren didn't return, and over the next few days, Valek regained some of his vigor. Enough so that he longed to sit up and move around, but Medic Mommy also dodged his questions about why he'd been secured.

When he woke next, the Commander stood at the foot of his bed.

"Interesting scar," he said, pointing to Valek's bare chest.

The blanket only covered the bottom half of him. He would worry, but the altered scar was the least of his problems at the moment.

"A wedding present for Yelena," Valek said.

"Ah, yes. I heard about that. And you've a baby on the way, too. Congratulations."

Nice words, but the tone was flat and…dangerous. "Thank you."

The Commander pulled a chair over to the bed and sat down. "I should thank you for killing that bastard, Owen."

"Are you—"

"Yes. *I'm* in full control." Fury blazed in his gaze for a moment. "Just when I start thinking that magicians aren't *all* corrupt and power-hungry, along comes proof that I'm right not to trust them."

"You agreed to work with Owen," Valek said. "If you'd executed—"

"I made a mistake," the Commander snapped. "And I paid for it." He smoothed an invisible wrinkle from his pant leg. "You saved me yet again. I should thank you for that, as well."

Should didn't mean he would. Valek rattled the cuffs. "Not the best way to express your gratitude."

"You're a traitor, Valek. You're helping Sitia, and you were a *magician*." He spat the word as if it tasted vile in his mouth.

But it wasn't the *m*-word that snagged Valek's attention.

MARIA V. SNYDER

Were. He reached for the power blanket. Nothing. Exhaustion or Harman sap? Did it matter?

Yes, it did. The answer surprised him.

"How long did you hide it from me?" the Commander asked.

"I didn't hide it. It happened on my return trip from the coast." He explained what had occurred by Vincent's grave. "All those who said my immunity to magic was a form of magic were right. No one was more astonished than I."

The Commander showed no emotion. "You still should have reported back to me."

"You were under Owen's influence, and I'm well aware of your views. It would have been a death sentence." The conversation had drained his energy. Valek wouldn't last much longer. "My corps?"

"Pardoned."

That was a relief. "Am I still first in line to be barbequed?"

A faint smile. "Hanged."

"Much better." And he meant it.

"The invasion of Sitia will continue as scheduled."

Valek closed his eyes as a wave of crushing dismay swept through him. Even though he'd killed Owen, he'd failed to stop the war.

"Magicians need to be neutralized," the Commander said. "The Sitian Council has proven to be ineffective at keeping them in check. It won't be a bloodbath, Valek. You know that's not my style. The Sitian people will be well taken care of, just like the Ixian people."

He wished it was that easy. Valek opened his eyes and met the Commander's gaze. "It'll be impossible to target all the magicians."

"A few will slip through the cracks," he agreed. "But what

I find very telling is that you didn't ask me *how* we planned to neutralize the magicians."

If he'd had more energy, Valek would have cursed.

"The Sitians know we have the Harman sap," the Commander said, more to himself than Valek. "That'll complicate things, but I'm confident once we target enough magicians, it will be easier to get them all. At least Owen delivered on his promise to produce an effective substance. He never fully trusted me, so he kept the details secret until recently. I suspect he'd just managed to get it to work." His cold smile failed to soften his expression. "Excellent timing for me."

Valek ignored the jab. "What about Rika?"

"She's been in Sitia, helping the Cartel."

Ah, that explained those illusion cloaks.

"Don't worry. She's on my list to be neutralized by the Harman sap," the Commander added. "You were the first, by the way."

"I'm honored."

A flash of amusement crossed his face before the Commander turned somber. "I've missed our conversations." He stood to leave. "I'm going to need a new assassin and security chief. Do you have any recommendations?"

"Onora."

Valek had managed to shock the Commander. He gaped at Valek, speechless. First. Time. Ever.

"I forced her to work for the resistance," Valek said. "She's not a traitor."

"I see."

And the Commander did—he was smart that way. A pang of grief rolled through Valek. Too bad he would have to assassinate the Commander.

27

LEIF

Leif opened his senses and waited for Master Magician Irys Jewelrose to contact him. His team hid in the woods near the back wall of the Featherstone garrison. He reached for Mara's hand and squeezed, reassuring her. The weak moon-light lit her face with a soft white glow. Strain etched lines of worry in her forehead, but if he'd suggested she remain at the inn, where it was safe, Mara would have growled at him.

The growling was new. And while he longed for the sweet woman he married, Valek's comments repeated in his mind. Trust. And perhaps with time, some of the sweetness would return.

Nearby, his father cradled the storm orb in his lap. Leif had constructed a null shield around Esau, Mara and the three Councilors—Featherstone, Cowan and Jewelrose. They also crouched in the underbrush. The buzz of insects was the only sound.

Leif glanced at the moon again, estimating its position in the sky. The attack was scheduled for tonight. They needed to launch it at a precise time or risk ruining the resistance's chances of success. What if Irys didn't contact him? What if she was compromised?

It didn't matter. Leif wouldn't miss the deadline.

He sniffed the air, seeking emotions or any signs that a patrol was close by. Refraining from reaching further, he drew back to avoid alerting the garrison's magicians that he was outside their walls.

The moon refused to move, or so it seemed to Leif. It clung to that one spot, just to annoy him. He suppressed a sigh and squirmed into a more comfortable position.

Leif, Irys's voice sounded in his mind. *We're ready.*

Cooling relief flowed through him. *The soldiers?* he asked.

They're regaining their senses, but a few are stubborn and insist they have to defend against the Commander's army. They might try to stop you.

Leif checked his tunic. Darts loaded with his sleeping draft had been threaded through the fabric. The rest of his team was similarly armed. *Let's hope by the time they figure out what's going on, it'll be too late.*

He signaled the Councilors to secure the slingshot. *Keep well away from the wall,* he told Irys.

Will do. See you on the flip side.

He clamped down on a chuckle.

Once the slingshot was strung between two trees, Leif took the orb from his father. Councilor Featherstone pulled the rubber sling back and angled it. Leif hoped the man's aim was as accurate as he'd claimed. A few other hopes followed in quick succession: hope that they were far enough back to avoid being flattened by the blast. Hope that no one was killed on the other side. Hope that they reached the main administration building before one of Bruns's magicians could warn the other garrisons.

Leif shoved all those worries deep inside. He placed the orb in the sling. The others moved deeper into the woods.

MARIA V. SNYDER

He held up a finger, signaling to the Councilor. One. Two fingers. Three.

Featherstone let go. The orb sailed through the air. Moonlight sparked off the glass, and for a heart-stopping moment, Leif thought it would fly over the wall. But then it smashed into the marble. Lightning exploded, blinding him two seconds before a roar slammed into him.

The force of the storm picked him up, carried him a few feet and hurled him to the ground hard enough to knock the air from his lungs in one whoosh. Bits of greenery floated in the clouds of dust while dirt and pieces of stone rained down on him. When he caught his breath, he sat up. Every muscle ached, and small cuts peppered his arms and legs.

Then he remembered the others. Panicked, he stood on shaky legs, searching for Mara and his father. She materialized from the fog. Blood streamed from a gash on her shoulder, but she waved away his hand.

"I'm fine," she said, reassuring him. "But your father's been knocked unconscious."

She led him to Esau. A nasty gash marked his temple. Leif felt his pulse. Strong. Thank fate. He rolled his father into a more comfortable position and covered him with foliage. "He should be fine. We need to go, or we'll lose the element of surprise."

They assembled and did a quick injury check. Councilor Featherstone and Leif had gotten the brunt of the blast, but nothing serious. The others had minor cuts and bruises.

"Stay close to me," Leif ordered.

Every one grabbed a dart, and the team raced for the ragged hole in the garrison's wall.

Bits of marble crunched underfoot as he led the others. Dust clouded the air, but fuzzy yellow dots marked the location of the torches and lanterns. Shouts and sounds of confusion echoed off the parts of the wall still standing. They climbed over the mounds of debris. Figures rushed toward them.

Leif aimed at the closest man, but Irys yelled, "He's one of ours." She strode into sight with a number of armed soldiers trailing her. Her long hair had been pulled up into a bun. Irys wore a generic Sitian uniform, but there was no mistaking the power in her emerald gaze, nor the commanding posture that only a Master Magician could pull off. She gestured to her men. "Provide cover."

Her soldiers surrounded them in a protective formation. Sweet.

"This way," she said, breaking into a jog.

His team chased her. They headed straight for the administration building where the garrison's high-ranking officers and magicians lived. A thick ring of guards two deep waited for them outside the building. They slowed to a stop. The defenders remained in position despite seeing Irys leading them.

Surprised, Leif asked Irys, "Is Cahil no longer on our side?"

"He sent his men on a mission, but Bruns ordered extra security, and he had to comply or risk being discovered." She glanced at him. "Bruns suspects something is going to happen, but I didn't tell Cahil which night, just in case."

Smart, but it didn't help with this obstacle. He looked over his shoulder, ensuring Mara remained right behind him.

Before he could stop him, Councilor Featherstone strode through their front line and approached the guards. "I'm Councilor Drake Featherstone. This is my garrison, and I'm in charge. Stand down at once."

No one moved.

"What now?" Leif asked Irys. "The noise of a skirmish will alert the magicians inside, and they'll send a message to Bruns."

Irys smiled. "I've a null shield around the building." She

gestured to the guards blocking them. Two of them flew through the air and crashed to the ground. They lay still. "I've been wanting to do that for months."

Ah, yes, so nice to be fighting with a Master Magician again. "Engage," Leif ordered.

The soldiers surrounding them surged forward. He glanced at Mara. "Stay with me."

"I've got your back," she said in a firm tone, even though she trembled.

Irys remained beside Leif as they fought through the chaos. Using the darts, Leif jabbed them into arms and legs while ducking blades. It worked, at least until he faced an aggressive opponent intent on skewering him. Irys's attention was elsewhere, so he pulled his machete to defend himself. Unwilling to inflict any major harm, Leif stayed on the defensive, searching for an opportunity to jab the man with a dart. Except the guard was smart enough to avoid getting too close.

Out of the corner of his eye, he spotted Mara. Distracted, Leif blocked left instead of right, and the man disarmed him. He backed away as the guard advanced. So focused on Leif, he didn't see Mara until she'd stabbed a dart into his neck. The man cursed and rounded on her, but she kicked him in the groin. Hard. He crumpled to the ground.

Mara grinned. "Told you I had your back."

Leif hugged his wife. "That's my girl!"

Working as a team, they wove through the clumps of fighters. Eventually they reached the entrance. Irys joined them soon after with two others.

"The null shield won't stop the magicians from using magic inside the building. I can't tighten it and keep the guards off balance." She hooked a thumb at the melee.

"I have a null shield around Mara, and I can construct another pretty fast if needed."

"Good. They'll be in the main command center on the third floor. Let's go."

Irys led the charge up the stairs. No one tried to stop them. When they reached the landing, the door was closed, but faint lantern light shone underneath.

Booby trapped? Leif asked Irys.

No. They're too busy arguing.

How many?

Four.

Leif turned the knob, opening the door into a large area filled with tables, chairs, desks and file cabinets. Beyond that was another door. It stood ajar, spilling a yellow glow.

Inside, four people gestured over a glass cube sitting on a pedestal. Their voices were clear. "...null shield, you idiot. We need to take this to the roof."

"And risk being shot by a bow and arrow? No thanks."

"Bruns needs to know!"

Leif gestured for Mara and the two soldiers to wait. Weaving through the furniture, Irys and Leif crossed the room without tripping over anything. They paused by the door.

Allow me, Irys thought.

Go right ahead. This was going to be good.

Irys swept into the room, surprising them. They turned and then froze, held immobile by Irys's magic. A number of big, comfortable-looking couches ringed the room, along with a few windows and doors.

"It's safe," Irys called to the others. "Leif, prick them with the darts, please."

Happy to oblige, he yanked a couple darts and approached. The air smelled like black licorice. Deceit. The four magicians were an illusion. He spun, crying a warning just as four people seemed to step from the walls. Another illusion? One swung a mace at Irys, catching the Master Magician on the temple.

She crashed to the ground and didn't move. Not an illusion. And now the null shield surrounding the building was gone.

The three others attacked Mara and the soldiers with such speed that by the time Leif yanked his machete, they were unarmed. Realizing his options were dwindling to nothing, Leif swiped the glass super messenger off the pedestal. Thank fate it was real. He hefted it in one hand.

"Stop, or I'll smash this into a million pieces." Leif hoped they didn't have another one nearby.

Rika Bloodgood pressed a knife to Mara's neck. "Put it down gently, or I'll slit her throat."

He met Mara's gaze. She mouthed the word *no*. But Leif couldn't sacrifice her life. Not even to stop a war. It was self-ish, and they'd probably die regardless. His heart twisted with anguish as he set the messenger back on the pedestal.

"Now drop your weapon."

Leif released his machete. It clattered to the floor, making the same hollow sound that echoed in his chest. He gestured to the walls. "Nice trick."

"Not a trick, but skill and talent. I fooled a Master Magician with that illusion."

Modest, too.

"Now move away from the messenger."

He obeyed.

28

YELENA

Crouched near the Citadel's southern gate, I waited. After twenty-three days of fretting, we finally moved into position after the sun had set. In a few short hours, we would launch the orbs and storm the castle...er...Citadel. Valek had decided a strike in the middle of the night would be more effective. Roused from sleep, the soldiers would be disoriented and disorganized. It had worked for the Greenblade garrison, but this time the garrisons had some warning and wouldn't be as scattered.

Fisk's helpers reported that the supply of Theobroma to the garrisons had trickled to a stop. But was it in enough time? A list of worries cycled through my mind. Had Valek reached Owen? Would the other teams be successful? Would the blood really work? Opal had assured us it would, but maybe the Harman sap would be strong enough to overpower the blood. It wasn't like we could experiment. I envisioned everything that could go wrong, and I was quite imaginative.

By the time we traveled to the Citadel, my desire to just get it over with pressed on my skin from the inside out. And I was about to burst. In this mood, I could bring down the walls with my bare hands—no storm orb needed.

Fisk strung the slingshot between two tree trunks. Bavol and Councilor Shaba Greenblade watched for patrols. They'd increased in frequency the closer we traveled to the Citadel. However, Shaba's magic was just strong enough to sense them, giving us enough time to avoid the soldiers. Hopefully Phelan's crew had also avoided the patrols and was now getting ready to target the northern gate.

When the appointed hour arrived, Heli placed the storm orb in the slingshot and, together with Fisk, drew it back and aimed at the Citadel's south gate. It had been barricaded closed, and no one should be around it at this time of the night. It was also the second-closest gate to the Council Hall. Remembering what had happened to Valek's back when we blasted the garrison's wall, I tried to get Fisk and Heli to scoot back a couple...okay, more like twenty feet. Heli assured me she'd be able to direct the storm's energy around them.

I crouched behind a tree as Fisk and Heli launched the orb. The moonlight reflected off the glass as it sailed through the air. The impact rattled my teeth as sound roared to life, ripped through the barricade and blew chunks of the Citadel's walls in every direction. Bits of marble and dust rained for a few minutes. However, a bubble of undisturbed vegetation surrounded Heli and Fisk.

"Wow. Teegan wasn't kidding," Fisk said in a hushed whisper. "That's...the coolest thing I've ever seen! Is anyone else's ears ringing?"

"Move now, marvel later," I said. "Those patrols are all making a beeline straight for us."

"Right."

The five of us dashed through the hole and into the Citadel. Businesses and factories occupied most of the area, but a few had been converted into apartments. People were already peering through the windows and coming to investigate the damage. Fisk led the way, and soon we disappeared through the alleys that he knew so well.

We arrived down the street from the Council Hall. Sliding into a shadow, we watched the main entrance. Soon after, a man raced up the steps and disappeared inside to report the blasts. After a few moments, guards streamed into the street. They split into two teams and raced off, leaving only a few behind at the entrance.

Bavol, Shaba and I stepped from the shadows. We climbed the stairs at a stately pace. By the time we reached the door, the four guards pointed swords at our chests.

"At ease, men," Bavol said in a commanding tone that promised pain if disobeyed. Impressive.

"You don't give orders," one man protested.

"I am *Councilman* Bavol Cacao Zaltana. This is *Councilwoman* Shaba Greenblade. We do indeed give the orders. Stand down. Now."

The tips of their weapons wavered.

"Fetch Bruns Jewelrose," Bavol ordered. "Tell him we await his immediate presence in my office." Bavol strode into the Council Hall without waiting for an acknowledgment.

Shaba and I followed him. We made it as far as the middle of the lobby. Bruns stood on the stairs amid an impressive array of armed soldiers, Cilly Cloud Mist and a few other magicians. A sly smile spread on Bruns's face.

I sucked in a breath. Showtime.

Cilly met my gaze. She pressed her lips together, and I sensed a light touch of magic in my mind before it was swallowed by the baby. Confusion creased her expression before she smoothed it out.

Baby, one. Cilly, zero.

"Ah, there you are, Bruns," Bavol said.

MARIA V. SNYDER

"Bavol, what a...surprise. You shouldn't have come. It's much too dangerous for you here."

So he was going to act civilized. At least, for now.

"Nonsense. This is where I and the rest of the Sitian Council *should* be. Don't you agree?"

"No. The Commander has spies and assassins everywhere."

"We accepted that risk when we were *voted* by *our people* to oversee Sitian affairs and protect our citizens. Thanks for stepping in, Bruns, but you're dismissed. Councilwoman Greenblade and I will take it from here until the others arrive." Bavol swept a hand out, indicating the crowd. "Everyone, report back to your stations until further notice."

No one moved.

Bruns clapped. "Bravo. A very convincing performance. However, you don't know your audience very well. All of them are loyal to me. No Theobroma needed."

It made sense, but we'd hoped at least a few had been coerced and were beginning to wake up. Time for plan B. Glancing over my shoulder, I confirmed that all the guards were focused on the action happening inside the hall. Then I reached under my tunic and withdrew a glass storm orb. My baby bump diminished by half the size.

Holding it high above my head in both hands, I said, "Surrender now, or I'll blow us all to bits!"

Many of the soldiers took a step back, but Bruns said, "She's bluffing. She wouldn't kill herself or her baby. This is truly pathetic, Yelena. What do you hope to accomplish?"

"Aww, shucks, Bruns, you saw right though me. You're right. I'm not going to kill us all. I just wanted to distract you." I tossed the orb at the staircase and grinned when they all flinched.

It shattered and released a thick white fog. The smoke swirled without direction for a second, but then raced up and down the steps with enough force to knock people down as they tried to flee. Heli stood near the door. She focused on controlling the air while Fisk and his helpers entered.

"The gas won't last long," I said over the roar of the wind. "Prick them with the Curare. It should work."

The kids moved like scavengers over the bodies. But there were two missing—Bruns and Cilly.

They hadn't come down, so they must have gone up to one of the upper floors.

"Bavol, stay here with Shaba. When the reinforcements arrive, you need to convince them you're in charge," I said. "Heli and Fisk, come with me."

Fisk pulled his knives, and I loaded my blowpipe. We sprinted up the steps, being careful not to step on anyone.

"How do you want to do this?" he asked. "Room by room?"

"Is there another exit?" Heli asked.

"The Masters' entrance," I said.

"This way!" Fisk cut down an empty hallway.

Why was I surprised Fisk knew about it? Little scamp enjoyed ferreting out little-known facts like that. At the end of the hall was a stairway to the ground floor. I paused a moment to listen. Not a sound. Not even the pounding of boots. Good or bad?

"Are you sure they went this way?" Heli asked me.

"No. But they can't escape, so if they didn't, they're still in the building."

We descended two stories. The stairwell ended in a large room where the Masters changed into their formal robes before attending Council meetings. The expensive silk material swayed in the breeze blowing in from the open door.

Fisk cursed and crossed the room at a run with Heli on his heels. Magic brushed my thoughts.

MARIA V. SNYDER

"I see them!" Fisk pointed outside.

"There they are," Heli said.

Before I could stop them, they raced into the empty street. The door slammed shut behind them, plunging the room into darkness.

I yanked my switchblade but wasn't quick enough. A knife poked my stomach with its sharp tip. I froze.

"Drop it," Bruns said on my left.

Could he see in the dark? I released my blowpipe. It clattered to the floor.

"And the knife."

Damn. I let go of that as well.

"I'd love to gut you right now, but I need you. Later," he promised. "Cilly, search her for weapons."

The woman was quite thorough. Too bad she didn't prick her finger on one of my darts. Once she'd collected most of them, Bruns instructed her to lead the way.

He grabbed my upper arm, but his knife remained in place. "Move." He pushed me up the stairs.

"But I thought—"

"You thought wrong," Bruns interrupted me. "My men will wake as soon as that gas wears off. Did you really think I wouldn't protect them against *all* your potions? Just because I didn't need Theobroma to convince them doesn't mean they don't consume it. And I was smart enough to stockpile it, just in case."

He dragged me to the lobby's staircase. Below, Bavol and Shaba waited for the reinforcements, but it didn't take them long to notice us.

"Don't do anything stupid," Bruns said to them. "Or I'll kill your Liaison. Cilly, take care of them."

They remained in place as the magician descended. She held a couple of my darts. She jabbed one into Bavol's arm and pricked Shaba with another. They both stiffened and toppled to the ground.

Feeling sick to my stomach over the turn of events, I stumbled a bit as Bruns led me to his office. Cilly lit a lantern as he pushed me into a chair. His weapon remained pressed against my skin.

"Secure her," he ordered.

Cilly picked up a pair of manacles and yanked my wrists through the wooden slats of the chair's back. The metal cuffs bit into my flesh. I could probably still stand, but my seat would come with me. When Bruns finally moved the blade away from the baby, I took my first deep breath since he'd jumped me.

"Go downstairs and wait for the others to wake," Bruns ordered Cilly. "Then take the Councilors down to the cells before returning."

She nodded and left. Bruns pointed to a glass super messenger on his desk. "I received word from Owen that he captured Valek. The Commander is going to execute him for treason at the opening of the fire festival."

I tried to keep my expression blank, but tears filled my eyes as grief crashed into me. Unable to stop them, they ran down my cheeks and dripped off my jaw.

Bruns studied me with a quizzical expression. "You stayed dry-eyed through far worse. Being forced to cooperate with me, seeing Valek after he'd been beaten...you never blinked. How do you even know I'm telling the truth?"

If I wasn't sobbing, I would have laughed at Bruns's attempt to console me. He actually appeared...upset. He'd had no trouble threatening a pregnant woman with a knife, but making one cry must have been one of those things his mother taught him was not nice. I took a few shaky breaths, trying to control my emotions. No doubt the baby was responsible for my outburst. Valek might have been caught, but he was a hard man to keep.

Bruns cleared his throat. "And through my magicians, I'm also aware of your attacks on the garrisons. They failed, by the way. And I'll blame the incidents on the Commander. So thank you for your help."

A gamut of emotions rolled through me. I bit down on my lip to keep them in check.

Bruns leaned back and tapped a finger on his chin. "In fact, those gaping holes in the walls won't be easy to defend. Especially with the enemy also on the inside. The Commander's forces should have no trouble conquering the Sitian army. You should be happy about that. Fewer lives lost."

"Thrilled," I said with plenty of sarcasm.

He grunted in amusement, but then turned serious. "There will be casualties, of course. You're not going to leave this room alive. I've learned my lesson and will not take any more chances with you."

"Then what are you waiting for?" I asked.

"Cilly. I promised her she can enact her revenge for her brother's death." Bruns frowned at the door. "How long until the gas wears off?"

Not long. However, the sleeping draft we gave them would keep them asleep for a couple more hours. But Bruns didn't need to know that we hadn't used Curare on his men. In fact, there were lots of things Bruns didn't know.

I shrugged. With my arms pinned behind me, it was harder than expected.

Cilly burst into the room. "They're...coming." She panted. "From all...directions."

Bruns was on his feet in a heartbeat. "Who?"

I answered for her. "The Sitian army." I savored his confusion. Getting caught wasn't part of the plan, but at least I had a front-row seat to his downfall.

He rounded on me. Pressing his knife to my throat, he asked, "What did you do?"

"Me? Other than tonight, not much. But my friends attacked the garrisons a few *days* ago. The Master Magicians were never under your control, Bruns. They've convinced your magicians to report the attacks tonight, instead of when they really happened."

"How? My people are loyal!"

"It's amazing how quickly the magicians switched sides once they learned about the Harman sap."

Bruns growled. "Die."

The blade burned through my skin. Pain ringed my neck. Guilt and grief over the baby dominated my thoughts.

Then a figure slammed into Bruns, knocking him away from me. He recovered and spun, aiming his knife at his attacker, but Onora blocked it with ease. She held a dagger in each hand. Bruns lunged and, while he had a bit of skill with the blade, it wasn't near enough to counter a well-trained assassin. In one smooth move, she sidestepped the attack and stabbed her knife right into his chest.

Cilly screamed and dove for Onora. The magician should have used her magic. Onora disarmed her in two moves and knocked her unconscious with the hilt of her weapon.

Everything had happened so fast that my heart was slow to catch up, but now it banged in my chest and made it difficult to breathe.

Onora stared at Bruns's corpse. An angry flush painted her cheeks. "He was going to kill you."

"Yes, he was." My throat throbbed, and the top of my tunic was wet with blood. My muscles trembled with shock.

Onora met my gaze. "Not on my watch."

MARIA V. SNYDER

29

VALEK

Valek's strength returned in bits and pieces. He'd have a good day, only to relapse the next. They moved his bed into a windowless room with one door. Medic Mommy cared for him, and she informed him he'd been her patient for ten days. The attack on the Citadel would happen in two days' time, and the Commander would invade in twelve days—unless Valek stopped him.

The next time Medic Mommy checked on him, he asked, "Why bother?"

"Excuse me?" She tucked a short strand of hair behind her ear.

"I'm going to die. Why bother to nurse me back to health?"

"Orders." Meeting his gaze, she asked, "Would you rather be tossed into a cell to fend for yourself?"

"Actually, yes." He grinned. "Better chance to escape."

She snorted. "Which is why I also have orders not to release you."

Pity. He tried another tactic. "At least you know the orders are coming from the Commander and not Owen Moon."

"It's better, that's for sure. No one is going to mourn that bastard."

"I'd hoped the Commander would be more grateful."

"You know his stance on magicians."

"But I'm no longer one." He considered. "Do you know if that's what happened to Yelena's magic?"

"I don't know." Medic Mommy glanced at the infirmary's door with a worried frown. "Did Yelena come with you to Ixia?"

"No. She's in Sitia."

The woman visibly relaxed. Valek remembered they were close friends. Time to capitalize on that sentiment. "She's not any safer there. Once the Commander takes over Sitia, she'll be executed, as well."

"He wouldn't do that." But the words lacked conviction.

"He has to. She's trouble." He gave her a wry grin. "Always has been. In order for the Commander to rule the Sitian clans without resistance, he needs to assassinate the Sitian Council, the Master Magicians, Yelena and a few other influential people."

"He'd wait until the babe's born," she said, as if trying to reassure herself.

"He can't risk the baby growing up and plotting revenge for the death of his or her parents. Plus, we both had magic at one point—the baby might turn out to be a powerful magician."

Medic Mommy's face creased in concern. She was all about saving lives. He played his final card. "Before I left, we picked names for the baby. Vincent for a boy and Liana for a girl. What do you think?"

"They're..." She swallowed. "Nice names. I...better get back to work." The medic bolted.

Valek hoped he'd planted a seed. At this point, he had no other options. But the next couple times she checked on him, she avoided all conversation, keeping focused on her duties.

Before she left the next day, he asked if she'd let him stand

MARIA V. SNYDER

up. "Just for a few minutes? Otherwise, you're going to have to carry me to the noose. I give my word not to do anything."

But she shook her head and dashed from the room. When the door opened, he counted four guards outside. The Commander wasn't taking any chances. Valek tensed and relaxed his muscles. Straining against his bonds also helped to keep his body limber. It passed the time. Once he'd flexed each muscle, he started over again. He feared the only chance he'd have to escape was the trip to the noose.

Time dripped by, leaving Valek with nothing to do but think. He didn't like where his thoughts led. The only scenario in which his friends and family didn't perish was if Sitia won. A possibility, if they weren't reeling from the attacks by the resistance. No. Valek doubted Sitia had the skills to beat the Commander's army.

Two, maybe three days later, a muffled sound woke Valek. The door swung open. He blinked in the lantern light as a couple dark figures entered. Only their eyes showed, but Valek recognized Adrik's broad build.

"Vacation's over," Adrik said. He unlocked the cuffs and helped Valek stand.

The world tilted, and he leaned on the bed for a moment.

"Here," Pasha said, thrusting a uniform into his hands.

Getting dressed required some help. But once he could stand on his own, he asked, "Weapons?"

Adrik handed him two knives. Not his, but Valek would rectify that as soon as he was able.

"Time to go." Pasha peered out the door. The four guards lay in a heap in the hallway.

They hurried through the silent and empty corridors. Adrik and Pasha moved as if they'd planned the route in advance. Soon they were outside.

"The gate?" Valek asked. The effort to keep up the pace had winded him.

"Taken care of," Adrik said.

Sure enough, there were a few prone forms on the ground. A handful of Valek's agents waited in the shadows. Most of them had been in the dungeon with him.

"About time, Boss," Qamra said. "Come on. We have reservations for dinner in Sitia, and I don't want to be late."

He scanned his loyal corps. "Thank you."

"Anytime. Now, come on." Adrik headed for the gate.

But Valek remained in place. "You go on without me."

Everyone stared at him.

"But—" Pasha started.

"Stay together and act as if I'm still with you. I'm going to need a couple days, so lead them on a merry chase."

Understanding smoothed her features.

"What do we do when we arrive in Sitia without you?" Adrik asked.

"Find Yelena. She'll make sure you're not arrested or harmed."

"You can't beat him," Qamra said.

"No, but I have to try. It's Sitia's only chance."

"What should we tell Yelena?" Pasha asked.

"That I'm doing this for a peaceful life. She'll understand."

Valek returned to the castle. He knew every inch of the building, from the dungeon's abyss to the rooftops. First he needed a place to hide. He had regained some of his strength while recuperating in the infirmary, but he had to get back into fighting shape before he faced the Commander.

Five days later, he was ready. Well, as ready as it was possible to be, considering his circumstances. Plus only four days remained until the Commander attacked Sitia. To conserve

MARIA V. SNYDER

his energy, Valek decided on a frontal assault versus climbing over the rooftops. Stealth was no longer needed.

After the Commander retired for the evening, Valek strode up to the two men guarding the entrance into his apartment. He hoped his reputation would scare them away, but he was prepared to fight dirty to save energy.

When he approached, he cursed under his breath. Just his luck—Sergeant Gerik was on duty. Valek wondered if the Commander had informed the man that Onora still lived. Gerik growled and pulled his sword when he spotted Valek. That would be a no. The second man also brandished his weapon, but he appeared a bit shaky.

"I should have let you fall to your death," Gerik said, sliding his feet into a fighting stance.

Gerik had been covering the wall the night Valek had visited the Commander. "Onora is alive and well."

That deflated some of the menace from Gerik. Not all, but it was a start.

"How do I know you're not lying?" the sergeant asked.

"Because *your sister* trusts me."

He jerked in surprise. "She told you?"

"Yes. Thank you for saving my life. Now get lost."

The other man took a step back, but Gerik put a big hand on his shoulder, anchoring him in place. "We can't," he said. "The Commander would hang us as traitors. And, no offense, Valek, but if Onora couldn't kill him, you can't, either."

"Gee, thanks for the vote of confidence." Valek drew a knife with one hand while he yanked a couple darts with the other. Before the men had a chance to react, he hit them both in the neck with Leif's sleeping draft.

Gerik yanked his out. "What's this?"

"It's supposed to make you fall asleep," Valek said.

An awkward silence ensued. Finally, Gerik's companion

swayed on his feet and leaned back on the wall. The guard struggled to keep his eyes open and failed. He toppled to the ground.

Showing no signs of drowsiness, Gerik glanced at his companion. "Supposed to?"

"Leif warned us that it doesn't work on everyone." And it was just his luck that he'd found someone who was immune. Valek didn't have the time or energy to spare to fight Gerik. Perhaps he should hit him with a second dart.

Shoving the dart back into his neck, Gerik stretched out on the floor.

Touched by the big man's gesture, Valek said, "Thank you again."

"It was nice knowing ya." Gerik closed his eyes.

Valek unlocked the door into the short hallway that contained only two doors that faced each other. Valek's suite was on the right and the Commander's on the left. He paused as sorrow swelled. Twenty-four years together, and they ended up right back where they started.

The Commander's door was unlocked. Keeping the knife in his hand, Valek entered without knocking, then drew the second blade. Ambrose sat in his favorite armchair by the hearth, sipping brandy. Valek's knives rested on the table in front of him.

Not surprised to see Valek, the Commander smiled instead. "I've been waiting for you." He gestured to an empty glass. "Drink?"

"No, thank you."

"All right, then." The Commander set his drink down and snatched the daggers from the table in one fluid motion. He stood. "Shall we?" He inclined his head toward the right side of the living area. The Commander had cleared away all the furniture.

MARIA V. SNYDER

"Can I convince you not to invade Sitia?" Valek asked.

"No."

"Then we shall." Keeping the Commander in sight, he moved to the cleared area. "I wish to reclaim my knives."

"Oh, you'll get them back soon enough." The Commander attacked.

When they had sparred before, the Commander preferred to remain on the defensive for the first series of exchanges, testing Valek. Not this time. Ambrose lunged, aiming for Valek's throat with the intent to kill in his cold hard gaze.

Valek shuffled back and blocked. The impact reverberated through Valek's bones. The grim knowledge that this fight wouldn't last long coiled around his heart and tightened, evicting the fear and doubt that had been dwelling there. Pure determination pulsed inside him as the Commander increased the pace, striking with unrelenting quick jabs—a brutal street style that Valek hadn't expected.

Unable to match the superfast speed, Valek scrambled to block but remained a hair too slow. The edges of Ambrose's blades sliced the skin on Valek's arms. Pain burned, but he ignored it. Valek had a much bigger problem. He was running out of room to maneuver. If that happened, Valek would leave a smear of blood on the wall as he sank to his death.

Deflecting the Commander's double thrust up instead of to the side, he kicked the Commander in the stomach. The solid impact pushed Ambrose back a few steps, giving Valek a little more room.

Valek sidestepped and dropped to one knee, thrusting his knife toward the Commander's thigh, aiming for the femoral artery. Ambrose dodged the attack and once again Valek was on the defensive. As the fight lengthened, Valek's energy ebbed. He sucked in air and his throat burned with the effort.

Valek rallied and tried a number of offensive techniques.

Familiar with each of them, the Commander countered with ease. The man wasn't even sweating.

After a few more exchanges, Valek sensed he was about to reach the limit of his skills. The certainty of failure brought desperation, which reminded Valek of his rooftop fight with Onora. It was clear there was no way he'd beat the Commander. Not with his knives. And not using conventional fighting tactics.

Bracing for pain, Valek blocked a double jab to his midsection, then dropped his weapons. He grabbed the Commander's wrists and found the pressure points. The tip of a blade pierced Valek's left bicep, but he clamped down hard, pressing his fingers and thumbs on the points.

Ambrose yelled as the all-consuming pain traveled up his arms. Using a pressure point created a unique sensation that dominated the entire body and scattered all thought and reason in the victim. Devlen had taught them to Valek a year ago. In any other fight, Valek would never have resorted to using them, because in any other fight, Valek wouldn't need them to save his own life and ensure his family's safety.

The Commander's weapons clattered to the floor. Valek kept his hold until the Commander sank to his knees. Then Valek released one wrist. He picked up the closest knife and rested the sharp edge on the Commander's neck. Valek let go of the man's other wrist. The fog of pain cleared from Ambrose's golden gaze. He stared at Valek, waiting for death. No fear shone in his eyes. No requests for mercy. No promise to stop the invasion of Sitia in exchange for his life. Not his style.

Valek tensed, preparing to end the Commander's life. But he was unable to execute that final move. Valek couldn't kill him. If he slit the Commander's throat, Valek would regret it. They'd shared too much history, friendship and even love. Ambrose was a part of Valek's family. Owen had ruined ev-

MARIA V. SNYDER

erything between them, but Valek wouldn't let the dead magician force his hand.

"Finish it, Valek," Ambrose said. "If you let me live, I'm going to invade Sitia."

And Valek would have to live with the consequences. War and death and no hope for a peaceful life. Or was there hope? Valek's comments to Leif about trust came to mind. Perhaps he should trust the Sitians. They'd certainly proven their resourcefulness in the past. Valek released the Commander. "You can try. Sitia will surprise you."

"Then why the assassination attempt?"

"Because I forgot."

"You forgot what?"

"That *I'm* a Sitian now, and we don't solve our problems by assassination." Valek found his knives and sheathed them. "I'm retiring as Chief of Security. Effective immediately." Valek headed for the door. He only had a few days to warn Sitia.

"I can't let you leave," Ambrose said.

Valek spun with weapons in hand.

The Commander stood and smoothed his uniform. The other knives remained on the floor. "You can't leave without having a drink with me."

Valek stared at Ambrose in confusion. The Commander strode to the chairs by the fire and poured two drinks. Was this an attempt to delay Valek long enough for the security guards to arrive?

"I—"

"Relax, Valek. I'm not going to invade Sitia. You're not going to be executed." He sat in his favorite chair, waiting for Valek to join him.

This seemed too good to be true. "Is this because I spared your life?"

"No. Once I learned Sitia knew about the Harman sap,

I figured that they would have already discovered a way to block the darts. An invasion would be a waste of time and resources right now. But if the Sitian Council loses control again, I *will* invade. They won't get another chance, and I can assure you that the magicians will be a casualty. But for now, I'm betting that when you're hired as Chief of Security for the Council, you will do a much better job of keeping the rogue magicians in check."

Valek tucked his knives away as he sorted through the Commander's comments. "Why did you let me believe you planned to invade?"

"Because I wanted to see what you would do."

Shocked, Valek searched for a proper response. All he managed was, "I almost killed you."

"But you didn't. And now I can trust you again."

Anger boiled up his throat. "Another test?"

"Partly. It was also for peace of mind. I know you won't be coming after me in the future. I'm not getting any younger, and don't wish to be constantly worrying about assassination."

"I'm not the only assassin."

"No. You're the only assassin that can beat Onora, and now me. In my mind, you're the only one who is a threat."

Valek had used two very desperate moves to win both fights. Moves he would be unable to utilize again against either the Commander or Onora, because they would be ready for them. His upper arm throbbed, and a dozen or more stinging cuts seeped blood that soaked his sleeves. Plus his magic and immunity were gone.

Valek certainly didn't feel like a threat.

Now that he didn't need to rush off to warn Sitia of an impending attack, Valek walked over to the armchairs. The Commander's comments had generated a number of unanswered questions. "Have you heard any news from Sitia?

There's no guarantee the Sitian Council and the others will defeat Bruns and his Cartel."

The Commander gave him a flat look. "Who planned the attack?"

"I did."

"Who did you leave in charge?"

"All right, I get it. There's a pretty good chance of success *if* everything goes well."

"I've received a report that the Sitian Council and Master Magicians have regained power and are rallying the troops to counter our invasion. I suspect they'll have a number of soldiers disappointed over the lack of action."

Valek gripped the back of the empty chair as relief threatened to turn his legs into mush. "Yelena?"

"She's been spotted in the Citadel, aiding the Council."

Unable to remain upright, Valek sank into the chair and rested his head in his hands for a moment.

"Onora was seen in her company. Please tell Onora to report back to Ixia immediately."

Valek lifted his head. "Ari and Janco?"

"If they wish to return, they'll be welcome. No charges will be filed against them or the agents who helped you escape a few days ago."

Good to know. "And if Ari and Janco want to stay in Sitia?"

Smiling, Ambrose raised his glass. "Good luck." He drank.

Valek laughed as six months of worry, tension and fear melted away. He grabbed his drink and took a long swig. The smooth white brandy slid down his throat, trailing fire. "The good stuff?"

"I thought the situation warranted it."

"You were that confident I wouldn't kill you?"

"Not at all. If this was going to be my last night, I didn't want to drink inferior brandy." He raised his glass again. "Here's to your new life in Sitia."

Valek clinked and took another swallow. He considered his future. Being with his family would be a highlight, but what else would he do? The vial of his blood might not return his magic. "I'm not sure that the Sitians trust me enough to put me in charge of security, or that I would even accept the position if they offered. My priorities have shifted."

"They'd be fools not to." The Commander sipped his drink. "Would they trust you more if you still had your magic?"

"Probably." Valek leaned back in his chair as fatigue washed through him. If not for his injuries, this could have been any night during the past twenty-four years. He realized with a pang that he was going to miss this.

"I'm not sorry for injecting you with the Harman sap," Ambrose said. "As far as I'm concerned, I've done you a favor."

"I know. I'm well aware of your views on magic." They shared a smile. It was an old argument.

"And you know I've been a hypocrite about it ever since I've learned my mother's soul shares my body. Something that is only possible because of magic."

Valek straightened. This was new.

"If Yelena's powers return, and she doesn't hate me, can you ask her to visit me? I'd like her to send my mother to the sky."

"I'm sure Yelena would be happy to help you if she's able." Valek tapped a finger on his glass. "What if her powers don't return? Would you be more accepting of magicians?"

"In that case, I will use the Harman sap on myself."

It seemed drastic. "That might kill your mother."

"She's already dead."

"No. That might destroy her soul, and she won't find peace in the sky. She'll cease to exist."

"Is your soul dead because of the Harman sap?" Ambrose asked.

"I…" Valek recalled Yelena's description of souls and how she influenced them. A body without a soul was like an empty cup—it lived, but had no awareness or emotions or personality. "No. I'm still…me."

"Exactly. The Harman sap will remove the magic that is holding my mother here." He tapped his chest. "That's the theory. But I'd rather Yelena do it, so I know for sure my mother is at peace." He smoothed a hand over his pants leg. "Speaking of peace, do you think Yelena will be willing to be the Liaison again?"

Good question. "I don't know, but I'll ask her. What if she says no? Who else would you accept?"

"You."

Valek's laugh died in his throat—it would be an interesting job. "I doubt the Sitian Council would agree."

"I'll also work with Ari, but if Janco is assigned the position, I'm declaring war."

Amused, Valek imagined Janco pouting from the insult. "I'll make sure to include that in my report."

They talked late into the night, healing the rift that had grown between them. The Commander then insisted Valek see the medic, and even escorted him to the infirmary. On the way, they stepped over the still forms of Gerik and his partner. Valek wondered what Gerik thought, seeing the two of them together. He guessed Gerik would pretend to sleep until the other man woke.

Medic Mommy's professional demeanor didn't alter when the Commander roused her from sleep and explained.

"I'll leave you in good hands. Good luck, Valek. You and your family are welcome to visit at any time." Ambrose shook his hand and left.

As soon as the door closed, Medic Mommy grinned. "I'm glad you two are friends again." Almost gleefully, she peeled off his shirt and cleaned and then sealed the cuts on his arms. But when she finished and Valek stood to leave, her jovial manner changed in a heartbeat.

She jabbed a finger at a bed. "Sleep." When he hesitated, she stepped closer. "Do I need to secure you?"

An empty threat, but Valek decided right there and then that his future would *not* include being captured, chained, manacled, jailed, beaten, stabbed or knocked unconscious ever again. And while he was dreaming, he included a future in which he spent his days locked in a tower with Yelena and their children. "No, sir."

"Good. Give me eight hours, and then you can leave."

His stiff and sore muscles protested the movement, but he managed to lie down and pull the blanket up before he fell into an exhausted sleep.

When he woke, Sergeant Gerik stood next to his bed. Valek reached for his knives, but the big man held up his empty hands.

"I'm here to escort you to the Citadel," Gerik said. He tried to keep a stern expression, but a glint of cheerfulness shone in his gaze. "The Commander's orders."

Ah. Gerik would see his sister sooner. "And escort the new Chief of Security home?"

"Yes."

The cuts on his arms flared to painful life as Valek pushed into a sitting position. His entire body ached. "Do your orders include carrying the ex-chief to Sitia?"

"If that's what it takes, sir."

"Good to know." Valek stood, although his body threat-

MARIA V. SNYDER

ened to revolt and send him reeling back into bed. He needed at least a couple more *years* of sleep.

Medic Mommy hurried over to inspect Valek's injuries before she discharged him from her care. "Send me a message with your new location. I'll come to deliver the baby."

He was about to remind her of Sitia's capable healers, but remembered the baby's magic-sucking abilities. If anything unexpected happened, they couldn't use magic to heal Yelena or the baby. "I will. Thank you."

They swung by Valek's hiding spot. Valek retrieved his pack and changed into a clean shirt. Then they left the castle.

"Horses?" Gerik asked as they crossed the complex.

"Not this time. Getting into Sitia is going to be tricky, even without horses. The Sitian army is prepared for an invasion, so they will attack anyone or anything exiting the Snake Forest."

A crowd of people waited by the southern gate. The guards on duty saluted Valek as he approached. Pasha and Adrik stood with Valek's other agents. Smiles shone in the bright morning sunlight. It appeared the Commander had orchestrated his rescue. Figured.

"We would have busted you out regardless," Adrik said.

"What if I decided to go to Sitia instead of remaining here?" he asked.

"Then we would have escorted you to Sitia," Pasha said. "But Adrik would have lost a couple of golds to the captain of the watch."

No surprise they'd been betting on him. He shook hands with everyone, thanking them for their years of loyal and excellent service. "Onora is more than capable. I'm sure she'll earn your respect in no time."

Maren waited for him outside the gate. She stood with her arms crossed, blocking the path. Gerik rested his hand on the hilt of his sword, but Maren ignored him.

Instead she asked Valek, "So this is it? You're done?"

"What do you think?"

"I think you broke your pledge to the Commander."

Valek considered. Was she trying to force a reaction? He kept his tone neutral. "I retired."

"Onora's not ready."

"Do you think *you* should be in charge?"

Maren dropped her arms. "Hell, no. No one can do that job."

"I'm flattered."

She huffed. "You're leaving all of us vulnerable. Onora's bound to make mistakes."

Gerik gripped his weapon. Valek put a hand on his arm, stopping the man from drawing the sword. Maren's comment explained quite a bit. "Yes, she will make mistakes," Valek said. "Just like I did when I first started. Just like I did a few days ago. You're right. No one can do the job on his or her own. Not even me. I built a support network to help me, and she will, too. She's already learned how valuable even Janco can be. And you'll be here to help her." Unless... "That is, if you want to stay. You're always welcome to come with me to Sitia."

"Not interested. I pledged my loyalty to the Commander."

Okay, then. "If you change your mind—"

"I won't." She stepped aside. "Tell Ari and Janco to get their asses back up here. Their vacation is over." Maren strode away without saying another word.

Gerik watched her go. "Does Onora need to worry about her?"

"No," Valek said. "Maren has a temper. She'll settle down."

"And if she doesn't?"

"Onora can handle herself." Valek met Gerik's concerned gaze. "Right now, your sister is the best in Ixia and Sitia."

MARIA V. SNYDER

"Right now?"

"There will always be a young hotshot eager to prove himself or herself. Part of the job. Someday, one of them will best her, but I don't think you need to worry about that happening anytime soon."

Gerik smiled. "You lasted twenty-four years."

"Exactly."

Valek calculated. He and Gerik would arrive at the Citadel right at the hot season's midpoint. The day the Firestorm had been scheduled—and a day longer than it should have taken, because he was unable to avoid the Sitian army. The soldiers had blanketed the land south of the Ixian border. The only way to get through without causing an incident was to creep into the encampment at night and find an officer to explain things to. The fact that the Snake Forest had emptied of all but a few border guards helped support his news of the canceled invasion. However, the unit he'd surrendered to didn't have a magician who could communicate with the people in charge.

Since they still didn't quite believe him, the captain sent him and Gerik to the Citadel with an armed escort. Valek longed to retrieve Onyx and reclaim his vial of blood, but as soon as he spotted the white marble walls of the Citadel in the distance, his focus and energy and thoughts all turned to one goal—holding Yelena in his arms.

30

YELENA

"What do you mean, the forest is empty?" I asked Ayven, sure I'd heard wrong.

"The Ixians withdrew all but a few patrols," the magician said.

Ayven stared into a glass super messenger, mentally communicating with Master Magician Irys Jewelrose on the front lines. Or what had *been* the front lines. We expected Ixia to attack in two days' time.

I glanced at Bavol and then at Onora, who'd stayed by my side as much as possible since she'd saved my life. We stood in Bavol's office in the Council Hall. Most of the other Sitian Councilors had joined their regiments in the field. We hadn't received any information or news from Valek since he'd left thirty-two long days ago. Many people assumed he was dead when the Ixian army remained in the forest.

Dare I hope?

"Perhaps Valek was successful after all," Bavol said.

The baby kicked as if in agreement, but I wasn't going to jump to conclusions. By concentrating on the impending invasion, I'd been able to function. And I avoided the dark thoughts that threatened to ambush me late at night.

"Ayven, please contact Master Zitora and ask her about that unit she and Teegan sensed hiding behind our front lines," I said. "See if they know where they are now."

"Okay." He focused on the messenger. A few minutes later, he looked up. "She says the unit has disappeared. She sent Devlen and Teegan to track them, and she's waiting to hear from Teegan."

Good or bad news? Hard to tell.

"Let me know if you learn anything new."

"Will do," Ayven said.

Over the next two days, more reports of the Ixian withdrawal arrived. It was the day of the planned Firestorm, and nothing happened. My emotions swung from confused to concerned to relieved, and settled into a general feeling of unease. Was this a trick? Perhaps the Commander had found a way to get all of his troops behind ours.

Zitora relayed a message from Teegan that the unit was headed east toward the Emerald Mountains. We had positioned a battalion near the tunnel the smugglers had used to get into Ixia. Perhaps we'd moved them too late—not that we'd had a ton of time. We'd only had ten days since we regained control of Sitia and the garrisons.

I sat at Bavol's desk that afternoon, staring at the map of Ixia and Sitia. Was there another tunnel beneath the border? Or another way past our defenses? Onora had left to fetch me some tea, but the baby's rhythmic hiccups made it difficult for me to concentrate. Poor little soul suffered with the hiccups at least once a day. I put a sympathetic hand on my mound. Calling it a bump no longer applied, I'd lost sight of my toes and couldn't touch them without great difficulty. And I still had ten weeks to go! If I grew any larger, I wouldn't be able to fit through the door.

A knock roused me from my musings. Fisk stood at the door with a pleased grin on his face as if he'd scored a good bargain.

"Don't tell me," I said, raising a hand. "You found the perfect hat for your latest client. What's her name?"

"Mrs. Catava." The glow dimmed just a bit. "Not yet. Soon—it's close, I can feel it. However, I found something better than a hat."

"Oh?"

"I found a husband." Fisk stepped aside with a flourish.

Valek stood in the doorway, and the rest of the world disappeared. The next thing I knew, I was wrapped in his arms. Not as close as I would have liked, though, because of the mass of baby between us.

He laughed and rested a hand over my girth. "You're—"

"Watch it," I warned.

"—more beautiful than I remembered," he said.

"Nice recovery."

Cupping my cheeks with his hands, he met my gaze. "I mean it."

Then he kissed me and proved he wasn't lying. By the time he broke away, I was gasping for breath and thinking of continuing our conversation in my bedroom.

A polite cough reminded us that we weren't alone. Fisk stood nearby with Sergeant Gerik.

"Do you know where Onora is?" Gerik asked me.

"The kitchen. She'll be ba—"

He disappeared.

"He thought she was dead," Valek explained. Exhaustion lined his face, and he was too thin. His hands slid down my arms, and he laced his fingers in mine. "I heard you defeated the Cartel. Did anyone... Are there any..."

I understood his reluctance to hear bad news. "Bain Blood-good had massive heart failure during the attack on the Krystal garrison."

"Ah, sorry to hear that."

"Everyone is still reeling. And now Zitora is First Magician."

"That's a heck of a homecoming." Valek braced for more bad news. "Anyone else?"

"A few soldiers were killed by the blasts from the orbs. It couldn't be avoided. And we can't find Hale in any of the garrisons. I suspect Bruns killed him soon after we escaped the Krystal garrison, but I can't ask him." I explained how Onora had saved our lives.

Valek squeezed my hand. "I owe her a debt of gratitude. How is she doing? Any problems with guilt?"

"I don't think so, but she's been acting like a mother bear protecting her cub. Guess who is her cub?" I tapped my chest.

"That's normal."

"Says the man who wants to lock me in a tower."

"That's normal, too."

"For *you*, maybe."

"Well, I'm glad she's been protecting you. Were there any... incidents at the other garrisons?"

"Other than a few injuries, none of our herd died. Thank fate."

"Injuries? How bad?"

"Janco has a couple of new scars to name. No doubt he'll be boasting about them when we see him. Mara cut her hands pretty badly. Seems Rika Bloodgood had a knife at her throat, but Mara wasn't going to let Leif surrender, so she took matters literally into her own hands."

"Good for her."

"She saved us all. If Rika had warned Bruns…" We all knew the consequences if that had happened. "Irys has already healed Mara, and Irys is talking about giving her a medal for her bravery."

"My siblings?"

"Fine. However, Zohav almost drowned Zethan, or so your brother claims, but I suspect he's exaggerating." I smiled, but sobered when I remembered Bain. We'd all miss him. "Now it's your turn. Owen?"

"Had a very bad case of overconfidence and died in my arms."

"I'm not sorry to hear it. I take it that's when the Commander woke up and recalled his army."

Valek tensed. "Not exactly."

"What happened?"

He sighed. "It's a long story. The short version is the invasion has been canceled, and Sitia can return to normal." He put his fingers on my lips. "I'll fill everyone in on the details once they're all back. Fisk?"

I'd forgotten he was there!

"Yes?" Fisk asked.

"Can you spread the word about the invasion? And please ask Ari and Janco to return to the Citadel with the twins."

"All right."

"Thanks." He returned his attention to me as Fisk left. "Do you have any plans for this afternoon?"

"Not anymore."

"Good." Valek tugged me into the hallway. "Have you been staying in the guest suites?"

"Yes. Are you tired?"

"Not anymore." His gaze met mine.

Heat flushed through me. "My room is this way."

MARIA V. SNYDER

★ ★ ★

Hunger woke me a few hours later. Valek didn't stir when I slipped from the bed. Exhaustion? Or was he finally able to relax?

I dressed and visited the kitchen—again. I imagined I'd worn a path in the rug, since I spent more time eating than sleeping these days. I grabbed a few extra pieces of fruit and cheese for Valek. At least, that was the plan. Since he didn't wake up until the next morning, I felt justified in eating his share.

Onora and Gerik visited us soon after we returned from breakfast. The guest suite had a living area, but they stood instead of making themselves comfortable. I suspected Onora had unwelcome news.

"The Commander has ordered me back to Ixia," she said.

I studied her. She tried to keep a stoic expression, but she appeared a little green, as if she was going to be sick to her stomach. "Are you worried he thinks you're a traitor?"

She glanced at Valek.

He shook his head. "I didn't have time to tell her."

"I'm the new Chief of Security," she said.

Surprised, I turned to Valek.

"I retired," he said.

Clearly we needed to catch up, but that would have to wait until later. I focused on Onora and was happy for her. "Congratulations."

She hesitated. "Thanks."

"Isn't that good news?" I asked, because she still looked queasy. "That's what you wanted. Right?"

"Yes. No. I don't know."

Ah. "The Commander would not have given you the job if he thought you couldn't handle it."

"I know. It's just…overwhelming."

"That'll pass in about five or six years," Valek said.

"Thanks," she said dryly.

"Just remember that you're not alone. And that I owe you one."

Onora peered at him in confusion.

"You saved Yelena's and our baby's lives. If you get into trouble and need help, send me a message, and I'll—"

"—*we'll* come and assist you," I finished for him.

He drew in a breath. I waited for overprotective Valek to frown at me, but instead he amended, "We'll come. And if it's bad, then we'll bring the whole herd with us."

"Herd?" Gerik asked.

Onora smiled in relief, and the color returned to her face. "He means his family and friends."

"*Our* family and friends." I corrected her. "You and Gerik are now part of the herd."

Shocked, Onora glanced at Valek. "We are?"

"Yes. The horses have named you Smoke Girl, but I don't know Gerik's horse name yet."

"Thanks." Another smile, this one with genuine warmth. She then asked Valek for advice on how to make the transition from his leadership to hers go smoothly.

He suggested she rely on Maren for guidance. "She's had years of experience, and my agents trust her. They'll trust you, too, once you've proven that you can handle difficult situations. Don't try to be their friend. Ask their opinions, listen to them, but once you've decided on a course of action, don't let them change your mind. Never show them you're uncertain. Issue orders with confidence, despite how you feel."

"Is that what you do?" I asked.

"Not at all."

"Uh-huh."

MARIA V. SNYDER

He flashed me a grin.

"Anything else?" Onora asked.

Valek sobered. "When you return to Ixia, you'll have a chance to show everyone what type of leader you'll be by how you deal with Captain Timmer."

She stiffened. I didn't blame her. Timmer had sexually abused her when she'd been a young solider in his unit.

"I thought the Commander..." Onora swiped a hand along her throat.

"He's waiting to see if you'd like to execute the captain yourself or if you want him publicly hanged. Or...if you wish to spare the man's life. What you decide will send a message to everyone in Ixia."

"No pressure," she muttered.

I grasped her hand. "You're protecting the citizens of Ixia now. They're in your care. Keep that in mind, and you'll do fine."

She hugged me. Or at least, she tried. Her arms weren't as long as Valek's. We laughed.

"Take care of the baby," Onora said. "If you need some extra protection or a dozen babyguards, just let me know."

I mock-groaned. "A dozen *baby*guards? Don't you start. I get enough of that overprotective nonsense from him." I jabbed my thumb in Valek's direction.

She gave me a smug Janco smile. "Too late."

"Go." I shooed her out the door.

Gerik shook our hands before following her.

After they left, I glanced at Valek. "What happened with the Commander?"

"I'll tell you on the way."

"To where?"

"To fetch Onyx."

★ ★ ★

We set off that afternoon. Valek borrowed a horse from the council's stables and I rode Kiki, who kept her gait as smooth as possible so I didn't go into premature labor. During the two-day ride to the farm where Valek had left Onyx, he filled me in on his adventures in Ixia. When he told me about the Commander's orders to execute him and still proceed with the invasion, I focused on the fact that Valek had survived and was with me. Otherwise, I'd plot a way to punch the Commander. Hard.

But then his next comment about being poisoned with the Harman sap turned my desire to punch the man into wanting to stab him.

"I hid the vial of my blood in Onyx's saddle," Valek said. "I'm…surprised that I'm anxious to find it. I never wished for magic, but once it was gone…"

"I understand completely."

"I know, love. There's still hope for you, as well."

However, there was no guarantee for either of us. Valek finished his story, and I mulled over the Commander's request to free his mother's soul. "If I can, I'll help him, but I can't promise not to punch him afterward."

Valek chuckled, but then he sobered. "If I do recover my magic, we shouldn't tell the Commander."

"He'll eventually learn about it. Plus, then he won't bother using the Harman sap on anyone."

"That's true. Of course, there's always the chance he'll find another way to neutralize magicians."

"Or someone else might discover a way. There's always going to be another problem to solve. We'll just have to tackle it when the time comes."

"We? I'm retired, love."

I stared at him. "*You'd* let someone else solve the problem?"

"I already have. Onora has my job."

"What about Sitia?"

"I'll help for now, but Teegan, Reema, Zethan, Zohav, Heli and Fisk are all poised to take over, and I'll be happy to let them."

I wasn't convinced that he could remain uninvolved. But only time would tell.

We retrieved Onyx, and Valek's vial remained hidden in the saddle. Both of us relaxed. However, we waited until we returned to the Citadel to inject his blood back into his body. If I missed his vein, it would ruin Valek's only chance to recover his magic.

When we arrived, we headed straight to the infirmary in the Council Hall. To our surprise and relief, Healer Hayes was back and helping at the Hall until the Keep was ready. Hayes instructed Valek to lie down on the bed while he filled a syringe with Valek's blood.

"Why lie down?" Valek asked.

"Just in case you pass out. Unless you want to hit your head on the floor?"

"I'm not the fainting type," Valek muttered, but he settled on the mattress.

"Have you been injected with your blood after losing your magic before?" Hayes asked, knowing full well Valek hadn't. "I don't know what's going to happen." He tied a band around Valek's bicep, right below a cut that had been sealed but still remained bright red. Hayes traced his thumb over the injury, and Valek sucked in a quick breath. "This is getting infected. Do you want me to heal it now or after?"

"Later. If my magic returns, I'll be able to heal myself."

"That's good to know. I can always use help in the infirmary."

"Walked right into that one, didn't I?"

"Yep." Hayes pressed the needle into Valek's arm and pushed the plunger. Red liquid disappeared into his vein.

I suppressed the impulse to hold his hand. The baby's magic-sucking ability might interfere. Instead, I hovered nearby.

Valek stiffened. He squeezed his eyes shut as his fingers curled into fists.

"Talk to me," Hayes said. "What's going on?"

"It burns." He arched his back. "Too hot…" A red flush swept over his pale skin, leaving beads of sweat in its wake. Valek jerked again. Then his head lolled back.

I dug my fingernails into the palms of my hands as I stood there, utterly useless. Glancing at Hayes's calm expression didn't help. "Is he all right?"

The Healer touched Valek's neck. "The toxin in his body is fighting the clean blood. It has overwhelmed his system."

"And that means?"

"He lost consciousness."

I bit back a sarcastic reply about stating the obvious. Instead I asked, "Will he wake up?"

"I hope so. Time will tell."

Must. Not. Strangle. Healer Hayes. Once I clamped down on my panic, I dragged a chair closer to Valek's bed and sat down to wait. There was nothing else I could do. As I watched my husband thrash about as if in the grip of a fever, I alternated between sitting and standing. Each position eventually caused my lower back to ache.

The hours added up. One day turned into two. I slept in the next bed, close but not touching. Visitors came as our friends and family returned from the various garrisons. Leif mixed his sustaining teas.

I paced around Valek's bed. After everything he'd gone

MARIA V. SNYDER

through—being knifed in his heart, being captured by Owen, fighting Onora and the Commander—to be taken out by his own blood? The desire to scream at fate clawed up my throat.

On the third day, Healer Hayes suggested I touch Valek. "The baby might neutralize the magic, and he'll wake up."

Without his magic. Better than without his life. But it was the "might" that caused me to hesitate. When I heard that Ari and Janco had returned, I asked Fisk to bring Janco right away.

I pounced on him as soon as he entered the infirmary. "You saw those survivors in the Greenblade forest. Did they say anything about the Harman sap that might help Valek?"

Janco's movements lacked his customary grace. He appeared tired and was probably in pain. The mischievous spark didn't flash from his gaze as he stood next to Valek's bed. "Wish I could help, but all I know is Selene reduced the concentration of the sap until it stopped killing her test subjects. She would know. Did she survive?"

"I don't know."

Energized, Janco squeezed my shoulder. "I'll find out."

"I doubt she'll cooperate."

"Oh, I don't think that will be a problem." A fierce expression gripped his face.

For the first time in days, I had a reason to hope. However, the next day Janco returned with Ari, and they both looked glum.

"Sorry, Yelena," Janco said. "The survivors of Selene's experiments were freed, and they managed to find and kill her."

There was nothing left to do but try Hayes's suggestion. I stood next to Valek's bed and cupped his sweaty cheek. He stilled and sighed. But he didn't wake.

"He might be exhausted," Hayes said. "Give him some time."

★ ★ ★

While we waited, there was a succession of meetings in the Council Hall. At one point, everyone who had been involved in stopping the Cartel, plus the two Master Magicians and Cahil, all assembled in the Hall. Twenty-eight people total, if you didn't include the three scribes who took turns writing everything down. Each of the teams reported what had happened at the garrisons. Fisk and I explained what had occurred at the Citadel. Then I related Valek's adventures in Ixia.

"Do you think the Commander plans to invade Sitia in the near future?" Councilor Tama Moon asked me.

"As long as the Sitian Council remains in power, he will not get involved or attempt to take control of Sitia. However, if you are compromised again, the Commander will act."

"Noted. And you say he's open to having a Liaison again."

"Yes."

"Yelena, would you be willing to resume your duties as the Liaison?" Councilor Featherstone asked.

Would I? I rested my hand on my belly. Hiccups vibrated against my palm. "Not at this time. I'm going to be busy with *other* duties the next few years."

Smiles ringed the room, but I couldn't share their good humor while Valek remained unconscious.

"All right. Please add that to the list of items the Council needs to discuss."

It took all day for everyone to report. The Council spent another day addressing the most immediate concerns. Cahil was charged with rebuilding the garrisons. The Master Magicians had already started clearing the Keep of debris, and the Council allocated a couple dozen soldiers to help them. The Masters aimed to reopen the school on the first day of the cooling season—twenty-three days away.

Opal, Devlen and their children returned to Fulgor. Teegan

would be back to continue his studies with the rest of the students, which now included Zohav and Zethan. They planned to fast-track Teegan's master-level training since they were in dire need of more masters. Reema had to wait a few more years before she could attend. The news didn't go over well with her, to say the least.

Heli returned to the coast, where Zethan would join her and the Stormdancers for the next storm season. Leif was asked to be the new Liaison. He accepted the job, as long as Mara could accompany him on all his missions. She beamed. I couldn't stop a twinge of jealously over their happiness. Once I acknowledged it, I moved on and was able to congratulate them both with genuine love and warmth in my heart.

I spent every night with Valek, sleeping pressed next to him. I talked to him, relating what had happened at the garrisons. Ari and Janco visited and told him how they'd attacked the Krystal garrison. Each took a turn telling their version of the story. Of course they kept interrupting each other to protest a comment or argue over a particular detail. I thought Valek would wake just to order them to shut up. He didn't.

That night, it took me a long time to find a comfortable position to sleep. My bulging belly made lying on my back or stomach impossible. It didn't help that my thoughts swirled with worry. I'd been avoiding making any decisions, since I couldn't face a future without Valek. I finally drifted into an uneasy sleep a few hours past midnight, but a cold touch jerked me from my nightmares. I yelled and almost punched the dark shape next to me until I realized it was Valek.

I struggled to sit up. "Valek?"

"Hmm?"

All the emotions I'd been holding in broke through my barrier. Clinging to Valek, I sobbed. He wrapped his arms around me. My cries were loud enough to bring Healer Hayes.

He carried a lantern. "What's wrong?"

Valek blinked in the bright light.

"About time. How do you feel?"

"Hungry."

"I bet. I'll be back." Hayes set the lantern on the night table and left.

Valek turned to me. He wiped the tears off my jaw with a thumb. "Thanks."

"For what? I took your magic."

He shook his head as if that didn't matter. "For guiding me home. I was lost in a world of fire and didn't know how to leave." Valek picked up my hand and rested it on his stubbly cheek. Then he covered it with his own. "You showed me the way."

Was he in the fire world? Or just lost in fever dreams? "That was days ago."

He frowned. "How long?"

"About a week."

Valek groaned. "I've spent most of the hot season lying in a bed." He threaded his fingers in mine. "There's only one good reason for being in bed. And it's not sleeping." He gave me a tired leer.

"I brought soup and some bread. Be careful not to eat too much," Hayes said, carrying a tray into the room.

Valek let go of me to sit up. Then he grinned.

"It's just chicken broth. No need to get that excited," Hayes said.

But I understood. "Your magic?"

"Looks like I'll be helping Healer Hayes after all."

A few days later, Valek was released from the infirmary. We returned to the guest suite, but eventually we would move to the apartment over Alethea's bookshop until classes started

MARIA V. SNYDER

at the Keep. Then we would stay in Irys's tower while Valek explored what he could and couldn't do with his magic. Irys speculated that Valek had gone into the fire world while he was unconscious, which was very similar to the master-level test. Because Valek couldn't leave without my help, his magic wasn't strong enough to be a master.

Soon after, my father left for home, but not before promising to be back with Mother when the baby was born. "I'll warn you now," Esau said to me in the living room of the guest suite. "Your mother will want to discuss plans for your wedding celebration."

"Even with a grandchild distracting her?" I asked.

"This is your mother we're talking about. She can be very persistent and stubborn."

Valek burst out laughing, and we both looked at him in confusion.

"Sorry," he said, wiping his eyes. "It's just I have a feeling that I'll be saying that very same thing to our son or daughter in the future."

"Hey," I said in mock outrage.

Esau clapped him on the back. "Just remember it's those qualities that made us fall in love with them in the first place."

"Really? I thought it was because she said I looked stunning in my dress uniform. Love at first compliment," Valek joked.

I marveled at my husband. I'd never seen him so happy and carefree.

Ari and Janco stopped by later that night for a visit. I'd relayed Valek's information to them about the Commander welcoming them back, but they'd wanted to wait for Valek to wake up before they decided anything.

"You certainly took your sweet time," Janco said to Valek as he plopped into one of the armchairs. He propped his feet up on the ottoman and sighed.

Ari shook his head. "The boy has no manners."

"What? I'm supposed to wait for an invitation to make myself comfortable?" Janco pished.

Sitting in another armchair, Ari made it appear small in comparison to his large frame. "You both look better," he said.

I opened my mouth to thank him, but Janco waved a hand. "Pah. Small talk. We're beyond small talk."

"True," Valek agreed. "You're here to say goodbye."

Janco straightened. "How did you know?"

Valek waited.

"Yeah, well, I guess we spent a lot of time working together." He frowned. "But we think we'd be bored here in Sitia."

"We?" Ari asked.

"Well, Ari is too polite to use the word *bored*, but we realize that you are going to build a nest and settle down."

"Nest?" I asked.

"Home, nest, you know what I mean. You don't need us getting in the way. And Little Miss Assassin needs us more."

I wasn't surprised by their decision. "I'm glad. Onora has a rough road ahead of her, and having friends will make it easier."

"We'll visit, of course. Someone has to teach the kid how to get away with stuff that you won't let him or her do."

I glanced at Valek. "Remind me to never leave Janco alone with our child."

"Hey!"

We all ignored him.

"And we'll drop everything and come if you need us," Ari said.

"Unless you need us to change diapers. Then forget it." Janco waved a hand under his nose.

MARIA V. SNYDER

"Just remember, we also can offer aid if you need it," Valek said to them.

"Will do." Janco saluted. "Our herd may roam, but we all know where is home."

The students returned to the Magician's Keep on the first day of the cooling season. The New Beginnings feast was a highly anticipated affair. I hadn't been to one in years. But this year's feast represented so much more than the start of a new school year. Everyone needed a night of celebration and fun after being under the Cartel's influence.

Before the party, Valek stood in front of the mirror in our rooms in Irys's tower. He wore a silver silk tunic with black piping, black pants and a silver belt—formal Sitian dress clothes—and they showed off his athletic physique. He'd regained weight and muscle tone since he'd recovered from the Harman sap. And I'd gained about a hundred pounds in baby weight...or so it seemed. He was sleek and sexy, and I was the size of a heifer.

"I feel ridiculous," he said, yanking at his high collar. "I'm the oldest student ever to attend the Keep. Can we skip the feast?"

"No. It'll be fun. Don't worry, you'll be working with Irys and Teegan and won't have to attend classes with the first-years."

"Thank fate."

We entered the dining room and wove through the clumps of people, stopping and talking as we headed for the buffet. Food first, dancing second. After we ate, Valek pulled me to the dance floor. He twirled me around as the music vibrated through the air.

Zethan mingled among the students and faculty with ease, but Zohav stayed on the edges of the room, frowning at anyone who approached her. Valek coaxed her onto the dance floor, while I partnered with Zethan.

"Don't worry about Zo," he said when he noticed the direction of my gaze. "She'll thaw eventually. It always takes her a while to adjust." Then he laughed. "And this has been the craziest year in our entire lives."

"I'd say. You've experienced a lot of changes. But you seem to have made friends already."

"Compared to being captured by pirates and then arrested by the scariest man in Ixia, who ends up being your older brother and involved in a dangerous plot to overthrow an evil Cartel? This is easy."

I laughed. "When you put it that way, I see your point."

"And it all worked out. I'm learning about my magic. I have a sister-in-law, and I'm gonna be an uncle!" He beamed at me.

His resemblance to Valek was unmistakable, and I hoped it didn't cause him trouble in the future. Many Sitians still feared Valek, despite all he'd done to save us. At the end of the song, I said, "Just remember, we are here if you and Zohav need anything."

"I know. There's only one thing I'm worried about."

Concerned, I put my hand on his arm. "What is that?"

"That after all the excitement of the past couple seasons, school will be boring in comparison."

I swatted him. "You're just like your brother."

"Thank you."

Boys.

After the feast, life slowly returned to normal. Valek kept busy attending sessions with Irys, and with helping to teach the students self-defense and fighting techniques in the training yard. I spent my time reading through Bain's history books. I

MARIA V. SNYDER

hoped to find some mention of another magician who might have had the same magic-sucking power as the baby.

I was propped up in bed scanning a book on the clans that traced the lines of magic in families when pain ringed my stomach. My first thought was that I'd been poisoned by White Fright again. Memories flashed of being locked in General Brazell's dungeon while it felt as if someone shredded my insides with a rusty knife. But that was nine years ago. My confusion cleared when another contraction hit, stronger than the last. It was the middle of the cooling season, and the baby was coming. Now.

Terror and panic mixed with relief—I'd gotten to the point where I couldn't stay in one position for long before something on my body hurt. Lumbering from bed, I put on my robe. Valek worked at a table in the living area. He concentrated on a wooden stick.

"Valek."

"Hmm?" He scowled at the thin branch. "Looks like lighting fires is truly beyond me. Pity. That would be a really useful skill to have."

Another contraction rolled through me. I sucked in deep breaths like Healer Hayes had instructed. Medic Mommy had arrived yesterday morning, but she hadn't thought I'd go into labor for another week. When I could speak again, I said, "Valek."

The strain in my voice caught his attention, and he was beside me in a heartbeat. "Is it time, love?" He remained calm. Typical.

"Yes."

"Almost there, Yelena, one more push. You can do it," Medic Mommy said.

She and Healer Hayes had taken turns soothing me while

I clung to Valek's hand as the contractions grew in frequency and severity.

"That's it. Breathe."

I grunted instead. After all these hours—I had no idea how many, except it was a lot—I thought I'd earned the right to grunt.

"Another push for the shoulders," she instructed. "The rest is easy."

And it was.

"The baby's a girl," she said, holding up a squirming little worm covered in goo.

Relief and joy pulsed through my tired body. Valek cut the cord, and I collapsed back on the bed, sweaty and achy. But all my woes disappeared when the baby cried. I lifted my head in concern. Was something wrong?

"Relax, Mom," Hayes said with a grin. "She's healthy." He weighed her. "Almost eight pounds. What's her name?"

"Liana Zaltana Icefaren," Valek said, leaning over and kissing my forehead.

Our gazes met and his eyes shone with unshed tears. *Even with her hair a mess, Yelena's still beautiful.*

Wait. I blinked at him.

"What's wrong?" he asked.

"Give me a minute." I reached for the blanket of power and concentrated. Magic flowed through me like a fresh, cool breeze. My magical senses awakened, and the world came alive around me. One of the best days of my life just became better. I met Valek's questioning gaze, then projected my thoughts toward him. I hit a solid barrier. Hard. Irys wasn't kidding when she'd said he was strong.

Valek straightened in surprise, but then he grinned. The wall disappeared.

Hi there, handsome, I thought.

MARIA V. SNYDER

Welcome back, love.

I smiled. Reaching out further, despite my low energy, I sought another.

Kiki?

Lavender Lady had foal. Approval flowed over our connection. *Better?*

Yes, I can hear you again!

She snorted as if she knew this would happen all along. *Bring foal.*

We'll visit soon.

Bring apples.

I promised to bring an entire bushel.

Healer Hayes cleaned Liana, wrapped her up so all that showed was her round pink face and handed her to me. Long black eyelashes arched from blue-green eyes, and dark hair covered her head. It was long enough to curl slightly. She was perfect. Liana stared at me for a moment, gazed at Valek for a few seconds, then promptly fell asleep. Unimpressed? Bored already? Or was it a sign that she'd be a good sleeper?

"We'll leave you alone now," Hayes said. "When she starts to fuss, that means she's hungry. Let us know if she has trouble latching on, and we'll come back and help."

Latching on sounded painful, but I nodded as if confident it would work. We marveled over our daughter for a while. It was love at first sight for both of us.

Valek touched her cheek with his finger. "She's so soft." His voice held awe. Then he crinkled his brow. "She's also blocking my magic." He pulled his hand back. "Is she blocking yours?"

I focused. "No." Then I placed my thumb on her chin. Her skin was soft, and my connection to the power blanket severed. "Yes, when I touch her."

"What happened to her sucking power?"

I thought about it. "Maybe since she didn't have direct contact with you, it seemed like she was sucking your magic, when in fact she was not being very effective in blocking it? You know, like when you build a dam of rocks, but water still leaks through?"

"Possible."

I laid my fingers on her forehead. "Try using magic on me."

Valek stared at me, but his voice didn't sound in my mind. "Now she's pulling my magic."

Unaffected by the magic around her, Liana remained asleep.

"What if you use magic, but don't direct it at us?"

He glanced at the door. "Healer Hayes and Medic Mommy are having a celebratory drink in his office." Valek laughed. "He's wondering if she'd consider moving to Sitia."

"I'd like that, especially if magic won't work on Liana."

"Do you think she's immune?" he asked in concern.

A good question. "Can you build a null shield around us?"

"Probably not without difficulty." He scanned the room. "I'll put one around the bassinet. Then I won't be able to lay her in there if she's immune."

The impulse to protect her surged through me—hot and fierce. I held her closer, "I don't want to hurt her."

His face softened. "Neither do I, love. But we need to know if she'll be trapped by a null shield."

True. He moved the bassinet to the farthest corner of the room. After a few moments, he returned to me. He lifted our daughter from my arms. Valek held her as if she'd break. "Wow, she's pretty solid. No wonder you were—"

"Watch it."

"—so uncomfortable."

"Nice."

But he wasn't listening. Valek gazed at Liana as if he held a precious jewel in his arms. He cuddled her a little longer before heading to the bassinet. Slowly, and with great care, he lowered her to the small mattress. I held my breath.

Valek straightened with his arms empty. "She popped the null shield and didn't even wake up." He grinned.

Was she a void? Did that mean she had no soul and would never find peace in the sky? I projected my awareness toward her and was blocked, but I sensed the spark of life that was her soul. I sagged back on the bed in relief. Did it really matter what she was? Not at all. As long as she was happy and healthy and safe from harm. We could determine the extent of her abilities when she was older.

Valek rolled the bassinet back beside my bed, then kicked off his boots and slid under the covers with me. Wrapping his arms around me, he pulled me close. I snuggled against him, listening to his heartbeat while breathing in his unique musky scent.

We'd survived so much, and I would never take moments like this for granted. I savored the peace, knowing full well that once the rest of the herd learned of Liana's arrival, we'd be inundated with visitors.

I was on the edge of sleep when Valek said, "I'm sorry I didn't keep my promise sooner."

I opened one eye. "What promise?"

"That we'd be together."

"I know I just had a baby and might not be thinking clearly, but I'm pretty sure we've been together for nine years."

"No. We've been living two different lives. I worked for the Commander while you were the Liaison. We were lucky to spend two weeks together at one time. If you add up all the days, it wouldn't fill two years."

He had a point. "And now?"

His arms tightened. "Now we're truly together. Body, mind and soul."

Liana hiccupped and started crying.

"And baby," I added.

"And babies," he amended. "She's going to need a brother."

EPILOGUE
VALEK

Valek watched as Yelena set Liana in the sling, securing the baby to her stomach before she mounted Kiki. Yelena's bat flew over and grabbed the edge of her hood. It hung upside-down from the fabric as it settled in for the trip. Much to Yelena's delight, the little creature had shown up mere hours after Liana was born. She hadn't seen it since the baby was conceived.

He checked the sling's straps, looking for weak or frayed spots. "Are you sure she'll be warm enough?" Valek asked his wife. The warming season had just ended, but the air was crisp despite the morning sunshine. Plus Liana was only five months old.

"Yes, she'll be fine."

"Are you sure you want to ride? I can get a wagon," he offered.

Kiki and Yelena stared at him. He didn't need to use magic to know what they were thinking, but he thought he'd asked a legitimate question.

"All right," he said. Valek checked through the saddle bags on Onyx. "Did you remember to pack—"

"Valek, get your butt in that saddle before we leave without you," Yelena said in exasperation, but then she relented. "It's my fault. I've spoiled you."

Confused, he asked, "What do you mean?"

"You've gotten your wish for the last five months. Other than trips to the market and Council Hall, Liana and I have been safe in Irys's tower while you've been learning about your magic. You're out of practice."

"Practice?"

"Yes. You haven't had to squelch your overprotectiveness during that time."

"It's not..." Well, that was part of it. "Sorry, love." He secured the bag's flap, then swung into the saddle.

Setting off at a walk, Onyx followed Kiki to the Keep's main entrance. The guards waved them through the gate. The horses navigated the busy Citadel's streets. A few Helper's Guild members waved to them as they hurried on their various errands. Fisk had rebuilt his guild, but he was also helping the Sitian Council. After regaining control of Sitia from the Cartel, the Councilors had realized their security measures were woefully inadequate. They hired Fisk to develop and implement new protocols. Fisk, in turn, hired Valek as his primary consultant. He'd enjoyed working with the young man. Plus it kept his skills sharp. Their first task had been to apprehend and arrest the members of the Problem Gang—a task Fisk had relished.

Valek and Yelena exited the Citadel through the northern gate. "Do you think we should keep this pace?" Valek asked her. "Trotting or galloping might jar the baby too much."

She peered at him as if he had two heads. Then her expression smoothed. "Why are you so nervous? *I'm* the one meeting them for the first time."

And there was the other part. "I...don't know." Which

MARIA V. SNYDER

was the heart of the problem. He had no idea what to expect. The last time he saw his parents, he'd been blindsided by the existence of his three younger siblings. With a storm of emotions raging inside him, Valek had stood next to his three older brothers' tombstones and finally come to terms with their deaths. That released his immunity and freed his ability to use magic. What might happen this time?

"Then again," she said, "they did spend a few days with Ari and Janco when they moved down to Sitia. Who knows what stories Janco told them about you?" She grinned.

"About *us*, love. Janco has just as many Yelena stories."

"Oh."

"Not so funny now, is it?"

"Maybe we should stay at a walk. It's such a lovely morning."

Kiki flicked her tail and broke into a smooth gallop. So much for that idea. At this pace, they'd be at his parents' new tannery by the afternoon. Wishing to be near their children, they had decided to move to Sitia without visiting first, as they'd originally planned. Valek had located a small complex that had been for sale. It was just outside Owl's Hill. It had a four-bedroom house, a storage shed and a building big enough to be used for his father's business. The Commander had approved the move, but it had taken a few months to transport the equipment, their furniture and dozens of crates full of their belongings. They'd lived in that house in Ixia for over forty-five years.

Valek could commiserate. The Commander had sent all of Valek's things, including his carving tools, soon after Liana was born. The boxes filled two entire floors of Irys's tower. Once Valek had completed his magical training, they would purchase a home somewhere in northern Sitia. It didn't matter where, as long as it was quiet and hidden. The Commander had given him a very generous retirement bonus, so they would be able to keep the apartment above Alethea's bookshop as their public address and for when they had business in town. Plus the Council planned to pay Yelena to resume her Soulfinder duties once he finished his training at the Keep.

His parents' tannery was on the northwest side of Owl's Hill. The path from the main road wove through the budding trees before it ended at a white picket fence that surrounded the complex. The house dominated the clearing. Valek's mother had insisted on at least four bedrooms so there would be plenty of room for her children and grandchildren to visit.

Kiki hopped the fence with ease, and Valek heard giggles. When Onyx cleared the barrier, he joined Yelena. She smiled at him. "Liana likes jumping."

Sure enough, his daughter's happy face peered from the sling, her blue-green eyes alight with glee. Figured. So far, she'd been a joy, easy to put to sleep and entertain. But Valek suspected that might change when she was older. He wondered if Liana would develop magical powers, or if her blocking skill was the extent of her abilities. Time would tell.

They stopped outside the main door of the house. Valek dismounted and helped Yelena down from Kiki. The squeal of a screen door alerted him. Yelena squeezed his arm. He drew in a deep breath and faced his parents.

His father strode toward them with a welcoming grin, while his mother hung back, uncertain. They both still wore their Ixian uniforms.

"About time you came to visit," Kalen said, slapping Valek on the back. "The twins were here two weeks ago. And you must be Yelena. Nice to finally meet you." He shook her hand with both of his. "Valek didn't exaggerate when he said you were beautiful. Ahh! There she is. Can I hold her?"

MARIA V. SNYDER

"Of course." Yelena removed the baby from the sling and handed her to Kalen.

His father's face lit up with an amazed joy as he gazed at Liana lying in his arms. She peered back, studying him with interest. Years of grief seemed to melt from Kalen's lined skin, and his brown eyes shone.

"Oh, she's a beauty. Olya, come see. She resembles your mother." Then he lowered his voice. "Let's hope that's as far as it goes."

"I heard that, Kalen," Olya said, joining them. She nodded at Valek and said hello to Yelena. But her reserved demeanor changed when she saw her granddaughter. "She's lovely." Olya plucked the baby from her husband's arms.

"Hey," he protested, but it was weak.

"Aren't you a sweetie!" She marveled at the baby, letting Liana clutch her finger.

Kalen gestured with a hand. "Let's get out of this sun. Come on into the house."

"Go on," Valek said to Yelena. "I'll take care of the horses."

Yelena gave him a don't-you-dare-leave-me-alone look. He suppressed a grin.

"No need," Kalen said. "Zebulon!"

Valek's brother exited the tannery, then strode over to them. He wore plain brown pants and a cream-colored tunic. Zebulon's black hair flopped about his head, and his brown-eyed gaze scanned them. With the same distant manner as their mother, he greeted Yelena and Valek, but warmth flashed when he spotted Liana.

"Zeb, can you take care of the horses?" Kalen asked.

"Uh." Zeb glanced at the horses with a queasy expression.

"Groom and feed them like the twins showed you, and then join us inside," Kalen said.

"All right."

Valek skimmed Zeb's surface thoughts. The twenty-year-old had only watched Zohav and Zethan care for the horses. Zeb had no idea what to do. Valek met Yelena's gaze, and she nodded.

Hurry up, she thought.

"I'll be right there," Valek said to his father. "I'll help Zeb—it'll go faster."

As they headed to the house, Kalen asked Yelena, "Is it always *this* hot here? I'm roasting."

"No."

"Thank fate!"

"It gets hotter."

He groaned. Yelena would be too polite to tell him he needed to wear Sitian clothing, but Valek would find some way to mention it. In the meantime, he showed Zeb how to remove the horses' saddles and tack. Then he handed his brother a curry comb and demonstrated how to use it. Zeb groomed Kiki. They worked for a while in companionable silence.

"What do you think of Sitia so far?" Valek asked.

"It's okay. I guess I need to learn how to ride, right? Isn't that how everyone gets around in Sitia?"

"Not everyone. You can walk, and there are travel shelters between cities." Valek sensed that wasn't what Zeb wanted to hear. "Although it's faster on horseback. Especially if you're going farther than Owl's Hill."

"There's not much to do in Owl's Hill."

Ah. "Would you like me to teach you how to ride?"

He hesitated. "Did you teach the twins?"

"I showed Zethan the basics when we traveled to Sitia, but they're learning the finer art of horsemanship at the Magician's Keep." Along with a number of other things, like fighting and self-defense techniques. Things the Ixian schools didn't cover unless it was required for your job. Since Zebulon didn't have magic, he wouldn't get this extra education. And since he was already twenty, he was too old to attend the Sitian schools.

"Yeah, they seem to be fitting right in at the Keep," Zeb said.

"Do you plan to stay here and work for Father?" Valek asked.

If the question surprised the young man, he didn't show it. "I don't know. Before, I sort of had to. I didn't have any other options in Ixia. Now..."

"Too many."

Zebulon laughed. "Yeah."

"What do you like to do?"

He shrugged, but then said, "I like working with my hands."

That was a start. As they groomed, fed and watered the horses, Valek asked a number of questions. By the time they finished, he had a better idea of Zebulon's interests, which didn't include the military, law enforcement or spying. Basically, not going into the family business.

"What about working with glass?" he asked Zeb as they brushed off all the horsehair from their clothes and washed the grime from their hands. "I've friends who own a glass factory in Fulgor and would be amenable to taking on an apprentice."

Zeb appeared interested. "It would be someplace to start. Is Fulgor like Owl's Hill?"

"No. It's much bigger. It's about a four-day ride west of here."

"I'd like that. Thanks."

They entered the house. It was cooler inside. Despite the fact that the family had moved in only a few weeks ago, all the crates and boxes had been unpacked. The familiar furniture and decorations from his childhood filled unfamiliar rooms, and the effect was disconcerting. Voices emanated from deep within, and Valek followed Zeb to the living area.

"...planned for the beginning of the hot season in the Magician's Keep," Yelena said. "You're all invited, of course."

"Invited to what?" Zebulon asked. He sat next to their mother on the couch.

Liana remained in Olya's lap. The baby chewed on her favorite yellow horse-shaped rattle. The number of gifts she'd gotten just for being born had been astounding. Janco had brought her what he called "baby's first set of lock picks." And the Commander sent her a pink diamond the size of Liana's fist.

Despite everyone's relaxed postures, an awkwardness thickened the air. Yelena sat in an armchair with a cup of tea on the table next to her. Kalen occupied the other chair.

"Our wedding celebration," Yelena said.

Valek hid his grin. Yelena's mother had refused to leave the Keep until plans had been set into motion for the celebration. And after a month of having her mother underfoot, Yelena would have agreed to anything to speed Perl's departure. Which was why the party was scheduled for when the Keep's students were gone. Perl's guest list was so long that they would need to use the student barracks to house them all.

"I thought you were already married," Olya said. She bounced Liana on her knee. The baby squealed in delight.

"In Ixia," Valek said. "Sitia has different rules."

"And they'll use any excuse to throw a party," Yelena joked.

Olya frowned at that. Valek suspected it would take his mother the most time to adjust to the Sitian way of life.

"Hot season, eh?" Kalen wiped his brow. "We'll come, but I can't guarantee we won't melt into puddles."

"We've invited a couple Stormdancers who will make sure

clouds block the sun and a cool breeze blows," Valek said. "Their powers are similar to Zethan's."

The tension increased with the mention of magic. Oh, boy.

Kalen cleared his throat. "Zethan mentioned you're working for the Sitian Council. What are you doing for them?" He adopted a casual tone, but the tightness in his shoulders said otherwise.

"I'm helping with security. What they had in place before the Cartel was not very effective."

"You mean like guarding the Councilors?"

Valek didn't need to read his father's thoughts to understand the real question. "More like setting up protocols, ensuring the guards are trustworthy and helping with training." He glanced at his mother's pinched face. "*Not* assassinating anyone." Unless they threatened the safety of his herd.

"Of course not," his father said too quickly. "I'm sure all that's behind you now that you have a beautiful wife and daughter."

Smooth recovery. Valek approved.

Kalen hopped to his feet. "How about a tour of the tannery? Yelena?"

She hesitated, glancing at Liana.

"Oh, she'll be fine. Olya's raised seven babies."

"All right. A tour would be nice."

Valek laced his fingers in Yelena's as they trailed his father. The equipment in the tannery remained the same as he'd remembered. The smells of the vats and the hides stretched over the drying racks brought many of his childhood memories bubbling to the surface of his mind. He and his brothers had devised many creative excuses to avoid working.

Kalen led them back outside. Three mounds of dirt marred the grass behind the tannery. The headstones of Valek's older brothers marked each one—Vincent, Viliam, and Victor. Yelena's grip tightened in his. Valek glanced at her in concern, but she shook her head. *Later.*

"I wanted to let you know we brought them with us," Kalen said. "We couldn't stand the thought of leaving them behind."

"Thank you." Valek swallowed the wedge of emotion in his throat. "I see you left Mooch behind."

Kalen laughed. "Yeah. The twins were upset, but I wasn't digging up that damn dog."

They returned to the house and spent the rest of the afternoon making awkward conversation. Valek offered to hire a couple of trustworthy people to help his parents.

"The tannery is smaller than the one in Ixia," his father said. "Zeb and I can handle it."

Valek exchanged a glance with Zeb, but his brother pressed his lips together, signaling it wasn't the right time to mention the glass apprenticeship. "They would be able to do more than work. They can advise you on the local customs, ensure you're not being cheated or taken advantage of and tell you where to purchase certain goods, like a fabric that breathes in this hot weather. Those wool uniforms are far too warm for the Sitian climate."

"We'll think about—" his father started.

"That would be nice," Olya said in a tone that warned her husband not to argue with her.

Wow. He hadn't expected his mother to agree so easily. Valek kept his expression neutral. "I'll make inquiries at Owl's Hill before we return to the Citadel tomorrow."

"Thank you." She stood with a sleepy Liana in her arms. "The baby needs a nap, and I need to start dinner."

"Would you like some company?" Yelena offered.

"Yes." Olya transferred Liana to Valek's arms. "You had those same long eyelashes when you were a baby. Everyone thought you were a girl, despite the fact that you wore your brothers' hand-me-downs." Then she went into the kitchen.

Yelena flashed him a grin before following his mother.

Do not *tell Janco*, he thought.

Sorry, I can't hear you. Too busy cooking.

Zeb and his father left to check on the next batch of hides, but Valek was content to remain on the couch and hold Liana as she napped. He drank in her clean, powdery scent and gazed at her. She was so precious to him. The urge to protect her burned in his veins, and he wondered if he'd survive her childhood. Just the thought of her learning how to walk and run and climb the stairs and sleep in a big bed and ride a horse already made him anxious with worry. If only she could remain a baby forever. Then again, forever's worth of dirty diapers was incentive enough to trust his daughter to reach those milestones without hurting herself too much.

After dinner that night, his mother escorted them to a guest room. "Zeb put your bags inside already and lit the lantern." She stood outside the door. "Kalen assembled the crib, so you might want to test that it's sturdy."

"I heard that," Kalen called from down the hall. "It wasn't my fault the legs broke off. The twins were too big to be in a crib, anyway."

A brief smile flashed. "Let us know if you need anything."

"Thank you," Yelena said.

Olya nodded and retreated to her bedroom.

When Yelena and Valek entered, he froze.

"What's wrong?" Yelena asked.

"It's…" He crossed to the armoire and opened the door. Scratches marked the inside, appearing random at first, but upon closer inspection, they were code words that Valek had etched into the wood when he'd spied on his older brothers.

Shock rolled through him. Valek scanned the rest of the room. The sloppy boat paintings Vincent had done in school hung on the walls, and the wooden toys Valek had carved lined a shelf—he'd forgotten all about them.

Except for the larger bed, nothing had changed. "It's *my* room. The one I shared with Vincent." It made sense that they'd kept the furnishings and Vincent's paintings, but he hadn't expected them to save his toys or leave the marks he'd made on the armoire alone.

Yelena tested the crib with one hand and then laid Liana down on the mattress. The baby sighed in her sleep. His wife took Valek's hands in her own. "They never stopped loving you."

He shook his head. "I'm no longer that boy. And my mother is still terrified of me."

"Despite her fear, her soul knows you." Yelena released his hands. She pressed her palm over his heart. "Her soul knows who you are right now, and she loves you. Your reputation has colored her thoughts, but she just needs time to adjust to all the changes in her life. Then she'll see what I see every day."

He pulled her close. "What do you see?"

"I see a loving husband and father who will do anything to protect the people he loves. A man worthy of love in return."

Unable to put his emotions into words, he kissed his wife with all the passion she stirred in his soul.

When they broke apart, she gazed at him. *It's time.*

To make love all night? I'm in. He tugged her toward the bed. She resisted. *No. Time to say goodbye to your brothers.*

He stopped as all the colors in the room drained away, leaving behind only shades of gray. *Is this—*

The shadow world. Yelena twined her fingers in his. *Look.*

Valek's three brothers stood in the room. So young and so… perfect. No wounds marked them. They grinned at him, but

MARIA V. SNYDER

he couldn't smile in return. He glanced at Yelena in horror. Instead of finding peace in the sky, they'd been trapped in the shadow world for the last twenty-nine years.

No. She tapped his chest. *They've been with* you *for the last twenty-nine years.*

But wouldn't you have seen them?

They were locked inside you. Don't worry, they have no memories of that time. According to them, they remember being murdered. Then they woke standing next to their graves in the shadow world. They were confused to see you much older and kneeling in front of Vincent's gravestone.

You've seen them since your magic returned? You've been talking to them? A sense of betrayal pulsed in his heart. Why hadn't she told him?

Of course not. I saw them for the first time this afternoon, by their graves. They've been waiting for you to come back. Your parents said goodbye when they moved here, and now it's your turn.

He thought he had made peace with them back in Ixia, when he'd lost his immunity to magic. Valek looked at Yelena. *Can I talk to them?*

Only through me. She squeezed his hand. *Go ahead.*

He turned to his brothers. *I'm sorry.*

For what, Little Brother? Vincent asked. *Marrying the prettiest girl in the world? Of course, if I'd been alive, she wouldn't have even looked at you.*

I'm sorry for being alive, when you... The horrible image of them lying dead in the snow flashed before him.

Stop that, Victor said. *Look at me.*

Valek focused on him. As the oldest of the four of them, Victor tended to take charge and calm everyone down.

We were beyond relieved that you weren't killed, as well.

Phantom pain spiked in Valek's shoulders where his mother had held him back. *But I should have—*

What? Gotten killed, too? Vincent asked. *Come on, Little Brother, we thought you were past all this.*

So did I. But seeing them again brought all those feelings back.

Well, I'm sure your lovely wife and beautiful daughter are happy you're still sucking air, Viliam said. He was younger than Victor by two minutes, but they were complete opposites in personality. He also had a good point.

Valek sensed Yelena's agreement.

Victor gestured to the three of them. *Remember us this way. No blood or gore.*

Good thing, since I faint at the sight of blood, Viliam said.

His twin frowned at Viliam. The gesture reminded Valek of Ari and Janco. How could he not see how much their personalities resembled his older brothers'? Again, Yelena's agreement pulsed inside him.

You can't change the past. We can't change it either, Victor said. *We're content and are ready to embrace peace in the sky. Are you ready to say goodbye?*

I... He'd have liked more time, but he had let them go back in Ixia. This goodbye shouldn't be any harder than the last. *Yes.*

Three matching grins.

Live for us, Vincent said.

I will.

They faded. Color returned to the world, brighter than before.

Yelena leaned against him. *Now, where were we? Oh, yes, you mentioned something about making love all night?*

He swept her off her feet and carried her to bed, savoring every moment with her. While spending all night engaged in intimate relations would have been a very romantic interlude,

MARIA V. SNYDER

the realities of their life—little Liana—made that quite impossible. They fell into an exhausted sleep after the first round.

Liana's hungry cries woke them a few hours later. Valek slid from the bed and carried the baby back to Yelena to nurse. He hoped Liana hadn't woken anyone else. Valek lowered his mental barriers and checked. His father and brother remained sound asleep, but his mother sat in the kitchen, sipping a cup of tea despite the late hour.

What's wrong? Yelena asked.

My mother is downstairs. I…need to talk to her.

Yes, you do.

Lovely. Her Soulfinding abilities didn't seem to be rusty after the long hiatus, he thought dryly.

I heard that, she said.

You were supposed to.

Uh-huh. Go on. We'll be fine.

He padded down the stairs soundlessly, but Valek made a little noise before reaching the kitchen. He didn't want to scare his mother. She turned her head as he entered. Fear flashed as she stiffened, but then she relaxed her grip on the cup she held.

Valek ignored her reaction. "Did the baby wake you?" he asked, knowing full well Olya was here before Liana had cried.

"Not at all. I…couldn't sleep."

Valek didn't need to read his mother's thoughts to know it was his presence in her house that was keeping her awake.

"Does Liana need something?" she asked.

"No, but I do."

She stared at him for a moment. "What do you need?"

He knelt next to her and took her free hand in both of his. "I need to thank you."

"You're always welcome to come visit us anytime."

"Not for your hospitality, although that's appreciated. I'm

thanking you for saving my life that awful day. I never did." He drew in a breath. "Thank you."

She put her cup down and rested her free hand on his shoulder, still marked with the scars from her fingernails. "You're welcome."

★ ★ ★ ★ ★

ACKNOWLEDGMENTS

I began this journey with Yelena and Valek twenty years ago, when the idea to write a fantasy novel about a food taster popped into my head. Little did I know that the characters in my first novel, *Poison Study*, would resonate with readers worldwide and be the impetus for eight more novels. It's been quite an adventure to chronicle their lives and acts of bravery, to cry with them and laugh over Janco's antics, to grieve and celebrate with them. I'm so honored and proud that my characters have inspired so many readers and have touched their lives. Their emails are the best reward for all the hard work.

This was a beast of a book, and not only is it longer than my others, but it was also difficult to write. To all those who provided feedback and guidance to help calm the beast—my agent, Robert Mecoy; my editor, Lauren Smulski; and my beta readers, Judi Fleming, Kathy Flowers, and my husband—thanks for all your help. You make me look good.

Speaking of looking good, I need to thank all the talented people at Harlequin who work behind the scenes. Your efforts are appreciated. And an extra-big thank you to the Australian team—I had a fantastic time when I visited! You made me feel right at home—you guys rock!

I'd also like to give a special shout-out to my Aussie friend, Natalie Bejin, for her help in keeping me organized and for finding all the inconsistencies—you're the best Chief Evil Minion an author can have.

Thanks to Meili for her expert advice on rabbits—Janco's glad you backed him up. And thanks to Abby, who gave me permission to use her quote in the book: "You put the *sass* in as*sass*in." Also thanks to Mike Farrar, who came up with the idea for the title.

This journey would never have happened without the following people in my life: my husband, Rodney; my parents; my sister, Karen; her husband, Chris; and my children, Luke and Jenna. Thank you all so very much!